EXODUS 2022

Kenneth G. Bennett

Huntington Public Library
143 Pidgeon Hill Road
Huntington Station, NY 11746

Booktrope Editions
Seattle WA 2014

Copyright 2014 Kenneth G. Bennett

This work is licensed under a Creative Commons Attribution-Noncommercial-No Derivative Works 3.0 Unported License.

Attribution — You must attribute the work in the manner specified by the author or licensor (but not in any way that suggests that they endorse you or your use of the work).

Noncommercial — You may not use this work for commercial purposes.

No Derivative Works — You may not alter, transform, or build upon this work.

Inquiries about additional permissions should be directed to: info@booktrope.com

Cover Design by Kathleen Grebe

Edited by Elizabeth Johnson

This is a work of fiction. Names, characters, places, brands, media, and incidents are either the product of the author's imagination or are used fictitiously. Any resemblance to similarly named places or to persons living or deceased is unintentional.

Print ISBN 978-1-62015-212-6

EPUB ISBN 978-1-62015-308-6

DISCOUNTS OR CUSTOMIZED EDITIONS MAY BE AVAILABLE FOR EDUCATIONAL AND OTHER GROUPS BASED ON BULK PURCHASE.

For further information please contact info@booktrope.com

Library of Congress Control Number: 2014905193

For my beautiful wife, Susan Marie Andersson, partner and cohort in countless wilderness adventures. Thank you for walking this path with me and for listening to my stories.

"God has to nearly kill us sometimes, to teach us lessons."

-John Muir

CHAPTER 1

JUNE, 2022. Joe Stanton opened his eyes and whispered his daughter's name. "Lorna Gwin."

No reply.

"Sweetie? You awake?"

Joe yawned and stared at the popcorn-tiled ceiling, stained here and there with sprawling amoeba-shaped rings, souvenirs of long-ago rainstorms.

He stretched. Shifted position in the bed.

Early morning sunshine stabbed through a crack in the blackout curtains, illuminating the spartan motel room like a searchlight in an abandoned mine. Ella slept quietly beside him, her dark-red hair spilling across two pillows.

"Lorna Gwin?" Joe whispered, louder now. He sat up and swung his feet to the carpet. The adjacent double bed was empty. Rumpled and ruffled, but empty. "Lorna G?"

Must be in the bathroom.

Joe got to his feet. Too fast. "Darlin'?" he croaked, head spinning, hands trembling.

No sound from the bathroom. Nothing.

Something's wrong.

He crossed the room in three strides, stepping through the bright slash of daylight.

I overslept. Something's happened.

The bathroom door stood open, revealing an empty tub, shower curtain swept to one side. No sign of the little girl.

"Lorna Gwin," Joe called, turning and scanning the main room in earnest now.

Ella stirred.

"Lorna?" Joe stepped to the window and shoved the heavy drapes apart, trying to keep his voice steady. "You hidin', sweetheart? Come on out now."

Ella rested on her elbows and tracked his movements with startled, sleep-filled eyes. "What is it? What's going on?"

"Lorna Gwin's missing."

Joe threw on a wrinkled T-shirt. Stepped into a pair of cargo shorts.

"What?"

"Lorna Gwin," Joe replied, exasperated.

He jammed his feet into a pair of Keens and tugged the laces tight. "Probably went down to the lobby to get a soda. I told her not to leave without telling us."

"What? Joe...Baby—"

The door slammed, and Joe stomped toward the stairs. It was 5:32 a.m.

CHAPTER 2

THE BELLS ABOVE THE MOTEL office door clanged and clattered.

"Lorna Gwin?" Joe whispered, stepping inside.

The lobby of the Breakwater had a homey 1950s-era motor-lodge feel to it. Glowing fir floors. Framed needlepoint art on the walls. Joe scanned the room, took it all in. Registration desk. Seating area. Fireplace.

A newspaper lay rolled and banded on the rug, where it had fallen through the mail slot. The Sunday edition of the *San Juan Islander*.

"Sweetie? You in here?"

No answer.

Silver-haired motel owner Walter Spinell stepped through the private door behind the registration desk.

"Mornin'," he said warmly. "Gimme one minute and I'll have the coffee on. We don't normally get moving quite so early on Sunday, but—"

"I'm looking for my daughter," said Joe. "Have you seen her?"

"Your daughter?" Spinell made his way around the desk.

"Little girl, five years old. Did she wander down here by any chance?"

"No," said Spinell, noting the concern in Joe's voice. "Don't think so. You're the first one in this morning. Those bells are pretty loud. My wife and I usually hear—"

"I need to find her. I think something's"—Joe hesitated and his face, just for a moment, went completely blank—"I think maybe something's wrong."

"Wrong? How do you mean?"

Spinell remembered Joe from check-in: Scruffy beard. Earring. Tattoos on one arm. He also remembered Joe's wife. She was a knockout. He'd given them Room 22, the last available unit. He couldn't recall a kid.

"When did you see your daughter last?"

"Last night." Joe stared out the window, raked his fingers through his thick, unruly hair, and nodded, as if confirming his own memory. "Last night. When we all went to bed."

"Okay," said Spinell. "I'm sure she's right around here someplace. Where's your wife looking?"

No response.

"Fella?"

Joe stared, face blank once more, and Spinell felt a thin wire of fear begin to coil in his gut.

"Could she have gone to your car? Did you check the lot? Where's your wife?"

Joe's eyes glinted like wet obsidian, and his mouth worked, but no sound came out. Spinell's concern ticked up a notch. The guest from 22 had the look of a shock victim. A meth head.

The guest's eyes cleared at last, but it was not a reassuring development.

"I know where my little girl is," said Joe. "I've seen her. She's dead."

CHAPTER 3

SPINELL'S FIRST IMPULSE was to jump for the phone and call 911, but the guest from 22 was marching for the front door. The old man shouted toward the back of the lobby. "Doris! I need you out here. Now!"

"Lorna Gwin!" Joe screamed, blasting through the door and stumbling toward the parking lot.

Spinell sprang after him. "Son. Please. It's five thirty in the morning. Keep your voice down. The other guests—"

"Lorna Gwin," Joe howled. "God in heaven!"

It was late June—the start of the summer season—and the place was completely full.

"I want my little girl back!" Joe roared, voice full of pain.

"Son!" cried Spinell. "For Christ's sake!"

Doors thumped open. Frightened guests peered around curtains and from behind safety chains.

"They've taken my girl," Joe wailed. "The bastards took my baby."

"Fella," said Spinell, setting a hand on Joe's shoulder. "Calm down!"

Spinell saw a wild-haired guest raise an iPhone and begin filming the spectacle through his window.

"Lorna Gwin!"

"Stop shouting!" Spinell yelled, almost as loud as Joe.

Doris Spinell burst from the motel office clad in a bathrobe, a look of shock on her face.

"Call 911!" Walter Spinell cried.

"Lorna G," Joe growled, low and anguished. Then, full-throated: "Lorna Gwin!"

Doris Spinell stared, frozen.

"Call the damn police," her husband commanded. "Now!"

Doris turned and ran.

"Mister," Spinell said, angry now, reaching for Joe. "I'm asking you—"

"They murdered my little girl!" Joe twisted away, bumping into cars, staggering like a drunk.

Spinell—red-faced, breathing hard, looking like he might have a coronary at any second—addressed his terrified guests. "Not sure what we've got here, folks. Police are on their way. It'll all be sorted out real soon."

Joe slumped against a cherry-red Corvette, triggering the car's alarm. Lights flashed. The horn wailed.

More doors thumped open.

Spinell saw Joe's wife at the railing on the second-floor walkway. Her hair was wet, as if she'd just stepped from the shower. She looked confused, then alarmed.

"Where's his little girl?" one of the downstairs guests yelled from behind her safety chain.

"That's what the police are gonna help us figure out," Spinell replied. "Everybody just needs to relax."

"Little difficult when somebody's screaming their kid's been murdered!"

The Corvette's owner silenced his car's alarm, and Spinell heard sirens, vehicles approaching fast.

"Please," he cried, "just go on back to bed."

Joe stumbled toward the far stairwell, clutching his head like a madman, muttering his daughter's name. Spinell saw Joe's wife moving for the stairs, tracking Joe as he crumpled against a cinderblock wall.

"Joe?" she called. "What happened? What's going on?"

There was no reply.

CHAPTER 4

"WE'RE NOT MARRIED," said Ella Tollefson.

They were sitting in the Breakwater lobby: two San Juan County sheriff's deputies and Detective Vince Palmer in folding chairs, Ella and Joe on a bench against the wall. The Spinells puttered behind the registration desk, eavesdropping on every word.

"We've been dating," said Ella, eyes cloudy from crying. "Getting pretty serious. But we're not married."

Joe leaned forward on the bench, head down. Ella held his hand.

"What about the child?" Detective Palmer asked.

"There is no child," Ella said softly. "I already explained that to your colleagues."

Palmer typed notes on a tablet PC. Looked at Joe. "Sir?"

Joe lifted his head slowly. Eyes glassy, vacant.

"Can you tell me about the little girl?" Palmer asked.

A radio crackled, and one of the deputies headed for the door. Palmer kept his eyes on Joe. "Can you tell me about this morning? About what happened here?"

A group of curiosity seekers sauntered past the entrance, the latest in a stream of looky-loos.

"Christ on a bike," Spinell muttered as Doris hurried out to talk to them.

Joe stared at Palmer. Stared hard, like he wanted to speak. His jaw quivered.

"Who is Lorna Gwin?" Palmer asked.

No reply.

Joe Stanton was a tall, athletic twenty-eight-year-old. Outdoorsy. Strong. Graceful. At the moment, though, he looked wasted. Weak and washed-out. More like a patient emerging from anesthesia than a vital twentysomething.

"Can you tell me what's going on here?" Palmer asked.

Joe said nothing, and after a few seconds Palmer turned back to Ella. The woman was stunning. Even with bloodshot eyes and no makeup, she was gorgeous. Reminded Palmer of the models in his wife's running-gear catalogs. Fit. Healthy. Looked like she could jog around the island and go dancing afterward.

Palmer said, "What's up with your friend?"

"I don't know," she whispered, squeezing Joe's hand. "I want to get him to the doctor."

Palmer nodded. "Couple more questions first." He adjusted his glasses. Glanced at his tablet.

"Got a wallet on him? I'd like to see some ID."

"Joe," Ella said gently. "Sweetie? Your wallet?" She put her hand on his shoulder.

Joe looked at her, eyes big, like wet marbles. Jaw slack.

"Your wallet?" Ella repeated. She turned to the detective. "I'd like to get him to a hospital. Now."

Joe finally seemed to process what she'd asked, fished his wallet out of his pocket, and passed it to her absently. She found his driver's license and handed it to Palmer.

The detective studied the license, then passed it to a deputy, who took it to a sherif's department SUV parked outside.

Palmer typed more notes, then regarded Ella again. "He's never acted like this before?"

"Never."

"What's he on?"

"On? Nothing."

"Prescription meds? Sleeping pills? Ambien? Something like that? Antidepressants?"

"No," said Ella. "I'm telling you, he hates taking anything. I'm a nurse. I'd know if he was on something. I can't even get him to take Advil when he's hurt." She turned to Joe. "He looks like he's had a stroke or something."

"Or too much crack," Spinell muttered. Ella glared at the old man.

"Please, Walt," said Palmer, as if Spinell was an old family friend. "Go check on your other guests or something, would you?" Spinell grumbled and focused on a pile of papers.

Palmer turned to Ella. "Mind if we take a look in your room?"

"Not at all." She handed Palmer her room key. "I don't know why Joe did what he did this morning, but he is *not* on drugs."

Palmer passed the key to a deputy. Whispered some instructions.

He looked at Ella again. "How long have you known Mr. Stanton?"

"We've been together about ten months. Almost eleven."

"And how long have you been on the island?"

"Since Thursday. We just came up for a long weekend."

The deputy who'd run the ID reentered the lobby and handed Palmer a one-page printout.

Palmer studied the page, then said to Ella, "And you were traveling from—"

"Bremerton. That's where we live."

"Purpose of your trip?"

Ella shrugged. "Vacation. Fun." She glanced at Joe. "His new congregation is doing really well. We wanted to celebrate."

"Congregation?"

"He's an Episcopal priest," Ella said. "A very gifted one."

Palmer watched for a reaction from Joe. Nothing.

Palmer said, "And again, as far as you know, Mr. Stanton does not have a child?"

"No."

"From an earlier marriage?"

"No."

"An adopted child?"

Ella shook her head.

"There was no child with you on this trip?"

"Definitely not."

"I want to press charges," Spinell cried.

"Easy, Walt."

"Damn nutcase, screaming like a lunatic. Scaring the hell out of everybody in my place."

"Walt, please," said Palmer. "I'm trying to get to the bottom of it."

Joe stood abruptly, pivoted, and teetered toward the restroom at the back of the lobby. Ella followed.

The restroom door banged open. A fan came on. Two seconds later Joe was vomiting.

"Christ!" Spinell cried. "Now the freak's puking up my john."

"He needs a doctor," Ella yelled. "Can't you see that? Call an ambulance!"

"He'll need a coroner if you don't get him the hell out of my motel!"

"Bring him out," Palmer told his deputies. "When he's done. We'll finish with the questions outside."

Doris Spinell burst into the lobby just then, eyes wet with tears. "Walter," she cried. "There's a video."

"Huh? Whatdya mean?"

"I saw it," Doris managed between sobs. "On one of the guest's computers. Our motel. That young man screaming. You can see our sign in the background."

"The Breakwater?" Spinell's voice sounded fragile. "In a video?"

"On YouTube."

Joe tottered past the desk just then and Spinell lunged for him, murder in his eyes. "Crackhead creep! Get off my property!"

Joe trundled on, oblivious, Ella at his arm.

Ella let go, just for a second, as they passed through the door. "Joe?" she said. "You okay?"

Joe's eyes rolled like cue balls, and he corkscrewed to the ground, too fast for Ella to break his fall. His body lurched forward, and his head smacked the curb.

His final, disturbing, fleeting thought before he lost consciousness was of a girl he'd never met. A girl named Lorna Gwin.

Are you out there? Joe wondered as his world went dark.

CHAPTER 5

NOT FAR FROM THE MOTEL, Lorna Gwin's mother fretted.

The contact with the new man had been solid, but fleeting.

Did the contact last long enough? she wondered. *Did I reach him? Did I push hard enough?*

She hoped so, because time was short.

There's something about this man that makes him different from the others. Better.

Lorna Gwin's mother tried to pin down the difference.

She thought back to when they'd met, yesterday, just for a moment. Mulled it over in her mind.

He's stronger, she thought. *The others were weak. Couldn't endure the contact. Now they're dead.*

Lorna Gwin's mother knew this to be true, though she had not *seen* them die. One minute she had been able to peer into their minds. The next, contact was broken. It could mean only one thing.

The contact killed them.

She felt no remorse for this. None whatsoever. Not after what had happened to her beloved Lorna Gwin.

Molten-red fury filled her mind and quickened her heart. *I hate them.*

She tried now to conjure this latest man's name. Focusing on what she'd gleaned during their encounter, she turned the information in her mind. Much of it was unintelligible: images and sounds and patterns she could not comprehend. *Did I get his name?* she wondered. *Would I even recognize it as a name?*

Strange sounds ricocheted in her brain.

She focused harder.

Gradually, the sounds took shape.

Stan…ton.

That was it. That was his name. *Stan-ton.*

There's something else different about Stan-ton, she thought, struggling with the realization. Not liking it.

He is…compassionate.

Lorna Gwin's mother shoved the notion from her mind. *Doesn't matter. I don't care. Stan-ton is just a tool. Like the others. Nothing more. If he dies, he dies.*

But she hoped he wouldn't die. Not yet. She needed his help. Desperately.

CHAPTER 6

URGENT CARE PHYSICIAN Myron Goss entered the cramped exam room where Joe and Ella waited and removed an ophthalmoscope from the pocket of his white lab coat without uttering a word. He smelled like hand sanitizer.

"Hi," said Ella.

Goss stepped in front of Joe, who was holding an ice pack against his forehead.

Joe looked exhausted, but the vacant stare was gone from his eyes. He was feeling like himself again, and the bizarre events of the morning swirled in his mind now like a half-remembered dream. The more he tried to conjure specific images, the more remote and surreal they seemed.

"Tilt your head back," said the doctor.

No smile. No "Please." No "Hello, I'm Dr. Goss. How're you doin' today? Heard you had a rough morning."

Goss switched off the overhead light and studied Joe's pupils, one at a time, through the ophthalmoscope.

"His eyes look normal to me," Ella said, as Goss turned the light back on. "What do you think?"

Goss said nothing, and Ella and Joe exchanged looks. "Excuse me," said Ella, getting to her feet.

Goss turned his back to her and took a stubby plastic stick from an instrument tray.

"Excuse me, what's the deal?"

Goss removed the lid from the plastic stick and lifted it quickly to Joe's left nostril.

Joe snorted and pulled back hard. "Whoa. What is that?"

Goss didn't answer, just raised the stick to Joe's other nostril.

Ella said, "Scratch-and-sniff test. Compromised sense of smell might mean frontal lobe damage. You smacked your forehead when you collapsed at the motel, so he's checking for concussion."

"She's a registered nurse," Joe said proudly. "Studying to be a nurse anesthetist."

If the news impressed Goss, he gave no sign. He merely sighed, plopped onto a swivel stool, and began typing notes into a laptop.

"This is bullshit," Ella said. "Is there another doctor we can see. Or a PA?"

"Nope," answered Goss, without looking up. "It's Sunday. I'm it."

"Well, what the hell?"

Joe touched her arm. "Ella—"

"Why are you treating us like this? What are you thinking?"

Goss swiveled on his stool, removed his glasses, and fixed Ella with a contemptuous gaze.

"I'm thinking," said the doctor, "that your pal here single-handedly trashed a wonderful island business this morning, and hurt a very good friend of mine in the process."

"Wait a second. Joe didn't—"

"I'm *thinking*," Goss continued, "that this is some kind of game you two are playing."

"Game?" Ella yelled.

"Doctor Goss," said Joe, "I can't explain what happened at the motel. I can't even remember most of it now. But I swear to you, I wasn't trying to hurt anyone, and I wasn't playing games."

Goss said, "I talked to the detective, Mr. Stanton. I read the health history you gave the nurse. You suffered, allegedly, a stupendous hallucination this morning. A hallucination you shared with everyone at the Breakwater. You screamed, at the top of your lungs, about a kidnapping. A murder. An imaginary kid. Acted completely out of your mind. Such a hallucination could mean that you were suffering from, say, posttraumatic stress disorder—except that you aren't in the military or any similarly stressful line of work. You could be psychotic, or schizophrenic, and yet you report no history whatsoever of mental illness."

"Doc—"

"You could have a high fever, or a catastrophic disease, yet clearly, you do not. This could be drug-induced. But, of course you both swear no drugs are involved."

"You can't just diagnose off the cuff like this," Ella said. "He needs tests. An MRI, a CAT scan. Joe could have a brain tumor or something."

The doctor shrugged. "Anything's possible. And if you're not both full of shit, I'd urge you to get it checked out. We don't have that equipment here. Catch the next ferry for Seattle. Or better yet, an air-evac helicopter. Get those tests. By all means. Right away."

CHAPTER 7

A NURSE FOLLOWED Joe and Ella outside, into the clinic parking lot. "I'd like to apologize," she said. "For Dr. Goss's behavior. I'm Carla."

They stopped and turned, Ella still furious. "What the hell *was* that?" she asked. "Why is that guy allowed to see patients? Why is such an asshole allowed to go anywhere *near* patients?"

"He should have retired a long time ago," admitted the nurse. "A lot of us think so. I'm really sorry."

The apology seemed to soothe Ella, and she and Carla discussed Joe's ordeal, talking in medical jargon about tests and procedures. Joe pretended to listen, but soon zoned out. Not because he was tired or disinterested. It was more than that.

The hallucination had come back.

The realization made him catch his breath, like a quick jab to the gut. *It's back.*

It was there, on the periphery of his conscious mind. A glimmer. A mirage shimmering in the distance.

Joe's heart began to thump.

I'm afraid, Joe thought.

Afraid of what? he asked himself.

Afraid of losing my mind. Afraid of—he went ahead and thought it—*dying.*

Don't write the script. It was something he told parishioners in counseling. *You don't know what this is.*

I know it's bad. I know hallucinations are rare. Drug addicts hallucinate. Serious alcoholics. Mental patients. If you're hallucinating and you're not any of those things, it means you're sick. Maybe really sick.

Don't write the script.

His heart thumped harder, his fear edging toward panic. Sweat beaded on his forehead. He could feel himself drifting into the hallucination again.

Breathe. You're in control. You're okay.

Ella and Carla kept chatting in the sunshine, oblivious to his discomfort.

I'm okay. I'm just afraid. And that's okay.

Breathe.

The self-talk worked, or seemed to. His progress toward the hallucination stopped. It was still there, like a storm beyond the next ridge, but it was no longer drawing him in.

Breathe. I'm in control.

What is this? Joe wondered.

Dr. Goss was wrong about the morning's events being a prank. And Spinell was wrong about Joe being a drug addict, but Joe understood how they'd arrived at their conclusions. He probably would have thought "drug addict" too, if he'd seen someone stumbling around a parking lot, shrieking about a nonexistent kid.

Can I look?

The question materialized out of thin air, startling him.

Can I see what this is and stay in control?

His limbs tingled. He shivered.

Can I look over the ridge? Into the storm? Into the hallucination? Can I do that without getting sucked in?

He wasn't sure, but he suddenly wanted to try. He had the feeling that if he could peer inside the thing, he might be able to understand what was going on.

Carla said, "What about an ambulance—or air-evac? I can make the call."

"Insurance would never pay for it," Ella replied. "And he doesn't have the money, and—"

Joe tuned out again.

Go for it. Look, but stay in control.

Stay in control.

In control.

He stepped over the ridge.

Stay in control.

"Well, I would definitely get in to see someone right away when you get back," Carla said. "And—"

He was close to the hallucination now, but also detached from it. *I'm observing this*, he thought. *Not living it. That's progress.*

He relaxed a little and let the hallucination envelop him. It felt like walking back into a dream and seeing every detail with perfect clarity.

Love.

The rawness of the feeling shocked him. Pure, deep love. The close, tender, unique love a parent feels for a child. The kind only a parent can understand. The kind that could induce one to step in front of a bus, or walk through fire, if the situation called for it.

Grief!

Grief flowed through him now. Stabbed his heart. The exquisite grief of a parent who has lost a child.

Joe was not a parent. Had never had a child. He knew what it felt like now, though. And he knew in his bones what it was like to see one's child die.

And now an image flitted by. A "picture" to accompany the tsunami of emotion. The picture was fragile. Unstable. Barely there. A fragment of a thought.

He tried to seize the image. Hold it. But the harder he tried, the more quickly it faded. It was like trying to catch mist in the sunrise. And then he was outside the hallucination again, on top of the ridge, and only one clear image remained: He was in his little rental house in Bremerton, standing near the entry, looking back down the hall, toward the small kitchen and the sliding glass door to the deck. The door stood open and the sun shone bright on his meager backyard. Ella swept past him, hand in hand with a little girl.

The girl had long red hair, like Ella, and she smiled as she passed, eyes bright and full of life.

They walked outside…and were gone. That was it. All there was.

It was the briefest sliver of a memory, though Joe felt certain there was more. The whole story was there, if only he could access it.

Is this our daughter? The little girl certainly resembled Ella. *Am I seeing the future?*

He turned the notion in his mind. Contemplated it. It was an answer, but he felt in his gut that it was not the right one. He couldn't explain it, but the image seemed wrong somehow. It seemed—fake.

The grief, loss, and agony that had consumed him in the Breakwater—that lingered in his mind and body still—*that* was real. But the image? It was a lie. Somehow, it was a lie. Joe knew this in his heart.

He tried to understand, but it was too much to process. He shifted his focus. Took a breath.

Breathe.

Breathe.

Is this a vision? A sign?

Or am I sick?

He focused on his faith. His belief in God.

I believe in God with all my heart, he thought. *But—*

But he was also a skeptic.

I believe that God speaks to us.

But not like this.

The tumult in his mind was too harsh. Too loud. Too abrasive to be of divine origin. He hoped so anyway. This hallucination, or vision, or whatever it was, was the equivalent of someone screaming in his face.

He stepped off the ridge and descended into the storm one final time.

Stay in control.

Ella and Carla stopped talking and turned Joe's way. His face had gone blank again.

He was peripherally aware of their attention. *I'll explain in a minute,* he thought.

Stay in control. In control.

The hallucination swept over him.

This loss is new. Fresh. Unbearable. It would be better to die than actually live through this kind of grief.

He tried to understand.

Who is Lorna Gwin?

Nothing.

He couldn't conjure another image. Just grief. Overwhelming grief.

"Joe?"

Ella and Carla were moving toward him now. "Joe? You okay? Joe!"

Joe let the vision slip away. Opened his eyes.

"It's all right," he said, steadying himself.

He stood there with Ella and Carla. In the sunshine. In the real world. Birds sang. A lawn mower droned nearby.

"I'm fine," he said. "Really."

CHAPTER 8

THEY DROVE IN Ella's blue Jetta, Ella at the wheel. She looked worried.

"Relax," said Joe. "Everything's gonna be fine."

Ella glanced at the blue-green knot on his forehead and winced. "Keep the ice on that," she said.

"Yes, Nurse Tollefson."

They wound their way through Friday Harbor, toward the ferry terminal. The sun shone bright and the sidewalks overflowed with tourists.

Joe said, "Thanks for defending me back there, in the clinic."

Ella shook her head. "What a jerk that doctor is. Should have his license revoked."

Joe gazed out the window. Kept the ice pack in place. "Made sense, a little bit, seeing as how he's friends with the motel owner. What happened with that guy anyway? And with the detective? I don't remember anything between when I hit the driveway, and the clinic."

Ella sighed, "The detective, Palmer, told me he has a full caseload and doesn't want to go through the hassle of prosecuting you. But Spinell insisted."

"Spinell's the motel owner?"

Ella nodded. "Palmer told me you're probably looking at some petty municipal court charges. Disorderly conduct. Disturbing the peace. You'll have to appear in court up here at some point. Or Spinell might calm down and drop the charges."

Joe stared out the passenger window. "Spinell has a right to be pissed," he said. "I would be if I was him."

"Spinell is a mean old man with no compassion. Same as his doctor friend."

"It's not that bad. I miss anything else?"

"Yeah. Palmer says we're supposed to stay away from the Breakwater for at least forty-eight hours, or risk trespass charges."

Joe laughed. "I'm thinking it'll be more like forty-eight *years* before I go back to the Breakwater. That's fine."

Joe watched Ella drive. Looked at the scenery. It was a beautiful day.

"I am so sorry about this," he said, after a while. "This was not my plan for the weekend."

"I know it wasn't, sweetie. I'm worried about you."

Joe nodded. "Yeah. I wish I knew what the heck just happened."

"You wanna talk about it?"

"I'd love to, if I could remember anything that made sense. The whole morning's like a dream. I see little shreds of it, but mostly it's just"—he shook his head—"Surreal. Like it didn't really happen to me. Like it was somebody else screaming and acting crazy. But then there are these clear fragments, so that I know it really *was* me."

"Who's Lorna Gwin?" Ella asked. "Do you know anyone named Lorna Gwin?"

"No." Joe laughed. "I have no freaking idea where that came from."

They rounded a bend and Ella slowed. "Oh great," she said. "Maybe we *should* try an air evac."

The ferry terminal was just ahead and vehicles clogged the vast lots of the holding area. Cars idled in the lanes leading to the ticket booths, and a giant reader board proclaimed a three-boat wait.

"Pull over for a second," said Joe.

Ella eased the Jetta onto the shoulder. "But we should get in line."

"No. Let's not waste half the day sitting in a parking lot."

"But—"

"It's still morning. It's a beautiful day. And we weren't even planning to leave until tomorrow."

"Joe, sweetie," Ella said patiently. "You need to see a doctor, okay?"

"I just saw one."

Ella rolled her eyes. "A *good* doctor. Seriously, we gotta get you home. Get you tested. Checked out."

"I know," said Joe. "I know. But I'm feeling better. Much better as the day goes on."

He smiled his most disarming smile. "I'm almost back to normal. Let's get some food, go for a drive, have a picnic on the beach. Nothing strenuous—just hang out together and chill."

He could tell the idea appealed to her. He said, "We'll let the traffic die down, that's all. Catch a late afternoon boat."

Ella leaned toward him, raised her sunglasses, and gently pulled the ice pack away from his forehead so she could see his bruise. "You really think you're doing better? How's your bump?"

"Great. No headache at all."

"Liar."

"Seriously. I feel good."

Ella sighed. "All right. We'll stay. But you have to promise to tell me if you feel any weirdness."

"I will."

"Dizziness, light-headedness, nausea. Anything at all."

"I promise."

The Jetta rolled back onto the highway and into a glorious Northwest summer day.

The two-lane road wound through groves of towering cedar and Douglas fir, and picturesque farms growing everything from lavender to llamas. In the distance: the vast, shimmering, living entity that was the Salish Sea. The gray-green gleam of the water lulled him into an almost hypnotic state.

CHAPTER 9

NINE HUNDRED MILES NORTHWEST of San Juan Island, in the wilderness of Southeast Alaska, Sheldon Beck peered through the scope of his rifle, tracking a wolf as it loped along a rocky, wild beach.

A black wolf.

The wolf trotted briskly along the high-tide line, nose down, looking for lunch.

Beck's pulse quickened.

The wolf moved closer, and Beck could see now that it was huge. Obviously a male. An alpha if ever there was one.

The head and pelt will look amazing in the gallery.

He steadied his rifle—a custom-built Holland & Holland Nitro Express Double—and focused on his breathing.

Has to be a clean kill.

He aimed for the beast's heart.

The wolf ambled closer.

Closer.

Beck settled into an almost Zen-like demeanor. Then, gently, ever so gently, he began to squeeze the trigger.

Breathe. Breathe. Steady.

A satellite phone buzzed, causing him to quiver and pull the trigger a millisecond early. The rifle boomed, and the bullet missed its mark and ricocheted off a barnacle-encrusted rock with a *zing*!

Beck lowered the gun and watched the wolf vanish into the alders. He clenched his jaw, sighed, and resisted the impulse to unsheathe his knife, whip around, and disembowel the moron with the phone. Instead, he turned slowly, and—in a soft voice—asked, "Whose phone was that?"

"Yours, sir," said Collins, the oldest and most senior member of his entourage. He displayed the suspect phone as evidence.

Beck arched an eyebrow. "Mine only buzzes if it's urgent."

"Yes, sir."

Beck glanced at his men: three rifle-toting ex-Special Forces soldiers, wearing camouflaged hunting gear, sunglasses, and impassive expressions.

"So?" said Beck, squatting close to the group and staring hard at Collins.

"There's been another incident."

Beck rested the butt of his rifle on the ground. The sterling-silver engraving and gold florets on the stock caught the morning light like polished mirrors. "Where?" He took the phone from Collins. "When?"

"San Juan Island. This morning. Same profile as the others."

Beck scrolled through the text message on the phone and forgot about the wolf.

"Look at the name, sir," said Collins. "At the bottom of the message. The name the guy yelled."

Beck glanced at him, then scanned down. "Lorna Gwin," he said softly, amazed. "Same name."

"Should we head back?"

Beck nodded, eyes shining. "Yeah. Definitely." He checked his Rolex. "And send Dodd and Drucker to the San Juans. Now. Use the Jet Ranger. I want them there. On the ground."

"Yes, sir."

"And tell Ring to pull out all the stops. I want to know everything about this guy in the San Juans. Everything."

CHAPTER 10

"**THIS WAS SUPPOSED TO BE** our bike day," said Joe, as they made their way along a winding two-lane road toward Roche Harbor.

Ella glanced at him. Smiled. Shifted gears. "We'll bike it another day. Anyhow, we get to see more of the island this way."

Joe looked at her and felt his mood improve. His mood always improved when he looked at Ella Tollefson. The woman was gorgeous. She was also sweet. Gentle. Funny as hell.

He thought, *Why the heck is she hanging out with me? And will she stick around now that I've behaved like a total nutcase?* But all he said was, "You're too good to be true."

When she glanced at him this time, she thought she saw—could it be?—tears.

"Baby, what is it?" she said, easing the car off the road again, into a gravel pullout. She'd never seen him cry before.

Joe said, "Wait. You're not, are you?"

Ella brought the Jetta to a full stop, turned the engine off, and gently caressed Joe's cheek with her fingertips.

"Not what?"

"Too good to be true?" He stared through the windshield, embarrassed. "I mean…you're really here. Right?"

Confident, strong, slightly cocky Joe Stanton—not-afraid-of-anything Joe Stanton—looked suddenly vulnerable. Like a little boy. It made Ella want to wrap her arms around him and hold him tight.

"I'm definitely really here," she said tenderly. "And I'm not going anywhere."

They stopped for groceries at a market in Roche Harbor. The checkout clerk was friendly and talkative, but while they were paying, Ella noticed two customers and another clerk staring at Joe from three aisles away, pointing and whispering. Joe noticed, too, but pretended not to.

"What's that saying?" said Ella. "Take a picture, it'll last longer? I should go tell them that."

"Small island," said Joe. "Word travels fast. And it's not every day you get to see a raving lunatic up close."

They headed south, to Lime Kiln Point State Park, found a parking space, and walked the short path to the lighthouse.

A few tourists were out, strolling the interpretive trail and admiring the proud century-old structure. Joe and Ella made their way along the rocky shore.

"I read about this place," said Ella, as they left the path and scrambled among the truck-sized boulders guarding the lighthouse from the surging waters of Haro Strait. "Lime Kiln was the last lighthouse in the U.S. to get electricity—in the forties. Guess they must've used lanterns up 'til then."

Joe gazed back at the tall octagonal tower. Ella took his hand and led the way to a flat-topped boulder with an unobstructed view of the strait. "Sounds kinda romantic," she said wistfully, "Out here on this lonely point, keeping the light on for the ships."

Joe studied the lighthouse as they spread a blanket on the rock. "I could do that job alone," he said. "But not with you. Never."

"Why not?" Ella asked, feigning offense. She saw the twinkle in Joe's eyes. "Don't you think I'm capable?"

"Oh you're definitely capable." He pulled her close and kissed her. The scent of her skin and hair, the feel of her body tight against his made him forget his problems. "And you're also *way* too distracting. I'd never remember to light the stupid lantern."

Ella giggled.

"There'd be shipwrecks everywhere. Lynch mobs after me."

They ate lunch, and the sun climbed higher—warming the rocks and making the water sparkle and shimmer like cut glass. Joe fell back onto the thick wool blanket and closed his eyes. Thirty seconds later he was asleep, breathing rhythmically. Ella studied the bruise on his forehead, thought about all that happened, and wondered if they'd made a mistake by lingering on the island. By not getting home as fast as possible. She thought about waking him and asking him to get back in the car, then thought better of it. He looked peaceful. Relaxed.

She took a paperback from her bag and curled up against him, feeling the warmth and strength of his body.

CHAPTER 11

SHELDON BECK GLANCED at a grainy video feed of the enemy he was about to kill, an enemy sulking in a tiny cell in the bowels of his 416-foot ship, *Arctic Marauder*. The prisoner's name was Dalton Ellis and he looked frail and defeated on the small black-and-white screen.

Beck removed his camouflage hunting jacket and polished the barrel and stock of the Holland & Holland with a fresh gun cloth.

He'd paid $190,000 for the custom-made English rifle at auction and it was a magnificent piece.

He hefted the gun, admiring its perfect balance—its seeming weightlessness in his hands—and aimed at the monitor.

Time's up, Ellis. Today's the day.

He lowered the weapon slowly.

Ellis would have to wait. First, he needed to know more about the guy in the San Juans.

He exited his private suite and beckoned Collins, who was loitering at a workstation nearby. "War Room," he said, moving into the corridor. "Do we have a name yet?"

Collins grabbed his tablet and hurried after his boss. "Stanton. Joseph Stanton. Guy's a priest."

Beck grunted. "That's different. Was he in the water?"

"We don't know yet. Details still coming in."

"What?" said Beck. The look on Collins's face worried him.

"It's your sister."

Beck stopped walking. "Kate? What about her?"

"She's on her way here."

Beck's jaw tightened. "Since when? Why wasn't I told?"

"We just found out. Her pilot radioed as they were taking off from Juneau."

"Juneau! Christ. She'll be here any minute."

Collins retreated a step and Beck paced the corridor. The word "bitch" made it to Collins's ears at least a half a dozen times.

"Why the fuck is she here?"

Collins made no reply. And Beck knew the answer anyway. He fumed a minute more, muttering under his breath.

"Fine," he said at last. "So, we'll show her."

"Sir?"

"She's coming. Nothing I can do about it. Not now. Showing her what we've found is the only way to get her off my back."

CHAPTER 12

BECK AND COLLINS MADE THEIR WAY down the gleaming steel-and-glass corridor. Shafts of summer sunlight stabbed through large convex windows, filling the hall with light.

From the outside, Beck's vessel—with its black dead-rise V hull and futuristic design—looked more like a starship than a boat. Inside, *Marauder* was all masculine lines and angles. A weird hybrid of luxury yacht and military vessel. In fact, it had been designed and built by a yacht maker and subsequently "enhanced," as Beck liked to say, with numerous modifications. Armor. Weapons systems. An extra helipad. And a slot for a six-person submarine, Beck's latest toy.

Marauder was also fast. Its aluminum alloy superstructure let it fly through the water, even in rough seas.

Marauder was Beck's home and office and command center. He owned other homes, but he was happiest aboard his ship. Running his divisions with freedom and autonomy. Not chained to a desk or office tower like his father and sister.

For the moment, *Marauder* was anchored in a quiet forested cove off Admiralty Island.

Beck and Collins passed the darkened lounge, where a Steinway grand with a custom Chihuly-glass lid glittered in the gloom. They rounded a corner into *Marauder*'s main hall. Kate Lerner was already there, waiting at the foot of the spiral staircase.

"Why haven't you returned my calls?" she asked.

"Heartfelt greetings to you, too," Beck replied.

He hugged Kate lightly and she tolerated the gesture. Barely. Beck stepped back. Forced a smile. "Always great to see my sister."

"Cut the bullshit, Sheldon."

Beck's smile tightened imperceptibly. No one, aside from his sister and father, called him by his first name. No one dared.

"There's no bullshit, Kate."

Kate handed her coat and briefcase to her bodyguard—a troll-like man with a neck as thick as a fire hydrant—smoothed her perfect corporate-lawyer suit, and drew herself up as if preparing to admonish a disobedient mailroom clerk. "Why," she asked again, "have you not returned our calls? Our e-mails?"

Beck smiled, thought about it. "You look good, Kate. Diet's definitely working for you."

"Sheldon—"

"Been working out?"

"Can we cut the crap, please?"

"Just trying to be sociable."

"Don't. I don't have time."

"Fine," said Beck. "What's on your mind?"

Kate stared at him. Laughed. Like his question was idiotic. When she spoke again, her voice was low and controlled, but there was a contemptuous edge to it.

"What's on my mind? The *contract* is what's on my mind. The four-hundred-million-dollar contract. The deployment that you begged Father to lead. That's supposed to start, end of next week."

Beck shrugged. "And? What about it?"

"Why are you holding here? Stonewalling. Playing with yourself. Whatever the hell you're doing."

Beck glanced at Collins and the bodyguard. Both men wore opaque, impassive expressions—like butlers for the Old Rich. But Beck knew what they were thinking. He knew: *Kate wears the pants in the family. Kate pulls the strings. Kate holds the power and has the cozy relationship with the board and their father. Kate has come to* Marauder *to put her irresponsible little brother in his place.*

He knew. It mattered not at all that he controlled entire thriving divisions of the family empire, that this was his private ship she'd come barging into. In this context, at this moment, he was just Sheldon Beck, impotent asshole. Black sheep. Third-in-command.

He knew. And inside, he was seething. Dad, at least, criticized him in private. But Kate seemed to enjoy berating him in the open, in front of his men. She'd done it before. She was doing it now.

"First of all," he said softly, "I'm technically still on vacation."

"Vacation—"

"I told everyone I'd be taking a few days after the Korean sim. Second, I *have*, in fact, returned your calls and e-mails."

"With half-answers and bullshit."

"With what I felt was appropriate." He gestured toward the lounge, determined to keep his cool. "Lunch? Something to drink, at least, while we talk?"

"Sheldon," said Kate, coming forward, like a teacher outlining last-ditch disciplinary measures to a problem student. "Let me be clear. This is not a pleasure trip for me. This is not a fun visit." She gestured at the panorama outside the windows. "Bum Fuck, Alaska, is the last place in the world I want to be right now."

"So—"

"I'm here," she said, ticking off points on the fingers of her left hand, "because you've ignored our meeting requests."

"There's a good reason."

"Given lame half-answers to our written and verbal queries."

"There's a good reason."

"Added people—very high-priced people—to the payroll without explanation."

"There's a good—"

"And, you've dropped the ball on the biggest deployment in Erebus history."

"I haven't dropped the ball. Just set it aside for a couple of days."

"You dropped the ball," Kate said flatly. "We've heard reports from some of your team leaders that you seem...unfocused. Disengaged."

Beck wondered who in his convoy was saying such things.

"I'm concerned," said Kate. "Father is concerned."

Father is concerned.

Beck waited to make sure she was finished.

"Why do you still call him Father?" he asked. "Makes you sound like you have a stick up your ass, you know?"

Collins stifled a laugh. Kate glared, shook her head. "Fine, Sheldon."

She ripped her coat from the troll's arm. "Great. You want to sit up here in the sticks and screw off, fine. Makes my job a lot simpler." She started up the stairs, bodyguard behind.

"There's a reason," said Beck, calling after her, "for everything I've done. For the delays. For the specialists on the payroll."

Kate paused. "*What* reason?"

He pointed to the sunlit corridor at the far end of the hall. "It's all in the War Room."

Kate resumed climbing. "I don't have time for games, Sheldon."

"It's no game, Kate. We've found something. Something you need to see."

Kate stopped again. Squinted at him. "*Found* something?" she said dismissively. "On the way back from the sim?"

"That's right."

"What?"

Beck took a breath. "A phenomenon. Something we can't explain."

Kate stared. "Sounds like more bullshit to me."

Beck stared back. "We found something, Kate. Something extraordinary. Please. You've come this far. You can spare ten more minutes."

Kate looked from her bodyguard to her brother to her watch. "Ten minutes," she said.

She stepped from the stairs, and Beck led the group to the War Room, where pictures of Joe Stanton already filled wall-sized screens.

CHAPTER 13

JOE STANTON LAY in the warm sunshine on the boulder overlooking Haro Strait and drifted into a dream.

It was a very strange dream.

I'm flying, Joe thought, as he fell through open sky—fell at great speed, then leveled off and soared, in perfect control, over a deep canyon.

I'm flying.

It was a glorious feeling, followed by shock, as he realized the truth.

Not flying. Swimming.

There were fish. Schools of fish. Above. Below. On the right. On the left. Joe laughed.

Ella, lying against Joe's chest, heard him laugh, and smiled, relieved that he was having a peaceful dream.

Fish!

Joe dreamed that he was zooming among schools of big, fat, beautiful fish. Fish that flashed like polished mirrors in the deep.

Feels like I'm flying, Joe thought. And it did.

So great was his speed and maneuverability in the water, so graceful and powerful was his body, so perfect his control, that it *felt* like he was zooming through the air, the finest, most gifted stunt pilot in the world. The most agile, nimble hawk ever to pirouette through the sky.

I'm flying…through the water.

Stanton focused on the fish, and the dream became stranger still.

Click!

The shimmering silver skin of the huge chinook salmon to his right disappeared, and Joe perceived the creature's skeleton and internal organs.

Click!

The skin reappeared. Joe gasped.

Click!

The school of herring flashing near the surface—directly overhead—became a school of skeletons.

The image lasted only a second, but the information revealed in that "snapshot" was astonishing. Joe could see everything. Every detail in every single fish: gills, brain, heart, liver, kidneys, intestines, stomach. The contents *within* each stomach.

He knew the number of fish in the school: three hundred eighty-two. He knew where they were going.

It's a miracle, Joe thought.

He wanted to stop and consider what he was seeing. But it was not to be. His speed was too great.

And now he found that he was no longer in control of his actions, that his dream was turning dark.

Click!

A jolt of adrenaline traveled the length of his body, like a blast of electric current. His limbs twitched and his heart thumped in his chest.

Ella felt Joe's body quiver and tense. Heard him cry out: "No!"

She dropped her book. Spun around. Caressed his face. "Joe. Sweetie? Joe? You okay?"

He couldn't hear her. He was deep underwater now, zooming toward a huge drifting shape. A shape he somehow recognized.

Click!

Skeleton. Brain. Lungs. Internal organs.

Heart.

Heart?

The heart's not beating. The heart is still.

"No!" Joe twisted and writhed, twitched and moaned. His face paled and a slick glaze of sweat coated his forehead.

"She's dead!" he cried, his voice a guttural, strangled gurgle. A sound Ella barely recognized.

She gripped him by his shoulders. Shook him. "Joe! It's me! You're having a bad dream. Wake up."

Joe stirred, and suddenly people up and down the beach were yelling.

For a moment, Ella thought they'd heard her worried cries and were yelling at her. But everyone was staring at the water. Pointing and smiling and cheering.

"Whales!" someone shouted. And Ella saw them.

Joe rose slowly to a sitting position and shook off his nightmare.

"Whales," said Ella, holding Joe tightly, clutching his hands in hers. She didn't like how cold his hands felt.

Tourists up and down the beach snapped pictures as a pod of orcas rolled through the sunlit channel.

A park ranger stepped from the lighthouse and trained a pair of binoculars on the pod.

"It's just like yesterday," said Ella, glad that Joe was awake, glad to have something to look at and talk about to take his mind off his nightmare and the day's events.

Joe was silent as he watched the whales. "Yesterday?" he said at last. "What's like yesterday?"

"Well…the whales," Ella replied. "Only, not quite as good, right? Had front-row seats yesterday. You especially." She glanced up and down the beach. "How many of these people have ever touched a whale, huh?"

Joe's body went so completely still that Ella let go of him and scooted around so that she could get a better look at his face. It was a face lined with worry and fear.

"Joe?" She took his hands and he stared past her. The whales were moving away now, steadily, in formation, soon to vanish around the point.

Joe said, "Talk about yesterday."

"When we saw the whales," said Ella. "You know. When we were kayaking. They came up under our boats. They were all around us. You touched one."

Joe kept his eyes on the whales. They rolled on, finally disappearing from sight. The tourists turned back to the lighthouse, and the excited chatter faded.

Ella held Joe in her arms again. After a long time, she said, "Sweetie…are you not remembering what happened yesterday?"

"Not a bit of it," he replied, shaking his head. "Nothing." He sounded close to tears.

Ella squeezed his hand. "It's gonna be fine. You're gonna be fine. But I think we better head for the ferry."

"Yeah. I think you're right."

CHAPTER 14

COLLINS PLACED HIS PALM FLAT against a sleek black pad set into the wall, and the War Room's beefy metal blast door slid open. The darkened room was spacious, solemn as a chapel, and bathed in the cool machine glow of high-def monitors and wall-sized screens. Soft classical music accompanied the faint hum of servers and the tapping of keyboards.

An immense glowing table dominated the center of the room——a giant touch screen that Beck and his team used to display charts, maps, and theaters of war, and to manipulate troop and resource placement. One of Beck's IT architects had dubbed the table "The Palantir" after the magical seeing stones in *The Lord of the Rings*. The name had stuck.

Technicians—some standing, some seated in large comfortable chairs—worked at stations around the room.

Kate stepped from the shadows, joining Beck alongside the Palantir, and a hush fell over the room, which was something, considering that the chamber was already library-quiet. Rustling stopped. Whispers ceased. Even the server-hum seemed to fade. A stifling, invisible tension replaced the sound, as if Kate were a storm cloud about to unleash lightning. Backs straightened. Screens refreshed. And everyone became suddenly, extraordinarily focused on the tasks before them.

A blonde woman looked up, unsmiling, from the flickering, ever-changing surface of the Palantir—the shimmer from the table reflected in her glasses—and addressed Beck directly. "He was kayaking," she said, in a crisp Slavic accent. "Joe Stanton—that's the subject's name—was on the water for at least three hours yesterday."

"Was he *in* the water?" Beck asked. He stepped to a wall of glass, where Joe Stanton's Facebook images filled multiple screens. "Did he dive?"

"Still checking," said the woman. "But not that we know of. Would you like to see when he cracked up?"

Beck looked surprised. "What do you mean? You have that?"

A lanky, pony-tailed computer technician standing at a console behind the blonde replied. "Yes Sir. Somebody recorded Stanton blowing his gasket and posted it on YouTube early this morning—just after the incident."

"Show me."

The technician, whose name was Brandon, tapped some buttons and a jittery image of the motel parking lot and the Breakwater sign appeared on one of the larger screens. In the foreground, an elderly man was trying to restrain a deranged twentysomething who was screaming and clutching his head.

"Stop shouting!" the older man yelled. Then, to someone out of frame: "Call 911!"

Beck recognized the younger man as Joe Stanton, from the Facebook pictures, though Joe's face here was a mask of anguish and pain.

"Lorna G," Joe growled. "Lorna Gwin!"

"Call the damn police!" the old man yelled to someone off-screen. "Now!"

"They murdered my little girl!" Joe Stanton screamed—and the amateur video bobbed and jumped.

"What little girl?" asked Kate.

"Jesus," muttered Collins, "Dude's whacked."

"Who *is* that?" Kate asked impatiently. "What are we watching?"

Beck stared at the drama on-screen and didn't respond.

Brandon paused the video.

"Is that it?" asked Beck.

"He stumbles around and sets off a car alarm," said Brandon, "but there are no more mentions of the little girl."

"*What* little girl?" demanded Kate.

"Lorna Gwin," Beck replied. "This is the fourth guy in a row—that we know of—to freak out and scream this kid's name."

"Well, who is she?" Kate sounded curious and irritated at the same time.

"We don't know."

A man and woman stepped from the shadows behind Beck and joined the group as if they belonged there.

"Dr. Phelps, Dr. Edelstein," said Beck, "welcome. I'd like you to meet my sister, Kate Lerner."

"Nick Phelps," said the man, a fit-looking fiftysomething guy with sandy hair and a neatly trimmed beard. He extended his hand to Kate and received a cold stare in return.

"Dr. Phelps is a professor of neuroanatomy," said Beck, "from MIT. Janice Edelstein is a professor of oceanography at Woods Hole."

Edelstein was a little older than Phelps and had a pleasant, intelligent face framed by thick gray hair, cut short. She smiled at Kate but made no attempt to shake her hand.

"They're still getting up to speed," said Beck.

"On what?" Kate asked. "Why are they on our payroll?"

Beck sighed. "Professors, you'll have to excuse my sister. Beneath her brusque, blunt exterior she's actually quite rude and demanding."

Kate glared at the professors. "What do *they* have to do with Erebus?" She waved at the monitors. "What does *that* have to do with Erebus?"

"Getting to it," Beck replied.

He signaled the computer tech, and snapshots of three different men—healthy, vigorous guys in their late twenties or early thirties—filled the top row of monitors.

"The divers we lost in the Bering Sea," said Kate, stepping closer to the screens and zeroing in on the first two men. "Why are their pictures here? And who's this other one?"

Beck tapped the images one at a time. "John Galbreth. Andy Stahl. Brad Whittaker," he said. "Whittaker was a gillnetter out of Yakutat."

"Was?"

"Died about a week ago."

"From what?" Kate asked. She studied Whittaker's pictures, some with very recent time stamps. He looked perfectly healthy. A man in his prime.

"Same thing that killed Galbreth and Stahl," said Beck. "We think so, anyway. You read the report on how our guys died?"

"Skimmed it," said Kate. "They were running security checks on the Sedco Forex TLPs."

"Right," said Beck. "Tension leg platforms," he explained, in response to Phelps's puzzled expression. "TLPs are deepwater oil rigs. They're potential terrorist targets. Feds stepped up security on oil platforms after 9/11, but the Coast Guard doesn't have enough assets to watch everything. They pay Erebus to help.

"The guys were fairly deep. Checking the tendons—the cables—that connect the TLPs to the seafloor. Separate platforms, two miles apart."

Beck turned to the glowing Palantir table, and brought up charts of the Bering Sea.

"The TLPs are here, and here," he said, pointing at the screen. "South southeast of Nunivak. These were routine dives. Nothing out of the ordinary. Not for our guys.

"They surfaced. Separate support ships, all good. All normal. Then, about an hour after they came up, they started wigging out."

"Like him," said Kate, staring at the freeze-frame of Joe Stanton and recalling the divers' autopsy reports.

"Yeah," said Beck, "real similar. They were screaming. Out of control. Ranting and raving about a kid. A daughter. A little girl named Lorna Gwin."

Kate shook her head. "That wasn't in the report. I'd remember that."

"Some of the facts came together later," said Beck. "After we interviewed support crew on the different ships. I was still at the South Korean sim when the divers flipped out. Details started coming in when we were on our way back. Our crews off Nunivak thought they were looking at DCS at first."

"Decompression sickness," said Edelstein.

"Right. Crew put 'em into hyperbaric chambers, just like they're supposed to, and after a while, the screaming stopped. They calmed down. Recovered. Or seemed to. Couple days later, they relapsed. We were on our way back by that time and I had them moved to the *Northern Mercy*. Stahl died ten days after his dive. Galbreth made it eleven. And both went crazy again…complete mental breakdowns."

Beck turned to the freeze-frame of Brad Whittaker, the robust young gillnetter. "Whittaker suffered a violent hallucination eight days after Galbreth died. Same symptoms. Same pathology."

"Was he diving?" Edelstein asked.

"Fishing," Beck replied. "But he fell out of his boat, apparently. Hauling in nets in rough seas. His brother saw it happen. Rescued him, in fact. Pulled him out of the water. A few hours later, the crazy stuff started."

Kate looked skeptical. "Don't tell me Whittaker yelled about a kid."

"Matter of fact, he did. On the street in Yakutat. In the clinic where they sedated him. Where he suffered a seizure. Eyewitnesses—Whittaker's friends—say he was completely out of his mind, screaming about a murdered daughter, a little girl. Lorna Gwin."

Kate and the others stared at the images of the men.

"What could cause such a thing?" Edelstein asked softly. "I mean…not just mental breakdown and hallucination, but the *same* hallucination. And a *fatal* hallucination."

"We don't know. We're trying to figure it out. It's the reason you and Dr. Phelps are here."

Kate turned to the glowing table map, and traced a line with her finger from Nunivak to Yakutat to the San Juans.

"It's fifteen hundred miles from the TLPs down to Yakutat," said Beck, "And another thousand to Friday Harbor in the San Juans. We set some of our computers to troll for new incidents matching the first three. Joe Stanton popped out of the woodwork this morning."

Kate and the others studied the map in silence.

Beck said, "Four guys. Four nearly identical mental breakdowns, along a twenty-five-hundred-mile trajectory, in the course of two weeks. And these are just the cases we know about. There may be more."

Kate turned her gaze to the YouTube freeze-frame of Joe Stanton in the Breakwater parking lot. "Mr. Stanton's going to die," she said.

Beck shrugged. "If he follows the pattern. Yeah. He's got ten days. Maybe twelve. At the most."

CHAPTER 15

JOE AND ELLA MADE THEIR WAY back to Friday Harbor in the slanting sunlight of late afternoon, to find the ferry line shorter, but not by much.

They waited in the holding area, listening to music in the car and playing gin rummy. Ella kept the conversation light, but inside she was deeply worried. She joked. Laughed. Clowned around. And prepared for the worst.

In her mind's eye, she measured the distance to the ferry ticket booth—the place she'd run for help if Joe had another breakdown. She kept her iPhone out in the open—in case she needed to call 911.

And she imagined the chaos that might ensue if Joe made it through the wait in the parking lot, but then had a breakdown on the ferry. How would she handle such a thing?

Ella's overriding hope and prayer was to make it through the afternoon and evening and get Joe to a hospital—a big state-of-the-art Seattle hospital—where they could run sophisticated tests and figure out what the hell was going on.

She watched Joe now, studying him closely. She wasn't the only one.

CHAPTER 16

KATE LERNER STOOD in the center of the War Room and considered the bizarre facts her brother had presented. "Is anyone else investigating this?" she asked. "State troopers? FBI?"

"No," Beck replied. "We didn't release the details about our divers, so nobody else is aware there's a pattern. Not yet, anyway."

Kate regarded her brother. "This is fascinating," she said, the reproach and anger gone from her voice. "Weird. But fascinating. It really is. If your reports are right—if the data's accurate—it's something that needs to be explored. Thoroughly investigated."

"I'm glad you think so."

"But not by us. You need to turn all of this over to law enforcement. I can see no relevance—"

"That's because you haven't seen everything," said Beck. "We have scans, Kate. Of Galbreth, Stahl, and Whittaker. Scans, and more."

Kate's eyes widened. "Whittaker was a private citizen. How did you get scans of Whittaker?"

"Doesn't matter now."

"Yes it *does*, Sheldon." Kate sounded pissed again. "How did you get him out of Yakutat?"

Beck shrugged. "I have fifteen gung-ho ex–Special Forces on board, Kate. Transporting a comatose civilian to the ship isn't all that hard."

"Sheldon—"

"We needed the scans, Kate. We got them. And we found something. Something similar in all three men. Something you need to see."

Kate glanced at Phelps and Edelstein. "Not now I don't."

Beck dismissed her concern with a wave. "Our guests have already signed a stack of NDAs this thick." He made a wide space with his thumb and index finger. "They're part of the team."

Phelps said, "I'm well aware of your firm's developments in thought capture. If that's your concern."

Kate ignored him. "Sheldon—"

Beck signaled to Brandon, and before Kate could intervene, big multicolored brain scans filled the monitors. The 3D scans began turning slowly.

Phelps took a step toward the screens, donned his glasses, and stepped closer still. He studied the images for a long time, moving from screen to screen.

"What is this structure?" he asked at last, pointing to a small mass deep within Whittaker's MRI.

Beck laughed. "We were hoping you could tell us that, Doc."

Phelps stepped to Galbreth's scan, then Stahl's. A walnut-sized orange mass was visible in all three scans.

Phelps returned to Whittaker's scan and asked Brandon to rotate and slice the images. Then, using a pen as a pointer, Phelps narrated as the brain segments came into focus. He might have been addressing a group of graduate students:

"Temporal lobes, corpus callosum, parietal lobes, occipital lobe," he said. "Also known as the visual cortex."

He stepped closer to the anomaly and ticked off the structures surrounding the fluorescing mass: "Thalamus, pineal gland, hypothalamus. Down here: the amygdala, hippocampus, basal ganglia...the brain stem. And..." He paused. "This...whatever it is"—he tapped the mysterious orange mass with the tip of the pen—"wedged between the caudate nucleus and the occipital lobe."

"Well," said Kate, "is it a tumor or something?"

"Or something." Phelps laughed and shook his head. "The identical tumor in three individuals? In exactly the same position?" He checked Stahl's scans again, then Galbreth's. "Not likely."

Brandon presented different views of the anomaly and Phelps continued his analysis. "No sign of perifocal brain edema. Not a meningioma. Not like any I've seen, anyhow." To Beck, he said, "I'd like to see the pathology reports."

"Of course."

"And you mentioned thought captures…"

Beck nodded at Brandon, and fresh images populated the screens surrounding the freeze-frame of Andy Stahl.

The screens showed a little girl, age five or six. A girl with pale white skin and brown hair, standing in a field, the only person in the scene. The sky behind the girl was dark, brooding. The perimeter of each image blurred, indistinct.

"Meet Lorna Gwin," said Beck. "As perceived by Erebus diver Andy Stahl."

"The mystery kid," said Kate, almost to herself.

"Yes," said Beck. "The one they're all screaming about. Except—"

"These are thought captures?" Edelstein sounded amazed. "I've read about the technology, of course. But I mean … How did you—"

"Stahl was dying," said Beck. "In the ICU on our hospital ship. We wanted to know what was going on. So we wired him for capture, just like we do with detainees. And we asked him straight-out. 'Who are you yelling about? Who is Lorna Gwin?'"

Beck nodded toward the screens. "These are the pictures he had in his head."

The images had a painterly, ghostlike quality.

"The other diver," said Kate. "He was in intensive care, too."

"Yes," Beck replied, as images of another girl populated the screens around the freeze-frame of John Galbreth. This girl was approximately the same age as the first child, but completely different in appearance.

The first girl was white. This girl was black, like Galbreth himself, with curly hair and a sweet, cherubic face.

"Meet Lorna Gwin number two," said Beck, as perceived by Erebus diver John Galbreth."

"I don't understand," said Kate.

"There's more," said Beck. He signaled to Brandon again and new images filled the screens around the freeze-frame of gillnetter Brad Whittaker.

"And *this* is Mr. Whittaker's Lorna Gwin," said Beck.

This girl was at a playground. Laughing. Spinning on a merry-go-round. She was about the same age as the first two girls, but this child was petite, with blonde hair, delicate features, and glasses.

They stared in silence for a long time.

"So they all screamed the same name," Phelps said at last. "All hallucinated about a kid. A dead girl named Lorna Gwin…But when you dig into their thoughts you find that there are actually three Lorna Gwins. Unique individuals. Which makes sense if each of these guys believes he lost a daughter." He sounded like he was trying to puzzle it out as he spoke.

"So are these real kids?" Edelstein asked.

"We don't think so," said Beck. "None of these guys had kids. None of their friends or family knew anything about kids that fit these descriptions."

Edelstein said, "So…despite how freaked out these guys all were, no kids actually died?"

"I didn't say that," said Beck, and he nodded toward the ghostlike images of the little girls. "I said *these* aren't real kids." He looked at his companions. Saw the confusion on their faces. "It didn't make sense to us either, at first."

"And now it does?" asked Kate.

Beck shrugged and glanced involuntarily toward a sprawling workstation on the far side of the War Room. "We have a theory," he replied.

Kate caught the glance and understood. By "We have a theory," her brother meant "Orondo Ring has a theory."

Orondo Ring was her brother's secret weapon. Ring was a genius, and Erebus's lead scientist. A math prodigy, with PhDs in artificial intelligence, physics, and IT infrastructure design, Ring's innovations had generated numerous patents for the company, and Sheldon Beck had gone out of his way to pull Ring into his sphere of control. Had, in fact, designed the room they were standing in with Ring in mind. To Ring's specifications.

"What's the theory?" Kate asked.

Beck looked at the group. Took his time.

"Thought capture," he said at last, "takes an enormous amount of processing power. Even for the new quantum computers, the requirements are staggering. It's one of the reasons the Feds didn't start using TC for interrogation until 2018. Took too long. Downloads too unwieldy." He tapped the side of his head. "Human thought is complex. Data-rich."

Kate sighed, impatient. "So?"

"So these particular captures—the images of the little girls—are all wrong. Way too light."

"What do you mean, 'light'?" Edelstein asked.

"I mean the downloads are small," said Beck. "Far too small to represent actual people."

He pointed at the picture of John Galbreth. "Take Galbreth. The guy was on his deathbed. Experiencing seizure after seizure. Nothing we could do. We hooked him up to the feed and started asking him questions. 'Who's Lorna Gwin? What happened to her? What happened to you?' And so on. And as we're asking these questions we're also watching the monitors, expecting a big jump in the fMRI patterns and a torrent of data to start roaring in."

Beck looked at his companions. "That's what happens in interrogation. You ask a terrorist where he planted the bomb, and the thought-capture hardware practically catches on fire, there's so much data. All those raw memories and emotions: Streets. Buildings. Faces. Thoughts. Fears. Colors. Smells. Sounds. It all comes flooding in at once. A deluge of information straight from the neurons in the visual cortex to the hardware and software that untangles it all. Sorts it. Catalogs it.

"Real memories, especially recent, vivid memories, take up an enormous amount of space. Galbreth's memories of his little girl—or at least of her physical presence— weren't like that. The images were hollow. Insubstantial."

Kate nodded at the screens. "So these kids are...what? Made up?"

"Right," said Beck. "They're constructions. Like characters your brain might generate to populate a dream. The emotions *underlying* the images are real. But the pictures are fake.

"For whatever reason, the men couldn't conjure an image of the actual dead child they were grieving. The *true* Lorna Gwin. So they fabricated a little girl to accompany the raw anguish flooding their minds. These images are...placeholders. We think so anyway."

The group fell silent again, digesting Beck's information.

After a while, Kate spoke, exasperated. "What could cause something like this?"

"We don't know," said Beck. "We're working on it."

Kate nodded toward Phelps. "He's part of your team now. What does the high-priced neuroscientist have to say?"

Phelps laughed. "This is a new one on me."

He stepped toward the screens. "If it were just a psychosomatic response to stimuli, I'd suspect a drug. A toxin. But the same—or virtually the same—hallucination across four individuals? I've never heard of anything like it."

Phelps turned to the monitors displaying the brain scans and tapped on the anomaly he'd identified earlier, the mass wedged between the caudate nucleus and the occipital lobe. "And then there's this little mystery."

Edelstein said, "Why would this tumor—or whatever it is—cause these guys to imagine a dead child?"

"We suspect," Beck replied, "that the grief hallucination is a sort of…icebreaker."

"A what?" said Kate.

Beck said, "Because here's the thing. The part I haven't shared with you yet. All of this stuff with the kids, all of the anguish and suffering…it's just what's on the surface. The thought captures uncovered a mother lode of material below that."

He gestured at the bank of monitors. "It's like these guys ran into a high-tension power line, only instead of filling up with electricity, their heads filled up with thoughts. Filled to bursting. The dead kid is on the surface, but there's an ocean of other stuff under that."

"What kind of stuff?" asked Phelps.

"Ah," said Beck. "This is where it gets really interesting." He nodded at Brandon, and fresh images filled the massive center screen.

CHAPTER 17

"WHAT IN THE WORLD?" said Kate.

On the screen hovered a phosphorescent tube, or chamber. Veil-thin. Delicate. Emerald green. The structure had a wide, gaping mouth and a long, tapering body, like a horn of plenty.

The broad open mouth of the object undulated gently. Rhythmically. Like a jellyfish drifting in the current. The walls of the structure glowed softly, but the area surrounding the strange object was dark, as if the tube, or chamber, or whatever it was, were floating in deep space, illuminated only by its own faint inner light. The image had a grainy, raw appearance, like a video transmission from one of the early Mars rovers.

The group stared in silence.

"This thought," Beck said finally, "this…memory, was identical in all of the victims."

"Well, what is it?" asked Kate. She stepped closer to the screen. "What are we looking at?"

"We don't know yet. But the data files are immense. And we haven't even cataloged everything yet. Whittaker's thoughts are the most complete. The downloads include an abundance of views. And the detail is good."

"But I don't understand," said Kate. "They were all screaming about a kid."

"Like I said," Beck replied, "the kid, the grief, was on the surface. Raw and painful. The first thing to hit them when they touched the metaphorical power line." He turned to the chamber images hovering before them. "This landed one level down—in their subconsciouses.

The men may not even have been aware of this. None of them said anything about it."

Brandon toggled between different views and angles, close-ups and wide shots.

The close-ups of the gently arcing "bell" or mouth of the structure revealed a lithe, opalescent wall that appeared to move and flow, and a dense latticework of glowing lines, thin as spider silk. The lines—there were thousands of them—ran like phosphorescent tracks from the outermost fringe of the bell into the heart of the tunnel.

The structure was unlike anything any of them had ever seen. It floated silently before them, looking like a cross between a living thing—an amorphous, liquid organism—and a fantastically exotic piece of architecture, a building designed and constructed without concern for the laws of gravity.

"Dead kids. Unbearable grief. And...this," said Kate, nodding at the giant screen. "That's one hell of an hallucination."

"I'd like to see all of the thought captures," said Phelps, "or at least what's been cataloged to date."

"Of course," said Beck.

"And," said Phelps, "I have to say, I agree with your sister that you need to open this up. Bring in other experts. Share this with the authorities."

Beck said nothing.

"The captures are elaborate," Phelps continued. "Complex. Unprecedented. And you say we've only seen a fraction. On top of that, and more importantly, this...phenomenon is lethal. Three guys dead—that you've identified. A new case this morning. What if there's another tomorrow? What if there are five more? What if—"

"Can you zoom in on this section, please?" It was Edelstein, and she was standing in front of a close-up of the chamber mouth. A low angle.

There was something in front of one tiny section of the structure's gracefully curving lower lip. Small randomly shaped protrusions. Bits of detritus backlit by the chamber's eerie glow.

Brandon tapped his keyboard, and the magnification increased. He boosted the resolution, made some adjustments, zoomed in even more.

"Anthosactis," said Edelstein. "In a whale fall. I'll be damned."

"Antho-what in a what?" asked Phelps.

"*Anthosactis pearseae*," she replied. "It's a type of anemone."

Brandon fine-tuned the picture until they could all see what Edelstein was talking about. The anemones were small, white, and roughly cube-shaped. They appeared to be growing—flourishing—amid a vast pile of bones.

"Anthosactis is about the size of a human molar," said Edelstein. "It even looks like a tooth."

They stared. There were thousands of the little white cubes—each with a small tentacle on one side—covering the jumble of bones. Stuck to them.

Brandon switched to a different angle, an even lower perspective. Now they were looking through the bone garden, toward the phosphorescent chamber mouth. The chamber opening looked vast and alien. Glowing fibers along the base of the chamber connected it to the seafloor. Like anchor lines. Like tethers. Like the chamber might float away if the lines didn't hold it secure.

Edelstein said, "Researchers discovered the species in Monterey Canyon, in 2007, twenty-five miles off the California coast, in about three-thousand meters of water. Living in a whale fall there, as well."

"You're talking about a dead whale?" said Phelps. "A whale skeleton?"

"Exactly." Edelstein pointed at an image of gigantic vertebrae, snaking along the seafloor. "The flesh of an animal like this decomposes within weeks, but the bones can last a hundred years. As the bones break down, they release sulfur. And creatures, including this anemone, use that to make energy. Just like terrestrial plants use the sun."

The group stared at the otherworldy scene: the bones, the eerie glow, the massive chamber mouth in the background. It was like something from a Salvador Dalí dreamscape.

"Find a wider angle," Beck said to Brandon.

"Yes, sir."

Brandon skimmed through images. Dozens per second flashed on screen, a blur of colors and shapes. Then he found what he was looking for and the stream of pictures stopped. He adjusted the resolution and brought the image up. It was a wide shot: the chamber, head-on, hovering in the darkness, shimmering softly, like the entrance to a fantastical labyrinth. The whale bones were there, in the foreground, but barely noticeable—insignificant bumps, tiny silhouetted protrusions against the immensity of the chamber mouth.

"Even if the bones are from a small whale," Phelps said quietly, "the chamber is—" his voice trailed off.

"Huge," said Beck. "Big enough to house a Trident submarine. Or two."

They stared in silence.

Kate shook her head. "Why would these images—any of this stuff—be in this guy's brain? In his memories?"

"Like I was saying," Phelps said, "you need to make some calls. Open this up and share what you've found. I can recommend some—"

"We're not sharing anything," said Beck.

They all looked at him.

"Not yet, anyway. There's one final piece to this that you haven't seen yet, something we found in the thought captures, in all three men."

He looked at Kate. "It's the reason, more than any other, that we've been holding here. Trying to puzzle this out."

"What reason?"

A deep, resonant tone boomed from the speakers around them, like the lowest note on the deepest bass instrument.

Throom! Throom! Throom!

"Sound," Beck replied. "We found sound with the images. Embedded in the thought captures."

Kate waited for the strange noises to subside. For the reverberations to fade.

"So there's sound. With their memories, or hallucinations or whatever they are. So what?"

Beck turned to Brandon again. "Play the other recording."

Brandon hit a button.

Throom! Throom! Throom! echoed throughout the War Room once again.

"It's the same sound," said Kate.

"Yes," said Beck. "But that one's from the real world."

They stared at him.

"The first series came from the thought captures. From inside the victim's heads. The second set, from hydrophones in the Bering Sea.

A NOAA research team noticed the sound first. Monitored it. Put it on their site to see if anyone could identify it. They have no idea what it is. Nobody does.

"Doesn't match anything in any database," said Beck. "Nothing natural. Nothing man-made."

Edelstein said, "Has NOAA pinpointed a location? A point of origin? Or have you?

"There appear to be multiple sources. All very deep. Spread across a huge area. Our hope is to find one we can reach, and check it out. Before anyone else."

He looked at his companions and gestured at the screens. "These aren't hallucinations. They're messages."

"Messages?"

"Messages. Transmissions. Thoughts and feelings and impressions foisted on these men, against their will. Without their knowledge. We don't understand the mechanism yet, but that's what happened. What *is* happening."

"A message implies a sender," said Edelstein. "Who's the sender?"

"We don't know. Not yet. What's clear is that something touched these men. Entered their minds. Changed them."

"*Killed* them," said Phelps. "The first three, anyway."

"Yes," said Beck.

The room went quiet.

Beck said, "Something or someone is causing this. Something real. Something no one's ever encountered before. We need to look into it." He regarded Phelps and Edelstein. "I need your help. I need you to work with Dr. Ring and the rest of my team. We've gotten this far, but we need your expertise."

He turned to his sister. "That is, unless you think it isn't worth it. That Father would want us to just walk away."

Kate spoke, all the venom gone from her voice, as if the wind had been knocked out of her. "I'll talk to him," she said.

CHAPTER 18

KATE COLLECTED HER TROLL-LIKE bodyguard at the entrance to the War Room and departed the *Arctic Marauder*. Beck watched her chopper lift off.

"There's an update," Collins said, in his most businesslike tone as he joined his boss in the sunlit hall adjacent to the helipad. "Joe Stanton is still on San Juan Island. Dodd spotted him in the ferry line, in Friday Harbor. We have some photos. He looks pretty messed up. And the woman with him looks exhausted. Hot as hell, but exhausted."

Beck thought about it. "Where's the *Northern Mercy*?"

Collins stepped to a monitor set into a wall and touched the screen. Pulled up maps. Scrolled through a couple.

"Thirty five miles south southwest of Tofino," he said. "About to make for San Diego. Quick resupply there, then on to Panama."

"Send it into the Straits. To the San Juans. Now."

"Yes, sir."

"And get Dodd and Drucker on the phone. Whichever one is watching Stanton this minute. I want to talk to them."

CHAPTER 19

JOE STANTON FORGOT about the engagement ring he'd hidden in his pack until they were on the ferry, bound for Anacortes.

He and Ella had endured a long, though blessedly uneventful wait in the Friday Harbor car holding area, finally boarding the MV *Elwha* for the 7:55 p.m. sailing.

"A beer sounds good," said Joe, as they climbed the stairs from the car deck to the passenger cabin.

The look on Ella's face made him reconsider. "Right," he said. "Alcohol with a head injury and hallucinations...probably not my best idea."

"Hot tea?" Ella asked.

"Sure. Good. I'll go grab us a seat."

He found an empty booth near a window, sat down, and pulled a fleece jacket from his pack. That's when he rediscovered the ring.

It was in a little box, inside a mesh compartment. Joe touched the package, but didn't bring it out.

He turned and watched Ella, standing in the galley checkout line. Even just glancing at Ella Tollefson made his heart jump, made him giddy and happy. Christmas morning kind of happy.

The woman was beautiful. The woman was smart. The—

Joe saw that at least three other guys in the bustling galley were ogling Ella. She hadn't noticed. Or maybe she had and was just ignoring them.

Joe felt like standing up and saying, "Excuse me. Hey! She's with me, okay? So just forget it."

Instead, he reached for the little box, turned it in his hand, and considered giving the ring to Ella here. On the boat. Tonight.

The idea died as quickly as it formed.

This isn't the time. Or the place. The circumstances are too weird. She deserves better.

Joe realized, gloomily, that if the weekend had gone according to plan, they'd be having a romantic dinner somewhere on San Juan Island right now. They'd be drinking wine and laughing. If the weekend had gone according to plan, he'd be steering the conversation to their relationship. Telling Ella that he was madly, hopelessly in love with her. That he wanted to spend the rest of his life with her.

But things had not gone as planned, and now they were on the ferry, quitting their vacation early, heading for Seattle and a bunch of medical tests.

Joe zipped the backpack shut as Ella reached the table with two steaming cups of tea.

They sipped in silence, held hands, and gazed out the window as golden summer light transformed the islands into a dreamscape from an Old Masters painting.

It was the last peace Joe Stanton would know for a very long time.

CHAPTER 20

BECK STRODE THROUGH *Marauder*'s main corridor in a sour mood, a throbbing, thrumming ache between his eyes. It felt like someone had jammed a penknife into his frontal lobe and was now twisting it slowly.

"Bring the prisoner to the weather deck," he told Collins. "And lock down the rest of the ship. No one up top except your team."

Beck had contemplated postponing his meeting with Dalton Ellis. He had a lot on his plate, after all. *Then again*, he said to himself, *now's as good a time as any to settle a score. Lively confrontation might burn off some stress, too. Stress courtesy of that bitch of a sister of mine.*

The prisoner stepped from an elevator onto *Marauder*'s weather deck, flanked by Collins and another ex-SEAL. He stood there. Blindfolded. Handcuffed.

Collins pushed the man further onto the deck.

The sky was clear, a rare thing in Southeast Alaska, and Eagle Peak lorded over Admiralty Island like a stoic king, its jagged snow-covered slopes jutting crisp and white against a pale-blue sky. Lush forest blanketed the lower slopes of the great island with trees so huge and healthy, one could almost taste the oxygen flowing from their limbs.

Three enormous brown bears prowled the banks of a brawling stream at the center of the cove, stabbing flashing salmon with daggerlike claws, oblivious to the mammoth ship a stone's throw away.

Beck nodded at Collins, who untied Ellis's blindfold but left his hands bound.

Ellis stood blinking in the sunlight, bewildered by what he was experiencing: the cries of seagulls and sea lions. The steady breeze against the ship. The verdant backdrop.

Ellis's eyes fell on Beck, and his body stiffened. "What the hell is this?" he asked.

"I pictured you bigger," replied Beck, strolling forward. "Big and pompous. Like your writing."

"Hell of a thing for you to call anyone pompous, Beck."

Ellis's face was pale, his eyes bloodshot. But he did not look afraid, and stood straight and tall. His demeanor in person did not match the weak, intimidated man Beck had perceived on the video feed, and this fact irritated Beck greatly.

"If you think my stories have damaged your...empire," said Ellis, "wait until this gets out."

Beck laughed. "What makes you think anything's going to get out, Mr. Ellis?"

Concern flickered in Ellis's eyes, but he made no reply.

"Look around you." Beck gestured at the sea and mountains. "This is Southeast Alaska. Admiralty Island, Icy Straits. Last anyone heard, you were in Kabul, Afghanistan. *Afghanistan!* Eight thousand miles from here. Your colleagues, your family—everyone believes you've been captured by the Taliban. No one, Mr. Ellis—no one outside of this ship—has the slightest inkling that you're here. Safe and sound, in the good ol' U.S. of A."

Ellis stared at Beck but didn't respond for a long time. Gulls whirled and cried overhead. The breeze picked up, whistling across the deck. "Fits," Ellis said at last. "It fits."

Beck waited.

"Spoiled rich kid. Unlimited resources. Unlimited ego. Knowing you, Beck, this whole endeavor will be paid for with tax dollars."

Sheldon Beck's smile vanished and a vein began pulsing in his neck.

Ellis kept going. "So what's the game here, Beck? You have your thugs capture me in Kabul in the middle of the night, bring me all the way here—for what? So you can kill me?"

"You attacked me," said Beck, pacing now. "Out of the blue, with no warning … planting your stories like roadside bombs. *You attacked me.*"

"I told the truth," Ellis cried, over the wind. "American public has a right to know about Erebus, don't you think? I mean, they're paying for your army—whether they want to or not. Don't you think they have a right to know what's going on? Doesn't that fit with your conservative principles?"

"Your stories are lies."

"What's a lie?" Ellis asked. "That Erebus has made billions off defense contracts? That your private, for-profit soldiers in Afghanistan outnumber the real military? That your troops routinely ignore US law? That Erebus operatives torture and kill when it suits them? Show me where I lied."

Beck's muscles contracted like heavy steel cables. His jaw quivered. "I love this country," he said softly. "I'm trying to save it. You and the rest of the Left are a…disease. Taking America down."

Ellis laughed. "Who's that speech for?" He glanced at Collins and the other fighters positioned around the deck. "These guys? I don't think they're buyin' it, man."

Beck stepped forward and clubbed Ellis across the face with the back of his hand. The reporter crashed to the deck, hands still bound, blood spraying in a wide arc as he fell. He discharged a strangled, raspy cough and said in a thick voice, "Another murder then. In cold blood. Only proves my point."

"Stand him up," Beck commanded, and Collins jerked the prisoner to his feet.

"Unbind him."

Collins removed the cuffs and Ellis massaged his wrists. Shook his hands out. Blood streamed from his nostrils, cascaded down his shirt and pooled on the polished teak deck, but he made no attempt to stanch the flow.

Beck moved closer, eyes locked on Ellis. "We're going to fight, you and I," he said. He removed his shirt and tossed it away, revealing heavy, thick muscles. "You attacked me—and my company—from afar. Now you can confront me face-to-face. Man-to-man."

"I'm not playing this game," said Ellis.

Beck glanced at one of the ex-SEALS waiting near the elevator: a compact bull of a man named Wilden. "Give him a weapon." Wilden turned and fished a fiberglass case from a compartment in the wall.

"I'm not a fighting man," Ellis said, voice calm, head high. "You're a trained killer. I won't fight you."

Beck circled closer. "You will attack me. Well-armed. With two weapons, if you like." He nodded at Wilden, who snapped the fiberglass case open, revealing a collection of gleaming blades.

"I will be unarmed," Beck continued. "And you will attack me." He stopped inches in front of Ellis's face. "Because, if you do not," he said softly, "your wife, Anne-Elise, and your daughter, Sarah, will vanish from your home in Silver Springs, in the middle of the night. Just as you disappeared from Kabul. And they will never, ever, be heard from again."

For the first time since he'd arrived on the solarium deck, Ellis's composure broke. His jaw tightened, his hands clenched into fists. "Beck," he said. "Please. Leave my family out of this. You have a problem with my articles, take it out on me. Kill me. Or tell me what you want."

"I *want* you to fight," said Beck. "Choose your weapons."

Ellis ripped two thick fiberglass-handled knives from the foam-lined case, tucked one into the top of his right boot, and crouched low, with the remaining blade outstretched.

"Certain guys on my crew," said Beck, "might like to get to know your wife, come to think of it. Beautiful woman." He chuckled. "Might like your daughter even better, knowing them. How old is she now, Ellis? Seventeen?"

Ellis leapt forward, gripping the knife as he drove for Beck's throat. Beck easily sidestepped the older man, grabbed his arm, and yanked him forward, pulling him off-balance. Ellis stumbled and Beck whirled and shoved him hard into a wall. Ellis thunked against a steel barrier and collapsed to the ground. The knife he'd been holding skittered across the deck and he lay on his back, moaning. Beck's men laughed.

Beck picked up the knife and tossed it back to his adversary. "I said *fight*."

Ellis rolled to his knees, then stood, slowly, clutching the knife once more. Mimicking Beck's actions—staying low and loose—Ellis came for his enemy more warily this time, jabbing with the blade, edging his opponent back, into a corner. He was sweating heavily now, heart thumping, redlining. When it seemed there was nowhere for Beck to go, Ellis lunged again, flying forward, slashing low, and rising as he charged.

Beck ducked, and twisted away hard at the last instant, smashing the reporter's outstretched arm with a hop kick, like a move from an Irish dance. Another spinning, booming kick hurled Ellis into a railing, where he collapsed like a rag doll.

Beck, barely winded, leaned over his bleeding, battered quarry and laughed. "What do I have to do to get you to fight, old man?"

Ellis blinked and his eyes swam in pale sockets. His brain stuttered. Tried to reengage. Like a computer restarting after a crash.

"Should've had that daylight-basement door fixed, Ellis," Beck said mildly, turning away. "Makes for very easy access, you know? Off the street, out of sight. Poorly lit. Haven't been keeping up on your home maintenance, have you?"

Ellis struggled to his feet, clearly suffering now.

"That's how my men went in," said Beck, "to place the cameras that are monitoring your family now. And how they'll go in tomorrow night to take your wife and daughter."

Ellis gasped, his voice a ragged whisper. "Beck, please. They've done nothing to you. Nothing at all. I'll do whatever you want. I'll write articles praising your company. I'll swear that everything I said was a lie."

Beck laughed. "Little late now, my friend. Your reporting cost us three billion in contracts."

"Beck—"

"Your reporting," Beck said slowly, his rage evident even in his controlled, measured delivery, "sparked investigations. Congressional hearings. I had to appear. It was messy. Awkward." He paused. "And now you want to make it all good? I don't think so."

"Please," said Ellis. "My family—"

"No good, man," said Beck. He stopped pacing and looked at Ellis. "What'd you call me in that last piece?"

Ellis gawked at him stupidly, his skin slick with sweat and blood.

"*Thug* is the word you used," said Beck. "You called me a thug."

Ellis licked his lips. Nodded. Wide-eyed, like a terrified child.

Beck said, "Would a *thug* offer his adversary a knife, while he himself remained unarmed?"

Ellis shook his head and kept his eyes locked on Beck. "No."

"Would a *thug* give his adversary two knives, while he struggled barehanded?"

"No. He wouldn't," said Ellis.

"Would he offer his adversary a gun? Bullets? While he fought with nothing?"

Ellis turned to find Wilden standing in front of him, face impassive, inscrutable. He held a metal case this time, and the lid was open.

Ellis's eyes flicked between Wilden's face and the objects nestled in the container's foam liner. A snubnose .38 and a handful of loosely scattered rounds. The bullets looked huge in the compact case, and the metal glinted in the late afternoon light.

Beck sauntered away from Ellis, toward the far railing. He called over his shoulder, yelling against the breeze. "They're real bullets, Ellis. And it's a real gun."

Ellis stared at the gun, ears ringing. He wondered if he had a concussion.

Beck said. "And if you can load it and fire before I get there, then you win."

Wilden set the case on the ground and backed away. Beck reached the far railing and began to turn. Slowly. Almost casually.

Ellis gawked a split second more, as if what he thought he'd heard Beck say couldn't possibly be right. Like he'd missed something. Like it was all a joke and he just hadn't figured it out yet. Like the case would explode in his face if he touched it, or one of Beck's men would stab him in the back when he knelt down.

The hesitation lasted only a nanosecond and then Ellis was dropping onto the case, falling on top of it and fumbling with the gun. He knew guns. Handguns specifically. He owned a Baby Browning .25 and a Ruger Speed Six .22. He'd taken a firearm-safety course with his daughter. They'd been to the range a few times.

Ellis struggled with the .38's cylinder—he couldn't find the latch—and registered a flicker of movement in his peripheral vision. A shape flying toward him. He focused on the gun. Fingers working. The .38 was different from his guns. He could figure it out, but—

He found the latch, the cylinder opened, and he slid a single round into the chamber. One bullet. No time to load more. Ellis slapped the cylinder closed, lifted the gun.

And Beck was there, coming like a freight train. He smashed into Ellis's chest, feetfirst.

The gun boomed. But the shot went high. Into the air.

Ellis bounced violently against a steel post, bones cracking on impact. Beck caught the gun, spun, and clubbed Ellis across the head with it, then scooped one of the knives from the deck and rammed it into his enemy's thigh.

Ellis howled in agony and crashed to the ground, blood spurting from his leg.

"No one," Beck roared, grabbing Ellis by his shirt and lifting him off the ground, "fucks with me and lives to tell about it!"

Muscles bulging, face taut with rage, Beck lurched toward the railing, holding Ellis a foot off the ground. "No one…fucks…with…me!"

Ellis regarded Beck with milky, terrified eyes. The left side of his face was smashed and bleeding. A jagged shard of bone pierced the skin like broken glass.

"Kill me," Ellis coughed, spitting blood. "But leave my family alone."

Beck laughed. "Oh, *I'm* not going to kill you, Ellis," he said cheerfully.

They'd reached the railing and Beck twisted Ellis's body around so that he was facing the shoreline, where the three enormous brown bears continued to feed.

"*They* are."

Beck heaved Ellis's mangled body from the deck and hurled him off the ship. The reporter tumbled through the air—too battered to try to right himself. Fifty feet he dropped, smacking the frigid blue-green water like a sack of cement. A Zodiac manned by two of Beck's crew waited by the side of the ship. They hauled Ellis out of the water and motored toward the salmon stream. And the bears.

Beck showered in the solarium and silently accepted a fresh change of clothes from a hovering attendant. Other staff appeared with rags and mops and began cleaning the deck, wiping up the blood. They didn't talk, and none of them so much as glanced at Beck.

Beck dressed, and the adrenaline and rage he'd felt while fighting Ellis dissipated. He needed a drink.

He picked up a pair of binoculars and studied the rocky beach where his men had deposited the prisoner.

Collins appeared at his side. Wilden was there, too. Beck said, "I told you to lock down the ship. No one on the weather deck except your team."

Collins and Wilden looked at Beck, glanced at each other.

"We *were* locked down, sir," said Collins. "Still are."

Beck stared at him, then flicked his eyes to Wilden. "There was a guy, near the aft helipad. I saw him, just for a second, when Ellis was going for the gun."

Collins and Wilden said nothing.

"Look at the surveillance tape. Find out who it was."

"Yes, sir."

Beck lifted the binoculars to his eyes again and found Ellis's boots and legs protruding from a thicket of alders just above the high-tide line. The bears were still there—fifty yards from Ellis's body—stabbing fat silver salmon with curved claws, scooping them from the creek. They seemed unperturbed. Completely uninterested in Ellis.

'Til nightfall, Beck thought. He hoped Ellis survived long enough to feel it.

CHAPTER 21

JOE AND ELLA SAT IN SILENCE, gazing out the window of the Washington State ferry *Elwha* as a fiery sun sank into a platinum sea. It was 8:30 p.m. and in the fading summer glow it felt like the *Elwha* was motoring through a magical archipelago, a fairy-tale ocean worthy of Narnia or Middle Earth.

Joe stood. Stretched. "Restroom," he said. "I'll be right back." Ella watched him walk toward the middle of the ship.

Beck's men were watching too. A few tables away. Dodd and Drucker—the guys Beck had dispatched from *Marauder*, the ones who'd located Joe and Ella in the ferry terminal parking lot.

Dodd studied a new message on his phone.

"Boss wants the party transported to the *Northern Mercy*."

Drucker grunted. "Yeah? And how the hell are we supposed to do that?"

"We're not. Not yet anyway. Just supposed to follow. It'll happen in Anacortes. Maybe in the parking lot. Plan's still coming together.

Drucker looked at his watch. "Boat docks in half an hour. Hope they work fast."

Joe exited the restroom and paused at a water fountain to get a drink.

"Excuse me," said a woman. "Could I ask you a huge favor?"

She was petite. Older. Gray hair pulled back in a ponytail.

"What's up?" Joe asked.

"My truck," the woman replied. "I'm driving my husband's old pickup, and the door is stuck."

"You lost the key?"

"No, no. I have the keys." She held up a huge jangling set of the things. "The door just binds, is all. It's an old truck, like I said. My husband always yells at me to pull harder. Usually it works, but I cannot get it open for the life of me, and I'm all alone, and—"

"I can give it a shot," said Joe. "Which part of the car deck?"

"Oh, you are a saint!" said the woman, beaming and touching Joe's arm. "Thank you so much."

She led him toward the rear stairwell. "It's near the back—won't take thirty seconds. Big strong guy like you."

Joe followed her down the stairs.

"You might want to try a little WD-40 on the door—if you have any," said Joe as he followed.

"I'll definitely do that," replied the woman, whose pace seemed to be increasing as they descended. She was a good twelve to fifteen steps ahead now, almost jogging. Joe wondered what the hurry was.

"Lady—" He emerged into the relative gloom of the car deck and looked around. There was no sign of the woman. And no sign of an old beater truck.

The steady rumble of the *Elwha*'s engines was loud down here, and Joe could feel the vibration of the huge motors through the soles of his feet.

There.

He saw a flash of movement among the last row of cars. A shape slipping past a white van. That had to be her.

Joe walked around the van and stopped. No woman. No truck.

What the heck?

There was only twenty-five feet of flat, open deck between Joe and the water now, and the roar of the propellers was constant.

Joe stared out, past the massive safety chain guarding the last row of cars, past the rounded steel stern, to where the wake boiled up, sculpting itself into a cornice of churning, roiling foam.

Joe heard, or sensed, a single footfall behind him. He turned, and an enormous bare fist smashed the side of his face. His head slapped the rear panel of the van, denting it.

"Freak bastard," the assailant growled, as Joe slid sideways and blood gushed from his nose. He heard alarms—shrieking bells—but couldn't tell if they were coming from his brain or from the ship. It felt like chunks of metal were grinding together in his head.

"Creep son-of-a-bitch," said the man, who loomed over Joe like an ogre. "Think it's hilarious to trash someone's business, huh?" He gripped Joe by the front of his shirt, jerked him upright, and reared back for another punch.

That's when Joe found his footing and struck back. Joe Stanton knew how to fight, and he hit back hard now, surprising his attacker with three staccato punches to the face.

The big man gaped. Blood trickled from his own nose and he loosened his hold on Joe's fleece jacket just a bit.

Joe pulled away but there was another shape to his right now: Ponytail Woman, lifting something, fast, toward his eyes. A can of pepper spray.

She pulled the trigger as Joe lurched back, tripping, falling, howling in pain and terror. Spray splattered his face, and his eyes felt like they'd been stabbed with white-hot skewers.

The big man crashed down on top of him, knocking the wind from his lungs and pinning him to the metal deck.

Joe was vaguely aware of Ponytail Woman pulling on the big man, telling him they had to get out of there.

The big man shoved her away and leaned close to Joe's face. "You trashed my folk's business so you could get yourself a funny clip on YouTube." He grinned. "You're gonna need some makeup for your next gig."

And then he clubbed Joe in the head again.

There was no pain this time. Just the odd sensation that the sky over the open end of the car deck had gone dark. Midnight dark. And the rumble of the engines was suddenly far away. A distant drone.

And then the engine noise was back—big and bright and raucous in Joe's ears.

He was being dragged along the deck—dragged by the man and Ponytail Woman onto a massive coil of rope behind one of the huge starboard cleats.

He opened his eyes again and his attackers were gone. Simply gone.

I blacked out, Joe thought.

He lay there: coughing, bleeding, eyes burning—nearly swollen shut—limbs strewn about the coil of yellow rope.

How long have I been here? he wondered.

And then all of his thoughts turned to Ella.

She must be frantic.

He got to his knees—clawing against the uneven pile of rope—and brushed his eyes with his sleeves. He had to get to water, to a restroom. The burning in his eyes was the worst. Far worse than the other wounds to his face. He lurched to a standing position and the car deck morphed and undulated before him, seesawing, tilting sharply, so that it seemed to Joe as if all those silent, driverless cars might just start rolling backward and plunge into the icy sound.

Panting, Joe steadied himself against a Ford Explorer and tried again to brush his eyes. No good. His right eye was swollen completely shut now, and his left felt like it had been coated with sticky cobwebs.

He swayed, contemplating his next step. The car deck was a graveyard. No activity except his own tentative movements. No sound except the relentless low-frequency roar of the motors.

Got to find Ella.

He took a wobbly old-man step. One step.

That's when the hallucination came back.

Help me, said a voice, clear and bright in Joe's mind.

Joe froze.

Not now, he replied, clutching his head. He stumbled forward, swerved. *We'll talk later. My eyes are on fire.*

The voice rang out again, clear and more present—like a radio signal that's finally been isolated and perfectly tuned. *Stan-ton. Please. Can you help?*

"Who are you?" Joe cried, choking on the words and weaving like a drunk across the rear of the deck. For a moment he even forgot the acid burn in his eyes. "Are you real?"

Flesh and blood, replied the voice. *Muscle and bone. Like you.*

The rush of the MV *Elwha*'s wake suddenly became a roar in Joe's ears. "Wrong way!" he screamed, pawing stupidly at his eyes and shivering with terror. "I'm going the wrong way!"

The deck had become a gray-green blur that blended with the water, which in turn blended with the sky. He couldn't tell what was moving and what was still, what was solid and what was infirm.

By chance or misfortune, he stepped over the lowest section of the burly safety chain, the last line of defense between the cars and the water.

Lorna Gwin has passed, said the voice, *but countless others may be saved.*

I need to save myself right now, Joe replied.

I need your help! cried the voice. It was a voice laden with anguish—the same horrible, all-consuming grief Joe had felt in the Breakwater parking lot.

I need your help!

The pain hit Joe like a fist and he swooned, teetered, and fell, clawing at the air as he plunged headlong into the *Elwha*'s wake, a raging, roaring geyser of white foam.

CHAPTER 22

DALE DEVELDT WAS SITTING in his 1978 Volkswagen Rabbit on the car deck of the MV *Elwha*, listening to music and smoking a cigarette. He caught Joe's fall in the Rabbit's passenger-side mirror and gawked, wide-eyed, the cigarette dangling from his lips.

"Holy shit," he yelled, smashing out the smoke and fumbling with the door. "Man overboard!"

An overall-clad ship's mechanic emerged from a stairwell thirty feet away and Dale sprinted toward him. "Man overboard!" he screamed again.

The mechanic removed his earplugs. Stared at Dale and saw smoke puffing out of his nostrils.

"You smokin'?" he asked, sniffing the air.

"Dude—"

"You know smoking on the car deck is a five-hundred-dollar fine?"

"Dude," Dale screamed. "I'm trying to tell you, Man overboard! A guy just fell off the back of your damn boat!"

Understanding finally dawned on the mechanic's greasy mug. "You sure?"

"Positive. Tell the captain to stop. The guy's a half mile back there by now."

The broad channel between Lopez and Blakely Islands was at flood tide, and the icy black water enveloped Joe Stanton like death and swept him south, toward Lopez Sound and away from the MV *Elwha*.

A speck of flotsam, he bobbed along, gasping for air as the fifty-four-degree water chilled the marrow in his bones, numbed every centimeter of his body and put him into instant shock.

My eyes are better at least, he thought, as the *Elwha* motored into the distance, a twinkling, glittering ornament on the horizon.

His eyes did feel better. He could see at least a little through both of them now. The water had eased the burn. But what he saw, as he bobbed away from the *Elwha*'s shimmering trail, did not give him hope.

The boat was disappearing into the night. A smattering of lights shone on Lopez Island—but it was at least a half mile away.

Treading water, he turned. Blakely Island was an amorphous gray mass to the east and even farther than Lopez. Decatur, to the southeast, was farther still.

It was almost dark and the frigid water crushed him, driving the wind from his lungs. Like a predator, it pinned him. Held him. Waiting for him to give up so that it could swallow and digest him once and for all.

Joe Stanton, on a normal day, might have made the swim to Lopez. He was extraordinarily strong and fit. A good swimmer. He'd surfed and scuba dived most of his life. The water didn't scare him.

But this was not a normal day. The beating he'd just endured, and the events of the morning, had taken their toll.

He swam toward Lopez, feeling the current, trying to move with the flow and edge toward land at the same time.

A leaden sky loomed overhead, and rolling black waves crested and fell around him, making it impossible to see. He gagged on the salty water, coughing and spluttering.

Far down the channel, the MV *Elwha* was turning at last. Turning hard, coming around to search for the missing passenger. Huge searchlights mounted above both wheelhouses flashed on, lighting up the channel like an oil platform at full production. Announcements blared. Alarms wailed.

Joe was oblivious to all of it. The current had carried him past the end of tiny Frost Island now, past Spencer Spit, well out of the main channel. He struggled to keep his arms moving in a coherent, steady stroke—to keep his feet kicking—but his limbs felt heavy and unwieldy, like tangled branches.

And now his mind was playing tricks on him again, this time due to the cold. He dreamed in bright bursts that he was swimming hard for shore, then awoke to find that, in reality, he was barely moving, just feebly treading water. He thought of Ella's sweet, serene face and tried again to swim, making a few frantic strokes.

At last his thoughts coalesced into a single dark blur. He stopped struggling, and began to sink.

Stan-ton must not die, murmured the strange voice in his mind, as the icy sea swallowed him, body and soul.

Stan-ton cannot die.

CHAPTER 23

JOE STANTON AWOKE TO SHOUTS and the sound of running feet, but for several seconds he could not find the strength to open his eyes.

"Damn! It's him!" yelled a man. "The guy off the ferry."

"He's alive!" cried a woman, as she dropped to the ground at Joe's side.

Together, the pair rolled Joe gently onto his back.

"Jesus, Hank," said the woman. "Look at his face."

The man stepped away and spoke into a cell phone. "Yes, I'd like to report an emergency," he said. "It's the guy from the ferry."

"Jesus, Hank," the woman repeated. "Looks like he's been run over or somethin'.

"Mister?" said the woman as Joe's eyes finally opened. "You okay? You're breathing at least. My daughter's gone to get a blanket."

A gravelly whisper was all Joe could manage. "Where am I?"

He was lying in tall grass, on his back, staring up through tree branches into a pale-blue sky. But when he tried to move, everything hurt.

"You're on Lopez," answered the man. "Lopez Island. And they're sending a medevac chopper for you right now. Plenty of room to land in our pasture."

The woman gripped Joe's hand, "You must be an awful good swimmer," she said. "Everyone thought sure you were dead."

Joe could hear waves lapping against a beach now, though that peaceful sound was soon overwhelmed by the noise of an approaching siren. Joe twisted his body around, enough to peer out. Beyond the grass, down a gentle slope, he could see haphazard piles of smooth driftwood, and a wet gravel beach. Lopez Sound stretched out wide and deep beyond that, the wave tops flashing like diamonds in the early morning light. He had no memory of swimming beyond mid-channel and no recollection whatsoever of climbing onto the shore.

The promised blanket arrived, and paramedics soon after. Joe looked up to find a face he recognized. A paramedic from the ambulance ride the previous morning.

"Well, hello there," she said warmly, rushing in to check his vital signs as her partner readied a gurney. A name badge stitched above her left shirt pocket read "Arnaz."

"San Juans used to be kinda boring 'til you showed up," she said. "You're definitely kickin' it up a notch on the ol' excitement meter." She studied the ugly blue-green bruises around Joe's eyes and lower jaw and touched his face gently with a latex-gloved hand. "Somebody throw you off that boat?" she asked, as her partner prepared a neck brace. "What the hell happened?"

The incident with Spinell's son replayed, painfully, in Joe's memory, but he decided he didn't want to discuss it. He gave a small shrug.

Arnaz stared at him, concern in her eyes.

"You lucked out," she said as she started an IV with practiced speed. "I do one shift a week on Lopez."

Joe managed a smile, though the effort hurt like hell. He searched her eyes. "My girlfriend. Ella. Is she—"

"Dude, everybody and their dog is looking for you. I'm sure your girl got the good news by now. She'll probably just head to the hospital when we know which one they're taking you to."

Joe gripped Arnaz's sleeve and whispered, "I can't do an air-evac."

Arnaz smiled and helped her partner lift him onto the gurney.

"Not up for debate, man," she said cheerfully. "We're looking at possible multiple fractures, shock, concussion, hypothermia, exposure—"

"I don't have insurance. I can't pay for it. I can't. And anyhow, I'm fine." He tried to sit up, to prove his point, and cried out in pain.

"Uh-huh," said Arnaz. "You bet you are. Ready to do an Ironman." Her radio crackled and she raised a hand, signaling for Joe to hang on. He followed her with his eyes as she retreated a few paces into the meadow. He could hear the *thump, thump, thump* of a helicopter now.

"Sounds like they're taking you to Bellingham," said Arnaz, returning to his side and checking his pulse again. "Super quick flight." She smiled. "I hear you're a priest. For real?"

Joe squinted at her. "The dispatcher tell you that?" He'd almost stopped shivering.

"Word gets around, dude," she said, "even up here in the sticks."

Arnaz and her partner hefted the gurney—with the landowner's help—and carried Joe toward the meadow.

"Your adventures are being tweeted about even as we speak. You made the Seattle news."

"Wonderful," said Joe, feeling suddenly sick to his stomach.

The helicopter—a bright red Sikorsky S-76—landed and a flight nurse jumped out and helped Arnaz and her partner lift Joe aboard.

Arnaz leaned through the door. "You're gonna be fine," she said, squeezing Joe's hand.

The chopper lifted off, bound for Bellingham. It never got there.

CHAPTER 24

"**HE'S IN CARDIAC ARREST,**" the flight nurse yelled, ten seconds into the flight. "We need to get him down."

Joe heard the pilot through a speaker mounted above the door. "We're seven minutes from St. Joe's."

"Not good enough," replied the nurse—a burly, bearded young guy with a photo ID badge clipped to his shirt. Joe saw that his name was Reggie Knutson.

"The *Northern Mercy*'s in Haro Strait," said Reggie. "Full cardiac unit. We can be there in three."

"A hospital ship?" said the pilot. "Lemme check."

Joe wasn't really in cardiac arrest. But it sounded plausible, given all he'd been through. And Reggie needed an excuse. A man had approached him at tiny San Juan airport moments before takeoff. The man had offered him five thousand dollars, cash, to get Joe Stanton to the hospital ship *Northern Mercy*. To show his sincerity, the man had given Reggie ten crisp new one-hundred-dollar bills. "Get him to the ship and you'll get the rest," the man had said. "Simple as that."

"What's this all about?" Reggie wanted to know.

"No questions," replied the man. "Do you want the money or not?"

Now, they were zooming toward the *Northern Mercy*, and Joe felt himself losing consciousness again. He'd heard Reggie say he was in cardiac arrest, but couldn't get his muddled brain around the idea. The pilot and nurse seemed to be talking about someone else. Whether it was Arnaz's IV or recent events that were scrambling his thoughts, Joe could not discern. But he felt curiously removed from the situation, and his eyes swam in their sockets.

"Big helicopter," said Joe.

Reggie nodded. "You got the freighter. This one can carry six patients and two attendants. But you're the star of the show today."

Joe blinked and the helicopter's beige vinyl ceiling swam before his eyes, warping and twisting and morphing into an odd grid pattern.

"*Stan-ton*," whispered the now familiar voice, deep within Joe's brain, as the ceiling continued to organize itself into a psychedelic tapestry worthy of *Alice in Wonderland*. Joe was dimly, peripherally aware of Reggie studying him intently, but he couldn't stop staring at the ceiling. Joe saw the nurse turn and look at the ceiling himself—fascinated by Joe's intense focus. Clearly, the nurse could not see what he was seeing.

I really do need a doctor, Joe thought to himself, as the grid pattern kaleidoscoped before his eyes. *Maybe I'm really, really messed up. Maybe someone dropped LSD in my coffee.*

His body convulsed and the grid pattern warped into a forest-green tunnel. The tunnel, in turn, bent and stretched, until it spanned a vast black chasm. Joe gaped, eyes fixed on the scene before him.

Like a living tentacle, the tunnel twisted and probed, arcing through the darkness, searching for something.

"It looks organic," Joe whispered, eyes riveted on the ceiling.

"What looks organic?" asked Reggie. "The ceiling?"

Joe didn't hear him. "But it glows like an LED. Not organic. Made. Created. But by whom?"

The nurse had vanished from Joe's field of vision along with the ceiling. Only the tunnel remained.

There was a faint glow at the end of the tunnel now. A daylight kind of glow. Joe wanted desperately to see it.

A light at the end of the tunnel? What could it be? Heaven?

Joe continued his slow, forward movement through the tunnel. *Or, maybe I don't want to see any light,* he thought. *Maybe if I get to the light, I'll be dead. Lord knows I've come close enough the last couple days.*

Then, for the third time in two days, Joe's mind went dark, and he lapsed into unconsciousness.

CHAPTER 25

JOE'S EYES SNAPPED OPEN. He felt peaceful and warm. Comfortable and content. He lay on his side as shapes swirled around him, transiting his field of awareness like planets spinning silently past the sun. The shapes were indistinct. Amorphous. Unthreatening.

He stayed like that for a long time, breathing, listening to his heartbeat, feeling no desire to move. Only his eyes were active.

Gradually the swirling shapes clarified.

People, Joe thought. *They're people.*

His focus improved. The people were wearing cotton gowns. Latex gloves. Surgical masks.

Clusters of lights—brilliant, blazing lights—hovered in the air above them.

One of the people came to a stop at Joe's side. Then a second person. Joe's eyes flicked up and he saw that they were regarding him intently.

They look surprised, Joe thought. *Surprised because I'm awake?* He couldn't be sure. It was hard to think. Hard to ponder anything. His thoughts seemed to dart away like shadows.

Joe lay there, trying to focus.

Soft classical music played on a speaker somewhere high overhead, but no one spoke. The people just stared. It was odd, but he felt no concern. No worry.

He looked past the people. There was a screen. A monitor displaying scans. X-rays. Medical images. He saw instruments. A robotic arm with tweezer-like fingers.

Joe focused. The robotic fingers were holding something. A miniscule wafer dangling a hair-thin wire.

Joe looked again at one of the gowned figures staring at him and saw a gloved hand pressing a button, pressing it slowly, steadily, like a syringe. He thought maybe he should be concerned; then he let it go. He was too comfortable. Too relaxed and peaceful. He saw liquid moving slowly through a clear plastic tube, and warmth and drowsiness overtook him again.

CHAPTER 26

"**LOOK CLOSELY** and you can see the fracture," said the doctor. She swung a computer monitor into position so that Ella could see the X-rays of Joe Stanton's skull more clearly. "A linear fracture. Here." She tapped on the screen. "Behind Joe's temporal bones. Should heal fully on its own. Assuming he avoids further trauma."

They were in a sunny private room aboard the hospital ship *Northern Mercy*. Joe slept peacefully in a bed with crisp white sheets. Ella and the doctor—a sixtysomething woman named Andrea Heintzel—sat nearby, and Detective Palmer watched via video feed from his office in Friday Harbor. Ella and Dr. Heintzel could see Palmer in the upper righthand corner of the monitor.

"We cleaned and dressed the wounds on Mr. Stanton's face and scalp," Heintzel told them, adding, to Ella, "Keep an eye on things. If the healing goes well you can remove the stitches in a few days."

Ella smiled. "I'll take good care of him."

Palmer spoke via the video link. "What about the hallucinations? The voices?"

"We did a complete neurological workup," said Heintzel. "The good news is, we see no sign of a stroke or tumor. None at all. All of Joe's neurological processes are robust. Exactly what we would expect in a healthy twenty-eight-year old."

"So how do you explain what happened?" Palmer asked. "At the motel? On the ferry? Some kind of…psychosis?"

"I don't think so. We've seen no evidence of that."

"What then?"

Heintzel sighed. "My strong suspicion, after considering this from every angle, is that Joe ate or drank something that caused the event."

Ella looked surprised. "What? Really?"

"Yes. Not knowingly. I'm suggesting that Joe ingested something tainted—without realizing it. A fast-food item spiked with one chemical or another, perhaps as a sick joke."

"A *joke*," said Ella. "Who would do that?"

"It happens," Heintzel replied. "Unfortunately. The public seems to think food tampering is a thing of the past, but I assure you, it is not."

Palmer nodded. "Happens to cops. I can vouch for that. I read about an arrest last month…Two Burger King employees in Fort Worth. They'd see police in line or in the drive-thru, and spit or urinate in the food. As a joke."

"That is beyond disgusting," said Ella.

"Of course," said Heintzel. "But it is a viable possibility. There are some very sick people out there. It may be that someone thought it would be amusing to drop a little psilocybin or PCP into the beverage or entrée of a young priest. Or perhaps it was totally random, and the perpetrator had no idea who would consume the tainted food. Maybe it was planted surreptitiously. Like with the Tylenol poisonings decades ago. I've ordered a toxicology screen for psychoactive substances—but we won't have the results for a day or two."

Ella frowned. "Screen shouldn't take that long, should it? It's usually an hour turnaround, max."

The question seemed to catch Heintzel off guard. "Yes, well, our lab is having computer issues at the moment. But things should be back to normal soon."

Ella looked at Joe, lying on the bed, bruised and battered, and tears welled in her eyes. She'd been on board twenty-four hours, almost as long as Joe, and she hadn't slept much. "Could this have messed him up permanently?"

"I don't think so," Heintzel replied. "I believe the substance—whatever it was—will work its way out of his system completely. I don't foresee any long-term damage."

Palmer said, "I'd like to get a list of the places he's eaten in the last few days."

"Short list," Ella replied. "After we left Bremerton we stopped at a Starbucks in Port Townsend and a Wendy's in Anacortes. We ate at two places in Friday Harbor." She rattled off the names.

Palmer took notes. But he wasn't the only one listening.

The tainted food explanation was Beck's idea. And now his operatives were considering Ella's restaurant list with interest.

"I want the cops, and the public, to have an explanation for Joe Stanton's behavior—so they don't start looking at other causes," Beck told Collins.

Within minutes, a plan was under way.

CHAPTER 27

SEVENTEEN HOURS LATER. Erebus operative Gavin Knox sat behind the wheel of a stolen Honda Accord in a darkened parking lot in Anacortes; a clear view of his target dead ahead.

It seemed a ridiculous target for someone of Knox's training.

But "target" was how Collins had referred to it. And Knox had prepared for the operation with all of his skill and professionalism. He'd scouted the place. Studied photographs. Spent time, inside and out. He'd broken into the restaurant manager's apartment and copied the restaurant's master key.

There were no video cameras at the Wendy's. And no alarm system. There *were* alarm company stickers on the doors and windows, but no functioning alarm. Knox had checked. Carefully.

He'd rehearsed his moves and knew how he'd get in—via the service door in back, away from the street. He knew where the walk-in freezer was, and what he'd find inside.

The ex-SEAL was prepared.

He was also upset. Pissed off. It was not an emotion he welcomed before a mission. Such an emotion could cause a loss of focus. A lapse in judgment. He lifted his phone and called Collins.

It took ten seconds for the call to connect. For the cell signal to find its way to Collins, on board *Marauder*, nine hundred miles northwest. For the special encryption software to do its thing.

Collins picked up on the first ring, sounding wide-awake even though it was the middle of the night. "There a problem?"

Knox laughed. "You always assume the worst."

Collins spoke evenly. "You haven't gone in yet."

"No."

"What then?"

Knox cleared his throat. "I scouted the restaurant today."

"I know."

"Families eat there. A lot of kids."

"So?"

Knox sighed. "So what the fuck, Collins? Why are we doing this?"

Silence on the line, then static, then, "Because Beck said to."

Knox was not a fearful person, never had been. But the way Collins enunciated this sentence sent a little shiver down his spine.

Collins's tone softened slightly. "Because a diversion is necessary. Because it's important."

"Yeah?" said Knox. "Well, I'm the wrong guy for this one."

"You're the right guy," said Collins, sounding more like a coach now. "Beck chose you specifically."

"Why?"

"Because of your expertise. Your attention to detail."

Knox gazed out the driver's-side window of the Honda. Checked the street. A soft rain was making halos of mist around each streetlight. It was still dark and the street was still dead, but he had to get moving. Sunrise came early in summer, bringing people with it. All he needed was for some asshole jogger to cruise past the Wendy's service entrance as he was walking out.

"I could just leave," Knox said finally. "Drive away."

Collins laughed. "Yeah, and you know how that would go down."

Knox knew.

Beck would find him. Or maybe not. Beck might ignore him completely and go after his ex-wife and three-year-old son instead. There was no telling. His ex and son lived far away. In a small town in Upstate New York. But the distance was no kind of barrier for Beck. Knox let it play out in his head. Two or three months would pass. Maybe more. Maybe a year. Nothing would happen. He'd start to believe that Beck had forgotten about him. Then, out of the blue, he'd get a call explaining that something terrible had happened to his kid. Or to his parents in Des Moines. His sister in Tampa.

Collins spoke again, staying in coach mode. "You're a pro, Knox. That's why Beck spent a shitload of money saving your ass after

Fallujah. And how much are you making now? What? Five times what you did when you were in? Think about that."

Knox said nothing.

"Are we on the same page here, Knox?"

"What happened with the reporter?" Knox asked. "After the fight?"

Collins seemed taken aback by the question. "What do you think happened? The reporter lost."

"No. I mean *after* the fight. The ship was locked down. Nobody but you guys on the weather deck."

"Yeah?"

"So I heard Beck saw a guy. Or claimed to. A stranger. I heard he was adamant about it."

Collins wondered who had told Knox this and made a mental note to find out. He didn't like gossip. Especially gossip about the boss.

"But the deck was locked down," Knox continued. "Nobody else saw anything. Cameras didn't record anything. There was no one there. No guy. It was impossible."

"What's your point?"

Knox hesitated, then said, "You ever think maybe the boss is off his rocker, Collins?"

Collins sighed. "We're done talking now, Knox. Gonna do your job, or not?"

"Fuck you, Collins."

Collins kept his voice even. Flat. "Are you doing the job, or not?"

"I'm doing it."

"Good."

The call went dead. Knox donned a pair of latex gloves, grabbed his backpack, and headed for the service entrance, sticking to the shadows as he crossed the lots. Inside the service door he slid cotton booties on over his shoes.

Four minutes later he was inside the restaurant's freezer, staring at neat stacks of perfectly formed all-beef patties. Hundreds of patties filled an entire column of stainless-steel shelves, floor to ceiling, each individual square of meat separated from the next by a single rectangle of wax paper.

The frosty walls of the freezer sparkled through Knox's night-vision goggles. He could see everything plainly, for a few seconds. Then the lenses fogged and he had to wipe them off, inside and out. He repeated this cleaning every ten seconds or so, silently cursing himself for not anticipating the problem.

He could simply turn the freezer light on, of course, or use his headlamp, but the light—any light—might reflect into the kitchen. Someone might see something from the street. He couldn't risk it.

Knox's heart thumped in his ears, a raucous noise against the stillness of the restaurant. The fog was throwing him off. Slowing him down.

He wiped the lenses for the umpteenth time, pulled the little plastic case Collins had given him from his vest pocket, and opened it, revealing a soft foam liner bearing an eyedropper and a single vial of clear liquid.

Knox extracted the vial and eyedropper with his right hand, shut the case and put it back in his pocket. Then he opened the vial, carefully, and filled the dropper.

He turned and focused on the hamburger patties, glowing green through his eyewear. Not the least bit appetizing. He placed the poison randomly. A drop here. A drop there. Some on this shelf. Some on that.

And then it was done and he was moving out, checking his trail, checking everything, shutting the freezer, heading for the exit.

He bolted the service door with the key he'd fabricated, checked the lot, and made for the Honda. One minute later he was on his way out of town, a shadow moving through the darkness and softly falling rain.

CHAPTER 28

JOE SAT ON HIS HOSPITAL BED, wide-awake and fully dressed. Tired, but relaxed. Ella was there, along with Dr. Heintzel, a nurse named Navarro, and a prim, nattily attired company liaison named Elton Gliss.

As Joe now understood it, he'd been airlifted off Lopez and was en route to a hospital in Bellingham when he'd gone into cardiac arrest. The chopper had diverted to the *Mercy*, which happened to be in the straits south of the San Juans. The ship's emergency-medicine team had attempted to stabilize Joe and send him on to a traditional hospital, but stabilization had proven difficult. Joe's heart irregularity—a side effect of the toxin he'd ingested, according to Heintzel—made transport unsafe. They'd sent a helicopter to collect Ella and bring her to the ship, instead.

The *Mercy* had continued on its southward path and was now approaching San Diego, en route to the Panama Canal and an eventual deployment along Ivory Coast.

Sun streamed through the windows and Joe felt his strength returning. The bruises on his face were healing, the soreness in his limbs dissipating with each passing hour. A lingering ache between his eyes was his only complaint now, and Heintzel had assured him that that, too, would fade.

Joe regarded Heintzel and the others. "I don't know how to thank you folks," he said. "You've shown real kindness to a complete stranger, and, you know—" Tears clouded his eyes and Ella put her arm around his shoulder.

"Mr. Beck was delighted to be able to help you in your time of need," Elton Gliss said, grinning with a toothsome politician's smile. "It is the Christian way, is it not?"

The nurse, Navarro, stared at the floor as Gliss spoke. Kept her head down. No eye contact. Joe wondered if she was just shy.

"Is Mr. Beck on the ship?" Joe asked. "I'd like to thank him personally."

"I'm afraid not," Gliss replied. "Mr. Beck is in Europe. On business. But he's been updated on your condition several times. I spoke with him just an hour ago, in fact, and he was thrilled to learn of your quick recovery."

"Well," said Joe, "I hope to meet him one day."

Sheldon Beck watched the conversation on a video screen in a different part of the ship. "Track them," he told Collins. "Monitor them, 24/7. Pass everything on to Ring. Keep me in the loop."

CHAPTER 29

HEINTZEL AND GLISS ESCORTED Joe and Ella to the *Mercy*'s helipad. Joe rode in a wheelchair pushed by the ever-smiling corporate liaison.

"I can walk," said Joe. "I feel fine."

"You may think you feel fine," Heintzel replied, as they navigated *Mercy*'s gleaming wood-paneled hallways. "But you must remember your ordeal and give yourself time to recover."

Ella said, "Don't worry, I'll remind him."

"You suffered hypothermia," said Heintzel. "Shock, exposure, multiple serious abrasions. You have a hairline skull fracture and thirty-five stitches. You nearly drowned. Before all of that, you endured a massive psychological trauma and stress to your heart as a result of the poison you ingested. In the words of my teenage niece, Mr. Stanton, you need to chill for a few days. Call in sick to work."

"Got it," said Joe, who seriously doubted he would still even have a job after his parishioners learned the full extent of his bizarre escapades.

They pushed on through the *Mercy*'s bustling corridors. Workers were cleaning rooms and surgical suites, fixing equipment, painting walls. Preparing for the looming deployment.

"Busy day on the *Mercy*," said Joe.

Gliss nodded. "Mr. Beck likes to keep his fleet in tip-top shape, especially the *Mercy*. Wounded service members deserve nothing less."

"It's impressive."

"More medical staff will deploy in Miami," said Gliss. "Our last stop before Ivory Coast. The population of this ship will double within a couple of days."

They emerged onto the upper deck and ascended a long ramp to the waiting helicopter.

The sky was bright, the air warm. Seagulls danced on the thermals, and whitecaps shimmered in the light. In the distance, far to the east, they could make out a flat brown line against the horizon—the California coast. Layered on top of the line, matching it perfectly, another layer. Haze. Smog. The layers made the coastline look like a section of geological strata.

Ella puzzled over their situation. Gliss had told her that after the chopper ride, an Erebus corporate jet would fly them home from California. Free of charge. All free of charge. Gliss attributed the generosity to Beck's religious convictions. *He's stepping up to help a man of the cloth*, Gliss had said. *It's a small act of compassion. A gift.*

Ella didn't buy his story. She'd seen things on the ship. Overheard snippets of conversations. Things that didn't add up. She wasn't worried, though, because she thought she had Beck's real motive figured out.

She'd Googled him. Read about his family, company, and military service. He'd accomplished great things. But there were stains on his record, too. Serious problems. The reports said Beck and a group of special operations soldiers under his control had been charged with killing innocent civilians in Afghanistan. Beck had been cleared, but questions remained. The press dogged him. Beck needed some good PR, Ella thought, and she expected to find reporters waiting in San Diego or Bremerton.

They stopped at the top of the ramp near the waiting helicopter. The engine began to whine.

Heintzel handed Joe a manila envelope and spoke over the din. "There's a DVD inside with copies of everything. Your history, scans, tests, my notes."

Joe rose from the wheelchair and gave Heintzel a hug. "Thank you," he said. "For all you've done. And stay safe…in the deployment."

Heintzel seemed taken aback by the gesture. She smiled fleetingly and smoothed her jacket. "I will try," she said.

The helicopter shrieked and an attendant in a flight suit adorned with the Erebus logo emerged from the craft to help Joe and Ella aboard.

Joe watched the gleaming white bulk of the *Mercy* recede, its bow rising and falling in the chop. Bold crosses on the top and sides of the craft marked the ship for what it was—very important in combat zones. It looked like a giant floating ambulance.

Joe stared at the tumultuous sea and thought it mirrored his recent past.

He'd endured the worst days of his life and yearned for things to get back to normal. He wanted to resume work. Step back into his familiar routine. Heal.

In fact, nothing would ever be the same again.

CHAPTER 30

BECK ACCOMPANIED HEINTZEL to her office and queried her as they walked. "Think Stanton and his girlfriend bought your story? She's a nurse, you know."

Heintzel shrugged. "They bought it, yes. I think so."

"The scans you gave them—"

"Altered, to appear normal, along with his records. There's nothing in there about his true condition."

"What about the implant?" Beck asked.

Heintzel led him into her office, closed the door, and with a few taps on her keyboard called Stanton's scans onto her monitor. Beck peered at the screen. Saw the tiny cluster of electrodes Heintzel had positioned against Stanton's temporal lobe.

"Lucky for us," said Heintzel, "Mr. Stanton suffered an assortment of deep cuts and contusions when he fell off the ferry. It wasn't difficult to widen one of the cuts and use it as an entry point for installing the device. We should be able to monitor his thoughts until he dies. Assuming there's a receiver nearby."

"Done," said Beck. "Hidden in Stanton's rental house this morning. Ring tested it. It works." He stared at the multi-colored scans spinning slowly on screen. "How long's he got?"

"If he follows the pattern, he'll be feeling pretty good for the next five to seven days. Almost back to normal. Then he'll decline. Fast. I'd give him a week, maybe a bit more."

"What if they do an autopsy after he kicks it? Find the chip?"

"The device is bioreactive," Heintzel replied. "It'll dissolve once cellular processes cease."

"When can we see Stanton's thought captures?" Beck asked. He knew it would be a while. Brain activity decoding—translating neural signals into sounds, words, and images—required a breathtaking amount of processing power. Even the supercomputer on board *Marauder* needed hours to process one series of e-scans.

"Eight to ten hours," Heintzel replied. "Though Dr. Ring can give you a more precise answer."

Beck nodded, satisfied.

Heintzel said, "There's something else you need to be aware of. Something that might affect Stanton's survival time." She looked at Beck. "The mass behind his visual cortex is growing."

Beck arched an eyebrow. "Growing?"

"I've sent pictures to Phelps and Ring, but there's no doubt about it. We measured a change during his stay here. This wasn't the case with any of the others."

"What would growth like that mean?"

"I don't know. That's Dr. Phelps's area of expertise. Neurophysiology. Molecular change within brain structures." She hesitated.

"What?" said Beck. The look on Heintzel's face worried him.

The doctor sighed and removed her glasses. Twirled them in one hand. She seemed suddenly reluctant to speak.

"What's on your mind?"

"Dr. Phelps."

"What about him?"

She turned to her monitor and tapped the color scans of the strange mass wedged between the caudate nucleus and the occipital lobe. "He's making good progress analyzing the anomaly."

"So?"

Heintzel looked at Beck. Sighed. "So he seems to think that we brought Mr. Stanton onto the *Mercy* to help him. To alert him to the dangers he's facing. He's concerned about Stanton's well-being."

Beck frowned. "Phelps needs to focus on his job. He's making a truckload of money."

"He's asking questions," said Heintzel. "Awkward questions: 'How did we treat Stanton's condition? What did we tell him? What are we doing to alert other possible victims?' Phelps e-mails me these things and I don't know how to respond." She looked at Beck. "If he finds out the truth…If he finds out—"

Beck shook his head. "Don't worry. He won't."

CHAPTER 31

THE EREBUS HELICOPTER carried Joe and Ella to San Diego International Airport, where it landed in an out-of-the way corner of the vast facility, next to a sleek Gulfstream G5 jet. The ground crew bustled around the tarmac, refueling and loading gear into the jet's open cargo bay.

Ella saw no sign of press. Only Erebus employees.

In Bremerton, she thought. *Reporters will be there, for sure.*

But when the jet touched down in Bremerton, it was the same story. No press. Not on the tarmac. Not in the little terminal. Ella felt relieved, but also baffled.

Why would Beck help Joe, she wondered, *for no reward or gain?* She still didn't buy Gliss's explanation, but she couldn't come up with a better one.

Joe and Ella said good-bye to the Erebus crew and caught a taxi to Joe's house, fifteen minutes away.

The cab turned down Joe's quiet, treelined street a little after seven. It was a warm, summer evening and people were outside. Dan Gerhard was mowing his lawn. Marella Martinez was washing her beater Volvo. Kids were skateboarding and jetting around on bikes.

Ella saw her Jetta waiting in Joe's driveway and made a mental note to buy flowers and a bottle of wine for her older sister, Jill. *Make that a case of wine*, she thought.

Jill had kindly retrieved the Jetta from Anacortes after the ferry mishap—a task that had caused her to miss half a day at the law firm where she worked.

The cab eased into the cul-de-sac fronting Joe's house and the neighbors stopped what they were doing to watch.

Joe gave the driver his credit card and waited for a receipt.

Jamala Gordon, three houses down—watched from her yard, arms folded. "Hi, Jamala," Joe, called, smiling. "Nice evening, huh?"

Jamala, normally talkative, just stared, then retreated to her porch.

Joe and Ella carried their things into the house. Two minutes later the doorbell rang and Ella answered. It was Janet Blevin, an elderly next-door neighbor and animal lover. She was holding a small pet carrier containing Joe's cat, Figaro.

"Hi, Janet. Hi, Figaro," said Ella, relieving Janet of the pet carrier and letting Figaro out on the hardwood floor. "Thank you so much for watching him. For the extra days, too."

"Oh, that's fine," said Janet, peering around none too subtly. "Figaro is a sweetie."

Janet set a paper bag full of bills and catalogs on the entry table. "Here's Joe's mail," she said, stepping further into the house.

Looking for Joe, Ella realized. *Nosy old thing.*

Joe was unpacking in the bedroom and Ella hoped he'd stay there. No sense revving up the neighborhood gossip machine any more than it already was.

Joe didn't stay in the bedroom.

"Hi, Janet," he said, emerging from the hallway. Figaro trotted to his side, rubbed against his leg, and began purring. "I meant to bring you something from the San Juans, but we—I—ran into a little trouble."

"Oh, I heard," said Janet, ogling Joe's bruised and bandaged face with morbid fascination. "I saw you on the news. And YouTube. Everyone did, I think."

Wonderful, thought Ella. *Perfect.*

Janet retreated a step, eyes fixed on Joe. "Are you…okay?"

Joe smiled. "Much better, thanks, Janet. Just want to get back to work and my routine."

Janet said nothing further. Just stared at Joe's battered, multihued face until the silence grew awkward.

"Well, thanks again," Ella said sharply, herding the old woman toward the door. "Joe has to unpack. And by the way—the doctors think he ate something poisonous that caused all this stuff. Not sure what you've heard. But that's what happened."

"She's old," Joe said gently, after Ella shut the door.

"She's rude," countered Ella. "I think she would've stared at your face all night if I let her."

Joe poured his mail onto the table, tossed the first few junk catalogs aside and gazed half-heartedly at the remaining heap. The house felt dark and musty, so Ella opened windows and turned on lights.

She moved methodically, lost in her thoughts. Joe scanned his mail, lost in his thoughts. The house fell silent. It was not the normal vibe for Joe Stanton and Ella Tollefson. Not at all.

Joe and Ella were young and in love. They couldn't stand being apart, and when they were together it was usually nonstop talking and laughing and touching and messing around.

"I have to go," Ella said abruptly. "Check my apartment and stuff."

Joe held her gaze a moment. Her expression worried him. "Okay," he said. "I'm just gonna...unpack."

Ella turned, but instead of leaving, marched into the small kitchen and began opening cupboards. "We should've had the cab stop somewhere," she said, sounding frustrated. "It's after seven! What are you gonna have for dinner?"

"I've got tons of stuff," Joe replied, following her.

"Like what? Cereal and stale milk?" She threw open a drawer. Then another.

"I *like* cereal and stale milk," he said. He reached for her gently. "Ella—"

Her eyes clouded and she looked to Joe suddenly vulnerable. Fragile.

"Baby—"

She fell into his arms, and the tears came.

"It's okay," he said, holding her, letting her cry. "It's okay."

She cried. He held her close.

"I didn't know you hated cereal *that* much," he said.

She laughed, then cried some more.

Joe led her into the den, and they sat together on the sofa. Joe held her hand. He said, "I got a clean bill of health, remember? I'm gonna be fine."

"I know."

"So what is it? The stress of the last few days? School? I know you missed classes."

Ella shook her head. "School's fine. I talked to my professors."

"So—"

Ella pulled away a little, shrugged. "Just stuff. We can talk about it later."

Joe withdrew slowly, misunderstanding. His expression hardened, and after a long silence he said softly, "You're leaving. I don't blame you. Considering what's happened, I mean—"

Ella abruptly stopped crying and gently lifted Joe's downcast face to hers. "Baby—let's get something straight, okay? I am *not* leaving you. Not now. Not ever…I don't care how weird you are."

They both laughed.

"I love you," she said. "I can't help it. You can't get rid of me."

Joe smiled, relieved. "Well, I mean, I can handle anything besides that."

Ella shook her head. "I'm not so sure. People called while you were recovering on the *Mercy*."

"Who? You mean with the church?"

"No. Joe, listen. The ferry system—they want you to pay for the search operation. They spent hours looking for you. Brought in other boats. They want you to pay.

"Their attorney—I talked to her. She says they'll sue to recoup their money if they have to. My sister thinks you could countersue—claim negligence on the ferry system's part. But you'll have to hire a lawyer for that, obviously."

Joe nodded slowly. "I mean, how much do they want me to pay?"

"Seventy, maybe eighty thousand dollars."

Joe laughed. "Should've told them the real reason I fell off the boat."

"What do you mean?"

He shrugged. "I got beat up. Pepper-sprayed. *Before* I fell off the ferry. It was an ambush, basically."

Ella's face paled. "Beat up?"

"Spinell's son," said Joe. "And, I don't know—his wife or sister or someone. She stopped me as I was walking back to you. Said the door on her truck was stuck. Asked if I could help get it open. I followed her down to the car deck and…"—he shook his head, embarrassed—"they jumped me."

"But…why didn't you say something? Tell the paramedics? The police?"

Joe sighed. "When I woke up on the beach, I was whacked out, just…out of it. I couldn't think straight. The helicopter came, I blacked out again. I don't know, but by the time I *really* regained my senses, on the ship, I just decided to let it go."

"How do you know it was Spinell's son?"

"He told me himself…in so many words. And there's a strong family resemblance."

Ella looked baffled. "You told everybody that your cuts and bruises came from your fall—from hitting the side of the boat."

Joe shrugged. "I wasn't mad at Spinell's son. I wanted to just get past the whole thing. I'm not mad now."

"Yeah?" Ella's expression hardened. "Well *I'm* mad. You almost died, Joe. He beat you. Threw you into forty-degree water in the middle of—"

"Whoa," Joe shook his head. "They didn't throw me off. I didn't say that. He beat me up. Pretty bad—but they left me on the deck. After they went away, I got up and stumbled around. I was dizzy. Couldn't see. Then I fell off." He decided not to mention the voice.

"Still," said Ella. "They're the reason you fell. If they hadn't beaten you up…You have to tell the police about this."

Joe said, "Spinell wanted to press charges against me, but you said he dropped those."

Ella laughed. "Yeah. Now I know why. His son almost killed you. Maybe he figured that was enough revenge."

"So let's drop it."

Ella took Joe's hands in hers and looked into his eyes. "Joe, listen. I love how compassionate and kind you are. How forgiving. It's one of the reasons I love you and it's one of the traits that makes you so great at what you do. You really think about other people and put yourself in other people's shoes. But this guy—Spinell Junior, whatever his name is—must be a total thug to do what he did. I don't care if he was pissed. That's not how you take out your anger. If you explain what happened, the ferry system might go after Junior instead of you."

"Baby—"

"Joe—the ferry bill isn't even your only problem. Remember the detective? Palmer?"

"Sure."

"He knows Heintzel thinks the hallucination was caused by something you ate. But he said the San Juan County prosecutor is considering filing charges against you anyway."

"For what?"

"Disorderly conduct. Misdemeanor, reckless…something. I had to sign an affidavit saying you'd come back to Friday Harbor to plead."

Joe shrugged. Smiled. "At least we get to go back to the San Juans."

Ella looked at him, exasperated. "Joe! This isn't funny."

"I know. It's just…I almost died."

Ella said nothing.

"But I *didn't* die, Ella. And I still have you." He studied her face. "With all the things you're telling me, I know I *shouldn't* feel happy. But I do. I can't help it. I just think everything will work out." Almost as an afterthought he said, "And at least the medical care was free."

"Right. The *Northern Mercy*," Ella replied. "I almost forgot."

Joe caught the sarcastic edge in her voice, and his smile vanished. "Wait. What? It's not free? You mean Beck's gonna charge me after all?"

"No. No. It was free. The flights, too. All gratis, apparently."

"So—"

"So it was also really weird."

"What was? I thought you said you liked the docs."

"I said the doctors seemed *qualified*," Ella replied. "And the gear was top-of-the-line—better than most hospitals."

"Yeah, so—"

"So it was still weird. Just the fact that the ship was there—it's a military ship."

"Luck," said Joe. "On its way to a deployment. You heard what they said."

"And that whole spiel Gliss gave us, about Beck donating your care because you're a priest. That's weird."

"He's religious."

Ella shook her head. "Joe, I researched Beck, okay? The guy doesn't have a page on Wikipedia, he has his own book. He made his fortune—or, actually, added to his family's fortune—as a defense contractor. Big-time defense contractor. He and his dad and sister run a bunch of companies, but the main one—Erebus Global Patriot—"

Joe arched an eyebrow. "Erebus Global Patriot?" He knew nothing about Beck, aside from the platitudes Gliss had volunteered on the *Mercy*.

"That's the name. They recruit private soldiers—mostly former Navy SEALs and Army Rangers—then deploy them around the world, in places where the Pentagon doesn't have enough regular military."

"I've read about military contractors," said Joe. "It's controversial."

"That's putting it mildly. And Erebus is in the hot seat more than the rest. Been accused of acting outside the law, doing whatever they want on the battlefield. Killing civilians when it suits them.

"One article I read says Beck's core team is made up of rogues. Misfits. Special forces guys who got zero medals—which is unusual. And general discharges."

"General discharges?"

"Means they're bad eggs," Ella replied. "It means they did stuff the military didn't like. Even if there weren't specific charges leveled."

"This is the guy who offered me free medical care?"

"Oh, you haven't heard anything. According to the entries, Beck is also a far-right Christian wing nut. Anti-gay, antiabortion, anti-women's rights. Not the kinda guy that would be likely to show up in your church on Sunday. No offense."

"Maybe he's moderated since the entries were written. Or maybe he just heard that a priest was in need and extended a hand without really knowing anything about me or my church."

"Fine," said Ella. "Maybe it's all good. But there's also this: I asked to see Beck when I got to the *Mercy*—to thank him for all he was doing. But Gliss told me he wasn't there. That he was in Europe."

"Yeah," said Joe. "Told me the same thing."

"But he *was* there, Joe. I saw him for a second—through the glass—up in the wheelhouse, when I got off the helicopter. I recognized him from the Google searches."

"Are you sure?"

"Positive."

"Why would Gliss lie? Doesn't make sense."

Ella nodded. "Neither did their questions. They asked me tons of questions."

"About what?"

"Your hallucination, about the sequence of events leading up to it. Really detailed, off-the-wall stuff: What were we doing in the San Juans? Why exactly were we there? How long had we been there? When did you start to flip out? What were you doing just before you flipped out? Had you ever mentioned the little girl before? Did you know anyone named Lorna Gwin? On and on. Over and over. The same questions again and again from different people. And then—oh yeah—tons of questions about water."

Joe frowned. "Water?"

"They went on and on about it," Ella replied. "Had you been swimming in the sound? Had you been diving? Could you have gone swimming or diving without me knowing about it?"

Joe shook his head.

"Weird, huh? See what I mean? I told them we'd been kayaking and they were all over that. Asked where we went, asked if you'd fallen out of your boat. Asked if you'd jumped in for fun, rolled the kayak."

"That makes no sense."

Ella leaned forward. "Here's the weirdest thing of all. I think so, anyway. Remember that nurse on the boat? Navarro?"

"Yeah, sure," said Joe. "She was really sweet to me. Didn't say much, but—"

"She was scared."

"Scared?" Joe raised his eyebrows again, which tugged on his stitches and made him wince. "Of what?"

"I don't know. And I can't prove it. That's just how she seemed to me. Nervous. Frightened. Maybe of Heintzel and Gliss. Did you notice she kind of averted her eyes when they were in the room?"

"Yeah," Joe said, "now that you mention it. I did wonder about that. Thought maybe she was just really shy."

"Do you remember right before we all left your room and walked to the helicopter? I went into the hall—to the little galley thing—to fill my water bottle?"

"I remember you left for a minute, yeah."

"Yeah. Well, she followed me."

"Navarro did?"

"Right. She looked pale, Joe. Really scared. Trembling. Kept glancing around like she was worried someone would overhear us. She put her hand on my arm when I was filling my water bottle and leaned really close and whispered to me. Said 'Mr. Stanton is the fourth one.'"

"Fourth one what?"

"I don't know. Just 'Mr. Stanton is the fourth one,' with these really big eyes and scared expression on her face. Her accent is thick but I'm sure I heard it right. I asked her what she meant, and she started to talk—but then Gliss walked into the hall and she practically ran away."

"Fourth one?" Joe repeated. "I wonder what..." His voice trailed off.

"I know it makes no sense," said Ella. "But the fear in that woman's eyes was real enough, Joe. I could feel it."

Joe leaned back into the sofa, puzzled. Thinking.

"You asked me to tell you what was wrong. Are you sorry you asked?"

Joe shook his head. "No. I can handle it. I want to know what's going on. I *need* to know."

Ella smiled and kissed him. Then she said good-bye and drove to her apartment to drop things off and check her mail.

The cameras and microphones Beck's men had placed around Joe's house worked perfectly, capturing Joe and Ella's conversation in its entirety. Beck and Collins watched the couple on Collins's laptop.

"Smart bitch," said Collins.

Beck nodded. "Yeah. But they have no idea what's really going on. And they're not gonna figure it out. We'll download as much as we can from Stanton—as fast as we can—and then get rid of them both."

Collins smiled, "Could keep the girl around for a few days. Just for fun."

Beck ignored the remark. "Make sure Ring has everything he needs. Phelps is here to assist, but Ring's running the investigation."

"Understood."

Beck's demeanor hardened. "The nurse, onboard *Mercy*."

"Navarro?" said Collins. "The one who tried to talk to Stanton's girl?"

"Yeah."

"Already taken care of."

Forty-five minutes later Ella was back at Joe's house with pad thai, chicken satays, and more of Joe's favorite dishes from Lila Ri's Tip Top Thai restaurant. She found Joe crashed out on his bed, snoring softly, face serene. Every light in the house was on and he was still fully dressed.

CHAPTER 32

TWO A.M. A soft, persistent chime woke Orondo Ring in his cabin aboard *Marauder*. He pawed the nightstand for his glasses and found his iPhone—the source of the chiming. Five minutes later he was at his workstation inside *Marauder*'s cavernous War Room.

The cool, dark room glowed like a fighter-jet cockpit. Machines hummed. Fans whirred softly. He saw what was on his computer screen, and his heart began to thump. He paused. Stood there in front of his sprawling desk, breathing deeply. Letting his mind clear.

He was close to understanding the mystery. Very close. He'd been the first to see the pattern: the link between the Erebus divers and the gillnetter from Yakutat.

He'd set the War Room's computers to troll for other incidents, which is how they'd found Stanton in Friday Harbor.

He'd urged Beck to run thought captures on all the men—despite the hassle and risk—and that had led to the discovery of the chamber images, the sound accompanying the images, and the matching sound in the deep ocean.

Ring sat down and saw two new folders waiting like neatly wrapped presents in the upper right hand corner of his huge monitor. The names read simply JSTANTON1 and JSTANTON2. Progress bars below the folders showed that more data—much more—was still coalescing.

Ring double-clicked on the first folder, and watched as images—captured thoughts from deep inside Joe Stanton's subconscious—unspooled across the screen. He gaped but uttered no sound, fingers fumbling across the touch pad. He dug his phone out of his jeans pocket and called Beck.

CHAPTER 33

JOE AWOKE IN THE QUIET DARKNESS of his bedroom to find Ella sleeping peacefully beside him. He guessed it was the middle of the night but he felt alert. Aware.

He remembered that he'd fallen asleep still dressed, with the lights on. And he remembered something sweeter: Ella helping him, gently, tenderly, out of his clothes and into the sheets. Ella leaning over him. Kissing him. Checking the cuts on his head.

He lay still now, and his thoughts began to drift to the painful experiences of the previous days.

No. Not gonna think about that now.

Shoving his worries aside, he focused on a subject far more pleasant. One he found endlessly fascinating: Ella.

He slid closer to her and curled against her back. Traced the smooth curve of her right hip with his fingers and kissed her gently on the neck. The rhythm of her breathing changed slightly but she didn't wake.

Joe lay there, intoxicated by the feel of her body and the delicious scent of her skin and hair—hair still damp from a shower. The woman was a dream. Beautiful. Smart. Athletic. Funny. He loved her for all of those things and for reasons far deeper.

He couldn't quite explain it, but in the ten months that they'd been together she'd somehow become a part of him. He *needed* to see Ella Tollefson every day like he needed air and light and water. Needed to touch her and hold her. Look into her mesmerizing green eyes. Hear her voice. Her laugh.

He'd had other girlfriends. Been in other serious relationships. But he'd never experienced anything like this. And the fact that Ella seemed to feel the same way about him only added to his amazement.

Joe lay there in the dark, thinking about a trait that had attracted him right from the start. Ella was strong and confident, gregarious and self-assured, no doubt. But her strength was balanced with a sweet vulnerability. A vulnerability tinged with sadness, tinged with loss. He hadn't understood the sadness until weeks after their first encounter, and learning the full story had only made him love her more.

I'm not the only one healing, he reminded himself, as he lay next to her in the dark.

He listened to Ella breathing, and his mind went back to the day they'd met.

The sky was blue, vivid blue, the smell of rain strong in the air.

The foreman shouted, straining to make himself heard over the roar of the river "On three! Everybody! Put your back into it. One. Two. Three!"

Joe and his crew pulled the heavy rope attached to the griphoist, the slack between the pulleys tightened, and the last stringer on the new bridge thudded into position atop the sills, next to two other massive Douglas fir logs.

They were deep inside Olympic National Park—Joe and a group of eight volunteers from St. Anthony's Episcopal Church—helping a team from the Seattle Mountaineers rebuild a washed-out bridge in a gorgeous valley known as the Upper Big Chinook.

The church group had signed onto the trip for the public-service component, and because they thought it would be a good team-building exercise. A way for some of St. Anthony's leaders to bond—with each other, and with their new priest.

The work had proven to be physically demanding. Grueling. Exhausting. Joe's back hurt. His muscles ached. And he'd never in his life been happier.

Being in the wild, hanging out with friends, and building useful stuff seemed like heaven to Joe Stanton. The group had eaten well, swapped stories and jokes, talked faith, and grown close. At night they retired to a cluster of tents in a corner of a vast meadow paralleling the creek, and slept like the dead.

Four days into the weeklong trip, another group of volunteers strolled into the worksite, and Joe's life changed forever.

He noticed her immediately. Every guy on the site noticed her.

She was tall and graceful, with a gorgeous smile, perfect features, creamy skin, and abundant red hair pulled back in a ponytail.

Her group—a half-dozen volunteers with axes, shovels, and other tools strapped to their packs—stopped to chat with the foreman and then edged single file onto the temporary bridge deck, bound for the meadow, where they would set up camp.

Joe was splitting rails on the opposite bank of the creek. He watched as she crossed the unfinished bridge, realized he was staring—ogling, in fact—and went back to swinging his axe. He couldn't resist looking up again, though, and when he lifted his eyes, she glanced his way and smiled.

His swing went wide—completely missed the log he was aiming for—and he stumbled forward with a grunt, burying the axhead in the dirt. She laughed—once she saw that he was okay—and continued on with her group.

The remaining days of Joe's stay proved frustrating. He wanted to talk to the woman with the red hair, but opportunities proved elusive. Their camps were far apart and they worked long hours with their respective crews in different parts of the valley.

When their groups crossed paths, Joe said "hello" or "good morning," and she always smiled. He thought he saw something in her eyes when she glanced his way; a bit more attention or interest than mandated by ordinary politeness, then decided he was imagining things. The woman with the red hair smiled at everyone. She was friendly. Sweet. Outgoing. What's more, there were young, fit guys in her group. Joe figured she had to be with one of them. Had to be.

This is a church trip, he told himself. *Not a singles vacation. I need to get her out of my head.*

The strategy worked, sort of, until the Goddess walked by, and his mind turned to mush. The fact that she wore baggy, grubby Pendleton work shirts, mud-caked Carhartts, hiking boots, gloves, and a baseball cap only made her look sexier, Joe decided. There was a radiance about her that no amount of dirt could hide, and her deep-green eyes sparkled, full of life, when she smiled or laughed.

They acknowledged each other, Joe and the woman with the red hair. And that was it. Nothing happened. Nothing at all. Until the final night of Joe's stay.

Joe liked to look at the stars, especially when he was in the middle of nowhere—where the sky was black and infinite. Where the stars of the Milky Way spanned the heavens like a river of diamonds. He'd intended to spend time stargazing throughout the week, but it hadn't happened. The work he and his teammates were doing was so tiring that when evening rolled around, it was all he could do to make dinner, clean up, brush his teeth, and crawl into his sleeping bag. He'd gotten up to pee around two o'clock one morning, seen the blazing stars through sleep-filled eyes, and vowed to himself that he would stay up late on his final night in camp.

Full dark that night. Joe pulled his Therm-a-Rest pad from his tent-careful not to wake his tentmates—and followed a game trail through the tall grass, happy to find that there was enough illumination from the sky alone to see where he was going without a flashlight.

He wound his way to the middle of the meadow and lay down on the grass, zipping his fleece all the way to the top and pulling on his wool hat. August or no, it was cool at night in the Olympics.

The sky shimmered—a fathomless vault of glittering, iridescent jewels—and soon Joe was lost in a blissful, almost meditative state.

He was aware of the soothing rush of the creek. The murmur of the wind in the trees. If he tilted his head back, or side-to-side, he could see the forest—a dark, impenetrable wall against the luminous, mysterious sky.

He lay there, lost in thought, feeling deeply content. Alive.

And then—an interruption. An intrusion. Someone walking out from one of the other camps, into the meadow. Joe cursed. Already the light from the walker's headlamp was messing up his night vision.

He lay still, in no mood for company. The meadow was huge and full of crisscrossing deer trails. Surely the person would take another path.

The walker came on, straight for Joe. He sighed and thought about taking his pad and quietly moving to a different area. But he liked the spot he'd chosen and didn't want to give it up just because of some clueless insomniac.

The walker drew close. A beam of light splashed across Joe's supine form, and the walker gasped. Stopped cold.

"Hi," said Joe.

"Are you okay?" asked the walker.

A small shiver traveled the length of Joe's spine and shot out to his arms and legs, fingers and toes.

It's her.

He sat up, shielding his eyes. "Yeah. Fine. Just looking at the stars."

She laughed and turned off her light. "Sorry I messed up your night vision."

"No worries," said Joe. "What are you doing?"

"Just walking. Thinking." She paused. "You're one of the bridge guys."

"Yeah," said Joe, getting to his feet. "I'm Joe. I'd shake your hand if I could see it."

The woman laughed again, extended her hand, found Joe's. They shook. Her hand was warm and soft and strong. "Ella," she said. "Nice to meet you."

Ella tilted her head to look at the sky and Joe caught a delicious fragrance in the air. Clean skin. Wet hair.

She went swimming, he thought. *Went for a swim after working on the trail all day. How the hell did I miss seeing that?*

The thought of this woman swimming in the creek made him feel light-headed. And then he felt embarrassed, because he knew for a fact that he himself smelled nothing close to fragrant. But Ella didn't seem to mind or notice.

"Jeez," she said. "Don't even need a headlamp at all, do you? It's so bright, once your eyes adjust."

"Yeah," said Joe. "Um, do you want to sit? The grass is kind of wet; but I brought something to sit on."

"Sure." He could hear the smile in her voice. "Thanks."

They sat together, a couple of feet apart, looking at the sky.

She asked how the work was going on the bridge. He asked how the work was going on the trail.

"What group are you with?" Ella asked.

"St. Anthony's Episcopal Church in Bremerton," said Joe. "What about you?"

"Washington Trails Alliance. I saw an ad on their website. Thought this would be a nice break between semesters. I live in Seattle." She explained that she was in a grueling nurse-anesthetist program and wanted to get away—far away—from books and computers. As Joe listened to her explanation, he sensed there was more to it. There was something in her voice. The faintest hint of...Sadness? Loss? Longing? He couldn't put his finger on it.

It flashed in Joe's mind that she'd come on the trip because she was looking for something. *Needed* something. He had no idea what the "something" was—he was far from certain that his hunch was even correct—and he didn't plan to ask about it. Not yet.

Joe's heart thumped. He was happy—elated—that Ella was there. He hoped she wouldn't leave.

He scanned the sky and said, "Amazing how much you can see without all the light pollution, isn't it?"

Ella laughed, "You mean like from morons wearing headlamps?"

Joe smiled. "Not what I meant. I'm *glad* you walked out here."

"Me too." The warmth of the moment hung in the air between them.

After a minute she asked, "So do you know many of the constellations?"

Joe shrugged. "Some. My mom was an astronomy buff. Used to drag me and my siblings outside at night. Taught us quite a few."

"But that's not why you look."

Joe couldn't tell if this was a question or a statement. "I look because it's beautiful," he said wistfully. "Because it's alive. Always changing."

Ella nodded.

"I look at the stars because they remind me how most of the stuff we worry about is so…trivial. How insignificant we are in this little splinter of time and space we occupy."

Ella laughed. "Okay…you don't *sound* depressed, but that's kind of a depressing sentiment, isn't it?"

"Not at all. The opposite." He leaned back. Spoke earnestly. "Fills me with wonder that I'm a part of something so big, that I'm awake and aware enough to sit here in a meadow in such a beautiful place and, you know, contemplate the mystery." He turned toward her. "It's a gift, I think. An amazing gift. Does that sound depressing?"

Ella leaned a little closer. "No," she said. "I like it."

He wanted to kiss her. The desire was practically overwhelming. But he didn't want to scare her away. The silence between them grew electric.

After a while she said, "The church you're with—St. Anthony's—what's that like?"

"It's an Episcopal—Anglican—church. Progressive. Everybody's welcome. Nobody's excluded. We're growing."

"And you joined? You're a member?"

Joe laughed. "An employee, actually. I'm the vicar."

"Get out." She sounded surprised but not put off. "Really?"

"Really."

"That's so cool. I've never met a young minister. Vicar, I mean."

"You just meet old ones?"

She laughed. "I guess so."

Joe anticipated the next question.

"So is it like the Catholic Church?"

"Some things are. Anglican and Catholic Christians follow the same creeds."

Ella nodded.

"Share the same central liturgy—a communion service. Catholics call it a mass."

"But I mean, in an Episcopal church can the vicar, you know—"

"Date? Yeah. Get married. Have a family. Definitely." Joe smiled. "The celibacy thing wouldn't have worked for me."

Ella laughed again.

They talked about school and work and their adventures in the wilderness. About Seattle and the Northwest and their dreams for the future. The darkness deepened, the fiery white stars danced their regal, perfect dance across the sky, the river murmured—soothingly, endlessly—and Joe completely lost track of time. Talking with Ella seemed the easiest, most natural thing in the world, like they'd been friends for years. And best of all, it seemed to Joe that she was enjoying the conversation as much he was.

At last, as if waking from a trance, Ella said, "I'm working tomorrow. Better go or I'm not gonna be much good to my crew."

"I'll walk you back to your tent," said Joe.

He stood, extended his hand, and Ella took it and held it, as they walked, side by side in the grass. The feel of her body so close in the darkness made Joe dizzy. He wanted to say something witty or romantic, but his thoughts were a blur. And then, too soon, they were at the edge of her camp. Joe could just make out the tents—inert gray mounds barely discernible against the alders and forest beyond.

She turned quickly, rose up onto her tiptoes, and kissed him on the lips. "Good night, Joe."

"Good night."

And then she was gone, moving away, into her camp, into the darkness.

Joe stood a moment, the stars hanging bright overhead, frozen in space; the river soft and muffled now, as if the universe was holding its breath, feeling the magic of the experience as keenly as Joe.

In a daze he walked back into the meadow, retrieved his sleeping pad, and headed for his own tent. He slept, and dreamed of Ella, the woman with the red hair.

When Joe awoke the next morning, Ella was gone. Her entire crew, someone told him, was already out on the trail. The really bad news was that her group had been sent to a new area, far from the route he and his team would take to get back to their vehicles.

Joe and his friends broke camp and readied their packs for the hike out. Joe chatted with his teammates and did his share of the work, but his mind was far away, his body on autopilot. He stayed in that mode for the entire walk, and for the drive back to Bremerton. All he could think about was Ella and the encounter in the meadow. *Ella.* The sound of her voice. The feel of her body. The sweetness of her kiss. He wondered, after a while, if maybe he'd dreamed the events of the previous night. If his friends hadn't handed him food, he would have forgotten to eat.

Back home, he called the Washington Trails Alliance, got bumped to voice mail, and left a message: "Hello. My name is Joe Stanton and I live in Bremerton. I was working on a trail project in the Upper Big Chinook region of the Olympics and met one of your members—a woman named Ella. I'd like to get in touch with her but don't have her contact information. Could someone please call me back?"

He hung up, cursing himself for not asking Ella for her phone number—or even her last name—when he'd had the chance. He'd assumed, foolishly, that he would see her again.

The day after he called, he got a message back. Terse. To the point. "Thank you for calling our office, but we do not share any member or volunteer information."

Joe called back, said he understood their policy and wondered if someone could at least send Ella a message on his behalf. No luck. He searched online. Studied the group's website for stories and photos that might include Ella's last name. Nothing.

Distraught, Joe resolved to go to the group's next meeting and plead his case in person. If that didn't work, he'd try Ella's university. In the end, however, neither thing was necessary.

She appeared out of nowhere, it seemed to Joe, during communion, at an early September service at St. Anthony's.

Joe had said the offering and prayer of thanksgiving. Performed the consecration of the bread and wine. Now he was moving around a wide circle of parishioners, Joe serving the bread, a lay minister following with the chalice.

Halfway around the circle, Joe offered a piece of bread to an elderly retired banker. A longtime St. Anthony's member. "Body of Christ," Joe intoned. "Bread of—"

He saw her out of the corner of his eye—two people away. His heart skipped a beat. Several beats. He turned. Looked.

She was really there. *Ella*. Looking his way. Smiling. Winking at him now.

The room spun, the parishioners disappeared, and Joe smiled back. Grinned like a child on Christmas morning. Then he remembered where he was. Regained his composure and finished his sentence. "—heaven."

The banker cocked an eyebrow but Joe didn't notice. When he got to Ella, he whispered, "I'm glad you're here."

"Me too," she replied.

She stayed for coffee hour after the service. Waited in the sanctuary as Joe stood at the door and said good-bye to each member of the congregation.

When the crowd had dwindled to a few volunteers stowing tables and chairs, he found her, took her hand, and led her outside into the garden.

"You look amazing," he said.

She laughed, "You clean up pretty well yourself. And I like the robe."

He pulled her close—not caring if the volunteers saw—and kissed her long and passionately.

"Would you have lunch with me?" he asked, as they caught their breath. "Or dinner? Or both, maybe, if you want."

She laughed again. "I was hoping you'd ask."

Joe said good-bye to the volunteers, hung up his robe, and in the warm afternoon sunshine left St. Anthony's hand in hand with Ella Tollefson.

They saw each other four more times that week, which wasn't nearly enough for Joe. He was falling hard for the beauty with the red hair. Falling fast. Enjoying every thrilling second of their budding romance.

What wasn't to love? Ella Tollefson was beautiful, intelligent, athletic, funny, playful, and occasionally silly.

She was also—as Joe had intuited during their first conversation—sad; burdened with a weight invisible to the casual observer. It wasn't something she discussed easily—and Joe never pressed.

After three weeks, with their romance growing more intense by the day, she told him the story. She shed no tears upon the telling. She had cried long enough and hard enough about it already. Joe listened, and wept, and fell even more deeply in love.

CHAPTER 34

THREE A.M. A disheveled, bleary-eyed group sat in a semicircle around Ring's workstation—Beck and Collins, Phelps and Edelstein—waiting for Ring to reveal why he'd summoned them at such a godforsaken hour.

Ring, who slept four hours a night, was wide-awake and chipper, humming to himself as he fiddled with a tablet PC.

Beck said, "You have something?"

Ring looked up from his tablet and blinked, as if noticing them all for the first time. "Ah."

"You've found something new in Stanton's captures?"

"Yes." Ring clicked a button, and the monitors flashed to life. "A bit more detail. And…something else."

There was a collective gasp as images filled the screens. "A bit more detail" was a spectacular understatement.

They stared.

And stared some more.

The familiar chamber mouth hovered before them. Same as what they'd seen in Whittaker's thought captures. And there was the whale fall, in the foreground. The bleached bones of the dead whale jutting against the gaping chamber entrance like broken teeth. The glowing fibers splaying out, like anchor lines tethering a hot air balloon to Earth.

It was the vast *interior* of the chamber that caused the gasp. That looked so different.

Ring adjusted some controls, accessed a different set of Joe Stanton's thoughts, and the perspective changed. No one spoke.

They were entering the chamber now, passing over the whale fall, drifting forward, hard against one wall.

The familiar phosphorescent strands were there, running like tracks from the gracefully curving bell of the structure deep into its core. But now the lithe, liquidy wall shimmered with color.

Where before there had been only muted shades of green, now there were splashes of blue and red and yellow.

The perspective changed again, and they were facing the wall head-on. Drifting over its surface, close enough to touch.

The wall was alive with light: Nodules of light. Ribbons of light. Points of light so numerous and diffuse it was like gazing into the Milky Way on the blackest winter night. It was impossible to tell how thick the wall was. It seemed infinitely deep, as if one could travel into the wall itself and be lost in a foam of stars, a universe vast and mesmerizing.

Nearer to the surface of the wall, a latticework of interlocking snowflake-like structures stretched away—geometrically perfect, multifaceted plates of light imbuing the fluid superstructure with an air of fantastic strength.

The perspective changed once more, and on into the chamber they drifted, on and on. The walls narrowed, gradually, elegantly, and the tracks of light coalesced, spiraling into a funnel that curved away before them, bending and arcing toward an unseen, unknown terminus.

Ring touched his keyboard and the familiar *throom, throom, throom* rumbled through the speakers. *Throom, throom, throom.* Steady and constant and soothing. Like a heartbeat, like a chant. The sound was pleasing. Reassuring. In just seconds, it penetrated the mind, conferring an almost subconscious sense of peace and tranquility to the listener.

But not to Beck.

The steady *throom, throom, throom* made Beck's head throb. He squeezed the skin between his eyes and felt his face flush, his mood sour. The sound caused him pain.

He tried to analyze it. Understand why. But it was impossible to think with such a vile noise assaulting his ears. Clogging his brain. He struggled to keep his composure.

"Turn the sound off. Please."

Ring turned it off.

"Any update on the sound?" asked Phelps, oblivious to Beck's discomfort. "In the ocean, I mean. The *real* sound."

Ring said, "Five transmission points in the Bering Sea right now, and three in the Gulf of Alaska. All very deep. At least three thousand meters. If the reports are accurate, there's a new source about fifteen miles southeast of Mauna Kea, in the Hawaiian Islands, as well."

Ring looked at his colleagues. "But the sources aren't stable. The sounds transmit from one spot for a few days, then wink off and start up somewhere else.

"NOAA's curious. But not curious enough to bring in special ROVs. The Navy knows about the sound, but isn't investigating. Not yet."

Beck asked, "Why not?"

Edelstein shrugged. "The ocean is full of sound. Man-made. Natural. Most people aren't aware of that, but it's true. Set aside all the human-generated noise and you still have countless sounds made by fish and mammals and invertebrates. Sound produced by geothermal activity, by pressure and wave action and the movement of the tectonic plates.

"Not all of it's been cataloged. Not every sound in the soundscape is understood. From the reports we've seen, NOAA is calling this a 'random-pattern, naturally occurring acoustical anomaly. Likely geothermal in origin.'"

"They're wrong, of course" said Ring.

"About what?" said Beck.

Ring laughed. "Everything. It's not random, for one thing."

They stared as he pulled a graphical representation of the sound onto his main computer screen—the *throom, throom, throom,* displayed as a colorful waveform. The waves were bunched into tight clusters above a baseline, and the clusters formed patterns distinctive and unique. The clustered waves resembled swarms of insects zooming over flat earth.

"There appears to be a five-day sound cycle," said Edelstein. "The same exact transmission is repeating every five days. NOAA just hasn't been listening long enough."

"They'll notice the pattern," said Phelps. "Or the Navy will."

"Of course," said Ring. "They will. And they'll notice something else as well. The pulse is getting louder. Right now it's background noise. A whisper in the soundscape Dr. Edelstein was telling us about. But that's changing. The cycle we're monitoring now—in the Bering

Sea—is a constant ninety decibels referenced at one micropascal. The first cycle was exactly half that loud. If the pattern holds, the next cycle will wake the dead."

Beck stared at one of Ring's smaller monitors mounted above the main screen. This monitor displayed an image of the chamber from a distance. From outside. It hovered there, alone in the darkness. An eerie, phosphorescent shape floating in space.

"Go back to the interior view," said Beck. "What you were showing us before you brought up the sound."

Ring tapped some commands. Once again they were inside the chamber, facing the graceful bend at the narrow end of the funnel.

All of the glowing lines and luminous crystalline shapes led the eye to that bend, to the place where the walls narrowed and the chamber constricted.

The glowing tracks spiraled through the constriction so that staring into the funnel was like staring into a vortex. Into the whirring, roaring stem of a tornado.

It was quiet now. But the way the light spiraled through the narrowing shaft gave them the feeling of impending acceleration, the sense that if they drifted just a bit farther, they'd be sucked through the funnel's gravitational field.

They drifted forward. Closer to the point of no return. And then they stopped and simply hovered, the great, luminous walls of the chamber close around them.

"Keep going," said Beck. "Into the funnel and around the bend. Show us what's there."

Ring sighed. "We don't have that yet."

He pointed to a little box on his monitor where Joe Stanton's latest thought captures were downloading. The progress bar under the box appeared frozen. If it was moving, the movement was imperceptible.

"There may be something in the next set of captures, but this is all there is right now. Nothing beyond this."

The curious funnel of light lay before them, straight as a rifle bore at first, then arcing away, bending, to an unseen terminus.

"What is that?" Phelps asked. "That other light, coming from around the bend?"

"The light at the end of the tunnel," said Collins, laughing at his own remark.

No one else laughed. No one said anything for several seconds.

"It's what I wanted to show you," said Ring.

The light intensified, pouring into the narrow end of the shaft from an unknown source. From a place they couldn't see.

"It looks like...daylight," said Edelstein. "Sunlight."

"It *is* sunlight," said Ring. "I analyzed it. The ratios match: visible light, ultraviolet and infrared radiation. And the color temperature—fifty-five hundred degrees kelvin—coincides with the sun at midday.

"There's a tint in the color signature that leads me to believe that what we're seeing here is sunlight shining through about fifty to sixty feet of seawater. Give or take."

Beck stared at Ring, confused. "Fifty to sixty feet? But the sounds we've identified are coming from *nine thousand* feet. Ten thousand feet. Maybe more."

"Yes."

Beck sighed, slumped back in his chair and massaged his forehead, which was throbbing again. "Ring," he said, "Do you believe that the chamber structure we're seeing in Stanton's thought captures matches what's really on the seabed?"

"Yes."

Beck pointed at the screen. "So you think if we follow the sound, go to the correct coordinates and down to that depth—to, say, nine thousand feet—we'll actually find one of these structures? A chamber? Or whatever it is?"

"Yes."

"So how do you account for sunlight entering such a chamber—nine thousand feet underwater?"

"I can't. Not yet." He tapped on the box showing Stanton's thought-capture downloads. "But I believe Mr. Stanton's going to tell us. Very soon now."

"Where is Mr. Stanton now?" Phelps asked after a long silence. "And what is his condition?"

The question seemed to hit Beck like a splash of ice water and he muttered something unintelligible.

Ring turned back to his computer. Collins seemed suddenly preoccupied with his phone. Phelps and Edelstein looked at Beck, waiting for his response.

"Where is he?" Beck mumbled.

"Yes," said Phelps. "He's no longer on the *Northern Mercy*. Where is he?"

"At Swedish Medical Center in Seattle," Beck lied. "We told Mr. Stanton everything we know about the phenomenon, about the anomaly, and we passed all of his charts and records on to Swedish."

Phelps gestured at the monitors. "So all of these thought captures were run with Stanton's permission—while he was aboard *Mercy*?"

"Of course," said Beck.

Phelps's expression was impossible to read. He said, "I have some new information on the anomaly—things I've learned studying the other victims. I'd like to share that information with Stanton's doctors. It might prove helpful in his treatment."

Beck smiled. "Whatever new information you have should go to Dr. Ring, and he will share it with Stanton's medical team." Beck leaned forward in his chair and looked at Phelps and Edelstein in turn.

"I'd ask you to please remember the documents you signed when you agreed to come to *Marauder*. When you agreed to the payment I offered. This project, this phenomenon, is…sensitive, to say the least. You can understand my wish to control the flow of information."

"How can it still be sensitive, if you've told Stanton everything?" Edelstein asked.

Beck continued smiling. "Suffice it say that I've made arrangements with Mr. Stanton and his doctors. We're on the same page. It's all under control. Please, just focus on your tasks, collect your well-deserved fees, and leave these details to me and my staff."

CHAPTER 35

"I CAN'T TELL YOU how awful it was seeing you like that," sniffed Zelda Finch, her eyes moist with tears as she hugged Joe Stanton for the third time in half an hour.

It was 9:20 a.m. and the eight-member St. Anthony's Episcopal Church "Bishop's Committee" had just listened to Joe's detailed account of the bizarre events in the San Juans.

St. Anthony's was an old working-class-neighborhood church, and the building was simple but elegant, consisting of a main sanctuary, a kitchen, and two meeting rooms. The committee was gathered in the larger of the two meeting rooms now—seated in a semicircle around a TV monitor on a stand. Morning light shone through the windows, imbuing the honey-colored fir floors with a warm glow.

The Bishop's Committee—dedicated volunteers who had recruited and hired Joe Stanton, and helped run the church—had just watched the infamous YouTube video of Joe's outburst together, though they'd all seen it multiple times before.

The video had elicited fresh tears from many of the committee members and prompted another round of reassuring hugs.

"We didn't know what to think," said seventy-two-year-old Rachel Bell, touching Joe's arm as if she needed to confirm that the young priest was still alive and really there.

"We thought you had a little girl you'd never told us about," added Cindy Dixon. "We were worried sick."

"I was worried sick," laughed Joe. "And poor Ella. She—" he fumbled for the words, and his cheeks reddened. "Well, Ella was amazing."

The committee members—especially the women—exchanged knowing smiles. They all knew Ella Tollefson. Most of the St. Anthony's congregation knew Ella. Ella attended most of Joe's services, stayed for coffee hour, and helped clean up afterward. The women on the committee were certain Joe and Ella would announce their engagement any day and gossiped about it at length.

"Ella's a strong woman," continued Joe. "A very strong woman. She stood by me through this whole miserable ordeal."

"We were all worried," said Chuck Walton, a burly, retired commercial fisherman. "But heck, now that Joe's on the mend…I mean…it's PR, right? And they say, all PR is good PR. Heck, everybody from here to Issaquah saw Joe's face on the news. Church will be packed on Sunday."

"Oh," said Cindy Dixon, dropping her knitting into her lap. "We'll need more bulletins. We should print fifty more."

Joe massaged the bandages on his scalp with his fingertips. He could feel the stitches underneath. "It's not how I envisioned putting St. Anthony's on the map," he said.

"And I'm not sure all PR is good," said Jenn Nelson, the youngest member of the committee at thirty-three and a woman who spoke her mind. "A lot of people who heard about Joe's incidents at the motel, and on the ferry, didn't hear the cause. The news didn't cover that part."

"People just think I lost my mind," said Joe.

Jenn shrugged. "Or that you were taking drugs."

"That's ridiculous," said Rachel Bell.

"Yeah," said Joe. "It is. I know that. And you guys know. Now that I've explained everything. But Jenn's right. Most people just saw snippets on the news or online—of me acting like a total maniac."

He turned to St. Anthony's office manager, Lindsey Oliver, working at a computer near the window. "Lindsey. How many people have unfriended St. Anthony's in the last three days?"

Lindsey opened Facebook and answered without turning. "Eighty-four. No, wait. Eighty-five." She sighed.

"Thanks," said Joe. He looked at the circle of caring, concerned parishioners around him. "You guys," he said, "I hate this whole thing. I hate it. You had faith in me. Hired me. Moved me across the country. We've all been working our tails off for, what, fourteen months now?

Building our membership, building a welcoming, compassionate church that people want to be a part of. And then this happens." He shook his head. "It has knocked us back. I'd be lying if I didn't admit that."

"It's not your fault," said Zelda Finch. "You were poisoned."

"I say we address this head-on," said Jenn Nelson, rolling up her sleeves as she spoke. "Use the Sunday service to lay it all out there. Tell the congregation everything you just told us."

Joe nodded. "I think you're right."

"Guys," said Lindsey Oliver. "Hey—you may want to take a look at this."

Joe and the committee members stepped to Lindsey's desk and stared over her shoulder. "KING 5 Breaking News," said Lindsey.

She scrolled down and clicked on a picture of a Wendy's restaurant.

"Hey," said Joe. "That's where we ate. That's the Wendy's in Anacortes."

"What's the article say?" asked Chuck Walton, stooping and squinting at the screen.

"I can't see without my glasses," said Rachel Bell.

Lindsey read the copy below the photo. "One person is dead and four others are in critical condition after an apparent poisoning at a popular Anacortes-area fast-food restaurant."

"Oh my God," said Cindy Dixon.

"How awful," murmured Rachel Bell. "How horrible."

Lindsey continued. "Police say two of the victims suffered seizures as they were leaving the restaurant just before six o'clock last night."

"Sounds familiar," said Chuck Walton.

"'The Anacortes Wendy's,'" Lindsey read, "'may also be the source of an alleged poisoning of a Bremerton-area priest last week, officials say.'"

Joe absorbed the news in silence. In disbelief. His stomach twisted. He found a chair and sat down. Committee members continued reading over Lindsey's shoulder, and the room went quiet.

"At least they're telling the whole story," said Zelda Finch, at last. "Now everyone will know what happened up there." She touched Joe's hand. "Everyone will realize now that none of it was your doing."

Joe nodded but spoke no reply. The whole thing made him sick. One person dead. Others seriously ill.

At the same time, he understood what the story meant for his reputation. If a maniac was poisoning people, then he was merely a victim, like the others. The outbursts in the San Juans would be considered in a new light.

The news represented vindication, but Joe was not cheered or relieved. Something deep inside told him that it didn't add up. That it didn't answer all the questions or solve the mystery of the voice. He *wanted* to believe that the news represented an end to the ordeal of the past few days, but in his heart of hearts he knew that it was not the last word.

CHAPTER 36

MILES WE MUST TRAVEL TODAY. So many miles.

Lorna Gwin's mother pushed to the front of the crowd, where she set a brisk, even pace.

She had not communicated with Stan-ton in days. But he was out there. Alive. Healthy.

At least for now.

Lorna Gwin's mother could feel it.

Stan-ton wasn't aware of her at the moment. Not consciously, anyway. At present, she was only a vague, undefined worry in the back of his brain. Lorna Gwin's mother knew this. But Stan-ton's lack of awareness didn't concern her. The connection had been made. The bond forged. It would not easily be broken.

Lorna Gwin's mother could feel Stan-ton, *out there*, and she placed him now like an air traffic controller placing a fuzzy, far-off blip on a radar screen. Each passing hour brought them closer together and soon she would send him a message.

Lorna Gwin's mother needed Stan-ton. She wished it wasn't so. She did not want to need anyone. But the fact could not be denied. She needed him. And soon he would feel her summons like a scream in his mind.

"Most people are on the world, not in it-- having no conscious sympathy or relationship to anything about them—undiffused, separate, and rigidly alone, like marbles of polished stone, touching but separate."

-John Muir

CHAPTER 37

"WE PRAISE YOU and bless you, holy and gracious God, source of life abundant," said Joe Stanton, in his best, most resonant vicar's voice.

Warm morning light streamed through St. Anthony's massive old windows and the congregation listened attentively. It was the midpoint of the Sunday service on July third.

"From before time you made ready the creation," Joe recited, steadily, evenly, looking at the congregation between glances at the printed text. "Your spirit moved over the deep and brought all things into being: sun, moon and stars; earth, wind and waters; and every living thing."

The congregation sat in a big horseshoe shape at St. Anthony's, with the vicar and lay ministers at the open end. Joe hated podiums and preached from the middle of the floor, turning as he spoke. The flock stood now, as Joe read the Eucharistic Prayer. Only two small bandages remained on his face, above his right eye, and his bruises were fading.

He could feel, as well as see, the congregation around him and was pleased with the vibe. The service was going well and turnout was greater than he'd hoped. Not a Christmas or Easter crowd, but more people than normal, including a few folks he didn't recognize.

Per the plan he'd discussed with the Bishop's Committee, he'd taken a few minutes before the homily to give his account of the events in the San Juans. Then he'd acknowledged the victims of the Anacortes restaurant poisoning and led the congregation in prayer. After that, he'd delivered a touching homily about the beauty and fragility of creation.

Now he was reading the words that always came just before communion at St. Anthony's. An Episcopal service is founded in ritual, and Joe loved this part of the ceremony.

"You made us in your image," proclaimed Joe, "male and female, and taught us to walk in your ways. But we rebelled against you, and wandered far away. And yet, as a mother cares for her children—"

Like I cared for mine? asked the voice, clear and bright in Joe's mind.

Joe's mouth snapped shut and he glanced around the room. The voice ringing in his skull was so fierce and full that he felt certain everyone had heard it. Judging by the expressions, however, everyone had not.

Half the congregation was already watching him intently. Those praying with heads bowed were now lifting their eyes and turning toward him.

I'm a mother, said the voice. *And my child is dead.*

"I'm sorry," Joe said softly.

He took in the faces around him—faces of friends and neighbors, people who loved him and cared about him—and time seemed to slow to one one-thousandth of normal speed. Thoughts and emotions lay before him like shining, shimmering objects, and now, in an instant that seemed to last hours, he examined them one by one.

The voice is back. For some reason, this fact filled Joe with relief, not terror.

The voice is real.

If the voice is real—if the voice belongs to someone alive who really lost a child, it means that I wasn't poisoned and didn't suffer a hallucination.

And yet...people have been poisoned and the evidence suggests I was, too.

This made no sense.

Can't untangle this now, Joe thought.

Time resumed its normal flow and suddenly Joe was acutely aware of the congregation staring at him, waiting. He had no idea what he'd said or how much time had passed. He took a breath.

Ella, four rows from the front, caught Joe's eye. The look on her face told him that she was concerned—but not freaking out. The look said that he still had time to make things right.

"I'm sorry," he said again, smiling at the assemblage. "Seem to have lost my place."

The congregation relaxed. He found his place and continued reading. "And yet, as a mother cares for her children, you would not forget us. Time and again you called us to live in the fullness of your love. Glory and honor and praise to you, holy and living God."

The service proceeded normally and ended as usual, with a brief celebration of the week's birthdays and anniversaries.

Most everyone stayed for coffee hour, and the mood around the food tables was warm and friendly.

Joe stood at the door of the church, chatting with parishioners as they departed. The young vicar received an abundance of warm, tearful hugs, and most everyone expressed the same sentiment: tremendous relief that he was back and on the mend.

By noon the only people remaining were Joe and Ella, and the music director, who was arranging hymnals and binders full of sheet music on a shelf across the room.

"What'd you think?" Joe asked Ella as he hung his formal robes in the storage closet.

"Beautiful service," she said, slipping her arm around his waist and kissing him. "You sounded great. The homily was inspired—everybody thought so."

"Really?" Joe looked pleased.

They exited the church and walked to the Jetta hand in hand. Ella said, "So how did everything seem to you?"

Joe shrugged. "Let's get in the car first."

As Joe drove, the tiny microphone hidden under the fabric of the Jetta's ceiling recorded every word of their conversation.

CHAPTER 38

JOE WANTED TO TELL ELLA about the voice, but didn't know where to start. "Some new faces at the service today," he said, instead.

"Yeah," said Ella. "I noticed."

"What?"

"Did you see those two guys?"

"Which two? Two new guys? There were probably fifteen people I didn't recognize at all."

"Yeah," said Ella, "but these two totally stood out."

Joe frowned. "Were they sitting together?"

"No. Opposite sides of the room. But they were together."

"How do you know?"

"They were trading looks. I watched them do it. Trading looks and studying you. It was weird. And their clothes were wrong. Like they wanted to fit into the neighborhood but missed it a little."

"Was one of 'em kind of big? Blond hair?"

"Yeah. One blond. The other almost bald. Both good-sized. I'd swear they were together."

"Together—but sitting apart? So—"

"I don't know," said Ella. "Reporters, maybe? Investigators for the ferry system. Employees of Sheldon Beck?" She looked at him. "More of Spinell's crazy sons?"

"Ella—"

She waved dismissively. "Just mentioning the possibilities."

"Maybe they signed the guest book," said Joe, as he steered the Jetta into a shopping center parking lot and toward a Starbucks.

Ella laughed. "Yeah, right."

They parked in front of a wall displaying a huge poster for upcoming Fourth of July and Seafair festivities. The poster featured a black-and-white photo of a Navy admiral in full dress attire. Big. Tough. Square-jawed. The caption read "Hometown hero and decorated Vietnam veteran, Rear Admiral Wesley H. Houghton, Seafair master of ceremonies. Meet Admiral Houghton aboard the U.S.S. Nimitz on the Seattle waterfront, July 4th."

Something about the poster caught Joe's eye. He studied it. Ella was focused on the Starbucks. "We had coffee at church," she said.

"Yeah. I could use another one, though."

"Me too." She started to open her door but Joe stopped her.

"Ella. Did you notice right before communion, when I was reading?"

"Uh-huh. You hesitated for a second."

"Yeah."

"Scared me at first," she said. "But then you went on and it was no big deal."

"It was a big deal to me."

"How?"

"I heard the voice again."

Ella's shoulders sagged and she searched his face. "Oh, wow."

"Yeah. Same voice as before. Only louder."

She took his hand. "Sweetie. Okay."

"It had a lot to say." He laughed without any trace of humor. "The voice has an agenda."

"But you only hesitated for a second. The congregation barely noticed."

"I'm glad. But it felt like an hour to me."

"We should go to the doctor," Ella said quietly.

"It's Sunday."

"An emergency room," she said. "Joe, this poison, this *drug* you were exposed to, is nasty. Here it is a week after the fact—after treatment—and it's still causing problems. You can't mess with this. I have Detective Palmer's cell number."

She pulled her iPhone out of her purse. "He may actually know what the poison is by now. He told me he'd call, but—"

"You want to know what the voice said?"

Ella lowered the phone, exasperated. "Joe…come on. This is your health we're talking about. Hearing voices is—"

"I wasn't poisoned," Joe said flatly.

"Joe—"

"I can't prove it, okay? But I'd be willing to bet my house I was not poisoned."

"You don't have a house."

"If I did."

A family passed in front of the Jetta, heading into Starbucks. A boy of five or six noticed the couple in the car and he smiled and waved. The boy had an endearing gap between his front teeth. Joe and Ella waved back.

"You think the voice is real?" said Ella, staring at the family. "Not just in your head?"

"I believe it's real," said Joe.

"So…Dr. Heintzel's diagnosis…The other Wendy's customers with similar symptoms?"

"I can't explain it. I'm just telling you what I believe, in my heart."

Ella shook her head. She seemed to be at a loss for words. "Joe-"

"She wants to meet. Tonight."

"*She*?"

"The voice."

"You never said anything about the voice being female."

"I never realized it. Until this morning."

Ella looked at him. "Where does *she* want to meet?"

"The Manette Bridge."

"You're serious?"

"Dead serious."

"The voice told you, 'the Manette Bridge'?"

"No." Joe sighed. "She said she wanted to meet. I asked where, and a picture of the Manette Bridge appeared in my mind. Big and bright. Just—*bam*—there it was. From a weird angle. But I recognized it. Definitely the Manette Bridge."

Ella considered it. "What time?"

"When the moon is full," Joe said abruptly, as if this revelation had only just dawned on him. "When the full moon shines on the bridge."

Ella seemed on the verge of tears and Joe looked like he'd experienced a mild electric shock. "I know how this sounds," he said quickly. "I know. But you have to trust me. I feel fine."

Ella blew her nose. "Having a woman talk inside your head—commanding you to meet on bridges in the middle of the night is not *fine*. So what does she look like?"

Joe thought about it. "I have absolutely no idea. The voice is loud in my head. Like…when she talks, everything else is pushed aside."

"You sure you're not channeling my mom?" Ella asked, laughing through her tears.

"But I can't *see* her. It's weird."

"Um. Yeah."

"I know. I know. And I promise you, if we go to the bridge tonight and nothing comes of it—if there's no one there—I'll be first in line at the doctor's office tomorrow morning. I'll insist on all the tests. I'll insist on a thorough psychological evaluation. Another one."

"If *we* go? You want me to go with you?"

"Yes," said Joe, as if it were obvious. "I won't go without you. Will you come?"

"To meet a disembodied voice on a bridge in the middle of the night? Oh yeah," replied Ella. She looked wrung out by the whole exchange. "Wouldn't miss it."

CHAPTER 39

"FASCINATING," SAID ORONDO RING, as Joe and Ella's conversation finished playing on speakers in *Marauder*'s War Room. Beck and Collins listened beside him.

"The Manette Bridge?" said Beck. "In Bremerton?"

"Yes," said Ring, nodding, as if the revelation held some special significance. He sipped an Orange Crush.

"Stanton sounds rational. The other victims never said anything that coherent or complete when it came to the voice."

"Yes. Fascinating."

"*What's* fascinating?"

"Stanton has a better receiver," said Ring. "He's receiving the messages more clearly."

Beck squinted at him. "What are you talking about?"

"Dr. Phelps has been analyzing the anomaly—the brain mass we identified in all of the victims."

"Yeah?"

"It appears likely that the anomaly is not a tumor at all. But rather an organ."

"An organ?"

"Yes."

Collins laughed. Ring glared at him.

Beck said, "You're saying that along with hallucinations these guys grew a new organ? A functioning organ?"

"Yes."

"What kind?"

Ring turned and brought scans of Whittaker's anomaly onto his monitor.

"Phelps sectioned Whittaker's anomaly into transverse slices and studied the compositional topography, using gas-liquid chromatography. He found three regions of distinctive lipid composition."

Beck stared at him. "In English, please."

"The lipids appear to be arranged in a most interesting way."

"What way? For Christ's sake, spit it out."

"In a sort of *lens*," said Ring. He pointed to the screen, to where a computer graphic of the anomaly was turning.

"We believe so, anyway. And there are analogous structures in other mammals. Mammals that employ echolocation. Bats, for example."

"Echo-what?" said Collins.

"*Echolocation*. Navigation by sound, Mr. Collins. *Sonar*." He pointed at the screen. "In certain mammals this type of structure, or lens, serves as an acoustical transducer, directing and refracting sound waves for the purpose of communication and echolocation."

"So," said Beck, puzzling it out. "You think the anomaly—the structure in Stanton's brain—is receiving sound waves?"

Ring shook his head. "No. I don't."

Beck put his head in his hands. "Jesus, Ring. Then what the fuck are you talking about?"

"Not sound waves. *Thought* waves."

Beck lifted his head. "Thought waves?"

"Thoughts travel in waves. Just like sound. And Stanton has been receiving thoughts and messages from outside his own person, for days."

Ring looked at his companions. "I initially believed that our divers and the gillnetter and Stanton encountered something out there"—he waved his hand at the wide ocean beyond Marauder's walls—"something that essentially *infected* them with the hallucinations.

"I thought it was a one-time occurrence. I figured they ran into something—most likely in the water—and the encounter blew their circuits and jammed their brains full of thoughts. And then killed them."

Beck said, "But now you think—what?"

"That it's not a one-time thing. That the communication continues. At least, in Mr. Stanton's case." Ring looked at Beck. "Stanton received a new message in church this morning. The lens is the likely mechanism. It's the receiver. The satellite dish, if you will."

Beck considered it. "You're talking about telepathy."

"Yes."

Collins chortled again but this time Beck and Ring both frowned at him. The room went quiet.

"Do you believe," Beck said at last, "that Stanton's actually going to meet the source of the hallucination on the bridge? The sender of the messages?"

Ring hesitated. "I believe that Stanton believes he's going to." He turned his gaze back to his monitors, where Joe's thought captures were still downloading, and took another sip of his soda. "And after all, something is causing all of this. Or some*one*."

CHAPTER 40

JOE AND ELLA made their way home to find a dozen or so neighbors standing in the street, staring at the sky.

"Cool!" said Joe, exiting the car just as three Blue Angel fighter jets rocketed overhead in tight formation. The roar of the jets hit seconds later, rattling windows and sending Joe's cat, Figaro, scurrying up a tree.

Joe and Ella watched as the F/A-18 Hornets—five of them this time—made another low, screaming pass over the neighborhood. Adults cheered. Kids jumped around and yelled for more. "I love Seafair," said Joe, squeezing Ella's hand.

In earlier years Seafair had been its own holiday—in August. The state had shifted it to the fourth of July to save money. Two celebrations at once. Now it was bigger and grander than ever.

The rumble of the jets subsided. Joe and Ella went inside, ate lunch, curled up together on the couch, and—without any further discussion of the voice or the pending rendezvous on the bridge—fell asleep.

Ella awoke after a time and lay there, thinking about the first time she and Joe had really talked: in the meadow in the wilderness, under the stars.

She'd found him charming and handsome. Gentle and rugged and sexy. He was a great listener, and, as she'd discovered on her first visit to St. Anthony's—a great speaker. She'd found his homily that morning brilliant, relevant, and deeply touching.

They dated. Their romance flourished, and within a few weeks she was madly, passionately in love.

Aside from the instant and powerful physical attraction they shared, she found it incredibly easy to talk with him. About anything.

She knew that he was intuitive. Sometimes it seemed that he could read her mind. Even before she told him, he'd been aware, somehow, of a secret she carried and divulged to almost no one. It hurt still to think about it, and most of the time she left it alone, acknowledging the awful event without really examining it. Without reliving it.

Now, though, lying there next to Joe, the memory of the thing unfurled in her mind, unbidden, and she let it flow.

Christmas shopping, at the mall. It's morning still but Ella has already had it up to here with the crowds. She hates malls—and can't wait to leave this one. But she's starving now and making her way to the food court before heading for the car. She's in a good mood. Her shopping's done. The bags in her hands are full of presents, beautifully wrapped. Gifts for the siblings, nieces, and nephews set to descend on her parents' house later in the week.

A quick bite, and then she'll be on her way.

She settles on P.F. Chang's because she likes their grilled salmon-on-rice. She places her order, checks her phone while she waits, puts the steaming dish on her tray, and heads for a table.

Any vacant table will do. She looks around.

11:30 a.m. and already the food court is mobbed—swarming and swirling with people. Young people. Old people. Teenagers and twentysomethings. Parents pushing strollers with screaming toddlers in tow.

A constant, cacophonous wall of sound envelops Ella and her fellow shoppers: conversation mixed with laughter mixed with whining mixed with Bing Crosby dreaming, for at least the fourth time that morning, of a white Christmas. And Ella wonders, absently, how mall employees maintain their sanity during the holidays.

At first it appears that there are no vacant tables and then, as if by magic, one appears just in front of her. A small table. The guy is leaving, getting up and heading out. Ella makes a beeline for it, sets down her tray, then her bags, and sits down to eat.

She digs her Kindle out of her purse and turns it on. Sets it on the table and props it up on her gloves.

Before settling in to read she glances around. There's a big family to her right, an older couple to her left, and a lone UPS employee one table beyond them. He's wearing the distinctive brown shirt with the UPS logo emblazoned on the front and he's smiling at her. She smiles back. He blushes—blushes, how cute—and she decides he's a nice guy. Not her type, but a nice guy.

She turns to her book, the new thriller-romance from Hugh Howey. The book is crazy-good. One of those stories you read as fast as you can—because you have to know what happens next—but hate to see end. Within a paragraph she's lost in the story.

The food court and all the people disappear. The noise drops to a whisper. Bing Crosby takes a siesta, and it's just Ella and her book and the grilled salmon, disappearing one slow bite at a time.

Then, like hard, sudden rain on corrugated metal, popping sounds. Popping sounds followed by screams followed by the noise of bodies and tables crashing, followed by crack, crack, crack and brilliant, searing flashes of light inches away.

She's lifting her head now, wide-eyed, dreamy terror washing over her, one hand still holding her fork. The gunman is there, rotating methodically her way, hands working, guns blazing, mowing down the family—parents, kids, all of them. And then he's standing over her, facing her, guns smoking, guns aimed at her head, concentrating. And she sees in his eyes that he's thrilled by the destruction he's causing, aroused by the mayhem, enjoying every second of his mad rampage.

The guns are inches from her face, so close that she can read the words engraved on the metal. And it's like he doesn't see her. Like she doesn't exist. She will explain this to the police, after the fact. To the counselors, and the psychiatrist retained by her parents.

"It's not like he let me live. Not like he said, 'Oh, you're beautiful, so you don't have to die.' No. It's like he didn't see me at all. Like I was in a blind spot—although I was right in front of him. Like he simply could not see me."

And now he's shooting again, shooting the old couple, and the UPS driver. The UPS driver is trying to get away, Ella sees, but too late. The bullets hit his back—hit the brown shirt and blossom red.

And then the gunman himself is crashing forward, flying forward, shot in the back by a mall security guard, and Ella looks down to find that she is covered in blood, none of it her own.

Ella lay there next to Joe, willing her heart rate to slow, letting the adrenaline dissipate. She remembered how Joe had listened to her story and how, in his way, he had helped her process what had happened better than her family and friends, better than the counselors or the psychiatrist. Joe had helped her realize that what had happened in the mall was something that would always be with her. That it was okay to acknowledge it. That by acknowledging the memory and naming it she could contain it, control it, instead of the other way around.

Joe had helped her understand this. Helped her heal. Now he was suffering, and she knew she would do whatever it took to help him through his ordeal.

CHAPTER 41

PHELPS AND EDELSTEIN sat at a table in *Marauder*'s main galley; a twenty-four-hour cafeteria frequented by the ship's crew, Beck's security team, and technicians from the War Room.

It was midday, the galley was bustling, and patrons were clustered around the space. Soldiers here. Technicians there. Overall-clad engine-room guys by the windows. Everyone divided into cliques. Like high school. Phelps and Edelstein occupied a small table in a far corner.

"Anybody watching us?" Phelps asked. His back was to the soldiers.

Edelstein picked at her salad. Took a bite. Glanced at the soldiers a few tables away. "Don't know. Feels like everyone is lately."

Phelps said, "They could be recording. I wouldn't put it past Beck, based on the stuff I've been reading."

Edelstein continued eating without enthusiasm. "Well then," she said, after a while. "On that note, should we talk, or not?"

Edelstein was a vibrant sixtysomething PhD with an important job, lots of friends, and a comfortable life. Unaccustomed to the kind of doubt and worry she was feeling now. The feeling made her grumpy.

Phelps sipped a cup of hot tea. "I think we need to talk. And this is probably the best place. Doesn't make sense that they'd have every table wired. And I'm not seeing anything in the ceiling."

Edelstein glanced up. Took another bite of her salad. "So Beck's lying to us?" she said.

"Yes. He is."

"You've thought that since he told us Stanton was at Swedish Hospital in Seattle, right? But it's just a hunch. I mean, you don't *know* it's a lie."

Phelps said, "It's more than a hunch now. I heard something else."

Edelstein set down her fork.

"One of Ring's techs said something. A slip of the tongue."

"What?"

"We were chatting and he mentioned he needed to find another drive for all the data coming in from Stanton's thought captures. That struck me as odd and I said, 'Oh, you mean for all the material you guys downloaded from Stanton on the *Northern Mercy*?' And the tech looked at me kinda weird—just for a second—and said, 'Yeah, that's right. That's what I meant.' But it wasn't what he meant."

"So you think Beck's still holding Stanton?"

"He's either holding Stanton on the *Mercy*, or they installed an implant and let him go on his merry way and they're recording his thoughts without his knowledge. Either way, I doubt Stanton has a clue about his true condition. Or the fact that he's likely to die in a few days."

Edelstein thought about it. "You really think Beck's that—I don't know—cold? That calculating? I mean, to bring the priest and his girlfriend onto the hospital ship under the pretense of helping them, while really all he wants is to study the guy?"

Phelps nodded, lowered his voice. "Pretty much, yes."

He took another sip of his tea and kept his voice low. "I mean, first off, based on the stuff I've read, it's his personality. And it's also his training. He killed people for a living. His company kills people for a living. It's supposed to be the bad guys they kill, but I'm not so sure Beck differentiates that much."

Phelps continued, "I wish I'd looked into it a bit more before I signed on. That I'd read more about Beck. But all I saw was the fee he was dangling out there. All I heard was 'Come and advise us on some neuroanatomy questions for a week or two and we'll pay you more than you earn in a year as a professor.'"

Edelstein's face paled. She'd had the same reaction to Beck's offer. She remembered the call from the Erebus representative—a smooth talker named Gliss: *"We've heard about your work,"* he'd told her, *"and are interested in hiring you to help with a fascinating field study in Alaska. One to two weeks max, and you'll live on a luxury ship during your stay."* When Gliss had announced the fee they were offering, she'd practically fallen out of her chair. She'd signed on immediately.

Edelstein took a deep breath. "Here's what I don't get," she said. "Beck's had all this negative press, right?"

Phelps nodded. "Yeah. A ton the last couple of years."

"So then, he and Ring stumble across this phenomenon. This remarkable discovery: shared hallucinations tied to something real and new and extraordinary in the ocean. Why wouldn't he share it? Open it up, like his sister advised? He'd be in the news."

Phelps laughed. "He's *been* in the news."

"Yes, but this would all be good press. It would solve his PR problems overnight. He'd be seen in a new light—as an explorer. A visionary. I can see the headline: 'Controversial defense contractor makes deep ocean discovery.' He'd be a hero."

"It's not gonna happen."

"Why not? Beck's a smart guy. Even if he's a mercenary he wants to keep his career intact. Wants his billion-dollar empire to continue. Why keep the lid on a weird, arcane scientific phenomenon when it could redeem your reputation?"

Phelps shook his head. "Because he and Ring believe it's more than that. They're convinced the chamber structures are real and that they *do* something. Can be used for something."

"What?"

"Ring isn't saying. He just keeps telling Beck that they have to get to one of the structures. It's why they're bringing in deep-water probes. And a submarine. Beck knows other people will investigate—no doubt already *are* investigating—and he wants to control the situation. He's a control freak, on top of everything else."

They sat in silence for a long time. Edelstein watched as the soldiers got up from their table and exited the cafeteria. A couple of them glanced her way, without expression. She'd learned early on that the groups on the ship—the soldiers and crew, engine-room guys and War Room technicians—kept to themselves. To their own cliques. They'd talk to you if they had to, and they were courteous enough, but it was all business. No idle chitchat.

"So what about us?" said Edelstein. "Beck brings us on board for our expertise, and we get up to speed, and start asking questions…I mean if Beck's really doing what you think he's doing with Stanton, using the man, exploiting him, letting him just…die, without disclosing his true condition…" She fell silent.

"How worried are you?" she asked at last. "I mean, are you worried for your safety?"

Phelps shook his head. "No. My whole department knows about this contract. They know where I am. My family knows where I am."

Edelstein nodded, relieved. Her situation was similar.

"My suspicion," said Phelps, "Is that Beck is monitoring our calls and e-mails and watching for the slightest breach of contract. I won't be surprised if Erebus lawyers debrief us before we leave the ship. I won't be surprised if Beck threatens me with lawsuits if I reveal anything I've seen or heard during my stay here."

Edelstein laughed, "I'm fine with that. At this point I just want to go home."

Phelps nodded. "I agree."

Edelstein said, "So let's call Collins. Or Gliss, if he's on board. Tell 'em we want off the boat. Request they put us on the next helicopter out of here."

Phelps smiled. "I like it. Beck might try to stiff us on payment, though."

"I'll worry about that when I'm back at Woods Hole," said Edelstein. "I just want the hell off this boat."

"Their mute gaze suggests a vision of reality beyond our imagining. What do they see in their ignorance that we in our wisdom are mostly blind to?"

-Frederick Buechner

CHAPTER 42

JOE AND ELLA WALKED, hand in hand, to the western edge of the Manette Bridge. It was a little after 1 a.m. on a cloudless Monday. The Fourth of July.

The bridge was quiet, but the sporadic boom of fireworks rattled the surrounding neighborhoods. Revelers sampling their arsenals for the big day ahead.

"Never seen the bridge this empty," whispered Joe.

Ella squeezed his hand. "Maybe because you've never been here in the middle of the night before." A massive firework rumbled in the distance.

A Seattle-bound ferry slid away from the city pier a mile to the south, and the ship's Coast Guard–mandated safety announcement echoed across the water. "Hello, and welcome aboard. May I have your attention, please?"

The announcement droned on and the ferry moved with surprising speed into the center of the inlet, diesel engines rumbling, light pouring from the passenger cabin. It looked like a floating all-night supermarket.

"Big bridge," said Ella, as a police car glided past, slowing to look at them. "Any idea where she wants to meet?"

Ella was trying to keep an open mind. The man she loved was hearing a voice in his head. Believing it to be real. And a part of her was caught up in his dream. The logical, rational part of her brain was complaining—pointing out all the reasons why *The Voice* couldn't be real—but Ella spoke no judgment or criticism. They were in this together. And they would know soon enough.

Joe looked at the sky as they walked. The night was clear, the moon huge and high. Moonlight glinted and danced on the dark face of the Washington Narrows, eighty-two feet below. But there was no romance for Joe and Ella in the lunar glow. Only mystery—and a growing sense of dread.

Beck's men were also there. Hidden in the weeds on either side of the 1,500-foot-long steel truss bridge. Waiting. Watching Joe and Ella through night-vision goggles. Filming the couple's every move.

More explosions reverberated across the channel. Bright fountains of light.

Joe and Ella walked on. Watched. Listened. They could hear the rumble of traffic in the distance, and big machines working in the naval shipyards, cranes and derricks humming and whining. Busy, despite the hour. Despite the holiday.

They were about halfway across the bridge now, near the structure's high point, the point at which they could see easily in both directions.

Nothing else moved on the bridge. No pedestrians. No cars.

Joe stopped walking. Ella stopped, too. Downtown Bremerton and the naval shipyard glowed in the west. The community of Manette shimmered over the bridge's eastern edge.

The city seemed to be taking a breath, calming itself in the small hours of the night, in advance of holiday parades and Seafair festivities.

Below, the deep, silent waters of the Washington Narrows rushed between Sinclair and Dyes Inlets.

They waited, the same thought tormenting both of them. *We're here because of a voice.*

A voice.

Joe's shoulders sagged. *I really am losing my mind,* he thought. *Crazy people hear voices. Lunatics. Drug addicts.*

Standing there, falling into despair, he envisioned tests. Procedures. Scans.

Ella imagined supporting him through his ordeal. Staying with him. Helping him recover.

Kawoof!

The sound brought them back to reality. Back to the moment. They turned toward the channel, toward the dark water flowing silently, far below.

Kawoof!

They knew the sound, but it was the last thing in the world either of them expected to hear in this place, at this time.

Kawoof! Deep and full.

Kawoof! Light and quick.

Kawoof! Rich and breathy.

"Whales," Joe whispered.

Kawoof! So close that Ella half expected the mist from the whale's exhale to waft up and hit her in the face.

"What are they doing here?" Ella asked, her voice soft with wonder. "In the narrows?"

They could hear other sounds now: sleek bodies slicing through icy water. Dorsal fins cutting the surface. And all at once, Ella could see the whales. See them in the moonlight. Ethereal shapes rising and falling, rolling ever closer to the bridge. The lead leviathan's spray seemed to fall in slow motion, water droplets glittering like a veil of diamonds in the moon's glow.

"It's her," said Joe, his face a mask of bewilderment. Bewilderment changing to wonder, changing to joy.

"Her?" said Ella, scanning the bridge deck in both directions, annoyed at the mention of "the voice" when there were whales to observe. Whales in such a strange setting, in such surreal circumstances.

A moving van rumbled across the bridge and Ella turned to look. When she turned back around, her heart froze.

Joe had climbed over the bridge's safety barrier and was clinging one-handed to the railing, leaning out, dangling like an insolent teenager. If he let go, he'd plummet eight stories to the channel below.

"Joe!" Ella sprang toward him, grabbing his arm, pulling with all her strength. "What are you doing? No! Joe!

"Help!" she screamed at the top of her lungs. "Help!"

Joe drew back to the rail and gripped it with both hands, which made Ella relax just a little bit.

"Joe—listen to me—"

"It's her," said Joe, a giddy gleam in his eye that simultaneously frightened and fascinated Ella.

"Who? Joe. Please. Just climb back over the rail."

Kawoof! Much louder now. The whales were almost to the bridge.

"She's here. But people are watching. This is the only way."

Joe pulled closer, and Ella thought he intended to climb back to safety. He kissed her passionately. "I love you," he said. Then, before she could react or move, he pushed off hard, springing back and dropping like a stone.

"Joe!" Ella lunged and grasped at thin air, almost toppling over the rail herself. "Help! No! Joe!"

Joe plunged into the icy water, into the heart of the moving mass of orca whales, and vanished from sight.

"Help!" Ella screamed, sprinting back along the bridge, back the way they'd come.

Beck's operatives—one man on each side of the river—had seen Joe climb over the rail and jump, but they didn't know the reason. Now they were sprinting for higher ground and a better view, trying to keep out of sight and also ascertain Stanton's whereabouts. They'd been briefed on Stanton, but no one had said anything about suicide.

Ella ran hard for the western end of the bridge, hoping against hope to see a car or pedestrian she could call to. There was no one. The bridge and feeder streets were silent. Empty.

"Help!"

She ran on, fishing in her jacket for her cell phone, not finding it. Not daring to stop and look.

As she neared the end of the structure she leapt the guardrail—where the earthen riverbank rose up to meet the steel mass of the bridge—and plunged downhill, toward the water. It was dark under the bridge, even with the moon.

"Joe!" Ella screamed, tumbling down the bank, plowing through chin-high weeds and trash, tripping on chunks of concrete and old tires.

"Joe! Help! Somebody!"

The water was just ahead now, and it was surprisingly, frighteningly vast—a dark, terrifying abyss opening before her. It was moving, too, flowing fast, like a river, as if the moon was exerting an especially strong pull.

"Joe!" Ella stumbled and flailed into the frigid channel, finally stopping when the water was over her knees.

"Joe!" she cried, frantically scanning the black liquid chasm, lurching this way and that, willing her eyes to penetrate the gloom.

What she saw filled her with dread: dark water surging against massive concrete bridge supports; a broad, flat river, rushing, hurrying out of Dyes Inlet, toward the larger sound.

What she didn't see was even more paralyzing: There was no sign of Joe. No sign of whales, no sign of any movement whatsoever—other than the flowing, roiling water itself.

"Joe!" She wailed, helplessly, choking on his name as the dark tide slapped the concrete monoliths before her, believing in her heart that he'd already been swept away, that his insane leap had stunned him—if it hadn't killed him outright—and that his inert, lifeless body was drifting now into Sinclair Inlet.

"Joe," she cried again, in a strangled, miserable voice no one could hear.

"Ella!"

Ella jumped.

"Ella!"

The voice was coming from upstream—a good hundred yards upstream by the sound of it, and it registered in the back of Ella's brain that this made no sense.

How can he be upstream? How, in this current, can he possibly be farther up the channel? He should be floating past the ferry terminal by now. No swimmer could swim against this.

She let it go.

He's alive. That's all that matters.

"Joe!" She plunged further into the channel, feeling the pull of the current. "I'm here! I'm right here!"

And then she saw him, swimming fast, with the flow, swimming diagonally for shore. "Ella!"

He was coming straight for her. He was going to make it. He was going to be fine.

Overwhelming relief was her first emotion as she watched him swimming confidently for shore. She could breathe again. Think again. Suddenly feel the frigid current swirling around her legs.

Anger was her second emotion. Anger bordering on fury. How could he have done such a thing? How could he have risked his life like that? Where was his sense of self-preservation? Where was the love and compassion he supposedly felt for her?

He really is sick, she thought. *Profoundly unstable. He must be.*

"Ella," he sputtered, staggering out of the water, stumbling and swaying as he found his footing.

She embraced his drenched, ice-cold body. Held him with every ounce of strength she possessed. The questions could wait. All that mattered now was getting him out of the water, up the bank, and into the car.

"Ella," Joe said. He coughed, loosening his embrace and peering at her in the moonlight. He was shivering violently, quaking and pulsing like a patient in midseizure. But his eyes glimmered with their own inner light. "She's here." He shoved his sopping wet hair out of his eyes with one hand. "Lorna Gwin's mother."

Kawoof!

Ella, still facing the channel, gave a muffled cry as a whale surfaced directly behind Joe, a great black mountain of a beast.

The leviathan turned slightly, steadying herself in the shallows with a snap of her great tail flukes. The mist from the whale's exhale showered the couple, and Ella suddenly found herself eyeball-to-eyeball with the creature. Ella moaned something inaudible and Joe felt her body quiver and quake—almost as violently as his own. He slid to one side so that she could make contact.

"This is Mia," he said, as Ella stepped forward and pressed her palm to the whale's sleek, black face. Ella's own face was a mask of utter bewilderment. She looked as if she'd just been struck by lightning. "Mia," Joe repeated thoughtfully, as if the facts were unfolding in his brain as he spoke. "Though that's not her real name. She's the one who's been calling me. She's the source of the voice in my mind."

Childlike joy animated Joe's speech, as if this miraculous epiphany had saved his sanity and set him free—which it had. "I know what she wants now. I understand."

Ella slowly retracted her hand, reluctantly severing contact with Mia. The whale drew breath into her sleek, shiny black body: a hollow, cavernous sucking sound. Then she slipped back into the channel, and was gone.

CHAPTER 43

BY THE TIME BECK'S OPERATIVES had scrambled to new vantage points, focused their night-vision gear, and located Joe and Ella, the couple was already exiting the water.

Allen Dodd had caught sight of a large, dark shape sliding into the water immediately behind the couple. He thought at first it was a boat, and spun the controls on his goggles, boosting the image and improving the focus. But when he looked again, the mysterious shape was gone. He scanned the dark recesses around the bridge supports. Nothing. He listened for the sound of a motor. No sound.

Dodd ducked down in the brush as Ella and Joe climbed the steep bank, silently, hand in hand, glancing at each other now and again, locking eyes momentarily, as if to agree that what they'd witnessed had not been a dream. Their legs felt weak and wobbly, but their faces glowed with wonder.

"Who teacheth us more than the beasts of the earth, and maketh us wiser than the fowls of heaven?"

-Job 35:11

CHAPTER 44

THE WHALE SPOKE TO ME, Ella thought, her head jammed with too many revelations to process. *Communicated with me. The voice is real; this is the whale we encountered while kayaking; Joe is not losing his mind; Joe was not poisoned; Dr. Heintzel's theory about poisoning is wrong.*

Ella's hand—the one she'd used to touch the whale—tingled with static electricity, a bang-your-funny-bone numbness. She looked at her hand in the moonlight, turned it, and wondered what sort of signal or impulse had passed between whale and human. She realized she had not the vaguest idea.

They stumbled onto Washington Avenue, just as a yellow cab rolled past, slowing to look at the half-drowned man and the disheveled woman in wet blue jeans, brambles clinging to her fleece jacket.

The cab turned a corner and Joe pulled Ella close and whispered in her ear. "We need to talk," he said, excited and out of breath. "But we can't. Not yet. We're being watched. And I'm sure your car is bugged."

Ella's body stiffened and she tried to pull away so that she could look into his eyes. He held her firm. "No time," he breathed. "Please just play along with what I say, even if it doesn't make sense. I'll explain later. It'll be all right."

She nodded and squeezed him harder. "She's real," she gasped. "The voice is real." The notion that her car might be bugged seemed trivial compared to this revelation.

"I know," said Joe. "But we can't talk about it. Did you hear what I said?"

"Yeah, I understand."

They resumed walking hand in hand and Ella peered at him curiously but did not speak. Joe massaged the side of his skull—where Heintzel had stitched his wounds. When they got to the Jetta, Ella drove.

Joe twisted the heater dial to full blast. "I'm so sorry!" he wailed, so abruptly that Ella jumped, jerking the steering wheel a little too far to the right and clipping the curb as she turned. For a split second she wondered what he was so sorry about. Then she realized he was acting.

"It's okay," she said.

"No it's not," Joe cried, with convincing anguish. "I tried to kill myself, Ella!"

"But you didn't kill yourself. You're here."

Joe sobbed. "It seems so hopeless. Everything that's happened. With my health, my church. All down the toilet."

"Baby," Ella said soothingly, "It's okay."

"As soon as I jumped," said Joe, his words warped and wobbly and miserable-sounding, "I knew it was a mistake. I knew I could never leave you."

"Thank God you're all right. Just…thank God." She found his hand and winked at him.

"I'm so cold," Joe moaned, redirecting the heater and turning on the defroster. In fact, he had stopped shivering.

He twisted in his seat and methodically scanned the darkened interior of the car. "I just want to go to sleep," he said, in weak, exhausted voice. "Sleep."

In reality, his face was bright and alert. Eyes sparkling. His methodical scanning ended when he reached the overhead reading light and gently probed the area around the fixture with his fingertips. Found a small bump under the fabric.

Ella glanced up, fascinated, as Joe loosened the molding and pried the fabric back. The microphone was there, attached to the fixture with a tiny strip of tape. The mic glinted like an earring.

Ella stared at it, feeling violated, wondering who'd planted the device and how long it had been there. She checked the mirror. A car was behind them, maybe a hundred feet back, but it kept going when she turned into Joe's neighborhood. According to the clock on the dash it was 2:13 a.m.

"I need to sleep," Joe repeated mournfully, as they pulled into his driveway. "Tomorrow begins the journey to restore my damaged life."

Ella thought this was over-the-top and made a slashing sign across her neck. Joe's eyes twinkled and he looked like he might burst out laughing. Clearly, he was enjoying playing for the microphone and did not seem alarmed by what it implied.

"I'll stay with you," Ella said soberly, shutting the Jetta off.

They went inside, took a hot shower together and crawled into bed, wondering how many more microphones lay hidden and listening inside Joe's house. They whispered, in the dark, under the covers, as they held each other close.

"Who's watching us?" Ella asked.

"Beck," said Joe.

The certainty in his voice surprised her. Frightened her. Beck was a far scarier possibility than Walter Spinell, who might have hired a detective to follow them, to build a case for a lawsuit; or Detective Palmer, who might have assigned a deputy to track them, as part of his investigation. Beck was a trained killer. A professional soldier surrounded by other soldiers, killers in their own right. Beck commanded his own private army.

"Why?"

"I don't know."

"How do you know it's him?"

"Mia told me."

Ella didn't laugh. "The whale told you Beck was following us?"

"Not with words. But she made it clear enough."

Joe massaged the side of his head, which was throbbing again.

"She—Mia—can see inside things. It's her sonar, I think. That's how whales hunt. How they navigate in the dark, you know?"

"I've heard about it, yeah."

"Yeah. And when I jumped into the water tonight Mia looked at me, outside and in. And she saw something that wasn't supposed to be there."

"What? Like another bug? Something in your clothes?"

"Worse," said Joe. "Way worse. Wires. Hardware. Inside my head. Next to my brain. Mia showed me a picture of it—sent me a picture—which I could see in my mind. There's no mistaking it. Somebody put it there."

Ella's body stiffened in the dark. "That can't be right," she said, knowing in her bones that it was right.

"Heintzel must've done it," said Joe, "When we were on the *Mercy*. She's the only one who could've done it."

"But why?"

"I don't know, but Mia said the wires were…alive. Hot. Sending out signals." He rubbed his head again. "She disabled them somehow. With her sonar. Cooked them. Didn't feel too good."

Ella pressed her body tight against Joe's and caressed his face. She was trembling.

"We need to get out of here," she whispered, "get our cell phones. You call the Bremerton Police. I'll call Palmer."

"No. Not yet."

"But Beck could kill us. Anytime he wants."

Joe could hear the terror in her voice. He said, "If he wanted that, he would've already done it. He put the wires in my head to monitor something. Watch for something."

"You think he knows about Mia?"

"He must."

"So why not go to the police?"

"We will. But Mia needs me to do something. Later today. If we involve the police now, it won't happen."

Ella was quiet for so long Joe thought she'd fallen asleep.

She whispered, "How can Mia communicate like that? So that we understand?"

"She knew someone," he said, as the answer formed in his mind. "A long time ago. Someone who taught her things. Taught her about people."

"Who?"

"A man. I don't know. I can see him in my mind, but I have no idea who he is."

"How can Mia put images in your mind? And what does she want you to do?"

"Ella—"

"Who named her Mia? And where did she go tonight? Can the other whales communicate like that?"

"Sweetheart—"

"Do you know you could've died jumping off that stupid bridge?"

Joe pressed his finger against Ella's lips, then kissed her gently. "Baby," he said, "we have to sleep. We'll talk more in the morning."

"But—"

He pulled her close and she melted into his arms.

One hour later Joe got up to pee. He stood unsteadily, then slumped back onto the bed, dizzy. Heart racing. Ella breathed peacefully, rhythmically, in the darkness nearby.

He stood again, using the edge of the nightstand for support, and faced the bathroom, ten paces away. The nightlight underneath the bathroom mirror appeared to be moving. Dancing. Zigzagging in the dark like a firefly. Joe felt his stomach flip and roll and tasted acid—bile—in his mouth.

He made it to the bathroom, dragging his hand along the wall for stability, like he was drunk, like he was back in college, paying the price for a big night on the town.

He left the door open and the lights off—the nightlight cast enough of a glow—and stood at the toilet peeing, staring at the framed picture on the wall. An antique map of Scotland. A souvenir from a semester abroad.

Joe's heart thumped harder when he realized he was seeing two maps on the wall. Two distinct and separate maps of Scotland in the dim light.

The frames floated lazily in front of his eyes, hovering, refusing to merge and become whole again.

I'm seeing double.

His stomach churned and bucked in his belly and his mouth felt now dry as desert sand.

He reached for the light switch, eager to check his pupils in the mirror and see if the double vision persisted in normal light.

Then he lowered his hand and left the lights off.

Go back to bed. Nothing you can do now. Turn on the light and you'll just get more worked up. More freaked out. Go back to bed. Things might be different in the morning.

He staggered back to the bed—room still spinning—and eased himself into the sheets. Felt Ella's warmth. He put his arm around her waist, closed his eyes, and fell back into an uneasy sleep.

CHAPTER 45

BECK, COLLINS, AND ORONDO RING huddled in the cool glow of Ring's workstation, watching the video of the events at the bridge.

"So there was no meeting," said a bleary-eyed, unshaven Beck. "Stanton went to the Manette Bridge to kill himself."

"So it would seem," murmured Ring, as he replayed the grainy green footage for the umpteenth time.

It was 3 a.m. and the War Room was quiet. Just the three men at Ring's workstation, and two technicians hovering about the Palantir, which shimmered like a reflecting pool.

They stared at Ring's big monitor—Collins and Beck looking haggard, Ring, sharp and alert as ever—and listened to the field agents' play-by-play from the time Joe and Ella stepped onto the bridge until they returned to Joe's house.

"This morning," said Beck, "after Stanton's epiphany, I actually believed that he might meet someone on the bridge. That we might discover the source of the hallucinations." He sighed. "This is a dead end."

"It's weird," said Collins. "I know Stanton's messed up—same as our divers and Whittaker—but I didn't peg him as suicidal."

Beck and Collins turned to Ring. Waited for him to say something. But Ring just sat there, watching the silent, grainy footage of the incident on the bridge, over and over again.

Ring restarted the video. Again. Beck and Collins watched with him. Again. The same fuzzy, low-light telephoto shot of Joe and Ella walking to the center of the bridge. The same thirty-some seconds of Joe climbing over the railing, hesitating, and then leaping off, slicing the darkness like an arrow.

Ring played the loop again.

Beck stood. His headache had returned. *Time to go.* "Ring—"

Ring turned suddenly. Faced them. Eyes sparkling. "He wasn't trying to kill himself," he said matter-of-factly.

"Huh?" Beck pointed at the screen. "Then how do you explain the jump? The stuff he said to his girl, in the car? He flat-out admitted it."

"He lied."

Beck sat back down.

"I analyzed his voice," said Ring. "Ran it through our software."

"Why would he lie to his girlfriend?" asked Collins.

Ring shook his head. "He wasn't lying to his girlfriend. He was lying to us. Or to the microphone, anyway. He knows he's under surveillance."

Beck slumped in his seat, irritated that Ring was apparently on to something he hadn't grasped, and wishing he had coffee. "What? Wait. So, even if he's lying, I mean, how do you explain the jump? Jumping off a high bridge into fifty-degree water in the middle of the night? What is that if not a suicide attempt?"

Ring rolled his high-backed leather chair away from his workstation. "Stanton," he said, "*did* meet someone tonight."

"When?" asked Beck. "Our guys had him under surveillance the entire time. We have video, for Christ's sake. There was no one else on the bridge."

"Take a look," said Ring. He swiveled and tapped commands on his keyboard.

Stanton's grainy suicide leap rolled again and Ring magnified the image. Slowed it down.

"Watch carefully," he said.

They saw Stanton's rigid body knife feetfirst into the channel.

"There. Did you see that?"

"See what? For fuck's sake, what are you talking about?"

Ring ran the video again—the same final frames of Joe Stanton's plunge. This time, he froze the image at the moment of impact—the point at which Stanton's feet and legs hit the water.

"See? There. A little to the right of Stanton, and behind."

Collins shrugged. "Mist or something. So what?"

"Watch it again," said Ring, "and focus on that spot." He tapped a small area of the screen.

He ran the video at one-eighth normal speed. Collins and Beck stared. And this time they saw it clearly: a plume of spray shooting up, out of the water behind and to the right of Joe Stanton.

"Spray?" said Beck.

"Breath," said Ring. "Exhale." His eyes shone brighter than ever and the excitement and confidence in his voice grabbed Beck.

"What, like from a dolphin or something? Our guys said they heard dolphins in the Narrows when Stanton was on the bridge." Beck nodded at the screen. "You think that plume came from a dolphin?"

"Precisely," said Ring.

"Which means?" said Collins, more flummoxed than ever. "So there's dolphins in the channel. Swimming past when Stanton tried to off himself. So what?"

"Not swimming past," said Ring. "Swimming *to* him. Coming to meet Joe Stanton."

Collins and Beck stared blankly at Ring, as if waiting for the punch line. Whatever it was, Beck wasn't going to laugh. It was the middle of the night, and Ring's bizarre ramblings were beginning to piss him off.

"Don't you see?" said Ring. "The voice—the source of the hallucinations—in all four men, belongs to a dolphin. An orca whale, if I'm right. Which technically is a dolphin. Did you know that orcas are the largest members of the dolphin family? Everyone thinks orcas are whales. But they're not."

Beck stared at him. "You think Stanton went to the Manette Bridge at one in the morning—to meet a whale?"

"Yes."

Beck slumped in his chair and Collins lowered his head, stifling a laugh.

"Are you smoking crack?" asked Beck.

Collins lost the battle to suppress his laughter and snorted long and exuberantly.

"Laugh all you like, Mr. Collins," said Ring. "I don't hear you advancing any theories. Come to think of it, I don't believe I've ever heard you offer a single cogent idea. On anything."

Collins lifted his head, red-faced, smile gone.

"Easy," said Beck. "Let's just take it easy, okay? Seriously, Doc. You gotta admit…this is…Talking to whales? Come on."

"It's the only explanation that makes sense," said Ring. He got to his feet, stepped to the Palantir, and called up a map of the North Pacific. Beck and Collins moved in beside him.

"Consider," he said, tapping a glowing image of Nunivak Island, "Galbreth and Stahl—the divers we lost in the Bering Sea—were in the water immediately before their hallucinations started. Crew reported heavy concentrations of orca around the platforms the entire day."

"I don't remember hearing anything about whales," said Collins.

"Perhaps because it seemed irrelevant," said Ring. "There are lots of whales in the Bering Sea. Who cares? Nevertheless, our crew reported seeing whales around the platforms. I just reread the files."

Ring manipulated the giant touch screen until Yakutat and South Central Alaska dominated the frame. "Whittaker—the gillnetter—fell out of his skiff in the middle of a pod of orca whales. His brother saw them. Talked about it."

Ring slid the glowing map to the San Juans.

"Eight days after Whittaker, Joe Stanton goes kayaking and encounters an entire pod of orca, here." He tapped on the map. "Off San Juan Island. Stanton's girlfriend said he touched a whale with his bare hand—that the whale rose up under his kayak and lingered there for several seconds."

Ring slid the map to Bremerton, deep within the Puget Sound.

"A few hours ago," he said, "Stanton responded to a summons and went to the Manette Bridge. What did he find there?"

Ring looked at Beck and Collins. "Whales…or, one specific whale, to be precise. A member of the species *Orcinus orca*, which is Latin for 'whale from the underworld of the dead.'

"The voice is real, gentlemen. The source of the madness and hallucinations. The voice is real. And it belongs to a leviathan. A creature of the deep."

CHAPTER 46

JOE AND ELLA STOOD in Joe's tiny kitchen, the radio blasting Elton John's "Philadelphia Freedom." Joe pulled Ella close, kissed her, and whispered in her ear, relying on the music to conceal his words from Beck's microphones. "Beck's not gonna let us leave. We have to ditch them."

Ella looked at him. Wide-eyed. Frightened. She squeezed his hand and nodded but didn't speak.

It was 10:00 a.m., July 4. Independence Day. The first day of Seafair. They'd slept six hours, waking to the roar and rumble of military jets. The morning paper lay open on the kitchen table, the front page all about the day's festivities. A picture of Bremerton hometown hero and Seafair master of ceremonies Rear Admiral Wesley E. Houghton, dominated the layout.

"I have an idea," Joe whispered, "to give us cover. Get us out of here. Be ready. We'll leave through the backyard." Ella nodded and began stuffing items into a daypack.

Allen Dodd sat slumped in the driver's seat of a beige Crown Vic. He'd spent the night—after the bizarre events at the Manette Bridge—sleeping in the car in front of a boarded-up adult video store on West Thornton Way, earbud in one ear in case the mics hidden around Joe's house picked up any suspicious conversation or sounds of departure. An iPad propped on the dash displayed alternating views of Joe's residence: Entry. Kitchen. Backyard.

Another Beck operative, Chad Kehler, waited in a Mustang on East Archer, one block south of Joe's house.

Beck wanted Stanton and his girlfriend brought to *Marauder*, alive and unharmed. Dodd and Kehler were confident they could do the job alone, but Beck had ordered them to wait for reinforcements.

Dodd looked at his watch. In twelve minutes, if all went according to plan, a FedEx van would enter Joe's street, back into his driveway, and park in front of his garage door. The man driving the van would knock on the front door, just as others jumped Joe's back fence and stormed the house from the rear. Joe and Ella would be taken captive, blindfolded, gagged, and herded into the van via the garage. The van would then deliver them to the Bremerton Airport and Beck's waiting helicopter. Clean. Simple. Quick. No drama. No freaked-out neighbors.

Dodd watched the video feed, fascinated, as Stanton rolled a charcoal grill onto the middle of his tiny back deck.

Ten minutes to extraction.

Dodd caught a glimpse of Ella stepping onto the deck and actually drooled, a thin stream of saliva trickling from the corner of his mouth.

Dodd wished Beck would haul Stanton away and leave him in charge of the girl. Even on the little screen she looked hotter than hell. Beautiful face. Long legs. Perfect breasts. Perfect ass. Great handfuls of red hair. Dressed now in shorts and a T-shirt and hiking boots.

Dodd ogled and daydreamed, oblivious to the fact that Joe Stanton was pouring gasoline from a jerry can onto his grill and intentionally sloshing it all over the deck.

CHAPTER 47

JOE STEPPED OFF HIS DECK and called 911 from his iPhone. "I'd like to report a fire," he told the dispatcher. "Burning out of control in my backyard. Please hurry."

He took a book of matches from his pocket.

"You sure about this?" Ella asked. The gas fumes were making her dizzy.

"Beck's guys are watching us," Joe replied with flat certainty. "They're not gonna let us leave. Or if they do, they'll track us."

He looked at Ella. "And Mia needs my help. *Our* help."

Ella nodded and Joe tore a match from the pack.

Seven minutes to extraction.

Dodd stared at Joe and Ella on the video feed and thought the girl looked scared. He'd seen the couple talking. Had seen Joe on the phone, but hadn't heard any of the call. There were no mics on the deck.

And then he heard sirens. Lots of sirens, coming fast, from multiple directions.

Dodd sat bolt upright in the driver's seat of the Crown Vic and called Kehler. "Dude, something's going down."

On the iPad he saw Joe Stanton light a match and toss it at his barbecue. The grill exploded in flame. Front and back. Top and bottom. Fire flowed down the legs of the cooker, a bright ribbon unspooling, and roared onto the deck, leaping and dancing like a thing alive.

The video feed skipped automatically to images from the other hidden cameras: Entry. Kitchen. When it flicked back to the deck, Joe and Ella were gone.

"Shit!" yelled Dodd. "Chad—they're in the alley! They're running."

Kehler threw the Mustang into gear and lurched from his parking spot, then jumped on the brakes as a cherry-red Bremerton Fire Department ladder truck swung through the intersection of Archer and 9th, fifty feet away, horns blaring, sirens screaming.

Kehler waited for the truck to pass, then blasted out of his space just in front of a second fire truck, this one a pumper, its air horns bellowing in complaint.

Kehler gunned the Mustang across oncoming traffic and into the narrow dirt alleyway behind Joe's house. He spotted Joe and Ella immediately: far end of the alley, three hundred feet away, running in the opposite direction.

"Got 'em!" Kehler yelled into the phone. "They're in the alley running east. I'm right behind."

The Mustang tore through the alley, clipping garbage cans and recycle bins as it shot forward. Black smoke billowed up from Stanton's backyard, just ahead.

"Aw, fuck!" Kehler cried, as a fire engine squeezed into the far end of the alley, trundling past Joe and Ella, who had to flatten themselves against a fence to let it pass.

"Shit!"

Kehler slammed the Mustang into reverse, then hit the brakes as an air horn blared behind him, so close it shook his car. The pumper truck—the one he'd cut in front of—was there.

He was trapped. Not going anywhere.

"Goddamnit, shit, motherfucker!" Kehler yelled, punching his door panel and steering wheel. He looked up to find a huge fireman glaring at him. In the side mirror, he could see cops squeezing past the pumper, coming for him. He tried to open the door, but the fireman blocked it with his thigh.

"You got some explainin' to do, pal," the big man grunted.

CHAPTER 48

ALLEN DODD DROVE the Crown Vic three blocks to Vance Boulevard, pulling over twice to avoid rampaging emergency vehicles. He heard Kehler swearing on the radio, and assumed his cohort had been delayed or detained, but didn't have time to sort it out. He had to find Stanton and the girl. Had to at least spot them and track them until the rest of Beck's team arrived.

Dodd turned left onto Vance and was forced over yet again, this time for an ambulance and the Fire Chief's Ford F-350, flashing like a Christmas tree. The vehicles' horns and sirens left his ears ringing.

Dodd scanned the hill ahead. Vance rose sharply, cresting at an intersection with Wheaton Way.

He stared. And saw them. Joe and Ella walking fast, hand-in-hand, turning right onto Wheaton.

The emergency vehicles passed and Dodd gunned the Crown Vic. Tires squealed, the car shot forward, and he was at the top of the hill in a couple of seconds. The light was green and he swung right, then hit the brakes.

"Aw, shit," he yelled.

There were people everywhere. Couples, families, kids. Old people, twentysomethings, teenagers. Big groups and small clusters, some carrying coolers, folding chairs, and picnic blankets. All out for a good time on the Fourth of July and the first day of Seafair, the biggest celebration in the Puget Sound. Stanton and the girl could be anywhere.

Dodd pulled to the curb and scanned left and right. Forward and back. He spotted the FedEx van and a Suburban ferrying Beck's operatives in oncoming traffic and reached for his radio, then hesitated as he thought about how Beck would react to the news that he'd lost a couple of unarmed civilians in a residential neighborhood.

He thought about running, but knew it would be no use. Beck would find him, and kill him, for sure.

"Guys," he said, into the radio. "We have a problem."

CHAPTER 49

JOE AND ELLA HURRIED ALONG Wheaton Way, cut right onto Edgewood, walk-jogged east for three blocks, turned onto Milton, and entered a well-used footpath leading into Wheaton Ravine Park.

Sirens wailed all the while, and dark thoughts swirled in Joe's mind: *I set my rental house on fire. I made a 911 call, then fled the scene. I'm running from the police now, as well as from Beck. I'm endangering Ella, putting her in harm's way and making her a party to an insane, incomprehensible mission.*

Then he remembered the implant, and his guilt eased. Beck's people had operated on him. Placed instruments in his head, without his knowledge or permission. Aboard the *Northern Mercy* they'd lied to his face. Lied to him, and Ella, and Detective Palmer. Joe touched the side of his head, near his right eye. It was still tender there, where Mia had fried the implants. Melted the wires.

Joe didn't know the reason for the implants, but one thing was clear: if Beck and crew were capable of such mutilation, such deceit, they were capable of anything. They would feel no compunction about hurting or killing him and Ella.

They emerged from Wheaton Ravine into the asphalt lot flanking St. Anthony's Episcopal Church and made a beeline for the church van, parked amid the weeds at the far corner of the lot.

Church members and staff used the Econoline for everything from youth backpacking trips to nursing-home visits, and Joe was one of three people with a key. As vicar of St. Anthony's, he had every right to use the vehicle, though as he climbed into the driver's seat now, he wasn't sure the Bishop's Committee would approve of this particular outing.

The air inside the van was warm. Stagnant. As if the vehicle hadn't been driven in a while. There was a newspaper on the dash, already yellowing from the sun, though it was only a few days old.

Joe grabbed the paper to toss it out of the way, then stopped and stared at the headline on the open page: "4th of July and Seafair Planning Guide." Joe scanned the article below the banner and his heart rate ticked up.

"Where to?" Ella asked.

"Ferry terminal," he said. "I'll explain when we're on the boat."

CHAPTER 50

COLLINS FOUND BECK in *Marauder*'s high-tech indoor shooting range, firing an MP5N submachine gun at lifelike projections of Taliban fighters.

Collins loitered behind a clear Kevlar safety shield until Beck noticed him and raised his hand. The simulation paused, midbattle.

"What?" said Beck, pulling his headset down around his neck.

Collins stepped around the shield. "Stanton, Sir. It seems he, um, started a fire."

The range was dark and cool, but Collins was sweating.

"A fire?"

"To mask his escape. He and the girl, um, got away. Apparently."

Beck repositioned his headset and stared at Collins through his thousand-dollar shooting glasses. Collins didn't like the look in his boss's eyes.

Beck signaled the controller, ensconced in a bulletproof booth at the back of the range, and the cacophonous sounds of an Afghan street market filled the chamber once more. A gunman leapt from behind a produce stand just ahead and Beck opened fire.

The noise was rock-concert loud, and Collins jammed his hands over his ears. It wasn't just Beck's MP5N, unleashing eight hundred nine-millimeter parabellum rounds per minute, but also alarms, horns, sirens, other weapons at close range, and people screaming. This was full-on combat immersion played with live ammunition.

Some on the ship referred to the range—which used state-of-the-art projection technology, lasers, and infrared cameras to track a shooter's score—as Beck's five-million-dollar video arcade, though never to his face.

Beck signaled for another pause, and confronted Collins.

"So, we had what…twelve guys on the ground there?" He waved the submachine gun's muzzle in Collins's direction. "Should I have sent fourteen?"

The range had gone abruptly, utterly silent, and Collins was suddenly aware of the *thump, thump, thump* of his heart and the sweat on his forehead.

"I don't know, sir."

"To bring in an unarmed priest and his girlfriend?"

Beck edged the MP5N closer to Collins.

"Maybe, what? *Eighteen* guys? Would that be enough?"

Collins didn't answer. He half expected Beck to kill him on the spot.

"So, where is he?"

"We don't know, sir. We're trying to figure it out."

"Trying to figure it out," Beck said softly. "Trying to figure it out."

He leaned forward and his whisper changed to a full-throated scream so abruptly that Collins nearly wet himself.

"He has a fucking chip in his head! *In his head!* It emits a fucking pulse every thirty or so fucking seconds. Makes a little chirp on our monitors. We should be able to track that, don't you think?"

"It's not working. Ring thinks it's been disabled."

Beck lowered his weapon. "How?"

"Ring thinks *she* did it."

"She?"

Collins averted his eyes. Ring's theory seemed so absurd he couldn't bring himself to say it to Beck's face.

"The whale. Ring thinks the whale may have disabled the chip and thought-capture hardware. With her sonar."

Beck handed the submachine gun to a flack jacket wearing range attendant and Collins felt his sphincter muscles relax a miniscule amount. Beck wasn't going to kill him. Not yet.

"Since when is the whale female?"

Collins shook his head. "Ring says he has more information now."

"Well, I'd better go talk to him then."

"Yes, sir,"

"And you, Mr. Collins, had better find Stanton and his girl and bring them in."

Collins exited the range, and Beck took his gun back from the attendant.

"Let's finish the scenario," said Beck, "and call it a day."

"Yes, sir."

The attendant vanished into the shadows, the countdown strobes flashed, and Beck was back in the Afghan market.

He stepped forward. Alert. Ready. Like stepping into a 3-D movie.

The market was deserted. The civilians had all fled after the firefight, and bodies of Taliban fighters and coalition soldiers covered the ground. Carts and stalls lay smashed and broken in the street. There was blood on every surface. Lots of it.

The simulations were astoundingly lifelike. Even the smells. A scent generator pumped odors into the range based on the particular scenario being run. Beck considered the scent generator a gimmick that didn't begin to approximate the stench of real combat (*thank God*, he thought). But it was a touch that impressed visitors and Erebus clients.

Beck took a step, and caught a flicker of movement out of the corner of his eye. Up high and to the left. A sniper.

He turned, fired, and dove for cover. The sniper crashed to earth, smashing through a market stall as he fell.

Not real combat, but close. And it always got Beck's adrenaline pumping.

He got to his feet. The sim was almost done. He could see the clock in the corner of the range ticking down. He was ready to leave and talk to Ring.

Almost done.

There was another fleeting twitch of movement, this time on his right. At the edge of his peripheral vision. He pivoted.

Beck was a soldier. The best of the best. Trained to assess and act in a split second.

But what he saw now paralyzed him. Bolted him to the ground and caused him to convulse, head to toe.

The computer-generated character lurking in the shadows a few feet away wasn't a Taliban fighter. Or a suicide bomber. Or another

SEAL. It was Dalton Ellis. The reporter. The enemy he'd fought and thrown overboard.

Ellis was just standing there in profile, staring into the distance, and Beck could see that there was something wrong with his face. Very wrong.

The reporter turned, stepping into the light, and Beck nearly dropped his gun.

Ellis's eyes were gone. His eyes were gone and maggots wriggled in both sockets. Filled both sockets completely.

Ellis's mouth formed a tight black "O," an expressionless, depthless pit. Shards of jaw and cheekbone glistened through ribbons of rotting flesh.

Beck experienced another convulsion. This time it was vomit rising in a wave. He choked it back.

The major injury he had personally delivered to Ellis—the stab wound to the reporter's thigh—stood out from the man's other wounds in almost fluorescent relief. The gash shone bright against the later insults—the tooth and claw gashes caused by the brown bears of Admiralty Island.

Beck stood frozen, willing his muscles to work, forcing—or trying to force—his brain to reengage.

Ellis's black pit of a mouth widened and worked and suddenly it was there in the front of Beck's mind. A whisper. A statement. A declaration.

You will carry me.

The statement was delivered with confidence. Arrogance.

Beck couldn't look away.

You will carry me! A little louder now. A little more force. Almost mocking this time.

There was more coming. More thoughts or words from that black pit of a mouth. But Beck didn't wait.

His paralysis ended. He lifted his MP5N, opened fire, and emptied the weapon into Ellis's body.

Almost before he'd begun, though, Ellis vanished—as if that part of the projection had simply winked out.

The roar of Beck's gun subsided, the scenario ended, and Beck screamed.

"What the hell was that?"

The range attendant hurried from the booth.

"What was what, sir?"

"Don't give me that shit!" Beck shouted, waving his rifle at the spot where Ellis had stood. "Who added that to the sim?"

"Sir?" The attendant looked like he might have a heart attack.

"Rewind the program, goddamnit! Replay the last sixty seconds. After the sniper."

The attendant scurried back to the control booth, and a few moments later the scenario lurched to life once more. The sounds and smells. The market in the immediate aftermath of the firefight.

The sniper fell from the rooftop and crashed through the market stall, just as Beck remembered.

He stood there, waiting for the rest of the scenario to unfold, for Ellis to step from the shadows on his right.

There.

A flicker of movement exactly where Ellis had been. In precisely the same spot.

Except it wasn't Ellis this time. It was an Afghan woman, covered, robed head to toe. Only her eyes visible. She was staring into the distance, just as Ellis had been. And then she turned, as Ellis had, stepped forward, and vanished into the market.

The scenario ended, the sound died, and the entire marketscape disappeared. The attendant hurried from the booth once more.

"The ending was different," said Beck. "What happened to the other ending?"

"Sir?"

"It was a woman that time, goddamnit. Where Ellis was standing."

The attendant looked confused. Frightened. He was just a kid.

"Sir, the ending was exactly the same. I mean, it can't change…The program—"

"Don't fucking tell me about the goddamned program!" Beck screamed. "Ellis was in the scenario. Someone added him. Someone's fucking with me."

"Yes, sir, but—"

"Show me the range recording. I want to see the last sixty seconds of the previous two loops."

"Yes, sir."

Beck followed the attendant into the booth and watched as he called the final moments of the scenarios onto his monitor.

There were multiple cameras mounted throughout the range—cameras whose sole purpose was to record a shooter's actions and performance during the simulation. The cameras were there to assist with training. To help soldiers see what they were doing wrong and improve.

The cameras captured multiple perspectives inside the range, and Beck was clearly visible in all of them.

He watched himself freeze. Watched himself look directly at the Afghan woman. Watched himself lift his MP5N, open fire, and tear her to shreds.

It didn't make sense. On the floor, in the range, he had seen Ellis.

But the cameras didn't lie. The cameras couldn't lie. The cameras showed the sim as it actually occurred. In real time.

I saw something that wasn't there. I heard something.

You will carry me.

Heart pounding, Beck left the range without saying a word. Without looking at the attendant. Without looking back.

He left with a raging headache, wondering if he was losing his mind.

CHAPTER 51

JOE AND ELLA SAT in the St. Anthony's church van at the very front of the car deck on the Bremerton-to-Seattle ferry.

They'd made it to the terminal okay, working their way through streets clogged with holiday revelers, and Joe was fairly certain that no one had followed them. Fairly certain that the St. Anthony's van was not bugged, and that Mia had successfully disabled all of the circuits embedded in his flesh.

The adrenaline that had propelled him since his leap from the Manette Bridge was finally wearing off and he felt tired. Very tired. But also relaxed. Perhaps the most relaxed he'd felt in days.

He cleared his mind, and let the sensation spread.

Ella sat next to him. Peaceful. Placid. Staring out the windshield as the MV *Chelan* motored through Rich Passage—the narrow, winding saltwater channel between Bainbridge Island and Manchester.

The Fourth was off to a brilliant, warm start, and boats were everywhere: Sailboats. Powerboats. Kayaks gliding close to shore. Sunlight danced on the wave tops.

Joe leaned back in his seat and closed his eyes.

Mia must have come this way last night, said Ella. *On her way to meet you. And on her way back out. Toward open water.*

Yes, she did, Joe replied. *She travels fast, Mia and her friends.*

What does she want, Joe?

Help.

With what?

Sound.

What sound? What do you mean?

I don't know. I'm not sure. I just know that it has to do with sound.
And if you help her with the sound, then what?
Something big will happen. Something monumental. Something that will change everything.

Silence. Save for the soothing rumble of the ferry's engines.
Can you help her? Can we help her?
I'm not sure. Maybe. We have to try.
Silence.

Ella lurched forward and slammed against her seat belt. Joe's eyes flew open.

"Joe," she gasped.

"Yeah?"

"What the hell was that?"

"What?"

"We were talking."

"Yeah."

"Except we weren't. I didn't say anything. And neither did you. Not out loud."

They looked at each other.

"I was daydreaming," said Joe. "Only"—he stared at her—"did you tell me that Mia must have come this way?"

"Yeah."

"And then you asked me what it is she wants and I said—"

"Sound," said Ella. "That she needs help with sound."

Joe nodded. "I thought I dreamed all that."

"Me too. Thought I was dreaming...and then it felt like a real conversation and I realized we weren't speaking."

They sat for a long time, gazing out at the water as the ferry cleared Restoration Point and angled toward Seattle.

An armada of gray Navy ships—in town for the Seafair celebrations—lay silhouetted against the waterfront far ahead. It was a big day. There would be hydroplane races on Lake Washington, flyovers by the Blue Angels, and multiple fireworks displays. Most of the Navy ships would be open for tours.

Ella scanned the vast expanse of Elliott Bay, looking for plumes of spray.

Mia communicates like this, said Ella, again without speaking the words.

Yes.

And now we can do it, too.

Apparently.

"That's *so* freaky," said Ella, switching back to speech. "I can hear your voice in my mind."

Joe took Ella's hand and they fell silent once more.

Stared at the water. At Alki Point. The Magnolia Bluffs. The Space Needle.

Downtown Seattle lay directly ahead now, looming larger and larger as the ferry motored on. The Cascade Mountains stood behind the city, a jagged, white-topped wall against the blue horizon.

Ella turned to Joe, a look of little-girl wonder in her eyes. "Will we always be able to do that, or is it just temporary?"

Joe laughed, shook his head. "I have no idea. Better enjoy it while we can."

Ella shut her eyes. "She's close," she said. "Mia, I mean."

"Yeah," said Joe. "I think you're right."

Ella looked at him again. "How does that work? How can we know where she is? Whether she's close or far away?"

"We're connected."

Ella laughed. "Yeah, I'm 'connected' to my mom and dad, too, Joe, and I think about them often—but I don't know where they are moment to moment. I'm thinking about them, but they could have flown to Ecuador yesterday and I wouldn't have a clue."

"When I think about Mia," said Joe, "I get an answer back."

Ella laughed at the strangeness of it. Nodded in agreement.

The fleet of gray Navy vessels grew closer. They could see sailors, dressed all in white, on several of the ships now.

Ella asked, "Why did you think Lorna Gwin was your daughter?"

"I have some ideas about that," Joe replied, gazing at the ships. "Mia has been trying to make contact with people for weeks, I think. I don't understand it, but I know her need is urgent. Dire.

"She knows about humans—a few things—from something that happened to her a long time ago."

He paused, thinking. Concentrating. Trying to understand. He had an image of an old man in his mind. The man had a beard and sunburned cheeks.

A scientist…a professor.

It was no one he had ever met. The image had simply appeared in his head.

Is this who Mia learned from?

Joe said. "Communicating with us—with humans—is hard. Nearly impossible. Think about how difficult it is for us to comprehend their whistles and clicks. It's the same for them. Human speech sounds like gibberish."

Ella said nothing.

"We're essentially alien to one another, right? I mean, we inhabit different worlds, lead utterly different lives. We share the same DNA, but we've evolved differently for…what? The last hundred million or so years?"

"Give or take," said Ella.

"So when she touched me, with these urgent, pressing thoughts in her mind, with this desperate need, it didn't translate quite right. Mia didn't know how to deliver her message to me, and I didn't know how to receive it. I didn't even know I'd been given a message, at first. I just thought I was going insane.

"All that came through when Mia spoke to me was grief. Loss. Pain. Sadness. Because those were the predominant thoughts in her mind.

"When we were kayaking and Mia came up out of the water—when she rose up and I touched her with my hand—I felt something. A jolt in my hand and arm and head."

Ella nodded. She'd felt the same sensation when she'd touched Mia the previous night.

"I didn't think about it at the time," said Joe. "Not with orcas surfacing all around our kayaks. I attributed the tingling in my arm to excitement. But I know now that it was more than that. Something passed between us."

"Communication," said Ella.

"Yeah. Mia planted thoughts…images…feelings—in my mind. And—this is my theory anyway—those emotions sort of percolated there in my subconscious. Coalesced. While I slept.

"By the time I woke up, at the Breakwater, Mia's messages had taken on a life of their own—inside my head."

"You believed you had a little girl."

"With all my heart," said Joe. "And I knew from the instant I opened my eyes that something awful had happened to her. That she was dead. Mia's grief became my grief."

Ella said, "To get into somebody's head like that, enter your mind, push aside all your other thoughts—"

Joe laughed without any trace of humor. "Mia," he said, "is a force of nature. Her thoughts hit you like a river at flood stage. Maybe it's how they all communicate. Whales, I mean.

"Last night," Joe said, "Mia was aware of you. Probably because you were the predominant thought in my mind."

Ella smiled.

"She wanted to meet you. I asked her to take it easy."

"Thanks," said Ella. She looked again at her hand, which still tingled, and wondered if more "communication" was coming.

Joe peered through the windshield and studied the Navy ships. They lay just ahead now. Gray. Huge. Intimidating.

The USS *Nimitz* was the biggest of all. It dominated the industrial waterfront south of the ferry terminal, dwarfing even the immense cranes and container ships lining the docks at the port.

Ella looked up in time to see two of the Blue Angels swoop into view above Safeco Field.

The jets fell into an invisible lane five hundred feet over Alaskan Way and accelerated, screaming along the waterfront.

"How can we help her?" Ella asked.

"*We* can't."

Joe lifted the newspaper, which was still open to the spread outlining the day's festivities and the picture of Rear Admiral Wesley H. Houghton. According to the caption, Houghton would be greeting members of the public aboard the USS *Nimitz* from twelve to four.

He might be able to accomplish what she's after. Joe put the thought in the front of his mind. Held it there.

Ella looked from the article to Joe and back. "You're serious?"

Joe nodded. "Yeah."

"Mia told you we need to talk to an admiral in the Navy?" She pointed at the paper. "This guy?"

"No. She told me what she needs. I thought about it and put two and two together. If anyone can accomplish what she wants, it's him. Or someone like him."

The ferry neared the dock and a new realization formed in Joe's mind, one that he withheld from Ella. One that he strove to conceal.

Mia was sad. Not for herself, but for him.

I'm going to die, thought Joe. *That's what she thinks. Mia feels bad because she believes I'm going to die. Soon. And she thinks it's her fault.*

And suddenly Joe could see them in his mind's eye: Stahl and Galbreth and Whittaker. The Erebus divers and the gillnetter.

Mia touched them, and now they're dead. She connected with them, just like she did with me. But the connections went wrong and the men died. The connection killed them.

Joe understood. Mia felt remorse for the deaths and feared that he would suffer the same fate. His heart rate jumped.

He breathed in and out. Kept his trembling hands firmly on the armrests.

Mia isn't just fearful that I'll suffer the same fate as the other men. She's certain of it.

CHAPTER 52

SHELDON BECK STOOD in the cool darkness of the War Room and stared at Orondo Ring's computer monitor. The screen displayed an image of a weather-beaten fishing vessel. Old. Wooden-hulled.

"What the hell's that?" said Beck, who still had a raging headache and was in an ugly, combative mood. The incident in the range, and the news that Joe and Ella had gotten away, tormented him like an acute, throbbing injury. He thought about summoning Collins so that he could break his neck. Thought about how cathartic that would be.

"It's a charter fishing boat," Ring said cheerfully, seemingly oblivious to his boss's mental state. "Diesel. Fifty-eight feet long. Works out of San Diego."

Beck massaged the painful knot between his eyes and kept his voice low, but there was an underlying rumble in his tone, like a volcano ready to erupt. "Please explain to me why I should give a Turkish crap about a goddamned piece-of-shit scow in San Diego."

"Ah, but it hasn't always been a charter fishing vessel," said Ring, sounding bright and buoyant. He clicked to a different image, to an angle where the name of the vessel was clearly visible.

Beck sucked breath in through his teeth as he read the moniker on the hull. "The *Lorna Gwin*."

"Yes," said Ring. "Fascinating history. But the part that I find most relevant is the ten-year interval before it was moved to Southern California."

Beck grabbed a chair and sat down, the throbbing between his eyes temporarily forgotten.

"Will Dieturlund," said Ring, opening a picture of a sturdy-looking man with a beard and sunburned cheeks, "was a marine biologist, whale researcher, and owner and captain of the *Lorna Gwin*. He and his crew—mostly graduate students—spent nearly a decade researching transient orcas in the North Pacific. Tracking the animals from on board the Lorna Gwin."

"*Transient* orcas?" Beck leaned toward the monitor as images of whales flashed on screen.

"Subspecies of killer whale," said Ring. "Highly specialized. Extraordinarily lethal—if you happen to be a seal. Transient orcas eat only mammals. Seals, sea lions, sea otters, porpoises, other whales. Sometimes they'll help themselves to a swimming moose or deer, as well. No fish, though. They hate fish."

Beck said nothing.

"Know how people figured that out?" Ring asked, as if he were revealing a fascinating bit of trivia at a cocktail party. "How they know transients won't eat fish?"

Beck waited. Too benumbed by his headache to think of a reply.

"It's unbelievable, really. Yet another example of the depth and breadth of human stupidity and arrogance."

Beck said nothing. He knew that there was no use rushing the genius when he was in storytelling mode. Anyone else delaying Beck with such casual blather might face bodily harm. But Beck *needed* Ring, depended on him to solve problems others couldn't manage. Ring knew this, and, consequently, feared Beck not at all.

"Back in the sixties," said Ring, "when orcas were being nabbed for display in marine parks, this one group of captured whales refused to eat. Flat-out refused. The moron zookeepers kept giving these whales fish. For seventy-eight straight days, it was nothing but fish on the menu. Fat, juicy salmon. Tuna. Herring. Cod. You name it. They tried everything. And you know what?"

Beck shook his head.

"The whales wouldn't touch any of it. Wouldn't take a single bite. Finally, the orcas in this group start dying of starvation, and it dawns on someone that maybe, just maybe, these whales are different from the others."

Beck sighed. "So Dieturlund studied transient orcas, and transient orcas only eat mammals. Who gives a shit? What does this have to do with Stanton?"

"Everything," said Ring, as if the linkage was perfectly obvious."

Beck squeezed the flesh between his eyes as his headache resumed with new ferocity.

"Our divers," said Beck, "and the gillnetter dude from Yakutat, and Stanton all hallucinated about a little girl named Lorna Gwin." He pointed at the boat. "What's the connection?"

"Ah," said Ring. "This is where it gets really interesting."

He turned back to his computer and opened a folder. "I've read Dieturlund's journals. They're all online. Plus he published scores of scientific papers. Absolutely fascinating."

"I'm sure," said Beck.

"Dieturlund wrote extensively about individual transient whales," said Ring. "But one particular whale got more ink than all the rest combined."

Ring clicked on a thumbnail image and the sleek black-and-white form of a single orca whale filled the screen.

"This is T-197," said Ring, "Dieturlund's favorite subject...and the sole focus of his final white papers."

"T-197?"

"'T' is for 'transient,'" said Ring. "Scientists label the resident clans—the fish eaters—alphabetically. 'A' clan is the largest in British Columbia. And then there are pods within the clans. A1 is the best-known killer whale family in all of Canada, probably. 'J' pod lives around the San Juans, and is responsible for an entire whale watching industry in its own right. But 'T' is reserved for transients—the hunters of mammals. According to Dieturlund, he had eleven separate up-close encounters with T-197 in the wild."

"What kind of encounters?" Beck asked. Despite himself, he was intrigued once again.

"Actual physical contact. Occasions when T-197 would purposely seek him out, come alongside his kayak or Zodiac and nuzzle against him. On three occasions Dieturlund swam with T-197 and her pod.

"Dieturlund was a by-the-book researcher, not prone to anthropomorphism or to giving his subjects names. But he named this whale. He called her 'Mia'."

Beck squinted at him. "Mia."

"And it seems that while Dieturlund and crew were studying T-197—or Mia—she and a male orca from a different pod got pregnant. Had a baby."

Beck leaned back in his chair.

"Officially," said Ring, "the baby was called T-204. But Dieturlund gave the baby another name, as well."

A shiver traveled the length of Beck's spine. "Lorna Gwin?"

"Precisely. He named Mia's baby after his boat." Ring shrugged. "Not the most creative choice in the world. But Dieturlund's a scientist, after all, not a poet."

Beck looked at the screen, which now displayed pictures of T-197 and T-204, taken from above. Probably from a helicopter. The baby was about one-fourth the size of her mother and appeared glued to the larger whale's side.

Mother and child. Mia and Lorna Gwin. Together. Swimming in calm turquoise water.

"When was this? When was the baby born?"

"Five years ago last April," said Ring. "These were taken near the mouth of Glacier Bay."

Beck thought about it. "Five years? So why are our divers, and the gillnetter, and Stanton hearing from this whale now—if that's really what's happening? Why the crazy hallucinations *now*?"

"I have a theory," said Ring. "But before we examine what happened to our divers and the others, it's important to know the rest of Will Dieturlund's story."

"The CliffsNotes version is fine," said Beck. "I've got a lot on my plate."

Ring nodded, "The fact is, Professor Dieturlund started to lose it. His methodical, dispassionate observations on *Orcinus orca* became infused with emotion. His careful white papers on cetacean behavior became more emotional. He began making fanciful claims."

"What kinds of claims?"

"Extravagant proclamations concerning cetacean intelligence and speech. Radical notions having to do with telepathy.

"Other scientists ridiculed Dieturlund's findings. Colleagues shunned him. Grant money evaporated. And the students who had always lined up to work with him went elsewhere. He was forced to sell his boat. His health suffered.

"He continued to write, however, generating white papers that read more like science fiction than critical fact-based analysis.

"He published treatises on the rich inner lives of whales and their astonishing cognitive and psychic abilities. There's a lengthy paper about a place Dieturlund calls 'The Dream Realm,' a region of ocean where whales of different species focus their collective mental energy to generate fields, or, distortions for purposes unknown."

Beck raised an eyebrow.

"That paper was the final nail in the coffin for the professor's scientific career," said Ring. "He became a laughingstock.

"During this phase, as he was losing everything, he began to suffer horrific nightmares and ultimately, hallucinations."

"Sounds familiar," said Beck.

"Yes, although Dieturlund's hallucinations never involved a little girl. His were more general, about death and loss and grief. It was about this time that Dieturlund's wife left him."

"Can't imagine why," said Beck. "So what happened? Why did he wig out?"

Ring leaned back. "This is where I'm guessing," he said.

"I'm listening."

"I believe that T-197, or, Mia, was reaching out to Dieturlund—communicating with him—and he didn't even know it. Or maybe deep down he did know it. But as a scientist, he couldn't acknowledge it outright."

"In other words?"

"In other words, the whale was talking to Dieturlund, but her communication manifested itself as changes in Dieturlund's mental state: new, colorful writing. Vivid, fantastical dreams."

Beck was struggling to follow. "So this whale—T-197—is filling Dieturlund's head with information, talking to him, only he doesn't even realize it. Just thinks he's losing his mind?"

"Right. And in the process, he loses his boat and his career. And Mia and Lorna Gwin and the rest of the pod go their merry way."

Beck scratched his head. "What? Then what? Nothing for five years and then Mia decides to pop out of obscurity and start mind-fucking more humans? Is she sadistic?"

"No. If I'm right, there was a pivotal event."

"What event?"

"Lorna Gwin—T-204—died."

Beck said nothing.

"There are other researchers tracking this pod. T-204 was reported missing two months ago."

"How'd she die?"

"Unknown."

"So what are you saying? An angry mother—enraged over the death of her child—blames people and seeks out our divers so she can touch them and blow the circuits in their brains? Is this about revenge?"

Ring turned to his computer and called up images of the strange, delicate, veil-like chambers.

"I might think that," said Ring. "Were it not for these." He enlarged the chamber images from Stanton's thoughts on-screen.

"No. It's not revenge. Mia has an agenda. And I'm convinced it has to do with these…structures."

Beck put his head in his hands. "But shit, Ring. If it's really about the chambers or tunnels—why did all these guys hallucinate about a kid?"

"Because. The communication isn't direct. It's between different species. This isn't English to French. Or even English to ancient Chinese. This is whale to human. And—in this case at least—the communication is occurring in images and feelings."

"But—"

"And because the dead baby is the overriding thought in this creature's mind, when she reaches out, that is what comes through first. And loudest. We need to look past that.

"Mia is reaching out to people because of *these*." Ring pointed at the chamber hovering on screen. "Structures that we know really exist."

"Collins told me that Stanton's thought-capture hardware is disabled," said Beck.

"Yes, but his final thought capture is still compiling. More will be revealed. Soon."

Beck looked at the monitors. "What will it show?"

Ring shrugged. "It's an immense amount of data. That's about all I can tell you."

"When will it be ready?"

"Five hours. Maybe a little less. In the meantime, there's someone we should see."

He brought up the picture of Dieturlund once more.

"He's alive? I assumed—"

"He's alive. In an assisted-living facility in Bellingham. I called...pretended I was a nephew. The receptionist wouldn't say much but told me he slips between periods of clarity and confusion."

Beck appeared skeptical. "Could be a waste of time."

"Possible. Or it could reveal a great many things." Ring looked at Beck. "Mr. Collins is tracking Stanton and the girl. And it will be hours before the final thought capture is in. It's a short flight to Bellingham, and it could be well worth our while."

Beck nodded. Sighed. "Let's go see him."

CHAPTER 53

JOE AND ELLA STOOD in the sunshine on the massive flight deck of the USS *Nimitz* at the end of a long row of gleaming, perfectly aligned F/A-18F Super Hornet fighter jets. Hordes of T-shirt-and-shorts-wearing tourists mingled with crisply attired Navy personnel.

The warm summer air smelled of sweat and sunscreen, hot aircraft aluminum and jet fuel, and every surface shone, from the fighter-jet cockpits to the shoes on the smartly dressed sailors.

At one end of the thousand-foot-long flight deck, a crowd had gathered to hear the prepared remarks of Rear Admiral Wesley Houghton. The presentation was nearly through.

Houghton stood behind a lectern, praising the organizers of Seafair and the people of Seattle for their hospitality.

The audience applauded. The admiral offered to stay and chat one-on-one. Most of the crowd dispersed, but thirty or so people queued up, including Joe and Ella.

It took a while.

Houghton was a war hero. A fighter pilot and decorated veteran of conflicts stretching back to Desert Storm. Several people wanted to reminisce and swap war stories.

Other tourists joined the line, and Joe let them go ahead. He was determined to go last. What he had to say to the admiral needed to be said quietly. Privately.

By the time it was his turn, the folding chairs and lectern had been put away and a first-class petty officer was coiling the velvet ropes surrounding the portable stage. Houghton's handlers were looking at their watches.

For a moment, Joe feared the admiral might just call it a day. But then the last of the other visitors walked off and the admiral turned toward them. Ella smiled, and Joe saw his chance.

"It's an honor to meet you, sir," he said. "We enjoyed your remarks."

"Well, I appreciate you folks coming out," said the admiral, barely taking his eyes off Ella. "And showing your support for the military."

"My name is Joe Stanton. And this is my friend Ella Tollefson. We live in Bremerton."

The admiral nodded, taking in the young man's long hair, beard, and earring while maintaining his warm smile. "It's a pleasure," he said.

"I'm an Episcopal priest," said Joe, wishing now that he had shaved, removed his earring, and worn a long-sleeved shirt to cover his tattoos. "And I'm proud to say that we have quite a few Navy families in our congregation."

The admiral gave Joe another look. "I'm glad to hear that. A strong faith community can make all the difference to a military family. All the difference. I commend you for your work."

"It's a privilege," said Joe.

The conversation stalled.

Joe wasn't sure how to proceed, and it was clear from the admiral's body language that he was about to exit the scene. The handlers were moving in.

Ella smiled her warmest, sweetest smile and said, "There was one thing we wanted to ask you about, sir. If you can spare another moment."

"Happy to. What's on your mind?"

Joe met the admiral's eyes. Coughed. "Well, sir. In addition to the Navy families I mentioned, we also have a number of other people in our congregation, with different interests."

The admiral nodded. "I see."

"And," said Joe, "we actually have a pretty strong environmental contingent within our church, with a keen interest in marine mammal protection."

Houghton never dropped his pleasant demeanor, never lost his warm PR smile. But one of the admiral's escort, a burly lieutenant in perfect, crisp whites, was watching them now.

Joe said, "Living in the Puget Sound like we do—such an incredible marine environment—there's a strong desire to protect the rich habitat."

"Well, that is certainly a goal we share," said the admiral.

"And there's growing concern that some of the Navy's sonar practices are harming marine mammals. Particularly whales."

The admiral relaxed. This was an issue he knew inside out. One he'd been asked about at countless press conferences. He had his boilerplate answer ready.

"Absolutely. I share your concern. The sonar issue is one we take very seriously. A lot of folks don't know this, but the Navy employs a staff of full-time marine biologists, and the focus of their work is to help mitigate the impacts of sonar testing. Fact is, the U.S. Navy is a leader in marine mammal research."

"That's great to hear," said Ella.

The admiral said, "I can tell you straight up that we've made changes based on the biologist's recommendations. Of course, it's always a balancing act between protecting national security and protecting the environment. But I assure you, the Navy is trying to do the right thing."

Joe smiled. And began to panic.

The conversation was over. The admiral was about to leave.

Ella turned to Joe with an expression that said, *Is that it? Is that what we came here for?* Joe didn't need telepathy to understand the look in her eyes.

Joe took a breath and focused his mind on Mia. Focused hard. He'd been aware for hours that she was concerned about sound. A particular sound. A horrific, relentless "pinging" emanating from a particular place far out to sea.

Joe could hear the sound too—had in fact been hearing it now for a long time a distant echo in the back of his mind. Constant. Steady. Irritating. He understood that it was preventing Mia from doing something she needed to do. Though he didn't know what the *something* was.

Joe thought, *So I can hear the sound? So what? What am I supposed to do, ask the admiral to shut off all the sonar in the world?*

He wanted to say more to the admiral, but what would be the point? What good would it do? The encounter had been a failure.

Joe froze, and felt a low frequency, molar-rattling hum inside his head.

She's here. Oh my God, she's here.

The sensation began at the base of his skull and quickly spread to his ears and jaw. It made his eyes water and his scalp tingle.

Somehow—he could not begin to comprehend the mechanism—Mia was inside his head. She'd arrived without warning. At the last possible instant.

So go ahead, he told her.

He felt a rush of blood and instantaneous nausea-inducing dizziness as the world before his eyes diminished.

It felt as if he'd fallen backward off a cliff and was now plummeting like a stone, watching helplessly as the world he knew receded to a dot; as if his mind were a control room on rails, flying in reverse as Mia—or Mia's mental energy—slid into position behind his eyes.

But it wasn't a clean transition.

There was bleed—overlap—between the two minds.

On the one hand, Joe was aware of the familiar shapes and structures before him: aware of the admiral with his square jaw, pale skin, and close-cropped hair. Aware of the wash of color on the big man's uniform: the perfectly aligned medals and insignias. Aware of the aircraft in the background. Wings and tails. Wheels and cockpits. Jet engines. The shapes were familiar. Decipherable.

And at the same time, the shapes made no sense. Filtered through Mia's brain, the objects in front of him amounted to a jumble of alien patterns. Houghton's face was comprehensible—Mia had seen human faces before—but the rest of the scene was nonsense. Noise.

The entire bizarre experience lasted only an instant. But in that instant Joe touched Mia's mind and felt the force of her intellect. Her curiosity.

Her unfamiliarity with the human world wouldn't last. Joe could see that. Given time, she would decipher the shapes. Interpret the patterns. It wouldn't take long.

He sensed that she wanted to stay. To gaze through human eyes out of sheer intellectual curiosity. For the novelty of it.

But it was not to be. There was work to be done. Things both of them had to accomplish.

Joe's mind lurched back into position and he was at the helm once more, in command of his neural processes and motor function.

But something had changed. Mia had left something for him. A thought.

Knowledge.

A kernel of information bright and shining, vivid and precise, in the front of his mind.

Joe didn't know how Mia had acquired the information but guessed it had to do with the professorial man. The old man, with the beard and sunburned face.

Joe blinked and saw the admiral and Ella studying him. Watching him curiously.

"You all right, son?" the admiral asked.

"I'm fine, sir. Fine."

He reached for the admiral's hand and shook it, matching the big man's bone-crushing grip with equal strength.

"In particular, sir, we're deeply concerned about a test site on the eastern edge of Kanaga Island, in the Aleutians."

The admiral stared at him, his warm, easy smile fading.

"The USNS *Impeccable* has been testing a Surveillance Towed Array Sensor System at 51.7665 degrees north, 177.2260 degrees west, for some weeks. This is a midfrequency active sonar, projecting at 3.8 kilohertz, and it's interfering with urgent and critical cetacean communication. We respectfully request that the sonar be turned off between 2 a.m. and 2 p.m. Pacific standard time, tomorrow."

The admiral's gaze flicked between Joe and Ella.

"Is this some kind of joke?"

"No, sir," said Joe. "It's a sincere request."

Joe watched the older man's eyes and knew what was going to happen. He was going to call security. He was going to have them arrested. His eyes reflected alarm. Surprise. His eyes said that Kanaga was classified. Nothing a civilian should know about. The game was up.

And then Joe felt a shiver pass through him, a pulse of energy and emotion. It traveled through his hand, and into the admiral—something else Mia had left for him, apparently.

The admiral's face changed and he looked suddenly confused. His skin paled. His confidence diminished.

It was not a look his men were used to.

Shakily, hesitantly, he said at last, "I'll see what I can do."

"Thank you, sir." Joe released the admiral's hand. Nodded. Stepped back. Ella smiled.

They said good-bye and retreated into the crowd, leaving the admiral staring after them, clenching and unclenching his fist.

CHAPTER 54

"**HELL OF A GRIP, FOR A PRIEST,**" Houghton muttered.

He lifted his hand. Studied it. Like he was seeing it for the first time. His aides exchanged looks.

"Everything okay, sir?" asked the big lieutenant.

The admiral turned to the man, his eyes cleared, and he said, "Get Admiral Walther on the line for me. Now."

The aide place the call, then handed a phone to Admiral Houghton as he and his entourage marched back to the bridge.

Houghton's warm PR smile was gone, the swarms of tourists forgotten.

The call connected. A gruff voice said, "Walther."

"Hayden. It's Wes."

"Wes! Hey, I hear you're at Seafair, making us look good. What can I do for ya?"

"Listen, Hayden, there still a SURTASS test happening off Kanaga?"

Hayden Walther's tone morphed from casual to businesslike. "This an encrypted call?"

Houghton lowered the phone and asked the chief petty officer walking beside him the same question. The chief assured him the call was secure.

"We're good, Hayden, go ahead."

"*Impeccable*'s still off Kanaga. Be there another week for a round-the-clock LFA survey. Pemberton wanted to keep it low-key. How'd you hear about it? Admiral Quitslund?"

"No. I heard about it from a tourist listening to my PR spiel here at Seafair."

Houghton lowered his phone again and looked at his men. "The guy I was just talking to, with the fashion-model girlfriend. Find them. No big scene, but find them. Detain them."

Hayden Walther was going nuts on the other end of the line. "What do you mean, tourist? Off-duty Navy? A contractor?"

"No. A priest, supposedly. Here for the meet-and-greet."

"How the hell does a priest know about classified LFA ops?"

"No damn clue. But I intend to find out. I'll call you back, Hayden."

Houghton handed the phone to an aide, resumed walking, then abruptly stopped.

Face blank, he lifted his right hand and studied it as if it were some sort of alien artifact. Clenched and unclenched his fist. Slowly rotated his hand. His men stared. Tourists did as well.

"You feeling okay, sir?" the big lieutenant asked again.

The admiral looked up, dazedly, mumbled a reply, and continued on to the bridge, oblivious to the buzzing crowds and fanfare. Five minutes later word reached him that Joe and Ella had slipped off the ship.

"Alert the Seattle Police, FBI, and NCIS," Houghton told his aides. "And check video from the security cameras. Get an ID on the priest."

Admiral Houghton retreated to his cabin and his computer. He entered passwords and called up classified data on the secure network.

He felt out of sorts, and his right side tingled still, as if a mild low-voltage electric current were coursing through his arm—a subtle, unending tremor running from his fingertips to his shoulder. But he ignored his physical issues and focused his mind.

And his anger.

A top-secret operation had somehow been compromised. Classified data stolen. The Navy—Houghton's de facto family for the majority of his life—was under assault. He intended to get to the root of the issue and, Fourth of July or no, he intended to start at once.

Seated at his computer, he called up charts of Kanaga and the islands around it. Studied Excel documents laden with arcane test data.

Why, Houghton wondered, would terrorists or anarchists or animal rights extremists—or whatever fringe group or faction the priest represented—be interested in such a site in the first place? In transmissions from one of the remotest places on the planet?

He recalled the priest's words: "*Urgent and critical cetacean communication.*"

What the hell did that mean?

Sounded like animal-rights eco-extremist bullshit to Houghton.

Or maybe Joe's request was a smoke screen for something else. A diversion of some sort.

Houghton leaned back in his chair. Thought about it. Then he looked at the charts some more. Read the CO's reports.

He stared and studied and contemplated. And eventually his mind wandered.

His face felt warm. A mild sunburn, perhaps? Made sense. He'd been standing on the deck, talking with visitors.

The warmth spread. Intensified. He felt sleepy.

Houghton fought the drowsiness. Resolved to power through.

But then he was snoozing in his chair. Nodding off at his computer. Dreaming.

In his dream he was a little boy again—age six or seven—sitting between his parents at church in Flagstaff, Arizona, where he'd grown up. It was a pre-Christmas evening service, the kind young Wesley Houghton loved most, and the church was packed and warmly, lavishly decorated. There were white lights and wreaths, and huge colorful floral bouquets on pedestals. The air smelled of candle wax and tangerines, cologne and perfume.

The vicar and lay ministers wore their finest, most colorful robes. The congregation was dressed to the nines. Lush music filled the hall.

Young Wesley swung his feet from the pew and listened and watched, wide-eyed, seeing everything, enjoying every moment.

He felt loved. Happy. Safe and warm. Included in every aspect of the proceedings.

Now the vicar—a gifted storyteller—was speaking, laying out the homily, talking about God and heaven and mysteries beyond human comprehension.

The little boy—the future U.S. Navy admiral—wasn't hearing every word, but the words were affecting him all the same—flowing over him, swirling around him, like a delicious summer breeze.

He felt alert. Attentive. Aware.

And in this state of heightened awareness, young Wesley's eyes fell on something curious.

The line.

The line that ran along the floor, through the center of the church.

Wesley Houghton had seen the line before, of course. Most everyone who entered the church saw it.

The line was a thin strip of metal—zinc, Wesley's father had told him—inset in the stone. It began at the elegant font in the garden in front of the church, and ran, along the ground, through the heart of the great structure.

The zinc line was a subtle and clever architectural element. A graceful means of connecting the spaces within the sanctuary: narthex and nave, chancel and altar.

At the back wall of the church, the zinc line left the floor and moved straight up the wall and into the great metal cross that towered over the apse.

The line was a thread. A connector. It tied everything together and it was always there.

Tonight though, something was different.

Tonight, the line was alive.

Little Wesley Houghton stared. Certain that the entire congregation was seeing what he was seeing, and marveling at their calm. Their restraint.

The line was glowing, burning brighter by the moment, thrumming with energy.

No one spoke. No one reacted.

The vicar told his story. The crowd listened and nodded. Smiled and laughed.

No one paid the line the slightest heed.

Am I the only seeing this? little Wesley Houghton wondered.

The notion thrilled and terrified him at the same time, but he couldn't think about it. Things were happening.

The line was practically on fire now.

The boy turned his head and saw that the light, the glow, the ribbon of diamond-bright radiance, extended from just inside the doors, from the narthex, clear to the cross.

Wesley guessed that the glow actually began at the font outside the building, but he couldn't be sure. The massive oak doors blocked his view.

The line marks a pathway, he thought.

A pathway that leads to…

To…

The vicar spoke confidently about humankind. Man's relationship with God.

And young Wesley had an epiphany. A fleeting look at a shining truth delivered from someplace far away.

Of the epiphany, he would remember nothing. But for an instant, a nanosecond, everything was clear.

The vicar is wrong.

Wrong about God and the universe and our place in it.

It's nothing like what they think. Not even close.

It's better.

The line had become a thread of white flame, so bright the young boy could scarcely stand to look at it.

No one else noticed, so Wesley watched, and waited.

The line marks a pathway.

A bridge.

An opening.

The line will cut through the wall at the back of the church and I'll see what's there.

The wall will fall away and I'll understand.

The wall will fall away and I'll remember.

He could hear music now. Soft, from beyond the wall. Growing stronger. Louder. Music familiar. Transcendent. Achingly beautiful.

Bright as the surface of the sun, the line cut through the sanctuary like a blade.

In a moment I will understand.

Then…

Struggle. Dissonance. Noise.

A jarring, brain-rattling, brutal sound that ruined everything.

Ping...ping...ping...

Like an obscenity the sound assaulted the music from beyond the wall. Jamming it. Desecrating it.

Ping...ping...ping...

Louder now.

The sound hurt Wesley's ears. Shattered his concentration. Worst of all: the sound caused the light to fade. The radiance diminished now as rapidly as it had flared.

The boy felt a visceral pain, as if he'd just been torn from his mother's side. He convulsed and cried out.

The dream stuttered on, and the admiral, dozing in his chair before his computer, writhed and moaned.

"We respectfully request that the sonar be turned off between 2 a.m. and 2 p.m. Pacific standard time, tomorrow."

Admiral Houghton's eyes snapped open, and he gasped. His hands trembled and his heart thumped. Sweat trickled into his eyes and he wiped his forehead with one arm. Blinked.

The priest is right, he thought. *The sonar must be turned off.*

It was a ridiculous notion. Utterly outrageous. Houghton understood this.

A ridiculous notion...An absurd request.

It's also absolutely true.

CHAPTER 55

JOE AND ELLA EXITED PIER 18 on foot and headed north, toward the Pike Place Market and the van. Ella glanced back, in the direction of the *Nimitz*.

"Anyone following us?" Joe asked. He was glad for the swarms of tourists jamming the sidewalk on Alaskan Way.

"No," Ella replied, "but I wouldn't be surprised. The admiral looked kind of stunned. Like no one outside the Navy would know about the sonar installation you mentioned. He seemed fine with the general questions, but when you named an exact site he kinda flipped. Seemed to me, anyway."

Joe took Ella's hand and picked up the pace, guiding her around and through clusters of strolling tourists. It was an unusually gorgeous Fourth of July, and no one, it seemed, was in a hurry. Except for the two of them. "How *could* you know about the sonar?" Ella asked. "Mia, right? But how could Mia know? The names, I mean? The English words? Kanaga—whatever that is?"

They wound their way through a huge happy crowd wearing identical T-shirts with Benton Family Reunion printed on the back.

Joe said, "The guy I mentioned earlier. The old guy Mia knew."

"Yeah?"

"He and Mia spent a lot of time together. Shared a lot of information."

They passed Pier 52 and the ferry terminal, and Ella glanced south one final time to find the *Nimitz* looming over the waterfront still, dominating the shipyards, rising above the container vessels and cranes like a colossal building.

"The guy," said Joe, "whoever he was, knew the place names. Knew the coastline like his own backyard."

Ella said, "And because he knew that stuff, you know it? How's that work?"

Joe stopped walking and his gaze froze on the waterfront structures ahead: Pier 55 and the Ferris wheel beyond. Ella clutched his hand.

Joe stared, like he might drill a hole in the buildings with his eyes. People flowed around them as if they were statues.

"It's real time," Joe whispered.

"Huh? What's real time?"

"Like a three-way call," said Joe, "only without the phones." He looked at Ella. "Dieturlund is alive."

"Who's Dieturlund?"

Joe laughed. He'd never heard the name before either. He knew it now, though, and it felt as familiar as a friend's name.

"Will Dieturlund. The man who knew Mia."

Ella nodded. "Okay, but what's real time?"

"I thought before that all of this information was old, but I misunderstood," Joe said. "Mia has been talking to him—to Dieturlund—or at least accessing his memories, to help her communicate with me...And because I'm connected to her, I guess I'm also connected to him."

Joe stared at the pier. Stared so intently passing tourists followed his gaze.

Joe said, "I can see where he lives. It's like a hospital. A rest home, maybe." He looked at Ella. "He's not well."

They started walking again, toward the Seattle Aquarium. Ella tried to conjure an image of the mystery man in his hospital room, but got nowhere.

"Is Dieturlund aware of you?" she asked.

Joe shrugged. "Don't know. Maybe. It's not that clear. The thoughts come in fits and starts. I can't explain it."

Ella nodded. "You seemed a little lost when you were talking to the admiral. Like you were reading a defective teleprompter."

Joe laughed. "Weirdest thing I've ever experienced, that's for sure. Memories keep popping into my mind. Thoughts. Only, they're not mine. Not at all."

They stepped into the street to get around a line of people ordering food at a waterfront grill. Kept moving.

"Last night," said Joe, "all I knew was that Mia needed my help. This morning I realized that the help had to do with sound. A sound Mia can't control."

"The Navy sonar," said Ella.

Joe nodded. "I can hear it in my head right now. Horrible. Drive me crazy if I had to listen to it all the time.

"Once I figured out the problem was sound—sonar—it seemed the Navy was the solution."

"So, Houghton," said Ella.

"Yeah. If Seafair wasn't happening, I would've gone to the base in Bremerton. Talked to an officer there."

"Where's Kanaga?"

They were nearing the aquarium and the Market Stairs—the steps leading up to the Pike Place Market.

"Alaska," said Joe. "Aleutians. Kanaga came to me at the last moment. One second all I knew was that it was sonar causing the problems. Then I had a name. I could see it. Could see the chart, like it was in front of me."

Joe took Ella's hand, and they crossed Alaskan Way, to the base of the steps. Tourists were everywhere.

"What does 'critical cetacean communication' mean?" Ella asked. "What does Mia need to communicate?"

Joe led Ella to a wooden bench adjacent to the broad climb, and they sat. Joe's face was pale.

"She needs to send a message."

Ella thought about it, fascinated. "A message to whom?"

"Don't know."

"What kind of a message?"

Joe laughed. "Don't know that either. Mia's not telling me. Or can't."

"But it's a moot point," said Ella. "It doesn't really matter what Mia wants, does it?"

Joe said nothing.

"I mean, Houghton's not gonna just shut down the sonar thing because you asked him to, right?"

"Maybe not."

"Why would he? We're nothing to him—except troublemakers."

"He might believe he needs to shut the sonar off."

"Why would he believe that?"

"I believed I had a daughter," said Joe.

Ella said, "Yes, because you touched Mia."

"Yeah," said Joe. "And Houghton touched me. And when he did, there was a little jolt. Electricity. Something passed from Mia to the admiral. Through me.

"Maybe it'll be enough. I wasn't asking the world, after all. Just for one sonar installation—a test site—to be shut down for a few hours.

"In any case, Mia believes the sonar will be shut down. She's moving for open water now. Moving fast, toward the straits. Getting into the clear so she can send her message."

Ella clutched Joe's hand and stared into the crowd surging around them. She looked frightened.

"What?" Joe asked gently. "Baby, what's wrong?"

Ella laughed. "I met Mia last night. Saw her with my own eyes, okay? Touched her. Connected with her in a way I can't even begin to comprehend.

"But if that hadn't happened, Joe, if it was you just telling me this stuff...I mean, it's insane. No one's going to believe it."

She shook her head. "But we're going to have to make them believe it, because we have to go to the police."

Joe made no reply.

"You said we would," said Ella. "After you helped Mia."

"I know."

"So?"

"We will."

"When?"

Joe sighed. "Ella—"

"We have to go to the police now, Joe. Explain about the *Nimitz*. About Beck. Explain why we started a fire and fled the scene. About the bugs in my car, and your house—and how they've been following us."

She touched Joe's face. "We need to tell them what he did to you—on his boat."

"They'll never buy it."

"They will. You aren't the only one this happened to, remember? The police will investigate and see what's true."

They sat quietly until at last Ella spoke again.

"Beck is evil."

Joe sighed and put a thought in the front of his mind.

Ella?

What?

We can't go to the police. Not yet.

Ella turned and faced Joe. He looked tired. Drained.

Out loud, Joe said, "It would take a lot of time, right? Going there? Explaining everything…several times. Waiting for them to verify what we're saying, or, the parts they can verify."

Ella shrugged. "Yeah. It'll take time. They might arrest us. Probably will."

I don't know if I have much time.

Why? What do you mean?

I told you about the other guys—the guys Mia contacted before me?

Yeah?

I didn't know what happened to them. But now I do. I can see their faces.

Ella waited.

They're dead, Ella. All of them.

Joe felt Ella's emotions rolling toward him like a tidal wave. Too many thoughts and feelings to process. He squeezed her hand and continued. *Mia is changing. At first she was all rage and grief. In agony over the loss of her child. She blamed people. All people. But it's different now. Now I sense compassion. Love.*

Ella replied, *She's gotten to know you.*

Joe smiled wanly. *And now she's worried for me. Because of what happened with the other men. With you, the contact was light. Easy. She was easy with you—because of me.*

Joe held Ella's gaze. *For me, and the guys before me, touching Mia was like touching lightning—only with a delayed reaction.*

Ella spoke out loud again, fighting to keep her voice steady. "So let's skip the police and go straight to the doctor. Find out how to stop what's happening."

"Doctors can't help," Joe said flatly. "Insanity and neural collapse by cetacean contact is not something they teach in med school."

Ella looked at him, tears clouding her eyes now.

"You don't know they can't help," she said angrily. "You don't know that. What are you saying? You can't just give up. We have to try."

Joe slid closer and put his hands on Ella's waist. His eyes were full of tears now, too. Passersby stared, but Joe and Ella paid no attention. "I'm *not* giving up," said Joe. "I plan to fight like hell. But not at some hospital. At least not yet."

Ella waited.

"There's one guy who actually understands this. Who touched Mia and lived. He might actually be able to help."

Ella thought about it. "Dieturlund?"

"Yeah. He had multiple contacts with Mia and survived. I need to talk to him. Ask him what to do. What the secret is."

Ella said nothing, but Joe could tell she wasn't convinced.

"If we go to the police now, we'll be delayed hours," he said. "Days, maybe. If we go to the hospital—more delays. I want to try Dieturlund first."

She sighed. "He's in Seattle?"

Joe considered it. Smiled. There was a new image in his mind now: a retirement home with a sign out front, and a distinctive city skyline in the distance. It was a memory of a building he'd never seen or visited. Not the first time such a memory had just popped into his mind, but the experience was jarring all the same. Startling. He didn't think he'd ever get used to it. The retirement home "memory" had just appeared, as clear and bright as if he were standing there in person.

"He's in Bellingham," said Joe. "A place called The Willows. On Seventh."

CHAPTER 56

THE SEATTLE OFFICE OF THE FBI is in the federal building at Third Avenue and Spring Street, four blocks from the waterfront. It took thirty minutes from the time Admiral Houghton's lieutenant phoned for agents Roger Chen and Sandra Timmons to wade through the holiday crowds and reach the *Nimitz*.

Now they were on the ship's bridge, reviewing security footage of Joe and Ella. Seattle Police were on hand as well.

"The sonar's not highly classified," Lieutenant Ollie Pedersen told them. "But there's no way a private citizen should know about it."

Agent Timmons studied her tablet computer. Joe and Ella had used their real names with Admiral Houghton and mentioned that they were from Bremerton. A simple Google search brought up pictures, links to the St. Anthony's website, and news reports concerning the events in the San Juans. A bit more digging, and Chen and Timmons found a link to the Breakwater YouTube video, news pieces about the alleged Wendy's poisonings, and a police report about the fire at Joe's house.

"The vicar's had an interesting week," said Chen. "A very interesting week."

CHAPTER 57

THE NINE-PASSENGER BELL 412 registered to Erebus Industries touched down at Goshen Field, eight miles northwest of downtown Bellingham, at 4:13 p.m.

Orondo Ring, Sheldon Beck, and two of Beck's men—Drucker and Knox—emerged from the helicopter. Beck told the flight crew to stay put and be ready for a quick departure.

Despite Ring's optimism, Beck wasn't convinced they'd be spending much time with Dieturlund. The man was old, frail and in an uncertain mental state. There was no guarantee he'd talk to them. And if he did talk, there was no guarantee he'd say anything of value.

A taxi waiting outside the miniscule terminal took them four miles, to a senior living facility called The Willows, in an older, well-manicured neighborhood of Bellingham.

There was a small high-end retail strip across the street, and solid 1960s-era houses with well-maintained yards on either side. Stately trees and flower beds.

Beck paid the cabdriver and told Drucker and Knox to wait in the Starbucks across the street. Then he and Ring headed for the entrance to The Willows.

The sign at the door read The Willows. A Home for Active Seniors, and the lobby was big and bright and airy. It felt to Beck like a cross between a hospital and a Hampton Inn. Nice carpeting and fresh-cut flowers, on the one hand. Fluorescent lights and Muzak on the other. The air smelled vaguely antiseptic.

A twentysomething attendant sat at the front desk, typing on a laptop. He shut his computer halfway and removed one earbud as Beck and Ring approached.

"Help you?"

Beck said, "We're here to see Will Dieturlund. What room is he in?"

The kid frowned. "You guys family?"

"Admirers of his work," said Beck. "My name is Stan Evans and this," he said, pointing at Ring, "is Lars Hillcraft."

The kid shook his head doubtfully. "Dr. D. doesn't usually see visitors. And plus, this is his naptime. You might want to come back in a couple hours."

"He's expecting us," Beck lied. "We spoke with him yesterday."

The kid looked skeptical, then shrugged. "Apartment J," he said. "Far right hallway."

They made their way down a long corridor, past a kitchen where an ancient woman was methodically preparing a snack.

Ring said, "Lars Hillcraft? Is that me?"

Beck nodded. "In case we piss Dieturlund off and he reports us."

"Stan Evans and Lars Hillcraft?"

Beck shrugged. "Best I could do on the spur of the moment."

They found Apartment J and Beck knocked softly.

No reply.

He knocked louder.

No response.

He tried the knob and found the door unlocked.

"Professor Dieturlund?" he called, sticking his head inside. "Hello?"

A husky voice answered. "Who's there?"

"Visitors," said Beck, easing the door open and stepping inside. "Friends."

"You're not my friends," said Dieturlund.

He was seated at a table next to a window, a gaunt, fragile-looking man with wispy white hair, age spots, and skin as thin as rice paper. Ring had said that Dieturlund was fifty-eight, but Beck figured the man before them could easily pass for seventy-eight, or older.

Beck proceeded through the small foyer and deeper into the efficiency apartment. Ring followed.

The air was stagnant. Stale. The room arranged more like an office than a residence. A messy, run-down office.

Stuff was everywhere. Piles of yellowing paper. Files. Official-looking reports. Professional journals. There were dented filing cabinets festooned with tattered *Far Side* cartoons. Graphs and charts and curling Cibachrome prints of whales covered the walls. Images of Northwest coastline.

Ring surveyed the space and imagined some of Dieturlund's graduate students—kids who still believed in the old man or who just felt sorry for him—moving his university office pretty much lock, stock, and barrel to The Willows retirement home.

"We're admirers," said Beck. "We'd like to talk to you about your work."

"That's nice," said Dieturlund, peering at Beck through nearly opaque glasses. "Thing is, I don't want to talk to you."

"We're fans of your research," said Ring.

"Bullshit," replied Dieturlund. "Who the hell let you in, anyway? That dumb-ass kid at the front?"

Ring pushed his way past Beck and said, "Professor Dieturlund, my name's Lars Hillcraft."

"So?"

"And this is my friend, Stan Evans. We were kayaking in the San Juans, sir, five days ago. We had an encounter with a pod of orca whales."

Dieturlund just stared at Ring through his Coke-bottle lenses.

"I touched one of the whales," said Ring. "Or rather, she touched me. Came up under my boat. I couldn't avoid her. The contact only lasted a few seconds, but I've had a hell of a time since then."

Dieturlund squinted at him. "What's a hell of a time?"

Ring stepped farther into the tiny apartment. There were no chairs, other than the battered leather high-back Dieturlund was sitting in, so Ring sat, awkwardly, on the foot of Dieturlund's twin bed.

"Bizarre dreams," said Ring. "Hallucinations. Nightmares. The morning after the encounter, I dreamed I had a little girl, which I don't. The dream, or hallucination, was very convincing. The girl had just died. I was devastated."

"It's true," said Beck. "He was out of his mind."

Ring said, "Stan was in another kayak a few feet away. But the whale didn't touch him."

Dieturlund looked from one to the other but said nothing.

Ring said, "My friend Stan here has been trying to help me make sense of my hallucinations. We started reading. Talking to people. A ranger told us the pod we encountered consisted of transient orcas. And then we read about your work with transients."

Dieturlund folded his hands in his lap. Sighed. Beck didn't know what to make of his body language.

Ring said, "The nightmares about the little girl faded, but then I started dreaming about something else."

Dieturlund narrowed his gaze as Ring said, "Tunnels."

The old man's jaw quivered. His body tensed, and he raised a trembling hand to his glasses.

"Vast undersea tunnels," said Ring. "Or chambers. Swaying in the current. Huge things. In my dream, I'm swimming toward one of the tunnels. It's dark all around me—because I'm so deep underwater. But the tunnel has its own illumination. A sort of phosphorescence. The entire fragile structure is moving with the sea, undulating gently, like a jellyfish. Glowing with its own inner light."

Dieturlund made no reply. Just kept his hands folded and his mouth shut.

Beck said, "So that's why we're here, Professor Dieturlund. We're hoping you can shed some light on"—he turned to Ring and abruptly forgot the alias he'd given him—"my friend's experience."

Dieturlund sighed again, leaned forward in his chair, and plucked a white grease pencil off a low table littered with scientific journals. He stared at the pencil and turned it slowly in his hands, this way and that. Beck imagined he was thinking, preparing to speak. But Dieturlund remained silent.

Beck and Ring exchanged glances.

"I know my story is 'out there,'" said Ring, "but I swear it's the truth."

Dieturlund lifted his head. Looked Ring in the eye. "I believe the story."

Ring smiled. "You do?"

"Yes. I just don't believe it happened to you."

Dieturlund lowered his head and resumed his deep contemplation of the grease pencil. He turned it slowly in his hands, this way and that, breathing noisily.

Beck could see the red emergency pendant Dieturlund wore on a tether around his neck—like a key fob with a single button in the middle. Push the button and help would come.

Beck guessed most every resident at The Willows wore such a device. He also guessed he could jump Dieturlund before the old man so much as lifted his hand. Rip the tether off his neck and make him talk.

It would be easy, but Beck wasn't sure it was worth it. He sighed. He'd had enough. The room felt claustrophobic. Stifling. There was a big window looking west, toward the San Juans and the Straits, but it was sealed shut.

Beck's headache suddenly resumed. Like he'd flipped a switch. And his temper flared. In a moment he'd either leave, or step forward and slap the professor around.

Ring said, "I'm sorry you doubt my veracity, professor. I only wanted to get your advice. I thought—"

"You can't follow her," Dieturlund said quietly.

Beck laughed, "Follow who, old man?"

Dieturlund kept his eyes on Ring. "It won't work. Can't be done."

Beck said, "What won't work?" He turned to Ring. "What the hell's he talking about?"

Ring waved Beck quiet and addressed Dieturlund again, respectfully. Softly.

"Where's she going, professor?"

Dieturlund said nothing.

"Where do the tunnels lead?"

"Away."

"Away where?"

"Away from here."

Ring stared at the old man in awe and nodded slowly. "Fascinating," he said, as if he suddenly understood things perfectly.

"*What's* fascinating?" demanded Beck.

Ring ignored him. "Please. Professor. I'm a scientist myself. Like you. I just want to understand. Where do the tunnels lead?"

Dieturlund turned his head slightly, as if acknowledging the ring of a phone in the next room.

"It's under way," he whispered. "In motion. Almost complete. You cannot follow."

"Where do the tunnels lead?" Ring asked.

Dieturlund gazed at nothing out the window.

Ring tried again. "Why does she want to leave?"

The question seemed to rouse the old man. "Why?" he laughed. "*Why?*" He seemed to find the question hilarious. He chuckled and chortled until his laugh became a labored wheeze.

He recovered at last and focused on Ring once more, his voice suddenly cold and hard and deadly serious. "She's found a way out. An escape. Why on earth would she ever stay?"

"I don't understand," said Ring.

Dieturlund sounded incredulous. "Wouldn't you want to leave your house if someone was pumping sewage in through the window?"

"Why does she want to leave? Why do they *all* want to leave?" He leaned forward, trembling now. "There's a shit pile of plastic debris the size of Texas floating in the middle of the Pacific Ocean. Another like it in the Atlantic. Oceans worldwide are acidifying. Coral reefs dying, fish stocks plummeting because we can't control ourselves. The fish and mammals that do remain—their tissues are full of PCBs and dioxins from pesticides and other chemicals. And orcas are at the pinnacle of the food chain. Which means they have the highest concentration of toxic crap in their systems."

Dieturlund was on a roll, and Ring made no attempt to stop him.

"Did you know, Mr. Hillcraft—or whatever the hell your real name is—that orca whales' bodies are so loaded with PCBs and heavy metals that when an orca dies and washes up on the beach it's considered toxic waste? They have to call a hazmat team to dispose of the corpse!

"Why does she want to leave?" he laughed. "My goodness, I can't imagine."

Beck squirmed. He hated environmentalists, and Dieturlund's rant was compounding his headache.

Ring said, "Where's she going, professor?"

"Where you can't find her."

Beck grunted. "Jesus Christ, what the fuck is he going on about?"

Ring waved Beck off again and kept his eyes on Dieturlund. "Why do you think we're lying?"

"I don't *think* you're lying. I *know* you're lying."

Ring sat studying the old man. After a minute he said, "They're social animals, aren't they, professor? Above all else, they're social creatures. Isn't that right?"

Dieturlund glared at Ring.

"T-197, or Mia, as you call her, will want to get her entire pod through. More likely, her entire extended clan. Every last individual. Wouldn't you say?"

Dieturlund kept his mouth shut.

Ring kept his focus on Dieturlund. "If one of Mia's relations were delayed somehow—"

"Get the hell out of here!" Dieturlund shouted, rising to his feet. "Before I call the police!"

Beck and Ring made for the exit in the lobby.

"What the hell was that all about?" Beck asked. "Why was he so upset?"

"Hit a nerve," said Ring.

They stopped on the sidewalk outside, waiting for Knox and Drucker to rejoin them.

Ring turned toward the sign for The Willows, and Beck followed his gaze.

"Stanton will come here," Ring said softly. "Or try to."

Beck made no reply.

"Stanton and Mia are in touch. And Mia and Professor Dieturlund are in touch. It stands to reason that Stanton and Dieturlund are in contact as well."

Beck raised an eyebrow. "You mean, telepathically?"

Ring nodded.

"Why would Stanton come here?"

"For help. It's a fair bet he knows about our divers and the gillnetter. Knows they died after touching Mia. If that's the case, he's probably worried about his own chances and wondering how it is that Dieturlund is still alive. He'll come looking for answers."

Knox and Drucker crossed the street, and Beck waited until they were close. Spoke to them quietly. "You're staying put. Want you to keep an eye on the entrance. If Stanton and the girl show up, let them visit the old man and then grab them when they come out."

Knox nodded. Drucker said, "Okay."

Beck said, "You'll need a vehicle."

"We'll find something," Knox replied.

Beck said, "Collins is poking around Bremerton, looking for Stanton there. Tell him to forget that and come here ASAP. You might need some help."

"So what did you say that made Dieturlund so upset?" Beck asked during the cab ride back to the heliport.

Ring shrugged. "I implied that there may be a way to keep Mia from leaving. Or at least to delay her departure long enough for us to go, too."

Beck stared at him, feeling lost once again. He massaged his temples and struggled to keep his voice even.

"Delay her departure to where?"

"To where the tunnels lead."

"Which is where?"

"Unknown."

Beck muttered a stream of profane words, but Ring paid no attention.

"We may know soon enough, though," said Ring, studying his smartphone. "Stanton's final thought capture just finished downloading."

CHAPTER 58

THE BELL 412 WAITED on the tarmac beyond the terminal, its engines already screaming.

"Restroom," said Beck, as he veered toward the building. "You go ahead."

The door to the restroom stood open, and a yellow plastic sandwich board sat on the threshold, Caution, Wet Floors printed on both sides.

Beck made for the nearest urinal. He saw a cleaning lady standing in the open door of the far toilet stall, back to the room, mopping the floor.

Beck didn't care. He needed to take a leak. Bad. He peed and peed, relishing the sensation of relief.

Mind full of thoughts, Beck was barely aware of his environment: the buzz of the fluorescents, the juicy slosh of the cleaning lady's mop as it slid across the tile floor.

But then another sound brought him out of his daydream. An out-of-place sound. A sound that prickled the hair on the back of his neck and sent a tiny instantaneous jolt of adrenaline down his spine.

The sound was a low grunt, followed by a fleshy wheeze.

Feet still planted firmly before the urinal, Beck turned his head and caught a whiff of a gag-inducing stench. A horrible, breathtaking stink. The unmistakable odor of moldering, gangrenous flesh.

Beck twisted his upper body further and looked in the mirror.

The cleaning lady was still in the far stall, her sturdy back still to the room. He watched her dunk her mop robotically into her bucket. Draw it back out.

There was no one else around.

Then the cleaning lady pivoted, and Beck forgot where he was and what he was doing. A gurgling moan escaped his throat.

It wasn't a cleaning lady. It was Navarro. The nurse from the *Northern Mercy*, the nurse who'd tried to warn Stanton.

She was dead. Obviously.

Yet she was here, standing in the stall, ribbons of flesh hanging loosely from her skull, yellow pus oozing from great cavernous black holes in her face and neck.

Her eyes were shut—the lids pallid and sagging.

Beck's combat-trained mind attempted a split-second analysis of the situation. An assessment. An explanation.

There was no explanation. So his brain froze. Stuttered. Lurched and locked up.

Already taken care of, Collins had told him.

Beck hadn't followed up on Navarro's fate. No need.

Already taken care of meant that Collins or one of his men had killed her aboard the *Northern Mercy*: most likely in the middle of the night. Most likely by knocking her unconscious, handcuffing weights to her hands and feet, and throwing her overboard. No muss, no fuss. No evidence. If coworkers asked questions, they'd say she'd gone back to the Philippines—or wherever the hell she'd come from.

Already taken care of.

And yet here she was.

What was left of her.

Navarro's eyes opened, and Beck screamed.

CHAPTER 59

IT WAS LATE AFTERNOON, but the sun was still high and the massive flight deck of the *Nimitz* still full of tourists. In a few hours' time, many of the visitors would be watching fireworks, gasping in amazement as Elliott Bay and downtown Seattle shimmered under a massive barrage launched from nearby Myrtle Edwards Park.

Agent Sandra Timmons had her laptop open and a new folder titled Joseph Stanton on-screen. The folder was filling fast with information about Joe and Ella.

"Bremerton Police are saying the fire at Stanton's house was intentionally set," Timmons told her colleague. "And a neighbor saw him leaving the scene with his girlfriend."

Agent Roger Chen shook his head. "Starts his house on fire and then comes straight here and asks about a secret sonar installation."

Pedersen said, "He didn't just ask about it. He demanded we shut it down to allow 'critical cetacean communication.'"

"Which is what?"

Pedersen shrugged. "Whale talk? Cetaceans are whales. I guess he's worried the whales can't talk to one another."

Agent Timmons laughed. "Sounds like somebody's off their meds."

Across the bridge, Admiral Houghton sat at a table, back straight, hands folded, with a faraway look in his eyes. Houghton's junior officers knew their admiral as a vigorous leader constantly in motion—not just keeping up but setting the pace. They were not accustomed to seeing him idle—frozen—as he appeared now.

Agent Chen asked Pedersen, "So *is* the Kanaga array affecting cetacean health?"

The lieutenant shrugged. "Maybe. Who knows? Environmentalists say all our sonar is hazardous to whales. Other marine life. They've been complaining about it for years. But their complaints are general. This Stanton character cited a specific install. A *classified* install. And he asked that it be turned off at a specific time."

Timmons asked, "Why, do you suppose? What good would that do? Who would it help?"

"Beats the hell out of us," Pedersen replied. "Kanaga's a test site where different ships operate towed arrays. It's not like shutting it down would affect national security. It's possible a foreign government is looking to analyze our capabilities, but my hunch is Stanton's a greenie wingnut. He and the girl are part of some fringe animal-rights group, probably. Sea Shepherd or one of those. Some of 'em are violent. Whether Stanton is or not, we'd like to know how he came by the classified intel."

Agent Chen nodded, began collecting his things.

"We're on it. Seattle Police, State Patrol, and NCIS are already in the loop. Kinda crazy with the holiday, but I expect we'll know something soon."

He handed Pedersen a card. "This has our contact info. Call if anything new comes up."

The agents and Pedersen passed Admiral Houghton on their way out. Walked in front of the big man sitting at his table. Ramrod straight, eyes fixed on the window and Elliott Bay beyond, he looked like a statue of a war hero.

Timmons said, "Thank you for your time, sir," as she crossed his line of sight.

The big man breathed. Blinked. Like he was waking from a dream. He looked at Timmons. "Hell of a grip for a priest," he whispered. "Hell of a grip, you know?"

"Yes, sir," she replied.

Pedersen escorted Chen and Timmons to the quarterdeck, and the two agents made their way off the ship. Timmons stared at her smartphone as they walked.

"Bremerton Police are saying the St. Anthony's church van is missing. Someone from the church went to use it this morning and it was gone."

"Stanton have a key?" Chen asked.

Timmons nodded. "One of three people at the church."

Chen said, "Check with the ferries—should be video of the van boarding a Bremerton or Bainbridge boat this morning. Maybe a shot of Stanton behind the wheel, if we're lucky."

"On it," said Timmons.

"And add it to the profile. I want every DOT camera in the state watching for that van."

CHAPTER 60

JOE AND ELLA CLIMBED the broad stairs leading into the heart of the Pike Place Market.

Progress was brutally slow, the stairs jammed with sweaty, noisy, sunburned tourists from every corner of the globe.

Joe took Ella's hand and focused his thoughts on Dieturlund, trying to glean more information from the new "memories" Mia had placed in his head.

He thought and contemplated and analyzed and climbed on, part of the sea of humanity, but also separate from it. In his own little world.

He could see Dieturlund shuffling around his tiny apartment. Bent, bearded, frail. In pain.

Lonely.

Dieturlund: Tenured professor. Department chair. Beloved mentor. Recipient of countless grants and awards.

Dieturlund: Cetacean researcher—one of the finest and most respected in the country—until—

Until he went off the deep end.

Until the embarrassing theories and nonsensical white papers. Until the personality shifts and volatile mood swings.

Dieturlund: Alone now. Subject of pity. A wasted old man suffering from what ex-colleagues whispered was early-onset dementia.

Joe could *see* Dieturlund's room. *Feel* its stale, stagnant air. Depressing.

He focused harder. Tried to see more.

Then his heart skipped a beat, and he had a sudden, terrifying epiphany. The hair on the back of his neck prickled. He squeezed

Ella's hand, and if he could've stopped walking he would have, but the crowd enveloping them—surging up behind them—had a life of its own.

"Don't let go of me," he whispered.

Ella nodded.

They climbed on, Joe's heart thrumming in his chest.

Someone's watching.

He'd experienced a similar feeling, from time to time in his life, believing he was alone in a room and then suddenly realizing someone else was there.

Someone's watching.

It was like that now, except…

Now the "someone" was in his head.

Not a thought or a message or a telepathic transmission—he was getting used to those.

Some one.

A foreign consciousness. Another mind. An individual, standing in the shadows. Waiting respectfully.

Waiting to be noticed.

The realization gave him the heebie-jeebies.

He squeezed Ella's hand tighter, mastered his fear, and faced the other presence.

It was Mia.

On the deck of the *Nimitz*, Mia had arrived in Joe's head unannounced. Without warning. At the last possible second.

Joe remembered. He'd been standing there, staring at the admiral, wondering what to say, when the lights flickered.

Neurons misfired. Thoughts stuttered. Ceased.

Like a massive solar flare blasting the power grid, Mia had entered his head—knocked the entity known as Joe Stanton momentarily off-line and slid into position behind his eyes, seizing control of his mind and body.

Through Joe's eyes, Mia had peered out, perceiving Admiral Houghton, the issue of the Kanaga sonar, and the entire situation as if it were some sort of vast combination lock, with dials waiting to be turned just so.

Click, and it was done: the name of the sonar array and precise coordinates placed front and center in Joe's neo-cortex. Images of the proper chart. A specific demand for Joe's mouth to speak.

"We respectfully request that the sonar be turned off between 2 a.m. and 2 p.m. Pacific standard time, tomorrow."

Like some fantastical supercomputer, Mia had lifted the relevant information from Dieturlund's head, placed it into Joe's, and simultaneously delivered a request—a command—to the admiral, through Joe's handshake.

Turn off the Kanaga sonar. The Kanaga sonar must be turned off.

She'd come and gone, in and out, arriving in the nick of time, and—having solved the emergency—departing an instant later.

That's what Joe had thought. But now he realized the truth.

She was still here: With him. Inside him. Awake and aware and watching. Quietly. Respectfully.

Hello, Mia.

Hello, Stan-ton.

The crowd continued uphill, a river flowing against gravity, carrying Joe along. Joe continued climbing. Feet moving, knees bending, body on autopilot.

The feeling that there was another living, breathing consciousness in his head, observing him, was all he could think about.

Relax, Mia told him. *We do this all the time.*

Do what all the time? Joe wondered to himself. *Inhabit another's mind? Look out at the world through another's eyes?*

He posed a question: *How can you be here if your body is somewhere else? In the ocean, far away?*

Joe heard laughter. Mia laughing. Not in a mocking way. This laughter was gentle. Benign. Full of joy.

I'm in both places at once. Do you see?

And then it was as if a small window opened in his mind.

Relax.

He was still on the stairs. Still climbing up to the Market. Still holding Ella's hand. Part of the Fourth of July crowd. But now—out of the corner of his eye—he could see…

A mountain of blue. Vast. Endless, dark underneath. Shapes around him, huge and powerful. And reflections: sunlight splintering across a surface at once familiar and alien.

It was too much to process. It was sensory overload. He didn't know what to look at. Didn't know what he was seeing.

May we trade a moment? she asked. A question posed in that same laughing, childlike voice.

And Joe understood. Or believed he did.

He turned to Ella. "She wants to trade places with me. Wants to see."

Ella stared at him, confused.

"Mia wants to see this place. Just for a minute, she'll be here, in my body, and I'll be far away."

Ella was shaking her head, eyes getting wider by the second. "What? No."

"Hold on to me," he said. "Guide me. Don't let go of my hand. I'll be right back."

Ella tried to protest.

Too late.

"Humans live largely inside their heads, from which they tell the rest of their bodies what to do, except for occasional passionate moments when the tables are turned. Animals, on the other hand, do not seem compartmentalized that way. Everything they are is in every move they make."

-Frederick Buechner

CHAPTER 61

JOE BLINKED, and when his eyes opened again, he screamed, or tried to. What became of the sound—if there was any sound—was a mystery he had no time to contemplate.

He was on top of a mountain—the mountain he had perceived moments before—moving now, diving, leaping headlong into space.

Into oblivion, his mind told him. *Death.*

This is where I die.

Everything he'd ever experienced—every molecule of muscle memory—told him that no other outcome was possible.

The body he now inhabited was huge—he realized that immediately—and heavy. Immensely heavy.

And it was hurtling off a cliff. Flying off a cliff. Shooting forward with stupendous velocity and momentum.

Joe's homo sapien brain registered the instant as a perverse physics equation: mass plus inertia equals death.

This is where I die.

And then his perception clarified slightly, and he screamed again. A scream of joy this time.

This mountain is alive.

This mountain is a wave.
This mountain is liquid. Fluid. Water. And water is where I live!
Understanding unfurled in his mind then like the seascape opening wide in every direction.

The body he was in—Mia's body—dolphined through the waves and took a breath. An enormous breath, a hundred times the amount of air his human lungs breathed during the most extreme exertion.

He looked around. Tried to process everything at once, seize the moment, knowing it wouldn't last. Couldn't last.

A moment is all I have.

He shoved everything else aside—cares, fears, worries—and took the helm of the body he was in, the creature he had temporarily become.

What an extraordinary creature it was.

Fast. Agile. Immensely, insanely powerful.

He felt an electric jolt as his, or rather, Mia's, tail fluke came down, driving her body forward—hurling it forward—like an afterburner catapulting a fighter jet—pectorals steering, dorsal fin slicing the water like a blade. A rush of speed that sent chills skittering along his spine like perfectly skipped stones.

Extraordinary.

Joe laughed. He'd always been a good swimmer. A strong swimmer. Swam for his high school team all four years and made varsity, no problem.

What a joke.

Calling what a human—any human—did in the water "swimming" was laughable. Like calling a chicken's spastic fluttering "flying."

Not the same thing. Not at all.

Joe sensed others around him and realized now that he was swimming in a group. Swimming in formation. He felt the rhythm of the pod, embraced it, and—gazing out through Mia's cetacean, utterly nonhuman eyes—perceived the world, the universe, in an entirely new light.

He was among hunters. Predators. Creatures patient, strategic, and cunning.

Bane of lesser whales, nightmare specter to seals, sea lions and all manner of creatures, the orcas were afraid of nothing. An entire school of great white sharks would stand no chance against one of these individuals.

Hunters? Yes. Apex predators? Definitely.

But Joe saw that the beings arrayed around him were many other things as well. As full of surprises and contradictions as any of their human cousins.

He could feel their minds, bright and inquisitive. Vessels of light illuminating the deep. And he longed for more time.

It was not to be.

Amid the blizzard of stimuli, amid the tsunami of information flooding his mind, a few things about the pack stood out. Facts. Truths that would linger in his memory.

First, there was love. Love all around him. Love tinged with humor, tinged with sadness, tinged with grace. Love deep and profound and ancient. Love between family members. Between mates. Between parent and offspring, young and aged, members of long-separated clans.

Love of Earth, sea, and sky.

The love that connected these creatures—to each other, to place—was palpable. An underlying vibe as steady and constant as a heartbeat.

Something else: he could tell that the whales around him—they all had names, though he didn't know the names, didn't know how to say them—were aware that Mia had gone away. That a foreign mind resided now, momentarily, in her body.

Joe felt the whales closing ranks around him, guiding, observing, shepherding him, until Mia's return.

Good thing, he thought. *Since I have no idea what to do or how to act or how to be, inside this body.*

The body he was in—Mia's body—could see extraordinarily well. Above the waves. Below the waves. Close up and far away.

But visual information was only part of the "seeing" he was experiencing now. Some of the pictures entering his head were of creatures and objects far below, or hundreds of feet to the right or left. Things he could not possibly know about via rods and cones and optic nerves alone.

Halibut on the seafloor. A school of herring hugging the cliffs in the inlet up ahead. Another pod of whales a mile to the right. He could "see" them all. Not vague, murky shapes, but crisp, colorful, spectacularly detailed images. Pictures rich and vibrant.

Sound travels four times faster in the water than in the air—he'd read that somewhere once. Maybe that physical law accounted for the speed with which images registered in his mind.

In any case, thirty million years of evolution had given these creatures gifts and talents humans could not begin to imagine.

Peering out through Mia's eyes, listening for the constant stream of clicks and whistles departing and returning to her body, Joe understood that for the orca there was no gloom, no inky blackness, no crevice or canyon cloaked by distance or depth or turbidity.

He'd heard people say that orcas "echolocate." It was a spectacular understatement. Like saying Michelangelo painted church ceilings.

The whales around him were talking, conversing as they moved, chatting in overlapping phrases—short bursts and long trains of complex-sounding dialogue. A symphony of whistles, clicks, and nanosecond pulses.

A few minutes here and I'll understand what they're saying, Joe thought.

A few minutes swimming with the pod, settling into Mia's head, and it will all come clear.

But he didn't have a few minutes. The clock was ticking. The trade couldn't last.

Joe focused on the conversation, the symphony coming at him from all sides. Let it flow over him. Through him.

Like listening to space aliens, he thought.

Incomprehensible.

No.

Wait.

The conversation resolved slightly, like a picture coming slowly into focus. He couldn't fully understand it yet, but the gist was clear.

They're saying good-bye.

The revelation surprised him.

They're saying good-bye, and they're full of sadness.

He let the conversation flow, let it swirl around in his mind.

The pod swam on.

They're saying good-bye to this place. Grieving for all the places they've ever been.

There was a finality about their "words," their phrases, that touched his heart. Broke his heart.

He realized something else.
It isn't speech I'm hearing.
It's song.
He listened.

It was true. The pod was singing. Singing a prayer. Singing together. Not just this group but all of the whales within a hundred miles.

All of them.

He listened. Tried to understand. Swam on.

Strange images filled his mind, images conveyed, or conjured, by the song itself.

This is the land and sea as it was, he thought, looking ahead and scanning the shoreline as the pod rolled forward.

This is the same place we're swimming through as it was ages and epochs ago, when the sea was healthy and brimming with life. When salmon choked the rivers and orcas numbered in the tens of thousands.

Where earlier he'd glimpsed lobotomized hillsides—shoreline eviscerated by clear-cuts, he saw now lush ancient forest and waterfalls too numerous to count. Streams choked with salmon, flashing like diamonds.

This is how it looked when the planet was healthy. When the sea was healthy. When life was abundant.

The pod swam on, and questions filled Joe's mind.

Did these creatures pass memories intact from one generation to the next? Was this the land and sea as it had actually looked?

He didn't know. There was so much he didn't know.

He marveled at his companions, Mia's kin, traveling with him, all around him; creatures full of light, they seemed.

Full of grace. More like angels than flesh and blood organisms.

And it struck him that they were in touch with mysteries humans no longer even recognized.

It's like a song inside them, a chant. Something we've forgotten.

He longed for more understanding.

The pod swam on. Joe listened. And all at once he discerned another thread in the conversation: a whispered stream paralleling the mournful song, happening at the same time. Words hushed and anxious and frenetic.

The meaning of this second thread crystallized in his mind.

They're excited.

There's something up ahead—not far now—something fantastic. Something calling to them. Calling to them all. Something they cannot wait to see.

He listened. Concentrating on the cacophony washing over him.

It's a destination. A place that will change the world.

And it dawned on Joe—though he was sure it had been there all along—that this was where they were headed now. The goal they were making for with all speed.

He listened, heard the call they were all hearing. A distant echo in the deep. A resonant tone, haunting and somehow familiar, sacred and joyful, nuanced and mysterious. A whisper in the deep, calling their names over and over.

But there was something impeding the call. Blocking it. Limiting its power and magic.

The sonar.

The Kanaga sonar.

A *ping…ping…ping* tainting the call like an obscenity. Tainting everything.

Joe realized then that it wasn't simply that the sonar was polluting the soundscape, or preventing the orcas from hearing the sacred voice—the call coming from someplace miles ahead.

It was more than that. Mia needed to do something. Mia needed to say something, to let others know what was happening. To alert them that the time had come.

This was her role. Her job. Her mission. The task that she had been preparing for all her life.

The time has come. The hour is at hand. Prepare yourself.

And Joe wondered: *Who will she call? Who is the message for?*

The answer formed in his mind as soon as the question was asked.

Everyone.

And Joe felt a shiver travel the length of Mia's great body.

Who are you? he asked his host.

Who is Mia? he asked the beings around him.

He felt them answering, placing the answer in his mind so that he could understand it.

Leader.

Matriarch.

Mia is the Messenger.
The one who knows the words, who knows the song. Who will show us the way.

Messenger for whom? Joe asked. *And what message is she carrying?*

Questions jammed his mind. There was so much he didn't know. So much he wanted to ask.

The pod swam on, but now, in his peripheral vision, Joe could see another place. A jarring panorama that seemed utterly alien at first glance. A place populated with bizarre shapes and strange forms.

And then it dawned on him. He was looking at a human environment. A location he recognized.

It filled his field of vision now, as he slid back into position behind his own eyes and reengaged with his own earthbound body once more.

The Pike Place Market.

CHAPTER 62

JOE SHOOK HIS HEAD like a fighter recovering from a punch and looked around. He was standing next to Ella, facing a wall of fresh produce. Peaches, cherries, heirloom tomatoes.

He noticed two things immediately.

First, Ella was no longer holding his hand, but was instead supporting him around the waist, bearing part of his weight as if he were an injured comrade.

Second, people were staring at them: Tourists. Merchants. Old people. Little kids. Staring at him, specifically. Gawking, actually, as if he were some sort of freak-show attraction.

"What happened?" he asked, turning to Ella. The expression on her face frightened him. She looked panicky.

"Joe? Is that you?"

He stared at her. "Yeah. It's me. What happened?"

"Let's go," she said.

Some of the gawkers were turning away now.

"What happened?" Joe repeated.

Ella let go of his waist, took his hand firmly in hers and led him forward, into the crowd, past the gawkers, toward First Avenue and the St. Anthony's van.

"You were acting like a mental patient," she said at last. "Blank stare. Drooling. Not a new look for the Market, but still—"

"I'm sorry," he said.

They walked.

Mia had vanished from his head.

He could feel her presence still, but not like before. She was far away again. Back in her own body, presumably. Leading her pod. Preparing to send her message—assuming the sonar went off.

And Joe was left with a question that superseded all the others: *Why did she want to trade places with me?*

Because she's curious?

No.

It was more than that.

Mia is the leader of a...

He couldn't find the word.

Migration?

Movement?

Exodus?

Was that the term?

She's the leader.

The leader.

The cog in the heart of the machine. The key that will unlock...

He didn't know what. But that was beside the point.

Mia's the leader. The matriarch.

The Messenger.

So why did she leave? Why trade places with me? Why risk such a thing when she's on the brink of finishing her life's work?

Because she felt curious? Inquisitive? Wanted to see a human environment?

No.

There's another reason. Joe felt sure of this.

She wanted to trade places with me for another reason. A more important reason.

He was absolutely certain of it. And equally certain that he had no idea what the reason was.

CHAPTER 63

IT WASN'T THE GROTESQUE STATE of Navarro's head, or neck or body, that made Beck scream. Not the ribbons of rotting flesh trailing down her limbs, like streamers, or the flaccid muscles and tendons unspooling around her joints, separating from her skeleton.

It was the eyes.

Unlike her skin and muscles and skeleton, the eyes were intact.

The eyes were whole.

The eyes were alive. Bright, fierce, and seeing.

The eyes were looking right at him.

Only, they weren't Navarro's eyes.

These eyes were unlike anything Beck had ever seen before.

The eyes of a beast.

A monster.

The eyes were staring at him in the mirror. Studying him. Appraisingly, like a predator scrutinizing prey.

The eyes flared, brightening like cinders reborn, and Beck felt a stabbing pain in his chest.

He lunged for the exit, pants and belt twisted to one side, falling off his waist, wet with urine.

He shrieked again—something loud and rambling and incoherent—and someone was there. At the door. Coming in. Someone from the tiny airport. A worker in blue coveralls—a mechanic, perhaps—coming to use the men's room.

Beck stumbled into the startled man's arms, face pale, babbling like a baby, gesturing wildly.

The man stepped quickly back, bewildered, and his gaze swung to where Beck was pointing. Beck turned.

There *was* someone standing in the far stall.

A cleaning lady.

Dark skin. Plain features. Hispanic or South American.

A woman. Not Navarro. Not a monstrosity. Just a cleaning lady clutching a mop, looking terrified, wondering what on earth the big man was screaming about and why he was pointing at her. Wondering what she'd done and if she was going to get fired.

Beck gaped, pointed, and struggled to speak. Then he gave it up and shoved his way past the mechanic, pulling his pants up as he stumbled out of the room.

With a loud *bang* he plowed through the terminal's double doors, weaving like a drunk toward the Erebus helicopter waiting outside.

CHAPTER 64

BECK STRAPPED HIMSELF into the seat next to Ring—or tried to.

His hands were shaking so violently he couldn't find the clasps at first. He fumbled and struggled until the harness finally snapped together with a *click*.

Beck's pilot, a man named Jeff Donaldson, turned to confirm that the boss was in his seat, and did a double take.

Beck's face was albino-pale, and he looked like he'd aged ten years in the preceding hour.

Donaldson didn't comment, just turned slowly back around, fiddled with some controls, said a couple of things to his copilot, and they took off.

Ring never so much as glanced at his boss.

Beck stank of urine—the front of his pants were soaked—but Ring was in his own world, tapping away on a laptop while balancing a tablet computer on the armrest, utterly oblivious to both Beck's condition and to the sparkling labyrinth of the Puget Sound opening out below them as the Bell 412 shot forward into the summer haze.

"New developments on *Marauder*," said Ring without turning.

Beck only half heard Ring's words.

He fumbled with a storage compartment in the bulkhead. Removed a metal flask, took a swig, and fell back into his seat, sweating profusely, heart still beating a mile a minute.

Then he lurched forward, dropped the flask, and snatched a barf bag out of a different compartment. Just in time.

Chunks of half-digested food hit the bottom of the bag so hard it looked like it might burst.

Ring's silo of concentration had been broken at last. He looked up—straight ahead—as if trying to get his bearings, then turned toward his boss and recoiled.

"What the hell?" he yelled over the roar of the helicopter. "Are you all right?"

Beck kept his mouth over the barf bag—long tendrils of putrid yellow spittle dangling from his lips and chin—and didn't even attempt to respond.

Ring opened another compartment, found some wet wipes, and handed Beck the case.

Beck grunted, grabbed a handful of wipes, and swabbed his face and neck. He leaned back in his seat again and shut his eyes.

Ring was annoyed by the distraction and disgusted by the smells assaulting him now. Disgusted also by what he'd just seen. Watching Beck, he felt his own stomach flip, and he clutched the armrests of his seat. Then he turned and stared out the window—something he hardly ever did.

Beck sealed the barf bag and set it on the floor.

"What new developments?" Beck whispered, swabbing his face with another wipe and running it over his teeth.

Ring looked at him.

"You said there were new developments on *Marauder*. What are they?"

Ring nodded. "The tunnels are stabilizing. Settling."

Beck said nothing.

"The pulse—the sound signature—was intermittent before. Winking on and off, as if the tunnel locations hadn't been fixed. As if the tunnels couldn't decide where to form."

"And that's different now?"

"Yes. We have three receivers in the Bering Sea. NOAA has hundreds up and down the coast. The sounds are stabilizing, no question about it. NOAA's scientists are buzzing about it. Wondering what it means. Thought it was some sort of transient geothermal activity before. Something organic in origin, maybe. But the pulses are louder now. Settling down.

"NOAA, the Navy, they're paying attention. Still attributing the sounds to natural phenomena but curious at the same time. It's still an internal, arcane discussion, from the chatter I'm seeing, but it won't stay that way much longer."

"So what *does* it mean?"

"That Mia's plan is unfolding. That something's about to happen."

Beck wanted to ask Ring to explain himself but guessed he'd get a complicated, opaque answer, so he didn't bother. He didn't have the strength. Instead he said, "You said *developments*, plural. What else?"

"One of the pulses is different. At least ten times louder than the others. If the tunnel is as big as the sound, it's enormous."

Ring lifted his tablet computer and showed it to Beck. A chart of the southern half of Vancouver Island filled the screen.

"Barclay Sound," said Beck. "Close to shore. Can't be that deep."

"It's not. Most life is near the surface, so few of the chambers will be very deep, once it starts."

Once it starts?

Beck's head ached, from the incident at the airport, from trying to follow Ring's update, from everything.

He said, "I thought the chambers were deep. Thousands of feet."

"Most of them are," said Ring. But they'll float up. Rise in the water column from the bathypelagic zone, where they are now, to the euphotic zone—between three hundred fifty meters and the surface. That's my theory anyway."

Beck said nothing.

"Remember the fibers on the exterior of the chamber? The phosphorescent strands running between the chamber and the seafloor?"

Beck shrugged. "I guess so."

"When it starts, those strands—or tethers, if I'm right—will break and the tunnels will rise. Kind of like hot-air balloons lifting off from the ground. They won't float all the way to the surface. Close, though, because that's where all the life is."

Beck didn't ask Ring how he'd arrived at his theory. "Barclay Sound," he said, instead, "is only a few hours from *Marauder*."

"Yes," said Ring. "My advice is to head there with all speed. If I'm right, we're very close to the end." He hesitated. "Or the beginning, depending on how you want to look at it."

Beck sat quiet, too drained and uncomfortable to focus or think critically. He stared out the window, at the vast, shimmering waterway—the Strait of Juan de Fuca—spread out below them.

He felt calmer. Steadier. But his head still throbbed, and he kept getting whiffs of his own awful smell: sweat mixed with urine mixed with vomit. He couldn't wait to get to *Marauder* and into a shower. He guessed they were thirty to forty minutes away.

Adrenaline gone, Beck felt suddenly very tired.

He settled back in his seat and slowly shut his eyes, then cried out and lurched forward, straining against his harness, vomit rising in his throat once more.

The copilot turned. Ring jumped.

"What is it?" Ring yelled. "What's wrong?"

Beck didn't respond, just sat there facing forward, shaking like a hypothermia victim.

"What happened?" Ring asked.

I saw the eyes again. The eyes living in Navarro's decomposing skull.

Beck thought this, but didn't say it. Didn't have the will or the energy to try to explain it to Ring.

The eyes.

He'd settled back in his seat to rest, to sleep a few minutes. Barely leaned back, and they were there. Clear. Bright. Huge.

Orbs.

Eyes.

Windows to a particularly sick and twisted soul. Liquid and alive and full of fire they were, floating in a molten membrane that made them gleam and glint.

The eyes are with me now.

He could feel the presence—whatever it was—lurking. Waiting.

Waiting for him to lower his guard.

He didn't dare rest again. Not now.

He sat there. Mouth dry. Hands shaking. Trying to think.

The eyes don't belong in Navarro's body. They're not Navarro's eyes.

He could feel the entity—the presence—close at hand. Closing in around him. Enveloping him in a putrid, smothering embrace.

The passenger cabin was empty, save for him and Ring. But *something* else was there. Something else. Something heavy and huge and foul. Something that could think and plan and see inside his head.

I'm losing my mind, Beck thought.

He was a strong man. A fighting man. A man trained to perform and flourish in stressful conditions. He forced himself now to relax. To analyze what was going on.

If Ring was right, Stanton and the gillnetter and the Erebus divers had suffered their breakdowns as a result of physical contact with an orca whale. They'd touched a whale and sometime thereafter begun to hallucinate. To see things that didn't exist.

He, on the other hand, had had no such contact.

Why am I hallucinating? Why am I having a breakdown in parallel with Stanton?

He thought about it.

Maybe it has nothing to do with Stanton. Maybe it's some kind of latent PTSD.

He'd seen plenty of combat in Iraq and Afghanistan, after all. Plenty of mayhem and death. He'd killed dozens of people. Been shot at hundreds of times.

Answers eluded him.

The only thing he knew for sure was that he wasn't going to shut his eyes again. Not here. Not now.

Maybe in my cabin, with the door locked, but not here.

He didn't want to see the eyes again. Eyes that burned. That could see inside him. That knew everything about him.

He wanted to avoid that at all costs.

He sat up straight in his seat and realized that Ring was staring at him. Not working. Not looking at his computers.

That's a first, thought Beck. *Ring idle. Ring staring at something besides a screen. This must be serious.*

"What's going on?" Ring asked. "Are you okay?"

After a long silence he said "Ring, why are we pursuing this?"

Ring didn't respond.

Beck said, "We have a deployment starting soon on the Ivory Coast. A huge deployment. Why did we sidetrack here?"

Ring squinted at him, like he couldn't quite grasp the question, like it was so ridiculous he didn't know how to answer.

"Because we stumbled on something extraordinary. You know. A phenomenon. Something no one's ever seen before."

Beck stared out the window. "A phenomenon?"

"Yes," said Ring. "Something unprecedented."

Beck said without turning, "I can see *you* delaying a deployment for such a thing. But why would *I* do that?"

Ring considered it. "Because I made a compelling argument? Piqued your curiosity?"

Beck said nothing.

Ring's logic was sound, but Beck didn't think it was correct.

In fact he was *positive* it wasn't correct.

Despite his stress and fatigue, he felt lucid. More awake and aware than he had in some time. Adrenaline, perhaps? He didn't know.

Whatever the reason, the facts—the salient elements of his current situation—arranged themselves in his mind now like objects on a table.

I'm a soldier and a businessman.

I like fighting.

I like killing.

I like making money.

Lingering in one place to explore arcane scientific phenomena is not me. Not something Sheldon Beck would do.

Kate was right to question me. To question my motives.

So there it was.

The truth, stark and painful.

I've jeopardized the biggest contract in Erebus history and squandered company resources.

Why?

Why?

He thought about it.

I'm hallucinating. Seeing and feeling things that aren't real.

But maybe the hallucination's not new. Maybe it's been going on for weeks. Maybe I didn't even realize it until now—when it's really bad.

He thought some more.

Did something trigger a breakdown? Am I cracking up?

He tried to puzzle it out. Struggled to focus his mind, then gave up, exhausted.

"What's wrong?" Ring asked again.

"Nothing," Beck lied. "I slept like crap last night and I don't feel well. Not myself."

"Yes, but—"

"I don't want to talk about it."

Ring sighed. Leaned back in his seat.

Beck asked, "Any other news from *Marauder*?"

Ring nodded. "Stanton's final thought capture finished downloading. My team is cataloging it now."

Something about the way Ring said this worried Beck. He didn't sound excited enough.

"Something wrong with the thought capture?" Beck asked.

"No, it's fine. The files are immense. Lots to look at."

"So? What's wrong?"

Ring hesitated, then said, "Phelps and Edelstein want off *Marauder*. They're demanding to be taken ashore. Want to use the Bell as soon as we're back."

Beck sighed. Phelps and Edelstein. Another issue. Another problem to solve. Soon.

"That all? Is anything else wrong?"

"Yes," said Ring.

Beck waited.

"Your father and sister are on *Marauder*. Landed about an hour ago. They're in the War Room now."

Ten minutes later Ring's tablet buzzed with a new message. A message from his lead assistant. He read the message, clicked on the attachment, and felt his heart begin to thump.

The pictures—there were about twenty or so—were poor quality. Crappy resolution. Murky lighting. Indistinct focus. Like snapshots of another galaxy taken through a powerful backyard telescope.

Still, these were the most important images he'd seen yet pertaining to the phenomenon.

The most important by far.

He scrolled through the pictures, examining each one. There wasn't much difference between them. The camera angles were limited. But the meaning was clear, and his pulse quickened.

The tunnels are real. They really do exist.

The images had been taken by a remotely operated underwater vehicle. An Erebus ROV in the Bering Sea, not far from the oil platforms where divers Stahl and Galbreth had encountered the whale. Hydrophones had picked up sounds of a tunnel in the area, and Ring had ordered some of the local crew to travel to the site and send down a probe.

The available ROV wasn't perfect for the job. Wasn't made for work below two thousand meters. That was a problem because the tunnel was on the seafloor, three thousand meters down. Thus the poor image quality. All of the photographs were taken from high overhead. From one thousand meters above the target.

Ring smiled.

The ROV's shortcomings didn't matter. Despite the distance, the tunnel was plainly visible. It dominated every eerie frame: an immense, phosphorescent shape sprawled across the seafloor, big as an ocean liner. Some of the images gave a view inside the structure's gaping, cavernous mouth. It rested there, delicate and fragile-looking, open and undulating, like some sort of extraordinarily exotic, rarely blossoming flower.

The tunnels are real. Joy crept into Ring's always-analytical brain. *The images in Stanton's head, the sounds we've captured—they connect to real structures in the real world.*

He'd believed this for a long time, of course, but now, in his hands, he held proof. Definitive proof.

The helicopter zoomed on and Ring turned to Beck and presented the tablet with both hands. "You need to see this," he said.

CHAPTER 65

TRAFFIC ON I-5 WAS LIGHT, thanks to the holiday, and Joe and Ella made the ninety-mile drive from Seattle to Bellingham in an hour and fifteen minutes.

A DOT camera two miles north of Arlington snapped a picture of the van and license plate, initiating an automated alert. Six minutes later, State Patrol officer Deanna Jacobs, driving south on I-5, spotted the vehicle on an overpass in Bellingham. She radioed the dispatcher, and within minutes, four Bellingham police cruisers were combing nearby streets.

Joe and Ella wound their way through a classy, low-rise retail district festooned with huge American flags and red, white, and blue bunting. Traffic barricades lined the sidewalks, and confetti swirled in the gutters like windblown snow.

Clearly, they were on the parade route, but the festivities had ended hours earlier and now city workers in fluorescent-orange vests outnumbered tourists by at least two to one. It looked to Joe like they had a lot of cleanup left to do.

They stopped at a Subway and ordered dinner. Both were starving and exhausted and well aware they couldn't rest. Not yet, at least. Not until they'd talked to Dieturlund. Assuming they could find him.

Joe hadn't given much thought to what they'd do or where they'd go after Dieturlund. He couldn't guess where they'd be one hour in the future much less one day, or three days, or a week.

Right now it was just one immediate task after the next: Eat. Find Dieturlund. Ask Dieturlund for his advice. For insight into their situation and Joe's condition.

Joe figured if they could accomplish these things—if by some miracle they succeeded and Dieturlund helped them—then they could rest.

Ella waited in line for the sandwiches, and Joe found a table.

He sat, intending to look up the address for The Willows, and was startled to observe his right hand shaking. Trembling noticeably.

He rotated the hand, studied it, and watched it quiver, feeling detached somehow, as if it was someone else's hand he was staring at. Not his own.

He shook his arm. Flexed his fingers. The tremor continued—a steady, constant shiver, as if he were out in the cold somewhere, freezing to death.

He set his iPhone down and tried to steady his right hand with his left. It was shaking, too.

His mouth felt suddenly dry as desert sand, and his heart thrummed in his chest.

What's happening to me?

He glanced at the cash-register line and found Ella looking his way, smiling.

He smiled back. Did his best to effect an easy, relaxed demeanor.

Easy. Everything's okay.

He gripped his phone with his left hand and watched the fingertips of his right dance and skitter involuntarily across the screen. Like he was nervous or hypothermic or deathly afraid. He willed himself to relax.

Steady. Easy. Calm down.

No luck.

He'd known parishioners with Parkinson's. The tremors he was experiencing now seemed similar to what those people lived with—when their medications weren't working. A constant, unrelenting shake, like his hands wouldn't listen to his brain. Couldn't listen.

He gave up trying to make the tremors stop and found the address despite them, though it took twice as long as normal.

Ella carried the sandwiches to the table and they ate, Joe doing his best to conceal his new problem.

Get to Dieturlund. Dieturlund will have answers. No sense making Ella any more worried than she already is.

The food tasted good, and Joe felt better—until the end of the meal, when the room began spinning and his stomach jerked and jumped in his belly. He put both hands flat on the table, stood, and smiled at Ella, burying his fear and alarm—or trying to.

"Restroom," he said. "Be right back."

He walked slowly to the back of the restaurant, the vertigo easing a bit as he moved. His stomach was still a tumultuous mess, though. Getting worse by the moment.

The men's room was occupied, so he went straight into the women's, locked the door, and crumpled in front of the toilet. Just in time. He vomited up his entire dinner, and then some. A violent ejection of solids and liquids that left him gasping— jagged and ragged and shakier than ever.

Get to Dieturlund. Dieturlund will have answers. Dieturlund will explain things, tell me what I need to do.

He hoped it was true.

He washed his face and headed back to the table, forcing himself to smile, to stay steady, to not let Ella see what was wrong.

Three minutes later they were back on the road.

CHAPTER 66

BELLINGHAM POLICE LIEUTENANT Kevin Simms spotted the St. Anthony's van as it entered The Willows parking lot, and got on the radio. Instructions came back fast: Observe. Monitor. Report. Wait for backup and for the FBI team already en route.

Simms parallel-parked his unmarked cruiser near the Starbucks across the street and watched the suspects make their way toward the building. Watched the male suspect stop and stare at the sign. Watched the couple finally head inside, through the front doors.

He wasn't the only witness.

Knox and Drucker were sitting in a stolen Ford F-350 extended cab at the far corner of The Willows lot, where they had a clear view of the entire scene. Like Simms, they waited.

Collins would be joining them soon. Any minute now. Fresh from Bremerton.

Inside The Willows, Joe and Ella made for the front desk.

The twentysomething receptionist was engrossed in Facebook. Typing fast. Expounding, perhaps, on being stuck inside a musty old-folks' home while his friends partied and played in the sunshine. His name badge identified him as Jordan Boutman, Resident Services Assistant.

He looked up to find Ella smiling at him and smiled back. Removed his earbuds.

Ella said, "Hi. We're here to see Dr. Dieturlund."

Jordan said, "Sure. Apartment J." He pointed. "That hall there. Big day for Dr. D."

"What do you mean?"

Jordan shrugged. "Dr. Dieturlund hardly ever gets visitors. But you're the second ones in today."

Ella glanced at Joe. "Do you happen to know who it was that stopped by earlier?"

"Two guys. About an hour ago. Can't remember their names, but they said they were admirers of his work."

Ella saw a monitor on the desk displaying alternating black-and-white video streams: the lobby, the courtyard, the dining hall. She smiled again and said, "Jordan, I'm really curious if it was my…colleague who came by. Would it be possible to check the footage real quick?"

Jordan shrugged again. Smiled at Ella. "Sure. No problem."

It took about thirty seconds for Jordan to rewind the day's footage and find the images Ella wanted to see. He slowed the rewind, went too far, stopped, and hit Play.

For several seconds the screen showed nothing but empty lobby. Then two men appeared in the frame.

"Beck," Ella said, almost to herself. She realized Jordan was watching her.

"It *is* him," she said. "My colleague. He did stop by, just like I thought."

It occurred to her that Beck might still be in the building. Still in Dieturlund's room. "Do you think they might still be here?" she asked, trying to look hopeful.

Jordan shook his head. "Nah. You definitely missed them. Left over an hour ago. Looked like they were kind of in a hurry. Late for something, maybe."

"For that which befalleth the sons of men befalleth the beasts. As the one dieth, so dieth the other. Yea, they all have one breath. All go unto one place; all are of dust, and all return to dust."

-Ecclesiastes, Chapter 3

CHAPTER 67

8:15 P.M. Joe knocked at apartment J.

"Come in," said a husky, tired voice.

Joe entered first, made it a couple of paces into the small foyer, and stopped cold, transfixed.

He'd never met Dieturlund before. Never visited his apartment. Never set foot inside The Willows until this day. And yet he knew the place. Knew the room. Knew the hunched old man in the battered chair. Recognized the maps and charts and pictures on the wall. It was all in his head. Memories of a place, of things, of a man, he'd never, ever seen in person.

Ella squeezed past Joe, into the living area. "Dr. Dieturlund, I'm Ella Tollefson, and this is my friend, Joe Stanton."

Dieturlund gave no reply, not so much as a nod, just stared—first at Ella, then at Joe. The warm light streaming through the windows cast a halo around him, accentuating the papery thinness of his skin.

Dieturlund's gaze lingered on Joe. Intense. Piercing.

The old man's body might be failing, but his eyes remained bright and alive.

Joe had told Ella earlier in the day that he could "see" inside Dieturlund's room. That he felt like he was on a "three-way call" with Mia and Dieturlund. She wondered if Joe and the old guy were communicating via telepathy now. She could detect nothing of the kind in her own mind. Nothing like what she'd experienced on the ferry, when she and Joe had first realized they could read each other's thoughts. If telepathy was happening now, Ella wasn't privy to the conversation.

She waited. Watched.

Dieturlund rose from his chair at last, and—without breaking eye contact with Joe—shuffled forward. He took the young priest's hands in his. Clasped them firmly.

Neither man spoke for more than a minute, and the room grew so quiet Ella could hear the fan whirring inside Dieturlund's computer.

At last the professor, in a hoarse whisper, said, "Mia loves you. Did you know?"

Neither Joe nor Ella spoke.

"Hatred has become love. Rage has turned to compassion. And she is profoundly, deeply grateful. I am also. Please. Sit."

Joe and Ella sat on the end of Dieturlund's bed as he shuffled back to his chair.

He settled and fixed his gaze on Joe once again. Another minute ticked by. Then—a childlike gleam in his eye—he asked, "What was it like? Swimming with them?"

Joe laughed, and his body relaxed. "Fast. Fast and scary. At first. Until I started to see what was going on." He thought about it. "Her strength is beyond anything. The power I felt. Moving through the water."

Dieturlund nodded, wonder in his eyes.

Joe said, "But it was sensory overload, you know? Sights and sounds I barely understood. So much happening. And then it was over. Boom. I wish I'd had more time."

Joe fell silent, and Dieturlund just sat there, on the edge of his chair, like he hoped Joe would continue.

Ella wanted to say something. Wanted to lead the conversation in a different direction entirely. Wanted to get right to the reason they'd traveled to The Willows—to Dieturlund—in the first place: Joe's health. Joe's condition. Joe's prognosis.

She was aware of the new tremor in Joe's hands. She'd seen him struggling with it in the restaurant, trying to hide it from her. Trying to put on a brave face. She'd kept quiet, aware of his desire to get to Dieturlund. But she wouldn't stay silent much longer. She was terrified. Wanted answers.

She couldn't bring herself to interrupt just yet, however. There was something happening between the two men. Something building. A sort of energy flow she could feel.

Joe spoke again, abruptly, sounding surprised by his own words. "They're spiritual creatures."

Dieturlund nodded. Smiled. "Yes."

Joe's gaze shifted to the windows, to some distant point light-years away.

The seconds ticked by.

"They can see into it," Joe said, "can't they? Something, at least. More than we can."

"A great deal more. Yes."

"See into what?" Ella asked.

The old man looked at her, like he'd forgotten she was there. "Why, the mystery, of course."

Ella raised an eyebrow. Started to ask what the heck he was talking about, but Joe spoke first.

"What is the Dream Realm?" He said the name as if it had only just surfaced in his mind. "I heard them talking about it. Mia's family, I mean."

"'Dream Realm' is my term," said Dieturlund. "There's no translation for the song they use to describe it."

"But what *is* it?"

Dieturlund shrugged. "A place. A place in the deep. Far from here. Whether they ever journey there in physical form is a riddle I could not decipher. Regardless, it is there that they meet." He laughed. "A white paper on the idea ended my career. Not that I give a shit."

Joe leaned forward. "But *why* do they go there? I caught a glimpse of it, when I was with the pod, but..." He shook his head, straining to remember. "What is it they find there?"

Dieturlund smiled and looked at the young priest. "Understanding. A peek behind the door, as it were."

It seemed to Ella then that the energy in the room had shifted, coalescing around the old man as he spoke.

"Our forebears knew how to find the Dream Realm," Dieturlund whispered. "How to visit. Look inside. Gain sustenance. A talent we have lost."

He hesitated. "Mia uncovered a secret there, after her baby died. Something sacred. Something old beyond reckoning."

He looked at them. "Something to change the world."

Neither Joe nor Ella spoke.

"Things are in motion now. Whether Mia actually started it, or is merely the bearer of the news, I cannot discern. But change is coming. Assuming she can send her message, say what must be said."

"The sonar," said Joe.

Dieturlund nodded. "Yes. If the sonar goes off—"

"But why is that so important?" said Ella. "If the orca can communicate via thought, why is sonar even an issue?"

"There are many species of whales," Dieturlund replied, "And countless other creatures. A very few of them are telepathic. Very few indeed. Sound is critical. Sound is key. Sound is the way they've communicated for time out of mind.

"Did you know," he said, sounding every bit the college professor, "that before the noise of ships and sonar, whales routinely communicated across vast distances? The low-frequency sounds they emit—in the sixteen to forty-hertz range—can travel twenty five hundred miles or more. Or *could*. In quieter seas."

Joe stepped to a chart on Dieturlund's wall. Big and colorful, it showed the undersea topography of the Pacific. Mountain ranges and valleys, towering peaks and bottomless chasms. A vast swath of the planet most humans know nothing about.

Joe touched the map with his fingers as another "memory" unfurled in his mind.

"The message will begin with her," he said quietly. "But others will repeat it. Carry it far and wide."

Ella said, "*What* message? What does she need to say?"

Joe shook his head in frustration—like he wanted to remember but couldn't manage it. He said, "I don't know."

The room went quiet once more. Completely still save for the sporadic, muffled boom of fireworks outside. In the distance.

The old man's head sagged to his chest, and he shut his eyes. His breathing grew heavy. Joe and Ella exchanged looks.

Has he fallen asleep? Just like that? Now what?

And then they both felt it: a tiny, almost imperceptible jolt, like a mild electric shock.

They froze as a wash of color exploded in their minds. Bursts of reds and greens, violets and yellows, jets of color electric and unstable.

The kaleidoscopic display disintegrated like confetti in the wind, leaving a single, potent image hovering in their brains.

An image.

An object.

A thought, courtesy of Professor Dieturlund.

A tunnel floating in the deep.

Big and bright, the tunnel hovered front and center in Joe's thoughts. In his mind's eye. In Ella's also.

Joe felt his stomach roll again. Felt dizzy. As if he'd stepped too quickly to the edge of a cliff and stared down, then pulled back.

He steadied himself. Took a breath.

It wasn't the strangeness of the image that confounded him, made him feel weightless. Unmoored from reality. Not the bright outline of the cornucopia shape, or the object's stunning clarity.

It was the feeling of déjà vu.

He'd seen this all before. In his dreams. In his subconscious.

"What is that?" Ella asked, her curiosity overriding the strangeness of the situation—the fact that the three of them were sitting in a room, contemplating an image only they could see.

"An escape hatch," Joe replied. "A way out."

This is what it's all about, Joe thought, understanding flowering in his mind, everything coming clear at last. *If the sonar goes off—if Mia sends her message—the tunnels can be completed and the doors will open.*

Joe said, "They're forming all over the world. Tunnels. Passageways. Portals. Whatever you want to call them."

Dieturlund roused himself. Nodded. "That's right. Yes. And once Mia gives the word—assuming she *can* give the word—it will begin. Nothing to stop it after that."

Ella said, "But I don't understand. An escape hatch? What do you mean?"

The tunnel hovering in their thoughts drifted lazily, turning in space so that they were looking now directly into the mouth, over the gently arcing bell.

Shimmering threads of light, fine as spider silk, lined the fluid walls of the structure, receding into infinity.

Joe said, "They'll swim into the tunnel—this one, others like it—and vanish. Disappear from the Earth. Mia will go last."

Ella laughed. Not because she didn't believe what Joe was saying, but because she did. Because the truth was so surprising.

When she'd touched Mia, she had established her own connection with the creature. And though the bond wasn't as potent or powerful as what Joe and Dieturlund felt, it was there. It was real. She didn't understand as completely as the two men—not yet—but she sensed the veracity of Joe's statement, and found the implications alarming.

"You're saying whales—the orcas—will leave."

Dieturlund shook his head. "No, my dear," he said softly. "Not *just* the orcas."

He held Ella's gaze, and when he spoke again, his voice was heavy with sadness. "Not just the orcas. And not just whales. Everything. Everything in the sea that can swim or crawl or walk. Predator and prey. Fish and mammal and invertebrate. Everything. In all of the seas."

The old man's words hung in the air, and Ella gawked at her companions, appalled. Stunned. "But the oceans will be dead."

Dieturlund laughed bitterly, "They're nearly dead now, child. We've seen to that. The oceans are terminally ill. A sickly, diseased mockery of what they used to be."

"Yes, but...leave?" Ella couldn't believe what she was hearing. "What will happen to us? To people?"

"We should have thought of that a long time ago. Shown more restraint. Less hubris."

Ella stared at him. "But they haven't given us a chance! If people knew what was happening—"

Dieturlund scowled. "People *know* what's happening, Ms. Tollefson. The ones in power. The ones who could actually do something. And they haven't lifted a finger." He rose from his chair and jabbed at another huge chart on the wall.

"The oceans are thirty percent more acidic now than they were a half century ago, thanks to climate change. To all the crap we pump into the air. Policy makers know this, and they have computer models that show where we'll be in another two decades, when the acidity is fifty percent or higher. Answer: everything dies in that kind of environment. Everything except for algae, single-celled organisms. They know this and they do nothing!

"What's happening to the oceans, Ms. Tollefson, to the Earth, is rape on an unprecedented scale. I don't blame Mia—I don't blame any of them—for wanting to get the hell out!"

The room went quiet again and the tension faded. The old man shrank back into his chair, looking tired. Worn out.

Ella sat quietly. Joe held her hand.

He said to Dieturlund, "You're worried about something, aren't you? Something to do with Mia's plan."

Dieturlund sighed. Looked away.

"Isn't that right?"

The old man nodded reluctantly. "The two men who were here earlier—"

"Beck," said Joe. "And his cohort."

"They didn't use their real names…"

Joe waited.

The old man sighed miserably. "I fear I told them too much."

Joe said nothing.

"One of the men is a scientist. A very smart man. He understands a great deal. More than I realized at first. I didn't take him seriously."

Joe waited.

Dieturlund shook his head, close to tears. "He's going to try to stop Mia, or interfere somehow. Try to keep the tunnels open so he can exploit them."

"*Could* he do that?"

The old man, his voice full of anguish, replied, "I don't know."

Ella barely heard Joe and Dieturlund's exchange. She couldn't get past what the old man had said. Couldn't process it.

They're leaving. Going away. Going somewhere else. Never coming back.

It was astounding news. Staggering news. Overwhelming. Difficult to process at the best of times. But now, after all that had transpired—

It was too much. She was so tired.

They're leaving, and the oceans will be empty. Desolate. Barren.

Too much.

Imagine the wars…the famine…once people figure out what's happened. It's—

Too much.

She pushed it aside and focused on Joe—on the reason they'd come to see Dieturlund in the first place. Thought about the trembling she'd seen in Joe's hands.

She lifted her eyes. The men were still talking, but she didn't care.

"Excuse me. Professor."

Dieturlund and Joe turned.

"You said earlier that Mia loves Joe. That she's grateful for all he's done."

"Yes. That's right."

"Joe thinks that she's also sad for him. Worried. Mia told him that she touched other men, before him, and that they all died. Joe said she's sad because she thinks the same thing is going to happen to him."

Dieturlund nodded and spoke softly, gently. "All of that is true, what you say about Mia's concern. I can feel it as well. She is deeply troubled."

Ella looked at him, expecting more. But he said nothing else.

She said, "But Mia's wrong to be concerned, isn't she?"

Dieturlund stared at his hands and remained silent.

"I mean, she doesn't know Joe. She can't know what will happen to him—just because of those other men."

Dieturlund stayed quiet.

"Talk to me, please." Her voice was trembling now.

Dieturlund sat in his chair. Sighed.

Ella looked at Joe, then at the old man, an edge of desperation in her voice. "Talk to us. Tell us what you know."

Dieturlund lifted his head reluctantly. Looked first at Joe, then at Ella.

"Mia's fear is well-founded. The other men *did* die, and she believes Joe will as well, that the contact they had will kill him."

Ella glared. "That's what *she* sees. But she doesn't know, does she? She can't know."

Dieturlund muttered under his breath. Looked away.

Ella stepped from the bed and knelt in front of him.

"You survived," she said. "You lived. You had multiple contacts with Mia and you're still here."

"Yes," he replied gently, turning to face her again. "But my experience was different. Mia knew nothing of people then—when we met—and she was happy. She reached out to me because she was curious. Eager to learn. When she approached humans again—years later—everything had changed."

Joe said, "Her baby had just died."

"Yes. And she was full of rage. Hate. She had a goal in mind from the beginning: knocking out the sonar. But her desire went beyond that. She wanted blood. Revenge. Wanted to inflict pain and death on people. So she approached the other men—and you—violently, antagonistically, wielding her thoughts like weapons. She is filled with regret now."

Ella lost the battle to keep her emotions—and her fatigue—in check, and tears flooded her eyes. "So that's it. Mia did her thing and now Joe's just…just done?"

Joe knelt next to Ella and put his arm around her waist. "Ella—listen—"

Dieturlund said, "I didn't say that. Joe is young and strong. And Mia does not know everything. You're right about that. There is a great deal she doesn't understand about humans. Joe might well have a different outcome than the other men."

Ella took a tissue from a box on Dieturlund's nightstand and wiped her eyes. "So now what do we do? Can you tell us that? Help us?"

Dieturlund looked at them. "I know contact changes our brains. *Physically* alters our brains. But I don't know the mechanism. I don't have that kind of expertise."

He sighed. "Mia wishes she could reverse what she set in motion, but she can't. But a doctor *might* be able to. If the physical change she caused is akin to a tumor, they could treat it. Keep it from progressing."

Anger flared inside Ella. *So we've wasted our time here. We should have gone to a doctor—to a hospital—in the first place. We've wasted our time!*

Joe read the thought and said "No. That's not true."

Ella burst into tears and Joe took her in his arms. "I know you're upset," he whispered, "and I'll go to the doctor now. But this was *not* a waste of time."

Ella's tears flowed and she lifted her eyes to his. "I saw you shaking, Joe—in the restaurant. I didn't say anything because we were almost here. Because I thought we'd get some answers here. But this is...We have nothing."

Joe held her tight. Let her cry.

Dieturlund watched them, tears in his own eyes now.

"Ella," Joe said gently, "I had to come here, okay? I had to know what was going on. Try to understand. This was the only way."

She nodded miserably, like she grasped what he was saying but loathed his reasoning. She cried some more. "I love you," she said. "I don't want you to die."

"Shh," Joe said as he stroked her hair. "I have no intention of dying, okay? I'm strong. Obstinate. You know that better than anyone."

Ella laughed, then cried some more.

Joe said, "I plan to fight like hell. And I'm a lot better armed now than when we walked in here."

They said good-bye to Dieturlund. Hugged him. Thanked him.

It was getting dark at last. The *pop* and *shriek* and *boom* of fireworks was all around now, as if a war were starting in the neighborhoods on every side. The big official city displays would be underway soon.

Hand in hand, Joe and Ella made for the exit in silence, both of them focused on what lay ahead. Doctors. Tests. Hospitals. They knew what they had to do, and there was nothing else to say—for the moment, anyway.

The receptionist—Jordan—had apparently gone home, and the front desk sat empty. Neat and tidy. Papers and supplies aligned just so, ready for the next attendant.

They passed through the front doors, into the gathering darkness, but never made it to the van.

CHAPTER 68

FBI AGENTS SWEPT IN from all sides, converging on Joe and Ella with authority. Boxing them in and stopping them in their tracks.

"Mr. Stanton, Ms. Tollefson, I'm Special Agent Chen with the FBI."

Joe stared blank-faced at the man presenting his badge and ID, unable to process the agent's words. He was exhausted. Wrung out. The agents' appearance now struck him as a bizarre mistake. An annoying delay that couldn't possibly have anything to do with them.

"We're placing you under arrest for conspiring to possess classified government information. We need you to come with us. Please."

Fireworks popped and boomed in the distance. Pedestrians stopped to watch the bust. A Bellingham cop—one of a contingent providing support for the arrest—headed toward the gawkers, ready to move them along.

"You've got the wrong people," said Ella. She took a step forward, like she meant to keep walking, but another agent blocked her path.

Chen spoke calmly. "We have eyewitness testimony and video surveillance related to your visit to the USS *Nimitz* earlier today."

"But—"

"You cited classified information during your exchange with Admiral Houghton, and we'd like to know how you came by that."

"We can explain," said Joe, wondering as he said this how he *would* explain.

The Kanaga sonar? Oh, I learned about that from an orca whale. A telepathic, genius orca whale. And she in turn got part of it from a frail old recluse in a retirement home. Also via telepathy. Of course.

Chen said, "You'll have plenty of time to explain everything back at our office."

Ella clutched Joe's hand, on the verge of tears again. "But we can't go with you," she said to Chen. "Joe is sick. We're on our way to the hospital now. To the emergency room."

Chen regarded Joe. "What's wrong with him?"

"Severe neurological issues, as a result of…an accident. Please. It's an emergency."

Joe said, "She's telling the truth."

Chen seemed to consider it. Studied Joe. "You look fine to me."

"That may be," said Ella, low and controlled. "But you're not a doctor and you don't know his history. I'm a registered nurse and I'm telling you, he is gravely ill."

Chen nodded, and his body language changed slightly. "I'll ask for a doctor to meet us in Seattle. Check him out there."

"But—"

"I'm afraid that's the best I can do right now."

They were searched. Handcuffed. And led to a black Suburban double-parked in The Willows's fire lane.

Joe noticed more people—presumably more FBI agents—searching the St. Anthony's van. They were wearing latex gloves. Working methodically. All business. The doors of the van stood open, the inside lit up like a convenience store.

Joe turned to find Agent Chen reciting Miranda rights from a note card. He finished and asked if they had any questions. Anything to say.

Ella nodded and spoke calmly through her tears. "Like I said, my friend is sick. Please. He needs medical treatment right away."

Chen replied, "He'll be evaluated in Seattle."

Ella started to argue but Joe caught her eye. "Baby, it's okay." He smiled, wanting to reassure her. "I'll be fine. I can wait that long."

The agents eased them into the back bench of the Suburban and shut the door.

Arrest accomplished, the police cleared out, leaving the FBI to manage prisoner transport on its own.

As the Suburban merged onto the road, a Buick LaCrosse followed—a couple hundred feet back.

Collins drove alone in the rented LaCrosse. Beck's right-hand man was satisfied—for the moment at least—because the Suburban was taking the route he'd hoped it would take. Predicted it would take. The quickest, most logical route back to I-5. The route leading straight through the city's industrial zone.

Collins had come up with the plan. Talked about it with Knox and Drucker. Sketched it quickly out on a sheet of paper while sitting in the F-350 in front of The Willows. They'd agreed there was no sense getting into a gunfight in the retirement-home parking lot. That was a battle they could easily lose. Would likely lose. The Feds had too much support.

They needed better odds, and given the direction the Suburban was heading now, Collins figured the odds had just improved mightily.

Watching his GPS and talking to Knox via cell phone at the same time, he called the approach:

"Six blocks. Five blocks. Four blocks…"

Knox, behind the wheel of the idling F-350, watched for approaching headlights and kept his foot on the brake. Lights off.

Knox had departed The Willows five minutes ahead of Collins and the FBI. He'd raced to the industrial zone and staked out a spot on the main drag. An intersection with a narrow dead-end drive that terminated in a warehouse loading dock. It was poorly lit. Empty as a graveyard.

Knox sat in the Ford, windows down, hoping the Feds would stay on the anticipated route, but ready to move out and pivot to plan B if they altered course.

Drucker was outside, crouched behind a parked car, pulling on gloves. He wore a hood that covered his face and head. Like a ski mask.

Knox gripped the wheel. Put the big truck into low gear and kept his foot on the brake.

The phone buzzed, but Knox no longer needed Collins's updates. He could see headlights now. The government Suburban coming on fast.

There was no stop sign at the intersection. Knox would have to time the collision just right.

He straightened his back, braced his head tight against the headrest. Felt for his gun.

He saw Drucker tensing his body behind the parked car. He had his gun out. Ready.

Knox breathed. The air bags would deploy—in the Ford and in the Suburban. But unlike the Feds, Knox knew what was about to happen and had thought it through. Rehearsed it in his head.

Knox listened to the rumble building in the surrounding neighborhoods. The cacophony of amateur fireworks was steady now—a constant barrage of booms, zings, pops, whirs, and whistles, on all sides.

There was nothing going on close-by though. The industrial zone was deserted. A no-man's-land for the remainder of the holiday weekend, Knox guessed.

Knox tracked the Suburban with his eyes, saw it glide quickly closer, windshield and shiny black hood glinting under the streetlights. He figured it was going about thirty-five.

Knox hit the gas and the F-350 roared forward and smashed into the Suburban. Four hundred horsepower, eight hundred pound-feet of torque, the three-ton truck bulldozed the Chevy across the intersection. Into a light pole.

Glass shattered. Air bags blossomed. Bumpers clattered onto asphalt.

The Suburban's alarm shrieked, then died, as the LaCross screeched in behind the wreck, swinging broadside and slamming to a stop.

Drucker was at the Suburban in seconds but the agents were already moving. Drawing weapons. Reaching for radios. Battling for control of themselves and the situation. They were disciplined. Superbly trained. Fast.

Unfortunately for them, so were Beck's men.

Drucker shot the agent who tumbled—gun drawn—from the right rear door, and then Collins and Knox were there, weapons ready, bellowing commands, ordering the others out and down, onto the pavement. They took the agent's guns, wallets, badges, shoes, cell phones, and radios. Threw everything into the LaCrosse's open trunk.

There was the hiss of radiators. The *tick, tick, tick* of cooling motors, the sound of fluid dripping onto the ground. The smell of gas—but not too strong.

Agent Chen lifted his head, and Drucker kicked him in the chest. Hard.

"Down," Drucker growled. "Don't make me say it again."

They worked fast, Collins, Drucker, and Knox. Silently.

They handcuffed the agents and duct-taped their mouths, yanking them up by the hair and running tape tightly around their heads.

Collins checked the agent Drucker had shot and found him groaning in pain, but not bleeding. The outline of a Kevlar vest was visible through the man's shirt. Collins cuffed and taped him as well.

And then they were lifting the agents to their feet and shoving them into the Suburban's cavernous cargo hold, locking them to the posts anchoring the vehicle's steel prisoner cage.

Heart thudding, Collins checked Sixth for the umpteenth time. No cars in either direction.

Fireworks were booming everywhere now. Continuously. On all sides. It sounded like a war.

"Follow me," said Collins. He sprinted for the open door of the LaCrosse. Drucker jumped behind the wheel of the Suburban, and Knox climbed back into the crumpled F-350, shoving a flaccid air bag out of his way with one hand.

Collins breathed when the Suburban and F-350 started.

The plan was working. The plan was on track. He drove a half block down sixth—the two battered, hissing, leaking vehicles close behind—and took the first available drive, a narrow lane between two utterly unremarkable warehouses. Behind the buildings, the lane bisected two parking lots. Collins chose the right-hand lot because it was darker. Just one dreary halogen in the far corner.

He drove to the darkest corner of the lot and got out. The truck and Suburban parked nearby.

Collins, still wearing his mask, opened the Suburban's undamaged rear door and leaned in, holding his gun loosely in his right hand. He surveyed Joe and Ella closely for the first time. Ella had a small cut above her eye where she'd slammed into the side panel on impact. The blood was already drying. Joe looked dazed but unharmed.

Ella started to speak. Collins cut her off.

"Not a word," he said through his mask. "Not a sound. Or I start shooting the guys in back. Blowing their brains out while you watch."

Ella shut her mouth, and Collins said, "Good." He waved his gun. "Both of you. Out. Now."

CHAPTER 69

JOE AND ELLA WERE HUSTLED into the back of the LaCrosse. Ella smelled bleach and caught a glimpse of another man working furiously in the front of the big truck. A spray bottle in one hand. Wiping everything down with rags.

And then doors were slamming all around. Ella heard quick chirps as Beck's men—she was sure they were Beck's men—locked the truck and the Suburban and piled into the LaCrosse. And then they were leaving the lot, exiting the lane and speeding back down sixth, crunching over broken glass in the intersection where the collision had occurred.

The men began removing their masks. Casting them aside.

Ella stared. They were big guys. Thick necks. Heavily muscled backs and shoulders. Flat, unemotional faces. Tough-looking.

The guy in back—seated next to Joe—checked his gun with practiced ease. Inspected it, removed and reinstalled the magazine, and tucked it into a shoulder holster with the fluid grace of a magician. A Vegas blackjack dealer. As if he'd done the same thing ten thousand times before.

Ella leaned across Joe and said, "Where are you taking us?"

The guy ran his hands through his hair but made no reply. Didn't turn, as if he hadn't even heard her question.

Joe and Ella looked at each other and silently agreed to let it be. For the moment, at least, it didn't seem like there was any other choice.

Ella looked at Beck's men again. Studied them. They were calm. Polished. Aloof. Professional soldiers, every one.

She recalled with horror that—in the immediate aftermath of the accident—she had almost said Beck's name. Almost said, "You're working with Beck." It had been on the tip of her tongue.

They would surely have killed the FBI agents if she had said that. If she'd identified them, in the heat of the moment, they would have felt compelled to do so.

She hadn't said anything. Joe hadn't said anything. And the agents were still alive. It was a miracle. She guessed that someone would find them the next day. By midmorning, probably.

Then a new alarm rang in her mind.

Beck's men had removed their masks. They were no longer hiding anything. They'd concealed their faces from the Feds, but such secrecy no longer seemed important.

The meaning of this—the obvious implication—sank in, and despair settled in Ella's mind like a dull, throbbing pain. She slumped against Joe and watched the city blur by, fireworks exploding here and there along the horizon.

Joe nuzzled Ella and whispered, "I love you, Ella." She pressed harder against his chest and Joe smelled the fear flowing from the pores in her skin. Felt the dampness on her face. New tears. "Shh," he whispered. "It's gonna be okay."

Joe remembered what Ella had told him about the shooting at the mall, how she'd felt invisible—as if the gunman couldn't see her at all. Joe wished with all his heart that that was the case now. That Beck's men would take him away and ignore her. Leave her. Turn a blind eye to her presence and let her go in peace. He felt responsible for the situation they were in and would at that moment have given anything for her safety.

He sat there, trying to think, trying to control his own fear and fatigue long enough to assess the situation. His head hurt—a sharp, cutting pain behind his eyes, as if he'd been staring at the noonday sun. And his hands shook still. He could feel the tremors even with his wrists tight behind his back. The shake was constant now.

And then the pain around his eyes subsided—just a little—and he felt oddly comforted.

A sudden flood of warmth spread outward from his core to his hands and feet, fingers and toes, piercing his somber mood like a blade of luxuriantly hot sunlight in a cold room.

There's someone else here. With us.

He could feel it. Another presence in the darkness.

Mia.

It *was* Mia. Mia, finding him. Connecting with him, yet again. Not understanding his predicament in the least, but sensing his terror and wanting to reassure.

Joe shut his eyes and let the connection stabilize. He didn't think about *why* Mia had come, or what her arrival in his mind might mean. He didn't have the energy to grapple with it.

He simply let the warmth flow, accepting Mia's offer of comfort with gratitude. Without reservation.

After a long minute, another feeling hit him:

I'm not the only one suffering here.

Mia was comforting him. Worried about him. Filled with regret over what she had done to him. That was all true. But she was also deeply worried for her own tribe, for the tasks she had yet to accomplish.

And then he heard it, clear and bright and excruciating: *ping… ping…ping.* Relentless and unending. A sort of torture lasting years.

Joe breathed, seeing now into Mia's mind. Perceiving her fears and worries just as she had perceived his.

He looked and watched, and understood.

Mia has her message to send. But she can't send it until the sonar goes off. Everything hinges on that. Everything.

He understood. It was like there was an avalanche ready to start. Ready to rumble. Ready to release a billion tons of kinetic energy and thunder down from the mountaintops.

But it can't start until Mia sends her message. And she can't send her message because the pinging is blocking her voice, like a wall.

He felt her despair, as she felt his. She wasn't giving up, not by any means. She and her pod were swimming on, farther into the open sea. But time was running out.

CHAPTER 70

ADMIRAL HOUGHTON SAT ALONE in his cabin aboard the *Nimitz*.

It was dark now, and the great ship rested in its deep-water moorage beneath the skyscrapers of Seattle, 102,000 tons of steel slowly cooling after a long, hot Fourth of July.

The ship was quiet, and if Admiral Houghton had ventured onto the deck, he could have seen fireworks bursting over the harbor and heard the excited murmur of spectators along Alaskan Way. He remained in his cabin instead.

He'd been invited to a barbecue and celebration at the Governor's Mansion in Olympia, but had asked an aide to send his regrets. Explain that he wasn't feeling well.

He *wasn't* feeling well. That was a fact. Wasn't feeling like himself at all. And he wanted to think.

He lay back on his bed, wondering about the priest and his girlfriend, about the odd tingling in his arm, and about the dream.

The dream.

Houghton couldn't remember the last time he'd dreamed. He'd read somewhere that everyone dreamed, every night, and he guessed that was probably true. But he rarely remembered his own dreams, and he had certainly never experienced one so vivid. So real.

The line.
The wall, slowly opening at the back of the church.
The line. On fire.

He hadn't thought about his childhood church in years. Decades, maybe. Why was he dreaming about that now? And what was the significance of the line—a minor feature in a building he barely remembered?

Why had he heard the sonar pulse in his dream, and why had it caused him such pain?

He lay there, trying to relax, analyzing the security implications of Joe Stanton's bizarre request with one part of his mind, and puzzling over his personal reaction to things with another.

There was no mistaking it. He'd felt something when he'd shaken the priest's hand. Something powerful. A sort of jolt that had scrambled his thoughts and shoved him back in time, to a Sunday morning long ago. To something he'd witnessed with his own eyes.

I remember now, he thought. *I was close…close to seeing… what?*

The line had pointed the way. The line. A blade of light singing with energy.

He'd almost seen something that day, caught a glimpse of something beautiful—like sunlit fields spied through a far-off window.

And he'd heard music.

Music not meant for human ears.

I almost saw it.

Almost heard it.

I was almost there.

There had been magic in the church that day. Magic and power. And the memory of it now slowed his breathing and quieted his mind, like clear water flowing over smooth stones.

At last he settled into sleep.

After a time, though, the *ping…ping…ping* began in his sleeping brain, faintly at first—an annoying earworm—then getting louder. His eyelids twitched and jumped in the dark.

CHAPTER 71

THE BELL 412 SETTLED like a great, buzzing insect onto *Marauder*'s aft helipad. It was dark, and the breeze funneling over and around the ship's sleek, muscular hull was brisk and unrelenting.

The ship was entering Trincomali Channel, sticking to the same course it had followed from Alaska, now bearing south-southeast through the Canadian Gulf Islands, toward the US border. It glided forward, nimble and elegant. A work of art. A fantastic piece of sculpture masquerading as a ship.

Within the hour *Marauder* would turn due south, then gradually steer southwest, passing Victoria and the southern end of Vancouver Island and heading west into the Strait of Juan de Fuca.

The shriek of the Bell's engine faded as Beck and Ring made their way across the deck. The helicopter would refuel, then immediately lift off again and return to Bellingham to retrieve Collins and crew.

Beck barreled downstairs from the helipad, leaving Ring far behind and scaring the shit out of everyone he passed.

He was a wreck. Hair disheveled, clothes rumpled and stained. His body reeking still of sweat and urine and vomit.

It was the look on his face, though, that made people jump out of the way. Made eyes snap open and jaws drop.

He looked deranged. Crazy. A fierce, gone-around-the-bend gleam in his eye that said he was a nanosecond away from exploding and breaking someone's neck.

Beck found Heintzel at her desk in the infirmary. At her computer. Staring at her screen, typing thoughtfully.

She glanced up to see who was there and forgot about her work.

"Jesus. What happened to you?" she asked, getting to her feet.

"Didn't sleep well," Beck replied. "I need something."

Heintzel squinted at him. Wrinkled her nose as she caught a whiff of the potpourri of odors wafting off his skin and clothes.

"You look like you've been in a war," she said. "What happened?"

"Fucked-up sleep. And I don't want to talk about it."

Heintzel steered him toward the nearest exam room. A tiny space packed with shelves and medical apparatus and a narrow bed.

"Have a seat, and let me check you out."

She shut the door. Turned and got some hand sanitizer from a wall-mounted dispenser. When she turned back, Beck was inches away, murder in his eyes.

He grabbed her wrist with his right hand—a move startling in its speed and ferocity—brought her arm slowly up to eye level, and began to bend it back. Stopped.

Heintzel could feel his strength. Sensed that he could snap her wrist like a twig if he wanted to.

"Andrea," he said softly. "I don't want an exam. I don't want to be checked out. Okay?"

She swallowed. Held his gaze. "Okay."

"What I want, is something to keep me going. Keep me awake and sharp and alert for twenty-four more hours."

She regarded him with concern. "But you're running ragged now. You should sleep."

Beck tightened his grip on her wrist, and the fire in his eyes intensified. "I *can't* sleep, Andrea. Not right now."

"Okay," Heintzel gasped. "Let me see what I can do."

Beck released her hand and slumped to a sitting position on the edge of the exam bed, his eyes dulling visibly. He looked like a wounded animal.

Heintzel massaged her wrist, tears in her eyes from the pain, and began assembling what she needed on a little metal tray: alcohol swabs. A syringe. Two glass vials from a minifridge.

A minute later the concoction was ready.

Heintzel rolled Beck's shirtsleeve out of the way and swabbed his bicep.

"Do you want to know what I'm giving you?" she asked.

Beck shook his head and said, voice flat, "No. I just want to know it's the best you have."

Heintzel nodded.

Beck said, in the same unemotional tone, "If I find out it's not, I'll come back down here and kill you."

Heintzel made no reply. Just steadied her hand as she finished the injection.

Andrea Heintzel had known Beck for years. Worked with him. Treated his injuries. Advised him on all manner of medical issues and willingly participated in procedures—certain prisoner interrogations and the like—of questionable legality. She was part of Beck's inner circle and enjoyed the power, authority and pay that came with that. She knew Beck for the charming, ruthless, volatile, egotistical leader that he was. She'd watched him verbally eviscerate employees and heard stories of far worse things. But she had never felt personally afraid of him. Until now.

She wiped the injection site on Beck's arm with a clean swab and applied a Band-Aid.

Looking up, she found his eyes dull still, as if the wounded animal had retreated to the back of its den and was hiding there, resting, gathering strength for the next outburst.

He's not looking at me, she thought.

But then he was looking at her. And the little hairs on the back of her neck lifted and her hands shook.

There's something wrong with his eyes.

It was true. There was something wrong—with the way the irises looked, with the pupils. With the cant of his head also. It was a demeanor, an aura, a vibe, that—just for a moment, just for an instant—made her feel that she was looking at someone else entirely. A different person. A stranger. A madman. A psychopath. She could feel it: madness wafting off his body as potently as the horrible stench.

Beck got to his feet. "Collins is bringing the priest here. To you. Reinstall his thought-capture hardware and fire it up. We're going to need him."

"Okay."

Beck exited the infirmary without another word.

Beck showered and put on clean clothes, pleased with how he felt, with the fresh energy surging through his veins. He was thinking clearly again and his headache had subsided to a faint, inconsequential twinge just beneath his scalp. The horror he'd felt in the restroom at the airport, and again on the helicopter, seemed like a distant memory. Like something he'd dreamed.

He smiled as he exited his cabin.

Clearly, whatever Heintzel had given him was working.

It occurred to Beck as he walked, as he headed for his rendezvous with Ring and his father and sister, that his mood didn't make sense.

His father and sister had come to his ship unannounced, barged into *his* War Room and ordered *his* staff around while he was away from the vessel.

I should be enraged, he thought. *Incensed. Livid.*

But I'm not.

Instead of rage, he felt an odd eagerness. A lustful exuberance.

He paused midstride, midcorridor, wondering at this and questioning himself. Questioning his mood and attitude.

The hesitation lasted only moments before the greedy, eager, lustful side won out and he continued on his way.

Still, there was doubt. A little voice in his head, warning him, suggesting, meekly, that he was becoming a sort of passenger or spectator in his own body. That the sick, afflicted part of his mind was growing stronger by the hour.

He ignored the little voice and strode on. He didn't know what was going to happen after he entered the War Room. That was a fact. And his mood was split now, evenly, sickeningly, between elation and terror.

CHAPTER 72

IT WAS THE DIAMONDS that turned Beck's father into a believer.

Diamonds on black sand.

Diamonds wet from a receding tide, sparkling and flashing in early morning sun.

The diamonds made Winston Beck set down his scotch and lean forward in his chair, closer to Ring's monitor and the breathtaking images populating the screen.

"Ring. Are those—"

"Diamonds. Yes."

Winston Beck fell silent, then finally said, "Are you saying that if someone were to go through one of these tunnels, they would come out in a place where things like that are just…what? Lying around on the beach?"

"Yes. It appears so."

Beck Sr. and his daughter exchanged glances.

They'd arrived on *Marauder* an hour earlier, Kate and Beck Sr., and made straight for the War Room, demanding to be brought up to speed on the "phenomenon," regardless of the younger Beck's whereabouts.

Kate had already told her father as much as she knew. Now Ring was filling in the blanks.

Ring waved at the wall of screens behind his console. "The diamonds and a plethora of other images were uncovered in Joe Stanton's final thought capture. The files are immense. My staff pulled some highlights while I was on my way back from Bellingham, but there's much more to review and analyze."

"This was all in Stanton's head?" Beck Sr. asked. "Or *is* in Stanton's head?"

"Yes. Though he's probably not even aware of most of it."

Beck Sr. lifted his scotch, then set it back down—an enormous gold ring on his right hand clinking the glass as he did so. "But why are these images in his head at all?"

Ring shrugged. "Stanton and the orca are connected. Able to communicate.

"After their initial encounter, Stanton's brain changed. Physically. Structurally. Grew a cluster of highly specialized cells that permit this flow of information to occur. Same thing happened to our divers. To the gillnetter.

"But the process is far from perfect. Works great, orca-to-orca. Not so great orca-to-human. There are…side effects."

"Yeah," said Kate. "Like death."

Ring nodded. "Most of the thoughts the whale transmits land in Stanton's subconscious. A good thing, considering the volume of information. If he were actually aware of it all, he'd go insane faster than he already is."

The room went quiet again, all eyes on the screens.

After a while, Kate said, "Why beach images? Why *these* pictures?"

Ring sipped an Orange Crush. "T-197—or Mia—did a test run with her inner circle. That's my theory, anyway."

"A test run?"

"Or a test dive, if you like." He pointed at a tunnel image on one massive screen.

"They went through, and out the other side to have a look around. To see if passage is actually possible."

Fresh images flowed onto the screens—more "highlights" from the mother lode of thoughts taken from Stanton's mind. And the spectators gasped.

They were looking at the broader landscape now—not just tight sections of beach. And the views were jaw-dropping. Southeast Alaska came to mind—it was like that—but Southeast Alaska on steroids.

Redwood-sized trees blanketed the coastline and stretched to the horizon in all directions. Vast tracts of stupendously tall, healthy, emerald forest. Verdant, mist-shrouded valleys.

Himalayan-sized mountains towered over the land, snowcapped peaks and glacier-draped ridges begetting dizzyingly tall waterfalls flashing like tinsel in the morning light.

More images materialized: Massive undersea cliffs, and sunlight filtering down through gently swaying forests of kelp. Rocky, wild shoreline, tide pools, and broad stretches of black sand. Some of the screens showed whales—members of Mia's entourage—holding themselves vertically in the water. Treading water like they were looking around. Big black eyes shining in the dawn.

"This behavior," said Ring, "is called 'spyhopping.' They're literally checking out their surroundings."

No one spoke as new images of jewel-speckled black sand flashed on-screen.

Sheldon Beck broke the silence from the darkness behind the other viewers. It was the first time he'd said anything since entering the room.

"I read somewhere that when the first Europeans arrived at the mouth of the Vaal River in South Africa, they found diamonds—gem-grade stones—in such abundance that they could fill a tin cup in a matter of minutes."

The group stared at the diamonds—at a coastline from a landscape painter's fantasy—and fell silent once more. But the vibe in the room had changed. There was tension in the air now. A fresh undercurrent of nervous energy. The younger Beck could feel it.

"How is this possible?" Beck Sr. asked. "What's the mechanism?"

Ring turned. "We don't know. We may never know." He waved at the screens behind him. "Wormholes form all the time—physicists have demonstrated that. Cosmic pathways that blink in and out of existence. But it's always at a subatomic level.

"T-197 may have tapped into such a phenomenon. Harnessed it. Magnified it. Replicated it. Or, she could simply be the catalyst for an anomaly destined to occur one way or the other."

Beck Sr. said, "So these images—the place we're seeing here—are, what? Another planet?"

Ring shrugged. "Yes, though where in the universe that planet resides is anyone's guess. It may not exist in our universe at all."

More images filled the screens, including some of the grainy tunnel pictures taken by the ROV. Taken in the real world—in the Bering Sea.

These snapshots lacked the crispness and quality of Stanton's thought pictures, but they added abundant credibility to the argument that the tunnels were real. Actual physical structures growing in the Earth's oceans, even as they spoke.

The tension in the room increased, until Kate asked a question. It was a question Beck had been waiting for. A question he'd suspected his sister or father would ask, sooner or later.

"You say the whales will use these tunnels. Other organisms, as well. What about people? Could people venture through?"

Ring manipulated the controls on his desktop and answered without turning. "It should be possible. I think so."

Ring turned and looked at her, his face backlit by the wall of monitors. "But the window of opportunity will be short-lived. I'm almost certain of that. The tunnels are coming on, powering up, to serve a purpose. But they won't stay open a moment longer than they need to.

"Think of the wormhole example. Hard to tame. Hard to control. T-197—Mia—will open the door and hold it open as long as she has to. But no longer."

Beck Sr. shifted in his seat. Rattled the ice in his glass and muttered, "Then it's futile. If what you're saying is accurate, the tunnels will open and close before anyone can use them. End of story."

Ring nodded. "Yes. Unless they can be forced to remain open."

Kate and Beck Sr. stared at the genius.

"You can do that?" asked Beck Sr., struggling to conceal the eagerness in his voice. "There's a way?"

"I think so," said Ring.

Kate and her father leaned close to one another in the darkness and whispered back and forth. The conversation lasted several minutes.

The younger Beck couldn't hear what they were saying, but the tone of the whispers and the body language told half the story.

He thought they resembled a king and queen debating the fate of their empire.

At last they stopped and looked his way. Both rose from their seats.

Winston Beck—scotch in one hand—took a step toward his son and tilted his head at the far side of the War Room. "May we speak with you privately?"

Beck stood. Smiled. Looked at his father and sister. "Absolutely. I've been waiting for this."

CHAPTER 73

INSIDE THE PRIVATE CONFERENCE ROOM with the door closed, Winston Beck looked his son in the eye. "You've done well," he said.

Beck the elder was a big man with a big head—literally and figuratively—and abundant steel-gray hair. He had a thick chest and shoulders, meaty hands and a heavy, gravelly voice. Used to giving orders and getting things done, he rarely engaged in pleasantries and hardly ever complimented anyone. But he was praising his son now, and the younger Beck didn't know what to make of it.

Beck Sr. said, "You stumbled on something intriguing and pursued it with tenacity and determination. I like that."

The younger Beck shrugged. "Ring had a lot to do with it."

"Of course. But you led the investigation. Brought in the requisite experts and shuffled your workload to push everything forward. Despite…external pressure."

Beck Sr. glanced at his daughter as he said this, and Beck caught the look. He was shocked. His father was giving him credit for something. Praising him and criticizing his sister. It was unprecedented. Never happened before. This wasn't how he'd envisioned the conversation would go. Not at all.

"To me," his father continued, "you've demonstrated evidence of a savvy, entrepreneurial streak. A streak I frankly didn't know was there."

Beck Jr. was at a loss for words so he said, simply, "Thank you."

The elder Beck nodded. "It's a style of thinking that could prove critical to the future of Erebus Industries."

Beck watched his sister as their father paid him this final compliment, and his attitude morphed from surprise to suspicion.

The words coming from Beck Sr.'s mouth were positive—no doubt about that—but Kate's body language didn't jibe with the unexpected praise. Based on what their dad was saying, she should look hurt. Defeated. Or at the very least, miffed. But she didn't. Quite the contrary. She appeared confident; cocky, even.

They have something up their sleeve, Beck thought. *Of course they do.*

The elder Beck said, "But now, we need to coordinate our efforts. Focus our energies."

Beck wondered what this meant. He waited.

"Katie and I will take this investigation from here. We need you to turn your attention to the Ivory Coast. You've got to carry the ball on that."

Silence.

So, there it was.

Kate finally lifted her eyes, a small, smug smile on her face.

Beck Jr. nodded slowly, as if considering all he'd just heard. "That all makes sense," he said. "I agree."

His father and sister looked surprised.

"Really?" said Kate.

Beck nodded. "Sure. I've thought a lot about this. We can't jeopardize the health of the company because of one exploratory venture—no matter how…unusual it is."

Beck Sr. wagged his head in agreement. "I'm glad you see this as a team effort, Sheldon. It's another example of your growth and development as a leader."

Inside, the old man was baffled by his son's reaction. His son had a horrific temper. He'd expected outrage; had even told his bodyguards to be ready to intervene, if necessary. Instead, the boy was agreeing with him. He didn't know what to make of it.

The younger Beck said, "The Ivory Coast deployment is huge. I agreed to lead it. And, I will."

Kate's eyes narrowed. "You're taking this pretty well."

Beck shrugged. "Father's plan is the only logical course of action. Divide and conquer. We need to explore this phenomenon–even if it proves to be a dead end. And, we must carry through with the deployment, or risk losing future contracts. I'm the most logical person to lead the Ivory Coast effort. I've been prepping for it for months."

Beck did his best to sound sincere while simultaneously trying to conceal his growing excitement—a perverse feeling of joy welling up inside him.

"I don't like the situation," he said to his dad and sister. "But it's the only course of action that makes sense."

Winston Beck nodded solemnly. "I think that's a very cogent assessment of the situation." He laughed and looked at his two grown children. "You know," he said, "there are people in the DOD who strategize about alien invasion. Absolutely true. Taxpayer money actually goes for that. There's enough of a perceived threat."

He waved at the monitors outside the conference room. "But here we have a threat from another sort of alien—another species—inside our own planet. From creatures no one has ever suspected. As the head of Erebus Industries, I need to lead this investigation. Explore what it means for national security."

Beck nodded and kept a congenial expression on his face. Inside, he felt only contempt.

Right, he thought. *National security. Doesn't have anything whatsoever to do with gaining access to a new, unexplored world with unimaginable natural resources. With wanting to plant your flagpole before anyone else.*

Out loud, he said, "Of course. And the good news is, you two are now almost up to speed on the investigation. I'll arrange transport to the *Outlier* tomorrow and run the deployment from there. It's a good ship."

Kate studied her brother. "What do you mean, *almost* up to speed?"

Beck sighed. Hesitated. Let the drama build. "We found something I haven't told you about. In the Bering Sea. Where our divers first got sick. Something neither of you has seen."

"Well, what is it?" asked Kate.

"Something we can't explain, but that may be important when it comes to navigating the tunnels." Beck looked at them. "Ring thinks it might be a sort of "key." Though his reasoning is beyond me. Would you like to see it?"

Winston Beck raised an eyebrow. "It's on board? Yes, of course we want to see it."

The younger Beck stood, tapped on his phone, and spoke to someone on the other end. "The hyperbaric chamber," he said. "Ten minutes."

Kate squinted at him. "It's in the hyperbaric chamber?"

"Under pressure," said Beck. "Ring's idea. We can observe it through the windows." He moved for the door and motioned for them to follow. "Come. See for yourself."

CHAPTER 74

THEY EMERGED ONTO *MARAUDER'S* broad weather deck: Kate and Beck Sr. and their two bodyguards, followed closely by the younger Beck and one of his men—Allen Dodd.

It was cold on the upper deck—summer or no—and wind whistled and shrieked around the craft's carbon-fiber bulwark as *Marauder* pushed south through Swanson Channel, driving hard in moderate seas against a strong incoming tide. The brisk, moist air tasted of the open ocean not far ahead.

They could see a smattering of lights on Moresby and Stuart Islands—cabins and vacation homes—and the warm glow of Victoria, BC, farther south. There was even the occasional sparkle and flash of fireworks to the southeast—on the U.S. side of the border.

Kate and her father didn't seem to notice the broader surroundings. They'd spied the hyperbaric chamber sitting midship, hard against the starboard rail, and were making for it now. The three-ton, six-person chamber's round steel door glimmered, and a soft golden light spilled from inside. The deck crane used to hoist the chamber—as well as speedboats and runabouts—hung dormant above it, the crane's massive steel hook swaying gently in the breeze.

Like moths toward a flame, they advanced on the light. Even the bodyguards seemed curious, wondering what further secrets might be waiting inside.

Beck Sr. reached the chamber door first, pressed his face to the porthole and scanned the tidy interior: padded seats for six divers. Gurneys with crisp white sheets. Oxygen masks. Fire extinguishers.

Gauges. Radios. All the standard accouterments. Nothing out of the ordinary.

He turned back to address his son. "I don't see anyth—

Beck Sr. froze and Kate turned to follow his gaze. So did the bodyguards.

Beck Jr. was standing with Allen Dodd a few paces away, wrapped in the glow of *Marauder*'s LED running lights. They were holding guns, pointing them at the group.

The younger Beck tugged the slide on his Colt 1911. Jacked a round into the chamber. "Hands where we can see 'em," he said calmly, loud enough to be heard over the wind and waves.

No one moved.

Beck flicked the 1911's muzzle a degree to the right and fired a round between his sister and the closest bodyguard. The gun roared, and his father and sister jumped. Neither bodyguard flinched.

"Hands where we can see 'em," he repeated. "Now."

Everyone complied.

Kate glared at her brother. "What the hell is this?"

"Sheldon," said Beck Sr. "What's going on? If this is a joke—"

"Shut up." Beck leveled the gun at his father.

The elder Beck went quiet, and Beck said, "Thank you."

He waved his gun at the bodyguards. "Boys, facedown on the deck. Arms loose at your sides."

The bodyguards did as they were told. As soon as they were on the deck, Dodd cuffed them—hands behind their backs—then rooted around for guns and wallets, phones and radios, tossing items into a pile as he worked.

"Sheldon," Kate yelled. "Have you lost your mind? What the fuck are you doing?"

Dodd jerked one of the bodyguards to his feet.

"I miss anything, Slim?" he asked, grinning at the outhouse-sized guard. The man had a Dutch Boy haircut that looked incongruous with his bulk. The bodyguard glared at Dodd and spat at his shoes. Dodd kicked him in the balls, hard, and the big man crumpled to his knees, groaning in pain.

The younger Beck laughed, and his father tried to catch his eye. "Sheldon! Please. I demand an explanation."

Beck turned to his father and sister. Stared at them. Kate was hugging her arms to her chest now, trying to stay warm in the wind and spray and darkness of the weather deck.

"An explanation?" Sheldon Beck stepped closer to his father, keeping the gun between them. "Sure, Pop. How about this? I don't like being dictated to. I don't like being shafted by my own family."

"Sheldon, listen," Beck Sr. said. "If you have a grievance, let's take it inside. Let's talk it through."

Beck laughed. "Tell you my grievances? That would take days, Dad. And I don't have days." He waved toward the front of the ship. "Got a schedule to keep."

The elder Beck nodded. "You want to investigate the phenomenon yourself? Is that it? Fine." He gestured toward the door leading to the lower decks. "Let's discuss it. Like civilized people."

"Too late for that. I know where you stand. Both of you."

"Sheldon—"

"You make the decisions. You call the shots—"

Beck Sr. protested. "Hang on a second—I ask for your input and counsel frequently."

The younger Beck nodded. "Yeah. And ignore it just as routinely."

"Sheldon—"

"Now, by gosh, my crew and I find something remarkable, something truly unusual and spectacular. And—oh, surprise!—you want me out of the picture."

"Sheldon—"

"But I don't think so, Pop. Not this time."

"Sheldon—"

"Sheldon, for God's sake," Kate yelled—the fury in her voice evident even over the relentless wind. "This is a company, remember? Erebus is a company. With a corporate hierarchy. Father is the CEO. I'm the president. You do not dictate to *us*."

Beck Sr. put his hand on his daughter's arm and eased her back. "Kate, please—"

"Hierarchy's changed, Kate," said the younger Beck. "As of tonight. As of this second."

The tone in his voice stopped them both.

He gestured toward the door of the hyperbaric chamber. Dodd was opening the door. "Get in, Kate. We're done talking."

Kate looked from the door to her brother and back. "What?"

"I said get in."

"Go to hell."

Beck smiled. "Don't worry, sis. It's got all the comforts of home. Beds. Shower. MREs—all you can eat. There's even some paperbacks. I wouldn't call it spa-like, but you should be comfortable enough while my team and I investigate the phenomenon."

Kate twisted away from her father and started toward her brother.

Beck twitched and fired another round, this one just over Kate's ear—the gun discharging inches from her face.

Kate screamed, stumbling back, and Beck shoved her hard toward the opening. Dodd heaved the bodyguard with the Dutch Boy haircut in after her, then slammed the heavy steel door and levered it shut—sealing the door against the surrounding frame as he did so. Dodd slid a padlock through the lever arm and snapped it closed. Pocketed the key.

Beck turned to his father and the remaining guard.

"Sheldon—" The old man had a quiver in his voice now.

"Save it, Pop."

Beck Sr. went quiet and his son took a step back. Breathed in the brisk sea air.

The wind was invigorating. Constant. Enveloping the ship like a lover. It was cold on the weather deck but Beck was sweating. His head was clear, though. That was for sure. Whatever Heintzel had given him was working. Keeping the bizarre thoughts and images he'd experienced earlier at bay. The monstrous eyes. The bad dream.

He wanted to think the monster was gone—vanquished—but he knew better. There was *something* with him, in his head, quiet, but there all the same. Lurking. Waiting. Hiding in a dark corner of his mind like a rabid animal.

For the moment, though, he felt in control. And he breathed, in and out.

I'll build on this, he thought. *Keep Dad and Sis locked up, safe and out of the way for a day or two while I examine the phenomenon for myself. Then…*

He turned to his father and the remaining bodyguard, suddenly aware of a little slip in his mind, of the rabid animal creeping forward from the corner, coming into the light. He breathed, sucked in the fresh sea air, and looked his father in the eye.

No hint of the elder Beck's usual arrogance or country-club demeanor remained. He looked pale in the glow of *Marauder*'s running lights. Worried.

Beck Sr. said, "Sheldon, you know I'm claustrophobic. Please—"

Beck Jr. smiled. "Relax, Pop, you don't have to go in yet."

His father looked relieved. "Good. So you want to talk?"

"No. I want you to make a phone call. To your helicopter pilot."

Beck Sr. looked puzzled. "My pilot?"

"He won't take an order from me."

Beck Sr. nodded and tentatively pulled his cell phone out of his pocket. Held it in his hand. "What do you want me to say?"

"Tell him he needs to make a quick flight tonight. Run a couple of people over to Port Angeles and drop 'em off."

"Sure, but—"

"Tell him to be at the helipad in fifteen minutes. There'll be two passengers waiting. A couple of scientists."

Beck Sr. nodded. Then hesitated.

Beck flicked his wrist to the right, almost casually, and shot the bodyguard in the face.

The top of the man's head exploded in a cloud of pink mist that vanished in the darkness and the wind. His body crashed to the deck.

Beck could see Kate fumbling around inside the hyperbaric chamber, struggling to see out the portholes.

"You killed him," moaned Winston Beck. "Jesus, Sheldon, you killed an employee."

Beck spoke calmly. "Make the call, Dad. Or we'll bring Katie out here next."

Winston Beck fumbled with his phone, and the younger Beck put his hand on his Dad's arm.

"Nice and casual. We don't want your pilot worrying about anything."

The elder Beck ducked against the side of the hyperbaric chamber to make himself heard over the wind. He relayed his son's instructions, then shut his phone.

"Great," said Beck Jr., raising his gun and pointing at the old man. "Now, get in."

He held the gun steady while Dodd opened the chamber door.

Kate lunged for the opening. "Sheldon!" she screamed. "Listen to me! This is your last chance. If—"

Beck shoved his father through the door, into Kate's arms, and Dodd resealed it. Levered it shut and reapplied the padlock. Kate's cries died instantly.

Beck and Dodd stepped back from the chamber, and Beck closed his eyes.

He was relieved to find that he saw only darkness as he did this. Heard only the sounds of his ship, running hard, the spray shushing over the bulwark and the wind whistling around the hyperbaric chamber.

He was relieved.

And then, he wasn't. The rabid animal was moving again.

There's something loose in my mind.

A kind of dreamy terror washed over him, a feeling both languid and repellent.

Someone's watching me.

He opened his eyes to find Dodd looking his way.

"Boss?"

"Yeah?"

Dodd's gaze fell on the dead guard. "Thinking we should move him, is all. Get rid of the body. You got people coming up here in"—he looked at his watch—"ten minutes."

Beck felt his stomach twist.

People coming up? He squinted at Dodd, wondering what the man was referring to.

And then it came to him, like a half-remembered dream. Dodd was talking about his father's helicopter pilot. He'd ordered his dad to make a call.

I want you to make a phone call. To your helicopter pilot.

He remembered asking his dad to make the call, but he had no idea *why* he had done it. He stared at Dodd some more.

"Right," he said at last, still confused. Unsure.

Did I arrange something with Phelps and Edelstein? Negotiate an agreement with them? Offer them payment in exchange for permanent silence about the phenomenon?

He couldn't recall.

And then he felt another adrenaline rush. The same sick anticipation he'd experienced walking to the War Room to meet his father and sister. The same perverse thrill.

He touched something in his lower vest pocket. A heavy, rectangular object, slightly larger than a deck of cards, a magnet on one side.

He didn't take it out. He didn't need to. He knew what it was.

The dreamy terror washed over him again, loosening his bowels.

Who put this in my pocket? Did I put this in my pocket?

He couldn't remember. He tried. Searched his mind, but found no answer.

Who put this in my pocket?

He looked at Dodd. Gestured at the dead guard.

"Help me get him on the catwalk."

Dodd looked from his boss to the steel catwalk attached to the hyperbaric chamber and shrugged.

Dodd didn't understand. If they were trying to hide the body, the catwalk was a poor choice. The corpse would be even more visible there than sprawled on the deck. But he knew better than to ask questions.

He bent and helped Beck drag the big guard. Grunting, they rolled him onto the catwalk, banging into the chamber as they worked.

Dodd could see Beck's sister and dad straining to peer through the portholes, Kate slapping the glass with the heel of her hand.

"Handcuffs," said Beck.

Dodd wondered if his boss was joking. He nodded at the dead guard. "For him?" I don't think he's gonna give you any trouble, boss."

Beck offered no smile, just held out his hand until Dodd set the cuffs there.

The ship motored forward, the city of Victoria—big, golden, and glowing—to the starboard now, just a few miles away. *Marauder* was veering west, around the tip of Vancouver, toward the open ocean.

"Go inside," Beck told his assistant.

Dodd stared at him.

"Go inside. I've got it from here."

Dodd nodded and surveyed the scene: Three people locked in the hyperbaric chamber. A dead guy chained to the catwalk. More people due topside in minutes.

His boss's behavior made no sense, but it was not his place to question. He turned and headed for the doors without looking back.

Beck stretched his arms and set his shoulders back, rolled his head on his neck in a slow circle, like he was doing an exercise warm-up. He could feel the balance of power shifting in his mind again.

It felt like he was dreaming, executing a nonsensical plan in a particularly vivid dream, surprising himself every step of the way. But part of him—the old Beck—knew that it wasn't a dream.

This is real.

He tried to analyze the situation, but thinking made his headache flare, dull and flat behind his eyes.

He looked at the hyperbaric chamber and the hulking body of the guard—blood oozing from the remaining sections of his skull—and understood Dodd's concerns.

His heart thumped.

People are coming.

The pilot and scientists.

What am I going to do?

The sick anticipation swelled in his belly then, and in a flash of illumination he remembered everything. The plan, tidily arranged in front of him.

Of course!

He climbed the short ladder on the deck crane and dropped into the control seat, turned a key and punched some buttons, brought the boom into position.

The crane clicked and whirred.

Beck stepped off the lift and thumped onto the top of the hyperbaric chamber. Gathered the cables hanging limp from the corners and clipped them to the beefy steel hook dangling from the boom.

He dropped into the control seat once more, threw more switches, nudged a joystick with two fingers and hauled in the excess cable. Drew it tight.

The three-ton chamber jerked, then lifted silently off the deck, tilting slightly as the cables tightened further.

Almost at once the chamber began rocking and swaying with the motion of the yacht, with the wind. Like a pendulum weight.

He could hear the prisoners inside the chamber scrabbling furiously, frantically.

Beck focused on the boom controls, aware now of a little voice in his mind sounding an alarm.

But the balance of power had shifted, and, for the moment, at least, the rabid animal was in control.

Beck embraced his new persona with a demented grin and lifted the chamber off the deck, the sick anticipation growing in his belly, sweat slick on his forehead.

He could see his father and sister in the chamber now. The bodyguard, too. They were frantic, scurrying about like trapped rats, trying to break out.

He teased the boom higher, and sent it telescoping out, over the water, timing the chamber's pendulous swings to avoid the bulwark.

Marauder dove through a swell, and the swings grew more violent. Light still pouring from the portholes, the chamber bobbed like a lantern at the end of a stick.

Beck waited, concentrating. He had to time the release just so. Release it on the wrong swing and the three-ton tank would glance against the ship, tearing a hole in the side, most likely.

He waited as *Marauder* smashed through two more large swells. The corpse handcuffed to the chamber's catwalk rolled, so that the body hung by the wrist, dangling from the chamber—a second pendulum weight below the first.

Beck punched the red release button at exactly the right moment.

The hyperbaric chamber hovered for an instant—like an alien spaceship come to take a closer look at *Marauder*—then dropped like a stone.

Beck screamed in a confused frenzy of terror and excitement and remorse as the chamber hit black ocean with a monumental splash.

Leaning from the crane, he watched the chamber sink, watched it plummet like a house with the lights on, vanishing beneath the waves forever.

Beck, mind numb, worked the boom. Drew it carefully back in.

The weather deck looked vast without the chamber, and salt spray settled over the place where it had been, erasing its footprint on the carbon-fiber deck.

Beck climbed off the crane and, following a plan he barely remembered, moved puppet-like toward the aft helipad.

The pad's LED landing lights were dim now, but they'd brighten as soon as the pilot and passengers exited the ready room.

He only had a minute. He felt along the gleaming steel underbelly of Winston Beck's sleek Bell 222B, and found the spot he was looking for. He took the heavy square from his pocket and attached it to the metal.

Click, and it was done. That simple.

He retreated to the solarium at the opposite end of the weather deck and found a chair in the shadows. Dragged it around so that it was facing the helipad and sat down.

Two minutes later Winston Beck's pilot was moving across the deck, followed by Phelps and Edelstein. The scientists dragged suitcases behind them. Bags hung from their shoulders.

The pad lights were bright now, bright as a Las Vegas stage. The yacht designer had spent a lot of time and money on lighting.

Beck watched the pilot and his passengers but could hear only the wind. The roar of *Marauder* driving hard for the strait.

Now two support crew from inside the ship were unclipping tie-downs, freeing rotors, conferring with the pilot, then stepping clear.

Beck heard the whine of the Bell's engine and saw the rotors start to turn, slowly at first.

The engine screamed and soon the blades were a blur.

Beck stared as the helicopter lifted off. It ascended a couple hundred feet, then nodded toward the Washington coast, and zoomed forward.

Beck watched.

Two minutes passed.

Three.

He could barely see the chopper now. Just a red blip against the glow of tiny Port Angeles.

And then—a fireball. A brief, intense explosion, orange against the horizon, in the middle of the shipping lanes. Then, nothing. Just dark sky and the stars over the Olympic Mountains to the south.

Beck rose from his chair and headed inside.

CHAPTER 75

FIFTEEN MINUTES AFTER Beck departed the weather deck, the Bell 412 carrying Joe and Ella settled onto the same helipad.

Even before the rotors had stopped spinning, Collins and his men were out, stepping low, reaching back into the passenger compartment and grabbing Joe and Ella.

Joe and Ella stayed as close to one another as they could.

Collins hustled them along, and the group split at the doors leading inside. Drucker and Knox stayed with Ella, took her to an elevator. Collins shoved Joe toward a different door.

"Where are you taking him?" Ella screamed.

Drucker and Knox stood impassive at the elevator. They looked tired. Like they wanted to finish their work—whatever that meant—and then retire to their cabins.

Ella wept as Joe disappeared into the ship, toward a spiral staircase.

Joe twisted away from Collins. Found Ella. Locked eyes with her.

"I love you, Ella!" he screamed. "I love you!"

Ella, tears flooding down her face, yelled back. "I love you, Joe!"

Collins pushed Joe downstairs.

Joe's hands were shaking, though they were bound behind his back, and his vision was cloudy, as if he were peering through gauze.

They hustled off the stairs and through a maze of passageways, past crew quarters and a small galley.

They came at last to the end of a long hall. An area bright and sterile and cold.

Joe saw a familiar face, and his spine chilled. Turned to ice.

It was Heintzel. Coming toward him. Unsmiling, not making eye contact. She wore a surgical mask and scrubs. Latex gloves. Glasses with magnifiers. Nurses and technicians were arrayed behind her, and a strong antiseptic smell stung Joe's nostrils.

Heintzel raised her hand, and Joe saw that she was holding a syringe.

CHAPTER 76

ADMIRAL HOUGHTON WOKE to a sound. A sudden, painful tone that rang from the four walls of his cabin. His eyes snapped open and he waited for the next blast. The next shriek of the alarm.

Nothing.

He breathed. Listened.

He'd believed, upon waking, that he was at sea. That the ship had come under attack.

Now that he was fully conscious, he realized the "sound" was in his head. Part of a dream. Another dream.

The cabin was quiet. Dark.

Houghton sat up and put his feet on the floor. Sat in the darkness in his boxer shorts and T-shirt and ran his hands through his hair, wondering at the sweat pouring from his scalp—*Am I running a fever?*—and the tingling in his arm.

He stood, steadying himself—one hand on his dresser—and flipped on a light. He dressed then—going through the motions without knowing why. Donning his uniform slowly, methodically, but feeling detached. Removed somehow from his own actions.

Houghton rarely drank—not like in his younger years—but it felt now as if he'd slammed a couple of gin and-tonics or taken a Percocet. Or both.

Why am I getting dressed at eleven thirty at night? he asked. But the question seemed immaterial. Like a question whispered by an audience member at a play.

He buttoned his shirt. Put on his belt. Opened his round hearing aid box and installed his hearing aid in his right ear, adjusting the volume as he did so. He donned his jacket. Checked himself in the mirror.

The audience member asked, "Where are we going?"

Admiral Houghton stared into the mirror and ignored the question. He took a hand towel from the rack next to the basin and dabbed the moisture from his forehead. He observed, with the same odd detachment, that his breathing was noisy. That his heart was thumping. As if he'd just climbed a bunch of stairs.

He squared his hat on his head and checked the mirror one final time.

Admiral Houghton stepped from the elevator onto the flag bridge and strolled into the center of the quiet, dimly lit room. The quartermaster of the watch and two lookouts turned at the same moment and reacted with surprise, hopping off their chairs and coming to attention.

"Attention on deck!" barked the quartermaster. Then, "Admiral Houghton. Good evening, sir."

Houghton stepped to the center window and stood staring at the flight deck and the Seattle waterfront stretching north and west beyond the ship. He could see the glow of Magnolia across Elliott Bay. The fireworks had long since ended.

"Get Commander Ferguson on the line for me. USNS *Impeccable*."

"Sir. Yes, sir."

The crew exchanged glances, but the quartermaster was already on the phone, speaking softly, relaying the order. After a couple of minutes, he handed the phone to Admiral Houghton.

"Sir. Commander Ferguson."

Houghton took the phone and the Quartermaster stepped out of the way.

The crew on the bridge heard Admiral Houghton's side of the call. It was a short conversation.

"Commander. Good evening. Fine, thank you. Commander, I want you to shut down your multistatic onboard source for twenty-four hours. That's correct. One hundred percent shut down on the Kanaga array until twenty three hundred hours, five July. Thank you, commander. That is all."

Houghton exited the flag bridge without another word, leaving a buzz of puzzled conversation in his wake.

He returned to his cabin. Went straight there, barely acknowledging the sailors he encountered as he walked.

The sense that he was observing someone else, standing off to the side, removed and remote from his physical body, was more potent than ever now.

Alone, inside his room, Houghton undressed, as carefully and methodically as he had gotten dressed. He hung up his uniform. Smoothed the pants over the hanger. Took off his dog tags and his hearing aid. Squared everything away. He brushed his teeth, poured himself a glass of water, and turned out the light.

He lay down on his bed and closed his eyes. Listened to the ship. And then he was dreaming. Or maybe not. He couldn't tell.

The line.

The line is on fire.

He was back in his childhood church once more, watching in anticipation, watching the line cut through the sanctuary like a laser knife.

His heart thumped in his chest, and his mouth went dry—not out of fear or alarm, but out of anticipation.

If this is a dream, I don't want to wake up.

The line was growing brighter and the walls were crumbling. Falling away.

I'm almost there, he thought, feeling a flood of relief.

The horrible, tormenting sound was gone—no longer blocking the music.

He smiled in his dream, letting the music envelop him utterly and watching as the walls at the back of the church gave way, at last.

Houghton moaned softly as a massive clot settled in his brain, blocking an artery and causing a stroke. His right hand slid from his chest to the side of the bed. The hand he had used to greet Joe Stanton. His arm went cold, and ten minutes later he was dead.

CHAPTER 77

MIA AND HER FAMILY swam steadily through the darkness, 622 million cubic kilometers of Pacific Ocean before them.

They swam, and listened, communicating little.

The time for discussion, for contemplation and planning, had long since passed. The time for action was upon them.

Almost.

They listened, and swam, and listened some more. Listened to the restless sea and its cacophony. Sounds they knew in their bones. Sounds they had heard every day of their lives: water moving beneath them, around them, water moving in streams and columns and great rushing rivers, all within the larger whole. Mammals and fish, and ships—all manner of craft—muddying and confusing the natural soundscape. Magma boiling up from the Earth's core, bubbling from cracks and vents and into the frigid darkness. The plates of the planet's crust shifting, settling, moving endlessly. The bones of the Earth itself grinding under pressures unimaginable.

The whales of Mia's family knew all of these sounds as they knew their own heartbeats, and registered them now as a city dweller registers the noise of traffic, which is to say, not at all.

The whales were focused on two other sounds: one that filled them with hope—with almost indescribable joy. And one that engendered dread. Despair.

The hopeful sound was the melody of the tunnels—the passageways to another world—turning on. Lighting up.

It was happening everywhere now, the sound—the music—of the tunnels. Spreading like a rumor in a crowded hall.

The sound that filled them with despair was the sonar. The *ping...ping...ping.* Sharp and painful and relentless.

The whales of Mia's family understood her role in the Exodus. She was the leader. The instigator and architect and champion. She had not made the tunnels, but she had tapped into the power that animated them and brought them to life. She was the catalyst at the heart of the reaction.

The whales of Mia's pod knew this. Mia was like others they had met—and yet unlike anyone or anything they had ever encountered. Mia was a singularity. A force of nature. And they swam with her now, poised between hope and despair, escape and imprisonment, life and death, with unspoken love and respect.

If the sonar stayed on, the Exodus would fail. The tunnels would wither and desiccate, never to be renewed.

If the sonar went quiet, Mia would make her call. Send a message that would reverberate around the planet. A message cousins north and south, east and west were waiting to receive and pass on.

Whatever happened, though, Mia was Mia. Matriarch. Mother. Grandmother. Sister. Cousin. And something beyond all of those things.

Her family—her entire pod and clan and community—revered her. Loved her. And regardless of the outcome, they would be at her side until the end.

They swam—listening, hoping—the balance in their minds shifting slowly, inexorably toward despair.

The sonar was unstoppable, most of them were beginning to think. Unending. A festering, malignant tumor in the collective consciousness.

We will never get out.

We will die here, as the humans turn the bright seas into putrid, lifeless holes.

We will die here.

And then it happened.

Ping...ping...ping...

Silence.

Silence.

Silence.

The whales swam on, wanting to believe but not jumping to conclusions, almost expecting the toxic noise to resume. The sound had plagued them for so long.

It did not resume, and a shiver of excitement traveled the length and breadth of the entire community. Starting low and building in intensity, the shiver intensified, an infectious explosion of happiness ricocheting throughout the community like the peal of a bell.

Mia cleared her mind and pulled to the front of the pack, visualized the long-rehearsed call one last time, and sent it in a single burst lasting thirty seconds. A song haunting and beautiful and poignant. Unlike any other whale song in the history of the world.

She waited a minute, then sent the same message again. And again. And out into the darkness the call moved, like a key gliding toward a lock.

Mia fell silent and dropped back once again, swimming on autopilot, swimming as if it were just an ordinary moment in her long life.

Silence.

Silence.

And then…a reply. Multiple replies. Calls, coming in from far away. Calls faint but discernible. Replies from fin whales and blue. Minke and gray. Replies from every orca clan within one thousand miles. Different dialects. Strange voices. All saying the same thing:

We understand and we will spread the word.

Another sound then, mixed with the replies: the music of the tunnels. Getting stronger, growing louder.

Throughout the world's oceans, the tunnels flared bright, like golden, unearthly embers reborn. Like miniature stars igniting in the deep.

The Exodus had begun.

CHAPTER 78

PROFESSOR DIETURLUND'S EYES flew open and he lay in the darkness of his room at The Willows, heart thudding in his chest.

It's begun.

He lay motionless, trying not to think or feel or analyze. Letting the news wash over him raw and unadorned.

The Exodus has begun.

He listened, breathless, allowing Mia's tidings to play across his mind like a story, feeling blessed to be connected to her still.

He felt her mind and spirit now like an electrifying physical presence, a supernatural entity throwing off light and heat in its ascendance.

Like the tunnels, Mia was flaring brighter by the moment, gaining power and strength. Mia, assuming her role. Donning her mantle.

She will be the last to pass the gates, Dieturlund realized. *The last to transit, before the tunnels vanish.*

Except…

There was something else. A puzzling revelation hidden in the torrent of thought flooding over him now. A whisper revealing news he couldn't comprehend.

Mia is a singularity.
But she has a twin.
A counterpart.
An equal.

It made no sense.

Dieturlund lay there trying to see, trying to understand. Getting nowhere.

Mia is Mia. Mia is the architect. The prophet. The leader. How can there be another?

In the darkness the old man remained. Listening. Waiting. Finding no answers.

CHAPTER 79

SUNRISE, THE DAY THE WORLD CHANGED, found *Marauder* anchored two miles from the outer edge of the Broken Group Islands, at the mouth of Barkley Sound.

It was only 5 a.m., and already Beck's crew was working full-tilt. Runabouts were in the water—two Boston Whalers with 150-horse Honda outboards, and an eighteen-foot Zodiac jet boat. And a specially trained team on the well deck was readying the *Velocity*, Beck's two-person thirty-foot-long supercavitating submarine.

Inside the bustling War Room, Ring's focus was split between a torrent of fresh images from two distinct sources: Joe Stanton's head and an ROV falling fast through the water column directly beneath *Marauder*'s hull.

Ring and his team were also monitoring news reports, a growing chorus of voices—some puzzled, some panicked—from around the globe.

Ring caught his breath as the ROV driver tilted the probe's 12x high-res camera down, toward the seafloor.

The ROV's fifteen-hundred-watt quartz halogens revealed a swarm of organisms—a stupendous undersea parade of fish and mammals, predators and prey—all steadily moving in the same direction.

Down.

Down.

Toward an explosion of light in the deep. A ghostly, phosphorescent nexus of illumination beckoning like an airfield on a stormy night.

Marauder's sonar had been tracking the flood of life since the ship's arrival, but it was different seeing the stark real-time images from the ROV.

Ring caught sight of Beck in his peripheral vision and addressed him without turning.

"Lots of chatter this morning. Twitter. CNN. FOX. MSNBC. Al Jazeera. Migration's pretty much all NOAA's talking about. Military channels are going nuts as well."

Beck slid into a chair next to Ring but said nothing.

One of Ring's techs brought up news feeds on a half dozen of the smaller monitors: reporters querying marine experts. Experts pontificating breathlessly. News anchors narrating grainy homemade videos from around the globe. The clips showed whales and other mammals massing, congregating, moving with a singularity of focus never before witnessed. One feed showed whales in marine parks going berserk, hurling themselves against the walls of their enclosures. But the bulk of the coverage was about the tumult in the sea.

"Shit's hitting the fan," said Ring.

"Anybody talking about the tunnels yet?" Beck asked. "Or is it all related to the migration?"

"*National Geographic* crew in Thailand's posted video of a tunnel, but they have no idea what it is. A diver in the eastern Mediterranean posted footage as well. Low-res. Can't see much. Give it an hour though. There'll be plenty more."

Beck stared at the monitors, feeling alert but jagged. Raw. He'd been on the phone for the past hour with various US authorities. Officials calling to tell him in remorseful tones that a helicopter registered to Erebus Industries had crashed in the Strait of Juan de Fuca. That Coast Guard vessels were on the scene and that an investigation had begun. *No survivors have been found,* they said, before assuring him that the search would continue throughout the day.

He hadn't slept, and Heintzel's magic potion—whatever the hell had been in that syringe—was propelling him still, but wouldn't last much longer. He could feel the crash coming: Collapse. Meltdown. And once that happened…he didn't know, and he couldn't bring himself to think about it. The possibility of seeing the eyes again—of the thing, whatever it was, prowling the corridors of his mind, unleashed—was too much to contemplate.

He said to Ring, "Will your plan work?"

Ring paused, a can of Orange Crush in his right hand, halfway to his mouth. "It should. If I'm right about Mia."

"Right about her how?"

"In thinking that she won't allow the doors to shut until her entire family is through. Every last member. If an individual is delayed, then the tunnels—or at least, this particular tunnel—will stay open. That's my belief."

"I wrote up a plan." He handed Beck a tablet computer with just two paragraphs displayed. An outline. "I went over this with Collins. He thinks they can pull it off."

Beck scanned the plan. Nodded. "So let's do it."

CHAPTER 80

JOE STANTON AWOKE to bright lights and a hospital smell that made him instantly sick to his stomach. He rolled onto his side, retching as he turned, appalled by the weakness and fatigue in his limbs. In his core.

There were people around him, he realized. Medical staff moving, working quietly, fiddling with equipment, adjusting his gurney. No one offered help or comfort.

"What's going on?" Joe asked. And it felt like someone had glued his tongue to the roof of his mouth. "What happened?"

The room was a blur, the medical staff a swirl of amorphous white-clad shapes.

No response. Just movement. People busying themselves. But Joe sensed that something was about to happen.

He lay back on his pillow and closed his eyes, though that did little to diminish the awful headache-inducing glare of the surgical lamps directly over his bed.

Ella?

Joe! Is that you? Joe?

Joe felt a wave of relief as Ella's voice registered in his mind. The interaction blew the cobwebs apart. Made it easier to think.

She sounds scared, Joe thought.

Of course she's scared.

He wanted to reassure her.

Hi, sweetie. Yeah, it's me. Where are you?

Here. On the ship. I'm okay.

Where on the ship?

I don't know. Lowest level, I think. Joe. What's happening? They won't tell me anything.

Joe's eyes snapped open as the gurney rocked forward and began rolling. The white-clad shapes were moving him. Taking him someplace.

Ella, he said. *I have to go. I love you. I love you so much.*

I love you, Joe. I love you.

Through the curtain of his own terror, he could feel Ella reaching out to him, touching him with her mind. Could almost feel her warm body next to his. He held her there, and shut his eyes.

CHAPTER 81

RING AND BECK and the War Room staff busied themselves in the command center, but dozens of other crew—from engine-room mechanics to dishwashers—were outside, on the decks, standing in the glow of a molten-copper sunrise, witnessing the strangest spectacle any of them had ever seen.

The ocean, shining platinum beneath the sky, was boiling. Seething. Not with waves or surging tides, but with life.

The sea—alive with purposeful movement.

The crew stood staring. Turning. Gawking. Snapping pictures. Not speaking.

A path—a trail of particularly vigorous churning—snaked away south toward the strait, and organisms of every description were jetting along this "highway" now, making for Barkley Sound.

Spectators standing on *Marauder*'s decks could see only a tiny fraction of the billion-creature flood, but even the surface display was stupendous, beginning with a dozen species of whales, rolling and breaching, leaping and diving. There were dolphins, seals, sea lions, otters, and fish—salmon and snapper, sharks and sturgeon—flashing like mirrors in the dawn as they shot along the trail, periodically breaking the surface.

More boats were out now. Powerboaters from Tofino. Kayakers from the Broken Group. People coming to observe the strange tumult in the water.

In the cool machine glow of the War Room, Ring surveyed the images of the surface—courtesy of a dozen cameras positioned around *Marauder*'s decks—but the bulk of his attention was on the pictures pouring in from the ROV.

The boxy, unsexy underwater vehicle the size of a home generator had settled to a depth of two hundred meters, and there it hovered in the water column, motors whirring softly. The

robot's forward-facing 12x camera showed the glowing, gently undulating tunnel mouth, perhaps a quarter mile distant. Vast and cavernous the opening looked. Mysterious as an alien city.

A torrent of organisms—creatures of every shape, size and description—swarmed through the tunnel's gently arcing bell and deep into the heart of the fantastic structure.

"It's happening all over the world," Ring said to his team. "But this is the mother tunnel. The nerve center of the whole operation."

Ring's ROV pilot ordered the craft slowly forward, closer to the tunnel's gaping maw.

"Because Mia's here?" Beck asked. "And she's the—"

"Catalyst," said Ring. "The nexus. Yes."

A commotion near the entrance to the War Room drew all eyes. A team from the infirmary was maneuvering a gurney into the darkened room, wheeling the narrow bed among the consoles and touch screens. Technicians stopped what they were doing to watch.

The infirmary crew lifted the gurney through a tight space, turned it, and came on, toward Ring's work area.

Ring glanced at Joe, then fixed his attention on a particular patch of screen, the ones showing the feed from the "Mia Cam," as Ring called it. Mia was sending a continuous, voluminous stream of thought to Joe Stanton now, and Heintzel's freshly installed thought-capture hardware was allowing Ring to eavesdrop on every bit of it.

The infirmary team parked Joe's gurney in the middle of Ring's workstation, set the brakes, and raised the end of the narrow bed so that Joe was sitting up. His head lolled to one side, and his mouth worked, but no sound came out.

Beck stepped from the shadows and took a close look at the young priest.

A two-inch square bandage covered the incision area above and behind Joe's right eye. The scalp around the bandage looked pink and tender and freshly shaved.

Joe's head sagged further and his shoulders slouched. If not for the strap across his chest, he might have rolled off the gurney.

"Christ's sake," said Beck. "Give him something to perk him up."

"Dr. Heintzel just did," said the lead attendant. "Should be seeing the effect of that fairly soon."

Beck studied Joe some more, and felt nauseated by the man's appearance: the greasy, matted beard. The scalped, bandaged area on his head. His pallid, emaciated frame. Beck thought he looked like a mental patient. A dangerous schizophrenic fresh from lobotomy surgery.

He felt no sympathy for the priest. He had no interest in easing his suffering or keeping him alive long term—only in his immediate utility.

So he watched him breathing now with cold, appraising eyes. He knew that Joe and Mia were linked, telepathically. Ring had told him that the reinstalled thought-capture hardware would allow them to track Mia's movements throughout the Exodus.

But as Beck observed Joe now, he wondered if the young man would even survive the next few minutes. He appeared to be at death's door.

Joe turned his head slightly, and his swollen lips moved again, like he wanted to speak.

"Get him some water," Beck told his infirmary team. "And wake him the hell up."

Beck's gaze flicked back to the ROV pictures.

The robot was hovering again. Holding steady in the water column roughly 150 meters from the chamber mouth. The pilot had positioned the craft to one side of the rush of creatures.

The remote's cameras revealed a densely packed ribbon of organisms. A long, unbroken trail of life forms flowing from the darkness of the sea toward the phosphorescent portal.

Beck turned to the screens, marveling at the surreal, impossible nature of the feed: predators and prey swimming side by side, submarine-sized whales flanked by seals flanked by sharks, surrounded by salmon and snapper, lamprey and herring, sculpin, wolf eels, greenlings, sole, tubefish, and ray. Orcas and otters and sea lions.

All seemed to be flying headlong toward the horn-of-plenty–shaped chamber, as if it were a colossal vacuum sucking in every last bit of life from a hundred miles around.

An elephant seal shot fluidly past the 12x lens, rolling and twisting and mugging for the camera. The beast's obsidian-black eyes shone with fierce intelligence. With excitement. It lingered a moment, then spun, merged into the parade of animals, and vanished.

The screens flashed to a wider view.

From this perspective, the fish and mammals crossing the phosphorescent bell resembled bits of interstellar detritus transiting a black hole's event horizon. Passing a threshold to another universe, never to return.

The flow of animals started to diminish and the War Room staff stared, mute and motionless, like witnesses to a catastrophic disaster.

Joe stirred on his bed and sat up straighter.

A new shape passed beneath the ROV then—through the glow of the ROV's halogens: Beck's submarine. *Velocity*.

Dark and sleek and nimble it looked. A worthy high-tech offspring of *Marauder*.

Beck glanced at Ring, sitting at his control panel, flitting from keyboard to keyboard.

"Your plan gonna work, Ring?"

"It should."

Beck nodded. Looked at Joe. The priest was awake now, soaking in the scene, gawking at news feeds. The White House press secretary was talking to reporters on one monitor, and a caption across the bottom of the screen read "Breaking News. Crisis in the Sea."

Beck said to Ring. "Send *Velocity* through. Let's do this."

Beck stepped to Joe's gurney as an attendant helped the priest sip water from a plastic cup.

Joe's eyes—tired but clear—widened slightly when they found Beck's face.

"Where's Ella?" he asked, voice thick and raspy.

"Here. On the ship. Safe and sound. For now, at least."

"What do you want?" Joe asked. The anesthesia was wearing off.

Beck leaned closer. "I'm Sheldon Beck," he said.

"I know who you are," Joe whispered. "You're a criminal. A murderer."

Beck laughed. "Bold words, Father. But you need to set your anger aside for the time being. We need each other, you and I."

Joe took another sip of water. Said nothing.

"You need your girl back. In one piece. I need your…insight, navigating in an unfamiliar environment."

Beck tapped a monitor on the nearest wall. "You see this? This is our Stanton feed. It's all you, my friend."

Joe looked from the screen to Beck and back. A group of adult orca whales were patrolling near the surface, along the edge of the flood of life. The Exodus tunnel was visible, but small and remote and far below, on the seafloor.

Joe realized Beck was telling the truth. The images *were* coming from him—from inside his own head—courtesy of Mia.

He lay still as the connection reengaged in his conscious mind. It was like tuning into a lost signal on the radio and finding it bright and clear and powerful.

Mia was communicating with him. Allowing him to see what she was seeing, real time.

They're shepherds, he thought as he watched the orcas patrolling the edge of the Exodus.

Yes. Shepherds.

The whales, members of Mia's pod, all of them, were shepherding the flood of life. Channeling the animals within it, spurring them on and guiding them to the tunnel.

Joe lay quiet. Thinking. Comprehending.

Mia and her family will wait until everyone else is through.

They'll do a sweep, check to see that everyone that could leave did leave. Then they'll depart. After all the others have crossed, they'll go. And then—

Joe felt Mia reaching out to him, finding him in the darkness and touching him with her mind.

He forgot about Beck and the War Room and closed his eyes. Let the connection build. He felt the warmth of Mia's spirit and suddenly saw her for what she was: a blend of bright-eyed child and sage old soul.

Inquisitive, playful, and wise beyond reckoning, Mia was in touch with secrets powerful and profound.

My friend, she seemed to be saying. *My friend.*

Joe felt Mia's message in his bones.

I am leaving.

I am sorry.

You are my friend.

I love you.

Stan-ton. I—

Joe cried out in pain as the communication broke. He opened his eyes to find Beck grinning at him, slapping his face.

"We're sending the submarine through, Father. To the other side. I need you to stay awake. Show us where the queen bee is. What she's doing."

Joe's head was pounding, his ears ringing from the abrupt separation, wishing he had the strength to throw a punch. He said flatly, "She's leaving, Beck. They're *all* leaving. She's sure as hell not going to hold the door for you."

Beck kept grinning. "We think she will. Meantime, I want to know what she's up to." He punched Joe on the shoulder. "So keep those pictures coming. For your girl's sake."

Joe said nothing, just lay there, trying to restart the conversation with Mia.

No luck. She was still sending him pictures via his subconscious—he could see them on the monitors all around—but the two-way communication was through, at least for the moment.

He took a breath and tried to find Ella with his mind, suddenly desperate to feel her presence. Hear her voice.

Ella?

Ella. It's me. Are you there?

No reply.

Beck's done something with her, he thought, and his heart skipped a beat.

Beck's done some—

He spotted Ella's image on a small black-and-white monitor near the bottom of one video wall. She was sitting on a chair in the middle of a drab-looking room. There was no one else around. She looked okay.

Joe breathed, and his heart slowed once more. He tried again to reach her.

Ella?

Ella. It's me.

Nothing.

He lay back, frustrated.

It's the situation, he thought. *Stress blocking my thoughts. Or hers.*

He focused again on the activity around him.

Beck and Ring were conferring with staff, talking low and urgently as screens blinked and techs busied themselves at a dozen nearby consoles.

The submarine, Joe saw with surprise, was already well inside the tunnel, traveling amid the swarm of fish and mammals as if it belonged there.

Mia and the other shepherds were aware of the submarine. Joe was positive of that. But they appeared utterly unperturbed by the craft's presence and trajectory. He could see the whales—on a different set of screens—patrolling near the surface, as before. Guiding the ever-dwindling tide of organisms.

Joe heard bursts of radio chatter—quick, excited exchanges between Ring and Beck and the submarine crew, but he couldn't make out what they were saying.

The sub moved deeper into the cavernous chamber, so deep that it was lost now to the ROV's cameras.

Cameras mounted on the sub itself revealed narrowing, light-filled walls and the now-familiar latticework of shimmering, glowing lines.

Fish and mammals clogged the gently spiraling passageway in front of the sub, and vanished around a graceful bend that seemed not far ahead.

The sub moved steadily on, and the radio chatter intensified. Ahead, a barrier. A shimmering, pearlescent wall.

He gasped as the creatures approaching the wall burst into flame—or appeared to—and vanished.

Joe's eyes danced from monitor to monitor. He could see that things were winding down. Coming to a close.

The torrent of life had diminished to a trickle.

Joe realized that in another minute or two Mia and her family would gulp their last lungful of Earthly air, dive six hundred feet, and enter the tunnel. A minute after that, they would swim into the barrier, or portal, or whatever it was, and vanish from the world.

Joe's attention flicked to Ring, who had risen from his command station and was standing now at the Palantir, talking urgently with a cluster of techs.

Their eyes met, and Joe panicked. Ring's eyes gave it all away.

It's happening, Joe thought. *Just like Dieturlund feared. They're going to try something.*

He had to warn Mia. Had to reestablish the connection.

He closed his eyes and, miraculously, found her. Touched her with his mind.

Mia.

Mia. Listen to me—

The same love and compassion he'd experienced earlier rolled toward him once more.

Stan-ton.

My friend.

We are leaving.

I am sorry.

Joe tried screaming at her with his thoughts.

Mia! Watch out! They're up to something!

No use.

The communication was muddled. Mia could feel his terror but didn't perceive it as a warning.

Mia, you have to—

Joe's eyes flew open and he cried out in pain as the connection shattered, the link with Mia severing instantly, brutally, as she exploded with rage.

Molten hot fury was the last emotion Joe felt. And she was gone.

"Beck!" Joe screamed. "You bastard! What are you doing to them?"

And then he saw. On the monitors it all came clear.

Beck's men were firing something off the weather deck. Firing into the water with what looked like a grenade launcher.

"Flash-bang," he heard someone say.

CHAPTER 82

THE LASER-GUIDED PROJECTILE landed a few yards from one of the last remaining orca pods—a group of Mia's cousins that included a two-week old calf known to researchers as T-13C or, more affectionately, Ninitat.

The projectile, a twenty-one-ounce tactical flash-bang grenade, detonated as it hit the water, blinding and disorienting the whales and temporarily incapacitating the eight-foot long, five-hundred-pound baby—which was exactly what Ring had intended.

Beck's crew in the Zodiac was on top of the listless calf ten seconds after detonation, looping canvas straps around the baby's sleek body, preparing to haul it aboard.

A Boston Whaler was on the scene moments later—more men to help hustle the calf into the sling and onto the inflatable. Ring had admonished the crew to work fast. To drag the baby aboard and jet back to *Marauder* with all speed.

Once at *Marauder*, Ring had explained, more crew would hoist the baby into a saltwater pool on the well deck. And there the calf would remain, a hostage, as Beck's sub transited the undersea portal at will.

Beck's men worked fast, but Mia and the other shepherds were faster.

The listless baby was in the canvas sling between the Zodiac and the Whaler when the first orca—a thirty-foot-long, ten-ton male—exploded from the fast-moving tidal churn behind the inflatable. He leapt completely over the craft, smashing the crew into the sea as he flew.

Orca after orca drove into the boats from below, flipping the Whaler as if it were a toy and upending the Zodiac.

One of the crew on the inflatable fired his sidearm into the attacking beasts as he fell, and red splattered against the orcas' white underbellies.

Then it was a frenzy.

Like goldfish in a piranha tank, the men in the water were ripped to pieces by jaws packed with three-inch-long conical teeth—jaws accustomed to crushing seals and sea lions and lesser whales.

The boats and equipment lolled broken and sinking in the chop.

An instant later, the whales were gone. Diving in unison. Diving fast. Guarding the baby, who had begun to come around.

For the tunnel they swam, with all speed.

CHAPTER 83

IN THE WAR ROOM, Beck was screaming at everyone and no one.

"What the hell was that? What the fuck just happened? Goddamnit! Goddamnit!"

Joe watched in silence as the ROV's cameras tracked Mia and the other shepherds.

Steadily, unhurriedly, they descended toward the tunnel—like spaceships approaching the entrance to an alien city. Gently, the tunnel swayed with the current.

So vast was the structure's phosphorescent bell that Mia and her family looked like minnows passing over it.

The stupendous flood of life summoned to the Exodus had departed. Mia and her kin were the last.

Beck planted his hands on Ring's console, leaned toward the scientist's face, and spoke in a voice tight and menacing.

"So what the fuck is plan B, asshole?"

Ring continued working as if nothing had happened.

Monitors around the room showed that the last whales were halfway through the tunnel now, moving steadily, confidently toward the glow at the end of the ethereal corridor.

"There isn't a plan B," said Ring.

"A bunch of my guys are dead," hissed Beck. "And my fucking submarine has vanished."

Ring nodded. "I guessed that we would lose contact with the sub after it crossed the barrier."

"But now they're over there," Beck waved at the tunnel. "Wherever the fuck *there* is. And we have zero leverage to keep the door open."

"Correct," said Ring.

Beck's voice broke. "So how the fuck are they supposed to get back? How are we supposed to use the tunnel?"

Ring shrugged. "I don't know. This didn't go as I had planned."

Beck glared at him, a breath away from ripping the man out of his high-backed leather chair and breaking his neck in front of a dozen witnesses.

"Didn't go as planned?" said Beck. "Is that a fucking fact?"

Ring appeared not to hear him. He was staring at a cluster of screens showing Mia's family deep inside the tunnel. These images weren't coming from the ROV, but from Joe Stanton's head.

Beck followed Ring's gaze. "She's still communicating with him?"

"Apparently," said Ring.

Beck stood, drew his 1911 from his shoulder holster and pivoted toward Joe, racking the slide on the weapon as he moved.

"Make her keep the tunnel open," he said, as he set the barrel of the gun against the priest's head.

Joe laughed. "How am I supposed to do that, Beck?"

Beck glanced at the screens. The whales were almost to the barrier.

"She's still communicating with you. She cares about you. Tell her that if the tunnel closes, your girl will die a slow, excruciating death. Tell her you'll die, too."

Joe twisted on the gurney, pushing against the gun. "Leave Ella out of this!"

Beck screamed and drove the weapon harder into Joe's skull. "Tell her to keep the fucking tunnel open!"

Joe shut his eyes and felt Mia's presence at once. Felt her thoughts rushing toward him.

Good-bye, Stan-ton.

My friend.

I am sorry.

The communication washed over him as before. But there was a finality about it this time.

Mia didn't blame him for the attack on the baby. He felt not a trace of the rage she'd exhibited moments earlier.

Good-bye, Stan-ton.

My friend.

Beck screamed again, spittle flying from his mouth.

"Make her keep it open! Tell her!"

On-screen, the whales were approaching the bend in the tunnel, the graceful curve that glowed with a holy luminescence.

Joe focused his mind.

Good-bye, Mia.

My friend.

May you find peace in your new world.

Mia and her family swam into the halo surrounding the barrier, and their bodies flared, meteor-like. When the flash faded, they were gone.

Instantly, the screens displaying Joe's subconscious thoughts went dark. Ring and his techs flitted between consoles, typing and troubleshooting, but it was no use.

Only the views from the ROV and *Marauder*'s deck cameras remained, plus muted news feeds on some of the smaller monitors.

The ROV's cameras revealed a tunnel empty, forlorn and adrift. Desolate. A lifeless husk.

Beck, sweating profusely, reeking of acid stress, banged the 1911 against Stanton's temple. "You better hope," he hissed, "that my submarine comes back and the tunnel stays open."

A collective gasp drew all eyes to the ROV feed. Beck lowered the gun and gawked.

The tunnel itself was flaring now, glowing brighter by the second, like a dying sun going nova. As it reached its zenith, the entire structure shuddered and convulsed, vomiting a stream of detritus, an asteroid-like field of debris that shotgunned out in all directions.

A dark cylinder whickered past the ROV's 12x lens, so close it looked like the objects would collide.

It was a section of the submarine. A jagged, twenty-foot-long fragment, twisted and burned and mangled. It looked, whirling by, as if it had been crushed in an avalanche, then set on fire.

Beck stared, speechless, as more ejecta from the tunnel wound past the ROV: *Velocity*'s propeller. A fragment of engine. A section of cockpit.

"Got your sub back," said Joe.

Beck spun on the priest and clubbed him with the 1911, knocking the gurney sideways and almost upending it completely. Face contorted with rage, eyes wide and burning, Beck lifted the gun, puppet-like, to Stanton's head.

War Room crew in the line of fire dove out of the way, scattering chairs and slamming desks.

"Good-bye, Mr. Stanton."

"Wait!" Ring screamed.

Beck pivoted toward Ring, then gaped as the images on the screens changed yet again.

The tunnel's luminescent glow dimmed, and the vast bell-shaped mouth shrank and shriveled, collapsing in on itself. The tunnel walls, and the radiant latticework that defined the passage, appeared to melt—disintegrating, before their eyes.

Moments later, all of the tunnel's light—all of the eerie phosphorescence—had been extinguished, and the "skin" of the structure was tearing, dissolving into pieces, like wet paper in a drain.

Beck watched as the pieces became a flaccid mess tumbling in the current. He turned back to Stanton but addressed Ring. "Why should I wait?" he asked, still aiming the gun at Stanton's head.

"Because we might need him."

"Why would we need him? The tunnel's gone."

"I'm seeing something I can't explain," said Ring.

A stream of data was tumbling down a small screen on his desktop.

"What?"

"Give me a minute," said Ring.

Beck's head was throbbing, only the thinnest membrane of sanity keeping him from killing the priest, from murdering everyone in the War Room, for that matter. He imagined how immensely cathartic that would feel.

Stanton lay sideways on the gurney, breathing in a ragged wheeze, blood trickling from his nose and mouth. He looked only half-alive.

Beck thought again about blowing Joe's brains out.

Ignore Ring and just do it.

He wanted desperately to kill. To find release for the failure with the tunnel. For the loss of his submarine.

Lifting his eyes to the monitors, he saw a cluster of boats where the Whaler and Zodiac had been, where debris now bobbed in the tide. People were there, looking for survivors. Bodies.

On another screen, remnants of tunnel wall fluttered in deep current. Ghostly fragments captured in the glow of the ROV's halogens.

The tunnel was no more.

Beck breathed, and the room spun carousel-like around him. For a moment, an instant, he saw everything clearly.

We put the deployment on hold to investigate a phenomenon.

It was me running the investigation, at first, but something changed.

He thought about the "mystery man" on the weather deck the day he'd killed Ellis. About the apparition he'd seen at the gun range, and the eyes in the desiccated skull in the Bellingham airport restroom. About the rabid lunatic beast loose in his mind.

It's in my head, he thought, numb with terror. *And when Heintzel's concoction wears off…*

He stood there, next to the priest on his gurney, oblivious to the gaze of the techs. It was suddenly difficult to breathe.

When my strength is gone and the beast slides into control behind my eyes, when it ascends to its place of control and my energy fades, I will be the one lurking in the corner and the beast will be in charge. A blend of Dahmer and Bundy and Manson. A thing sick and twisted and diseased.

I killed my father and sister, he thought with remorse.

I killed Ellis. Navarro. Phelps and Edelstein.

The beast murmured discontentedly in his head. Beck fought against it.

I was a rogue before. Pushed the boundaries of the law. Abused my enemies. But what's happened now is irreparable.

He analyzed his situation with cold lucidity. Like a cancer, the illness—the schizophrenia, or whatever it was—had metastasized, growing, flourishing, sinking its tentacles into the folds of his brain like an invasive weed.

The beast murmured again, then suddenly surged forward. Beck screamed.

I want blood, the beast whispered.

I want killing and death and pain.

But I want something else even more.

Beck waited, panting, shaking with terror.

I want to go across.

I want to go through the tunnel. Transit the barrier. And step into the new world.

And Beck understood.

It had been the disease all along. The lunatic part of him whispering in his ear, urging him to delay a massive deployment to investigate the phenomenon.

And now it was the beast moderating his actions, keeping him from killing Stanton, on the off chance that Ring was right.

We might need him, Ring had said. Though glancing at the monitors now, Beck didn't see why.

The tunnels were no more. Even the tattered fragments of tunnel wall had now dissolved into nothing.

The tunnels were no more.

Still, Ring was busy with *something*, frantic with something on his desk.

Beck decided he would spare Stanton, for the moment.

He turned to Ring, feeling the sick craving again, spreading now like a blast of whiskey, to his fingers and toes. He said matter-of-factly, "We don't need the *girl* for anything."

Stanton twisted on his bed, thrashing against his restraints. "She's done nothing to you!"

Beck leaned toward Joe with cold, pitiless eyes. "Bring the tunnel back to life."

Joe closed his eyes, and focused all his thoughts on Mia. But the lines were dead. The strange telepathic flow they'd shared was gone. He had his own thoughts. Nothing more.

He lifted his head and focused on the black-and-white video feed showing Ella in her tiny holding cell. She was just sitting there, staring intently at something offscreen.

Beck followed Joe's gaze. Sighed. "Have it your way, Father." He patted Joe on the arm. "I'm going to enjoy this."

"Please," said Joe, trembling now. "Please. For God's sake. She's innocent. She hasn't done anything."

"No," said Beck. "This is about you. About you reneging on our agreement."

Beck turned to the infirmary crew. "Take him into the conference room. Make sure he watches everything."

"Beck, please! Kill me! If you want blood, kill me. Leave her alone."

Beck strode purposefully toward the exit.

Blood rushed from Joe's head, the room rolled and undulated before his eyes, and he gave a strangled cry.

CHAPTER 84

THERE WAS A COLLECTIVE GASP. Beck paused at the exit, one hand on the massive steel door. Turned.

Screens throughout the War Room were filling with new images. Images that had nothing to do with the sea.

Beck called to Ring. "What the hell's that?"

Onscreen: A western landscape at sunrise. High, open prairie, reminiscent of Montana or Wyoming. Fog clinging to the ground and dew glistening on tall grass in the flat gray half-light.

The screens refreshed, revealing another section of prairie, this one terminating in a cliff. A ragged precipice where the land fell eight hundred feet—as if a giant fist had long ago smashed the plain in two at this precise spot.

The stone in the cliff face was old. Hammered and broken by millennia of rain and snow, ice and wind and scorching sun. The scrub at the base of the cliff was littered with boulders. Jagged slabs of sedimentary rock born during the Paleozoic.

Beck stepped back into the middle of the room. "Ring," he said. "What are we looking at?" He pointed at Stanton. "These images coming from him?"

Ring nodded. "Yes, from Mr. Stanton. But, I don't know where this is."

A young tech working at one of the computer terminals said softly, "I do."

Everyone turned.

"I grew up not far from that," said the tech.

"What's your name?" Beck asked.

"Thomas, Sir."

"Speak up, Thomas."

The kid stood. Stammered. Pointed at the screens. "It's called the Madison Buffalo Jump." He stepped to the nearest monitor. "It's a few miles from Bozeman."

"The Madison *what*?" Beck asked. Ring was already searching online.

"Buffalo Jump," said the kid. "The Madison jump's one of the most famous ones. It's a state park now."

"What the hell is a 'buffalo jump'?"

"Has to do with the Indians who lived in Montana," said the kid. "Before whites. They used these cliffs to kill buffalo."

Beck arched an eyebrow. "Kill them how?"

The kid pointed at the flat, open plan stretching away at the top of the cliff. "It was organized. Choreographed. They'd start miles out on the upper plain, see? A few warriors would find a big herd, maybe ten miles out, get 'em riled up by yelling and throwing rocks and spears. The buffalo would start running, this way and that. But the Indians would gradually steer them into this broad lane bordered by these cairns they'd built—piles of stone that kind of funneled the herd along.

"The lane started so wide the buffalo barely noticed. But it got narrower and narrower as they approached the cliff.

"Warriors closed in behind the herd, screaming bloody murder, dogs barking. Pretty soon the buffalo would be in a full-on stampede.

"Buffalo aren't as stupid as people think, though. They knew the cliff was up ahead, so they'd try to stop or turn aside. But the Indians had another trick. The last mile or so along the lane, warriors wearing wolf skins would leap up, howling. That kept the panic going. Kept the herd galloping forward. Then, before the buffalo could change course, they were shooting over the cliff. Dozens of them, plummeting over the edge, dying instantly on the rocks.

"The Indians–the women mainly–would get to work then, butchering the buffalo, cutting up the meat. Cleaning the hides. One hunt and the tribe had clothing and meat for the winter. And then some."

The screens suddenly refreshed again to reveal fog drifting over cold stone, tendrils of mist coiling and unwinding in the half-light.

The only sounds: the harsh, throaty call of a raven, and the rush of water flowing over jagged rock.

And then, a halo. A band of light, pale and pearly, like moonlight, arcing across the top of the cliff.

The adrenaline in Joe's veins—the panic he'd experienced as Beck threatened to harm Ella—was slowly dissipating.

As his mind quieted, he could feel the new connection, could sense it in the base of his skull like a low-frequency hum. Someone, or something, was sending him messages again. Images. Thoughts. Using the same channel—the same subconscious frequency—Mia had used. But there were big differences.

Joe couldn't "see" the sender, but he was certain the sender was female. Different from Mia, yet every bit as fierce and intelligent.

He lay there letting the connection build, sensing the bright mind that had found him in the darkness, like a radar breaking through the fog of his anesthesia and illness and filling him with hope. Heintzel had reinstalled the thought-capture hardware, and Beck and Ring were now strip-mining the images in his head, splashing them around the room for all to see.

But they weren't seeing everything.

There were secrets hidden in the new transmission. Whispers beneath the cacophonous roar.

Joe focused on these, trying to understand.

"Fascinating," said Ring, eyes darting between five screens at once.

"Part two," said Beck. The answer coming not from him, but from the rabid thing usurping his mind. Beck felt the thing shudder exuberantly inside his head, as it solved the riddle of the Buffalo Jump.

Ring looked shocked to hear the boss—or anyone, for that matter—solve a puzzle before him.

"Yes," he said. "I believe you're right."

"I'd been wondering about terrestrial animals," said Ring. "Birds, mammals, reptiles, insects. Mia engineered an oceanic Exodus. But what about everything else? Everything on land?"

The halo over the cliff shone brighter now.

"It's another gate," said Ring. "Probably the main terrestrial gate."

The room went completely still.

Beck said slowly, "Yes. Another gate. But into the same place the whales went?"

Ring shrugged. "It stands to reason, yes. An Exodus in two stages, to the same end place."

Beck said, "If it's like what happened in the sea, there will be thousands of these, all over the globe."

"Yes."

Beck waved at the screens. "Where's this coming from? What's the source?"

"I don't know."

"The whale?"

Ring shook his head. "Mia's gone. In another galaxy now. Another universe, perhaps."

He turned to one of his computers. "In any case, the brain patterns are different. Very different."

Beck squinted at him. "The whale and Stanton were linked. The whale needed his help, so she established a connection. But this…Why would he be privy to *anything* having to do with a terrestrial Exodus?"

"I don't know," said Ring.

"But you have a theory?" said Beck.

"Yes."

Beck waited.

Ring said, "Mia knew as she was leaving that Stanton was in serious trouble. She wanted to help. So maybe she opened a connection with her counterpart."

"Counterpart?"

"Mia was the leader for the marine Exodus. The entity around whom the entire undertaking was organized. It stands to reason that there would be a similar entity on land. Another leader."

He waved at the screens above his workstation. "Mia and the terrestrial leader were in contact. Coordinating their efforts. When Mia realized how grave Stanton's condition had become, she connected her counterpart—her coleader—with Stanton. It's like she said to her counterpart 'I have to leave. Can you look after my friend?'"

Beck considered it. "This is the help? Pictures?"

Ring shrugged. "I can see no other explanation."

Beck nodded, satisfied. "When will the terrestrial Exodus happen?"

"Soon, I should think. And when it begins, it will unfold quickly. Much more quickly than the marine Exodus."

"Why?"

"The gates," said Ring, "have already been tested. By Mia and her clan. The gates work. The leaders know what's on the other side, and they like it. The process has been fine-tuned."

"Also, on land, speed will be a necessity." Ring pointed at an image of empty seafloor. "The oceanic gates were remote. Virtually inaccessible. So the Exodus could unfold gradually without being noticed.

"Not so on dry land. The terrestrial gates will be noticed immediately. Analyzed. Meddled with. Whoever's organizing the Exodus doesn't want that. There will be a rush to get through as quickly as possible and shut them down."

Ring said, "Helicopter to Port Angeles. Your father's jet to Bozeman. Charter helicopters to the Buffalo Jump. We could be there, on the ground, in four or five hours."

Beck winced at the mention of his father's jet, but he nodded in agreement. "And when we get there—to the Buffalo Jump—then what?"

Ring said, "The gate won't close until the leader—the nexus animal—has crossed. Same as before. And it should be far easier to stop and detain a land animal than a creature of the sea."

Beck thought about it. "Put together a team," he said.

CHAPTER 85

BECK DISAPPEARED FROM the War Room, Ring and the others busied themselves with preparations, and Joe was temporarily forgotten, watching the screens. He could see crew hoisting the damaged skiffs and runabout out of the water. He could see inert bundles covered with yellow tarps lying on the deck. Bodies, he presumed. Beck's crew was rushing cleanup, he guessed, to avoid scrutiny by the authorities.

Joe scanned the video wall and focused on the images from his subconscious. He stared. Tried to think. To decipher the new messages, and the identity of the sender.

Mia's "counterpart," Ring had said. A "terrestrial leader."

Joe felt in his bones that Ring was right.

But there was more. There was subtlety and nuance in the new connection. A thread within the larger flow that struck him as somehow familiar.

He tried to focus, but his head felt like it was on fire. The anesthesia he'd been given was wearing off, and the pain from the surgery, and Beck's backhand smash, was nearly unbearable. On top of the pain—on top of everything—he was worried about Ella.

He lay there. Sweating. Thirsty. Nauseated. And he tried again to shove it all aside to listen to the deep voice. The "whisper" the thought-capture hardware hadn't yet detected.

He closed his eyes. *Mia is brilliant*, Dieturlund had told them. *One of a kind. But there's more to her than even she comprehends.* And he thought about something Ring had said. *"The terrestrial gates will be noticed immediately. Analyzed. Meddled with. Whoever's organizing the Exodus doesn't want that."*

Whoever's organizing the Exodus…

Joe thought about Mia: A leader. A genius. An anomaly. But she wasn't acting alone. He tried to imagine the leader of the terrestrial Exodus: *Female, like Mia. Powerful. Highly intelligent. Together they've tapped into something. Something larger than the two of them combined, something—*

Beck's voice jerked him back to reality.

"Give him the same stuff you gave me," Beck was saying.

Joe opened his eyes and jumped at the sight of Heintzel hovering over him—observing him as if he were a bacterium on a petri dish.

"Hi, doc," he said weakly.

Heintzel avoided his gaze as she readied a syringe.

"Didn't you have to take an oath in med school?" Joe asked. "Something about 'do no harm'?"

Heintzel spoke to Beck. "We took fresh scans last night, before we reinstalled his thought-capture hardware."

"Yeah?" said Beck.

"The mass in his brain has grown, inducing complications consistent with an astrocytic tumor or craniopharyngioma. Deterioration of the substantia nigra is manifesting in tremors in his extremities. And his EKG showed evidence of hypertrophic cardiomyopathy."

"So?" said Beck.

Heintzel lifted the syringe, expelling a minute drop of amber-colored liquid from the tip of the hair-thin needle.

"This could well send him into cardiac arrest. Cause a seizure. A stroke. Other issues I can't anticipate."

Beck cocked his head. Seemed to consider it. "It's worth the risk," he said coolly. "We need him awake."

Heintzel nodded and leaned in toward Joe's arm.

Joe focused on Heintzel's eyes—though she seemed to be looking right through him. "Thanks for the thorough history, doc. I'm touched by your concern and compassion. Truly."

The needle pierced his skin.

"How do you sleep at night?" he asked.

Heintzel finished Joe's injection, turned, and gawked at her boss, who was rolling up his own sleeve.

"Give me another blast, too," said Beck.

"Not a good idea," she replied. "Not a good idea at all. You haven't slept in…how many hours now?"

"Never mind that," said Beck, grinning—leering—at her with the same lunatic expression she'd seen in the infirmary.

"Fine," she said softly. "Have it your way then."

She gave Beck another injection, and the two of them departed Joe's bedside without another word or glance.

Seconds later, members of the infirmary team grabbed the corners of the gurney and hustled Joe toward the door.

"I need to use the toilet," said Joe.

"No time," said one of the men.

"Then I'm going to wet myself."

They took him to the restroom just outside the War Room, unclipped the straps holding him down, and helped him stand. He could feel Heintzel's concoction coursing through his veins, making his heart thump like an air hammer at a construction site.

His first step was wobbly, and the corridor swam before his eyes in shifting black-and-gray patterns that refused to settle. Then his head cleared. A little.

He pushed his way into the restroom, found the urinal, and peed, breathing heavily, one hand clutching the metal divider for support. His urine stank and issued forth in an almost fluorescent orange stream.

Need to drink more water, he thought, marveling, in the back of his mind, at his lack of concern.

He hobbled to the sink to wash his hands, looked in the mirror, and fear swallowed him whole.

"Aw shit," he whispered, willing himself to confront the gaunt, grizzle-faced stranger in the glass.

"Aw shit."

His hair was tangled, matted, and greasy; his beard uneven and flecked with gray.

Gray hair? At twenty-eight?

His skin had the color and consistency of wet ash, and there were sores on his cheeks. His lips were chapped and bleeding.

Lord help me, he thought, arching his eyebrows simply to confirm that the ghostly visage in the mirror was really his.

Lord, please help me now.

He exited the restroom to find the attendants waiting.

"Lie back down," one of them said, waving at the gurney.

"I can walk," said Joe, willing himself to stand up straight. He put his shoulders back and lifted his head.

"Lie down," said the attendant.

"Please," said Joe, holding the man's gaze. "Let me walk. I need to walk."

The man traded looks with the other attendant. Shrugged. "Suit yourself. But let's get moving."

The elevator opened to the bright sunshine of the helideck and Joe winced and nearly cried out in pain. It felt like someone had driven a bolt through his head, just behind his eyes.

They hustled him toward the Bell 412 he and Ella had ridden from Bellingham, shoved him aboard, and strapped him into a back-row seat.

The pain behind his eyes eased a bit as he grew accustomed to the light, and he looked around.

Beck's men were throwing crates and heavy canvas bags into the gear compartment. More crew were inspecting the craft. Doing a preflight check.

Joe lifted his eyes and stared at the sea.

Marauder sat anchored still at the edge of a broad inlet dotted with lush, heavily-forested islands and islets.

Nothing's changed, Joe thought. *And absolutely everything's changed.*

Humans didn't know it just yet, but the oceans—all of the Earth's oceans—had been transformed.

He saw boats bobbing, listless, in the chop. Skiffs, kayaks, and sailboats bearing residents, tourists, and curiosity seekers. All of them flummoxed—dumbfounded—by the morning's events.

Rumors of an unprecedented migration had sent them scurrying into their boats and out toward the flood of life.

But now astonishment was turning to dread.

The parade had ended, and the sea was quiet. Fish-finders showed an empty, sterile water column. A desert.

There didn't seem to be any life, anywhere, and the boats and their passengers looked small and lost on the wide sea.

CHAPTER 86

THE BELL'S CARGO COMPARTMENT slammed shut, and the pilot and copilot climbed aboard.

Joe saw Ella approaching from the far side of the weather deck—men accompanying her, one on either side—and his heart jumped into an even higher gear than its already tachycardic rate.

She looked tired but determined. Defiant. Beautiful. She saw Joe through the passenger-compartment window—found him immediately as if she could sense his presence—and smiled.

I missed you, she said with her mind, tears welling in her eyes.

God, it's good to see you, he replied.

They shoved her into one of the forward seats.

I love you, Joe. They haven't told me anything, but I'm glad we're together. Do you know where we're going?

Bozeman.

She turned, straining against her harness to look his way, ignoring her guards. *No fooling? I've always wanted to go to Bozeman.* She winked, and Joe grinned back.

The helicopter rose, the sea opened out all around them, and Joe stared at Ella from the back row, amazed.

The woman had endured days of hardship and mental anguish, been arrested, kidnapped at gunpoint after a violent car crash, and imprisoned in a cell. And yet here she was, smiling and making light, concealing her fear. Holding her head up.

Any feelings of self-pity left Joe in that instant. His demise, he told himself, might be imminent. Inevitable, even. But Ella's was not. And he would do everything in his power to see that she went free.

It took forty-two minutes to get from *Marauder* to Port Angeles through clear July skies. They landed a few feet from the Erebus Gulfstream G5, in a remote corner of the airfield, and Beck's men set about transferring gear before the Bell's rotors had even stopped spinning.

Because they were far from the tiny terminal building and potential onlookers, Beck's men could hustle Joe and Ella from the chopper to the jet without attracting attention. Even so, they approached the transfer cautiously, leaving the couple where they were until everything else was ready.

Then, all four of Beck's men—Collins, Wilden, Kehler, and Dodd—worked together, surrounding the couple and rushing them from one location to the next. Like Secret Service moving the First Family through a sensitive area.

Joe was pleased to find that his legs felt a little less wobbly than when he'd first dismounted the gurney. It felt as if a tiny bit of strength had returned to his body. Heintzel's injection was the source of his newfound energy, he presumed. And it wouldn't last.

Still, it was a welcome development.

Ella boarded the jet first, and Joe let her get a few paces ahead. Then he stopped hard in front of Ring and Beck, seated near the front of the craft.

"Beck," he said, teetering toward the man as Dodd tried to shove him forward. "I'll do anything you want. I'll cooperate one hundred percent. Just let Ella go here in Port Angeles. Let her go."

Beck motioned for Dodd to stop pushing Joe. "Nice to see you up and around, Father."

"Beck, please—"

"Reverend Stanton, I didn't bring your girl along because she's nice to look at—although she is—but to help keep you motivated at the new location."

"Beck—"

"Do your job right and I promise you, none of my men will lay a finger on her." Beck grinned broadly. "At least not yet."

Two minutes after they'd buckled in, the G5 was blasting down the runway.

Ring opened his laptops as soon as the jet leveled off, and soon had three machines arrayed around him—a miniature version of the War Room. He marveled at the strength of the images flowing through Joe Stanton's subconscious, and puzzled over the identity of the sender.

The screens displayed images of the same ancient cliffs they'd seen in the War Room. But the sky behind the cliffs seethed now with towering purple-gray clouds. Thin wires of lightning cut the gray here and there, illuminating the dark plain below.

Ring felt a little shiver of fear as the G5 raced on, almost due east, toward the growing storm.

Beck began pacing the aisle three minutes after takeoff, pausing at the front of the craft after each round-trip to peer over Ring's shoulder.

Beck needed to walk. The second injection—the one he'd ordered Heintzel to give him—was making his skin crawl and the veins in his neck and forehead pulse with every frantic heartbeat. It felt as if his eyeballs were growing, as if his eyes might burst right out of their sockets and slap Jello-like against the wall. His bones and ligaments felt stretched, pulled nearly to the breaking point.

Ignoring the looks from his men, he continued pacing, back and forth, back and forth, always pausing briefly to stare at Ring's screens.

Billowing black thunderheads now loomed over the Buffalo Jump like a tribunal of angry gods. Beck wondered, with his rational mind, why he was leading his team into such a maelstrom. If Ring's screens depicted an accurate view of the Jump—an accurate picture of how things would look at the opening of the terrestrial gate—then why proceed? The sky hinted of tornadoes. Torrential rain. High winds. Hail. Why venture into such an environment? Why risk life and limb?

And then, with a stomach-twisting spasm of disequilibrium, he felt the beast lurch into position behind his eyes once more. It scanned the passenger compartment, found Ring's computer screens, and settled its gaze there. With interest and intensity, it studied the Buffalo Jump and looming storm, just as Beck had done.

But the beast's reaction was completely different from Beck's own. The beast thrilled at the sight of the warlike sky. Seemed energized and stimulated by the tumult and chaos.

Smaller than ever Beck felt then, shunted to one side in his own mind as another entity assumed the controls. Told his head and eyes and limbs what to do.

With tremendous effort, Beck forced himself to turn away from Ring's screens and continue pacing.

One lap. Two. Three.

He tried again to think, to solve the riddle of his affliction.

What is happening to me?
Why is it happening to me?
Why am I suffering a breakdown in parallel with Stanton?
Why am I fighting myself? Killing myself?

He paced, made the round-trip a dozen more times, and stopped suddenly, midaisle. Midstep.

His heart skittered and jumped as the truth unfolded in his mind.

Not mental illness, he thought.
This isn't an illness.
I've been lying to myself.

Bile rose in his throat, acid and burning.

Since the onset of his hallucinations, his self-talk had centered around illness. The idea that he was suffering from some form of PTSD. Schizophrenia. Bipolar disorder.

I'm sick, he'd told himself. *Seeing things that aren't there. And as soon as this is over, I'll go the doctor. Find a really good shrink. Get help.*

But the truth staring him in the face now was worse than any mental disorder.

Not a disease.
An invasion.

The demon in his head wasn't the sort faced by alcoholics or drug addicts. This was a living thing. An entity. An independent organism with a mind and agenda all its own.

He hadn't imagined the eyes in Navarro's rotting skull. He'd glimpsed—for a split second—an actual creature.

He might not be able to see it as readily as he could see Ring or Collins, but it was there nonetheless. And it was using him. Had a plan for him. He could feel it watching him now, grinning imperiously, studying him with cruel, sadistic fascination, waiting to see how he would handle the news.

He handled it by going into shock. By freezing.

The truth was too much to bear, and despite his strength and youth and fitness, despite countless hours of training and experience in fantastically stressful situations and environments, he froze.

His mind stuttered and seized up. He had no strategy for engaging such an enemy. This wasn't a foe he could outwit or shoot or stab or wrestle to the ground.

And he was already stretched to the breaking point. Hadn't slept in days. Was functioning now only because of Heintzel's drugs.

This was too much. And as he stood there, frozen, in the aisle of the G5, all of his internal systems redlining, he believed he was going to die. That in three or four seconds his body would succumb to a seizure or aneurism or heart attack.

The beast seemed to believe this, too, and its imperious grin vanished. In the blink of an eye, it retreated into the farthest, deepest corner of Beck's mind.

Beck tottered and steadied himself, hands against the fuselage.

Tentatively, at first, he regained control of himself. Breathed in and out, in and out, and felt his heart rate slow. Felt the electricity burning through his nerves, jangling his extremities, diminish and quiet.

He breathed, feeling weak and thin and stretched, but also deeply relieved.

He sat down next to Ring. The sweat on his skin cooled. Evaporated. His pulse and blood pressure dropped within an almost normal range.

It's not really gone, he thought.

The thought spurred a fresh uptick in his heart rate.

The Thing—whatever it is—has retreated. Pulled back. But it hasn't gone away. Hasn't really left.

Beck shut his eyes as the jet roared forward at 488 knots. As long as he continued to the terrestrial gate, he thought, the beast would bide its time. slumber in the folds of his brain, one eye open. Watching.

You will carry me, the beast had said.

I'm a delivery system, Beck realized with horror. *A means to an end. And unless I can rid myself of this thing, the next time it comes forward I will shatter like a glass statue. The old me will be no more.*

CHAPTER 87

IT WAS EIGHTY DEGREES and sunny when the G5 touched down at Bozeman Yellowstone International Airport in the midafternoon, with no hint whatsoever that a monster storm might be in the offing.

The airport's lone helicopter charter service didn't have a Bell 412 for rent, so Beck's advance team had procured two smaller helicopters instead: a Bell 206B-3 JetRanger and a Bell 206L4 LongRanger.

Allen Dodd stayed in the jet with Joe and Ella while Beck's flight crew filled out forms inside the office. "When the time's right," he said, "you're going to walk to the helicopters like you want to be there. Like it's the most natural thing in the world. No running or screaming or trying to signal anyone." He grinned at Ella, as if she were the most likely to cause trouble. "Deviate from that, at all, sweet pea, and I will personally smash your pal's kneecaps to a bloody pulp."

Ella paled and turned away. Said nothing. Joe stayed silent as well. Through the window he watched Ring and Beck, conferring near the hangar door. Beck looked terrible in the sunlight. Puffy, bloodshot eyes. Pale skin. A slump to his shoulders that suggested massive fatigue.

Dodd sauntered to the front of the jet, chuckling to himself, and Ella watched him go. Made sure his back was turned. Then she leaned out and grabbed a stationery set from a compartment across the aisle. Tugged a sheet of Erebus stationery free, uncapped the attached pen, and started writing with the paper barely balanced on her knee.

Emergency! We are being held against our will, en route to the Madison Buffalo Jump near Bozeman. Call the police. She marked the date and time at the top of the note, signed their names and Joe's address and folded the sheet quickly. Stuffed it into her back pocket just as Dodd turned.

Outside, Beck signaled Dodd with a thumbs-up, and Joe and Ella were led to the 206L4.

Five minutes later both rental choppers were in the air.

Not all of Beck's team was in the helicopters. The G5 flight crew stayed with the jet. Taxied it to another corner of the airport to wait.

Collins remained on the ground as well and headed straight for the main terminal and Enterprise Rent-A-Car. If the advance team had done its job, he'd find a four-wheel-drive GMC extended-cab pickup with an extralong bed reserved and waiting.

Collins looked at his phone as he walked. Found the business name and address Ring's team had sent to him. Gallatin Veterinary Supply. The store was only eight miles away, and Ring had given him a concise shopping list. One of the items on the list seemed problematic, but Collins figured he'd deal with it when the time came.

If all went according to plan, he'd be on his way to the Buffalo Jump with the supplies within the hour.

"This grand show is eternal. It is always sunrise somewhere; the dew is never dried all at once; a shower is forever falling; vapor is ever rising. Eternal sunrise, eternal dawn and gloaming, on sea and continents and islands, each in its turn, as the round earth rolls."

-John Muir

CHAPTER 88

THE THIRTY-TWO-MILE FLIGHT to the Madison Buffalo Jump went quickly. One minute into the journey, they were leaving the neighborhoods and streets of Bozeman behind and zooming over lush, picturesque farms and ranches. Roads changed from pavement to dirt, and the land seemed to expand before their eyes. Grow exponentially.

Almost due west they flew, Beck's helicopter in the lead. Hobby ranches gave way to vast, verdant estates stretching as far as the eye could see—from the rolling foothills of the Bridger Mountains to the north, to Yellowstone National Park and the jagged, snow-covered Gallatin Range to the south. The Gallatin River glittered in the afternoon light, flowing strong and swift with snowmelt.

Ten minutes into the trip, the helicopters angled south, and now they could see the Madison River winding through the green bottomlands, lazy and inviting. A cool treelined corridor bisecting the vast wide open.

It wasn't hard to spot Madison Buffalo Jump State Park. Fenced, neatly delineated ranchland gave way to stone and sage, rugged brush-choked fissures and ravines, and a broad swath of wild high prairie. It was a place that seemed familiar at once, a landscape burned into the American psyche through countless Hollywood westerns.

Entering the park's airspace, the helicopters zoomed over the plain, following the same broad pathway the Hidatsa and Shoshone, Lakota and Blackfoot had used to drive buffalo to their death.

Flat as a baking sheet the ground below them was now. An alley of wild waist-high grass that tossed and rippled as the helicopters roared past.

And then, the Jump. The ground giving way, the prairie vanishing so abruptly beneath them, that even aboard the helicopters they felt a twinge of vertigo, a sudden blast of adrenaline.

Eight hundred feet the land fell, leaving a jagged escarpment, ancient and weatherworn, a gaping, mile-wide jawbone of limestone the color of fossilized ivory.

Beck ordered his pilot, Jeff Donaldson, to make two slow passes along the cliff face.

South to north they drifted first. Then back the other way. Beck studied the land above and below the cliffs.

There were tourists at the Jump, all below the escarpment.

Beck could see a dirt parking area with perhaps fifteen cars, a large covered gazebo, cinder-block restrooms, interpretive kiosks. The Buffalo Jump was not a major tourist attraction. Accessible from I-90 via twelve miles of dusty dirt road, only a tiny fraction of the four million visitors who trekked annually to Yellowstone stopped here. But it was a steady trickle nonetheless. History buffs. Geology enthusiasts. New Age believers hoping to tap into some mystical Native American vibe.

Some people waved at the helicopters. Snapped pictures. Beck paid not the slightest attention.

He stared at the precipice. At the upper plain. At a school-bus-sized boulder in the middle of the broad alley above the Jump, a hundred or so feet from the cliff edge. The flattopped stone stood out, big and bold. An island in a sea of grass.

Beck tried to imagine herds of terrified, stampeding buffalo roaring down the prairie, splintering into two streams at the boulder, and raining over the precipice—waterfalls of two-thousand-pound bison crashing to their deaths. And then he tried to imagine the gate. The terrestrial portal hinted at in Stanton's thought captures.

The Buffalo Jump in the blazing late afternoon sunshine of July 5 provided no hint of the tumult foretold on Ring's monitors.

Farther away, though, clouds were building on the hundred-mile long Gallatin Range, hugging the shoulders of the mountains, casting the snow-covered peaks into shadow, defying the summer sun. Beck stared. Ring did also. They hadn't noticed the clouds there before.

Beck ordered the helicopters to land on a broad, flat sagebrush-covered bench a half mile into the plain above the cliffs.

Donaldson's voice crackled over the radio. "State park. We're not supposed to land here without a permit. Could be looking at a fine."

"I'll take the risk," Beck replied. "Set 'em down."

The helicopters settled onto the bench like giant dragonflies, coming to rest a hundred feet apart. The pilots powered down the engines, and the roar of the machines died away. The rotors continued spinning, silently. Finally stopped. The dust settled, and everybody got out.

The bench made for an ideal observation platform—a flat pedestal of land with views east and west of the wide alley leading to the Jump.

There were no tourists here. No road. There *was* a footpath—a trail leading up from the parking area, deep into the six-thousand-acre park, but no one was on it. No one, it seemed, wanted to make the climb in the blazing afternoon sun.

"Find a place to sit," Dodd told Joe and Ella.

The couple held hands as they stepped slowly away from the helicopter. The sun felt good on Joe's skin, and he lifted his face to the sky. Reveled in the warmth. In the fresh air and fragrant, rain-washed smell of the prairie.

Standing there, basking in the light, Joe felt better than he had in days. He was weak and washed-out, yes; bruised and sore from the surgery and from Beck's backhand blow in the War Room, but otherwise okay. For a moment he imagined that if Beck would simply let them go free, he'd recover completely. Regain his health.

The fantasy played in his mind. He and Ella would hike down to the visitor parking area. Hitch a ride to Bozeman. Find a place to stay. To sleep and rest. Soon, he'd be as good as new. The sickly prisoner-of-war visage he'd seen in the mirror would fade. The gray in his hair would revert to black. His vision—cloudy now for days—would return to twenty-twenty.

Then he remembered the drug Heintzel had given him, and his mood sank like a stone. The drug was propping him up. Enlivening his mind and body like a river of caffeine. But the buzz—the illusion of vitality—wouldn't last. His prognosis hadn't changed. The tremor in his hands hadn't disappeared. His downward trajectory had not been altered.

And of course, Beck wasn't about to let them go free. Joe's thoughts—the pictures flowing through his subconscious—were the reason they'd come to the Buffalo Jump in the first place.

Joe looked out at the prairie and wondered where the pictures were coming from.

Mia's "counterpart," Ring had said. *The leader of the terrestrial Exodus.*
Where is she?
What sort of creature is she?
When will the gate form?
And where are all the animals? he wondered, *if another Exodus is about to happen.* The questions were endless, the answers, not forthcoming.

He struggled with it, then gave up and focused instead on the luxurious warmth caressing his skin. He squeezed Ella's hand, led her to a patch of grass amid the sagebrush, and together they sat down.

Ten minutes after the cacophony of the helicopters had faded, the soundscape returned to normal. Birds sang. Insects chirped. Prairie grass rustled in the warm afternoon breeze.

Beck's men worked quietly. Efficiently. Pulling bags of gear from cargo holds and unpacking just the right equipment in just the right order.

On an open, level patch of ground, they set up folding tables and a chair for Ring and his computer equipment. Pitched a ten-by-ten open-sided tent over everything and anchored the legs of the structure with rocks and sandbags.

Another table was set with boxes of food: Energy bars and chips. Bagels, apples, blocks of cheese. Coolers full of drinks were positioned close by.

There were weapons, also. Crates of ammunition and hand grenades. Heavy canvas bags full of rifles and machine guns. Joe caught a whiff of gun oil as Beck's men unzipped the bags on a wide, flat rock nearby. The weapons were quickly checked, then covered with a tarp.

Jeff Donaldson and the other helicopter pilot, Aaron Wicks, grabbed snacks and retreated to the Bell 206L4. Climbed into the cockpit and sat in the seats like they didn't know what else to do.

Ring and Beck wandered downslope, toward the mile-wide grass-filled lane leading to the cliffs, and stood taking it all in. Ring lifted an enormous pair of binoculars toward the Gallatin Range. The clouds massing there were still a far-off threat—a vague rumor of events that might or might not unfold.

"We wasting our time here?" Beck asked.

Ring shrugged. "Maybe. I don't think so."

"So where are the animals? Where's the migration? Shouldn't we be seeing something?"

Aside from a pair of hawks riding the thermals above the cliffs, there was no wildlife visible anywhere.

Someone flipped on a radio in Ring's newly assembled workstation, and the top-of-the hour news played. The entire report was about the marine Exodus. And the voices of the scientists, pundits, and politicians featured in the newscast reflected anxiety. Fear—bordering on panic. The world had changed suddenly, jarringly, and the experts didn't have a clue what was going on.

Ring said, "Stanton's thought captures don't reveal a specific timetable. We don't know when this phase of the Exodus will start. Though, if I had to guess, I'd say that it will happen soon. Very soon."

Beck said nothing. The throbbing pain in his head—around his eyes—had returned, and he felt suddenly agitated. Gazing once more at the plain, his agitation changed to anger. Anger founded in deep and abiding terror. The thing living in his head might have retreated to the deepest recesses of his mind, but it had not departed. Unless he could find a way to expel the thing once and for all, it would simply wait for him to weaken, then it would lurch forward and break him like a twig.

Kneeling near the weapons, Dodd watched Ella inspect Joe's injuries. Watched her caress Joe's face and check his incision. Watched her touch Joe's bleeding lips gently with one finger and ask if he was thirsty.

Dodd grabbed a plastic water bottle from the cooler and tossed it at Joe, hard and fast.

Joe wasn't looking, and the water bottle hit him squarely in the side of the head. Right on the incision site. Joe grunted with the pain, slumped back, and put his hand to his head.

Ella spun on Dodd, murder in her eyes. "Do you mind, asshole? Why did you do that? Can't you see he's hurt?"

Dodd and Kehler laughed. Wilden, standing nearby, stayed quiet.

Dodd plucked another water bottle from the cooler and brought it to Ella. Kneeling, he presented it to her with mock concern.

"Your boy's not doing too well. Maybe after he croaks, you and me can hook up. What do you say?" He grinned. "I think all the guys are looking forward to that, actually, but I'd like to be first."

Joe lifted his head and glared at Dodd. "Touch her," he said, "lay one finger on her, and I will kill you. I swear it."

Dodd tugged on his baseball cap and considered the threat with feigned alarm before breaking into another grin. "Can you do that? As a priest, I mean? Doesn't that violate some kind of vow or something?"

Ella, tears in her eyes now, said, "Just get away from us. Please. Leave us alone."

Fresh blood was oozing through Joe's bandages. Dodd stood, still smiling, and said to Ella, "Gimme a kiss and I'll bring ya the first-aid kit. Whatdya say?"

"Get away from us," Ella repeated.

Dodd laughed and sauntered off. Traded high-fives and more laughs with Kehler.

Ella turned at the sound of footsteps. It was Wilden. His face was serious. Impassive. No sign of malice in his eyes.

Ella looked from Wilden's face to the first-aid kit in his hand and back. Then took the kit.

"Thank you," she said.

Wilden nodded and walked off.

Dodd and Kehler watched him go, and Ella thought she saw resentment in their expressions. A little hostility. She found the looks encouraging. And she wondered, as she opened the kit and scrounged for alcohol swabs and fresh bandages, if Wilden was someone she could talk to. Reason with.

Maybe Beck's guys weren't uniformly sadistic. Maybe Wilden was different. Maybe if she could pull him aside she could get him to see things her way. Maybe—

"Guys," said a voice, loud enough so that everyone turned. It was Donaldson calling from the open door of the Bell 206L4. "Look sharp. We got company."

Following Donaldson's gaze, they saw a lone hiker switchbacking down from the ridge overlooking the helicopters, winding his way through the scrub.

CHAPTER 89

COLLINS FOUND GALLATIN VETERINARY SUPPLY in a shabby industrial park on the edge of town. The one-story beige stucco building had a large gravel parking lot in front, a driveway on one side, and a chain-link fence topped with razor wire all around.

Collins could think of only one reason such a store would need razor wire: Drugs. Narcotics. He guessed they'd probably been broken into at some point and decided to put up a fence. At the moment, the wheeled gate at the edge of the lot was open, the lights inside the building on, and the glass-front door propped wide. There were no other cars in the lot.

Collins parked his rental truck a few paces from the door and studied the front of the building. No surveillance cameras. Not that he could see, anyway. Maybe the owners had decided the fence was enough. Figured they didn't need cameras. Collins hoped that was the case.

He climbed out of the truck and walked inside.

The business was laid out like an auto supply store: Aisles full of products in the front half of the establishment. A long service counter in the middle. Floor-to-ceiling shelves in back. At the moment, there were two employees in public view: a pimply, greasy-haired twentysomething seated at a desk, working at a computer, and a dumpy, balding lab-coat-wearing salesclerk standing at the service counter.

Bouncy, insipid Muzak played on speakers mounted near the ceiling.

"Help you?" the dumpy clerk asked, as soon as Collins had crossed the threshold.

Collins reviewed the list Ring had given him, on his iPhone, as he walked. "Yeah," he replied. "Understand you guys carry a five-by-eight steel cage made by LB Barn and Ranch."

The pimply kid stopped typing to look at Collins as the clerk replied, a trace of superiority in his voice. "We've got the five-by-eight Exotic Animal Enclosure, if that's what you mean. Don't really call 'em cages anymore."

Collins stopped at the counter, directly opposite the clerk. Stared at the pudgy man, whose name badge identified him as Harlan Beale.

"Exotic Animal Enclosure," he said. "Good to know. So you have it in stock?"

Harlan glanced at the monitor over the cash drawer. Tapped some keys on the keyboard. "Yep. Got three in the yard. One assembled and ready to go." He eyed Collins through worn black-framed glasses. "What ya need it for?"

Collins considered answering, "None of your business," but decided to keep it cordial. He needed Harlan's help.

"Predator issues on the ranch I'm working at," he lied. "Up north." He waved out the window in the direction of the Bridger Mountains.

"Oh?" said Harlan. "Which ranch is that?"

The pimply kid snickered under his breath, and Collins glanced at him, wondering what was funny. He turned back to Harlan. Smiled and kept his cool. "You know," he said. "I'm new in town and actually just running errands for someone else who works at the ranch. So I don't have a lot of details."

The pimply kid snickered again, without looking up from his computer. Collins thought about jumping the counter and smashing his head in. It was tempting. Instead, he focused on Harlan. Kept his voice even. "So, if you could just help me out, with my list and all, I'll get out of your hair."

Harlan typed something on the keyboard, stared at the screen, and said, "The five-by-eight galvanized is seven hundred and ninety-nine dollars. Not including tax."

"Great," said Collins. "I'll take it."

Harlan raised an eyebrow. "Okay. Pull around back. I'll meet ya."

Collins did as Harlan instructed, and together they hefted the steel cage into the bed of the GMC. The cage was well made and heavy—six-gauge welded wire mesh all around—but manageable for two people. It fit perfectly in the back of the truck.

Collins shut the tailgate and asked, as casually and conversationally as he could, "Just you and the kid manning the store today?"

"Yup," Harlan replied. "Not that busy right now, with the holiday and all. "Boss took the week off."

Collins drove to the front again and went back inside. Harlan was at the counter, waiting for him.

"So," Harlan asked. "What else you need?"

Collins glanced at his phone. "Tranquilizer rifle. Best one you got."

Pimple Boy snickered, louder this time, and Collins glared at him. "I say something funny?"

The kid kept his eyes on his computer screen, but Collins could see a smirk on his face.

Harlan smiled. "Tranquilizer guns aren't called *rifles*. They're called *projectors*.

Collins nodded. "Okay. Lot's to learn. So show me a projector. Top of the line."

"What kind of predator they dealing with"—Harlan waved vaguely out the window, as Collins had done—"at that ranch of yours?"

"Cougar," said Collins. "Big mother, apparently."

Harlan nodded and headed for a row of floor-to-ceiling shelves.

Collins turned 360 degrees while Harlan was gone. Scanned the walls and ceiling. No interior surveillance cameras. Not that he could see.

Harlan returned with what looked to Collins very much like a rifle. It was wrapped in clear plastic and festooned with tags and labels. Harlan set it on the counter.

"This is the X-Caliber, by Pneu-Dart," he said, as he slid the gun out of the bag and handed it to Collins. "Most popular gas-based dart projector on the market. Versatile, pressure-gauged, full-volume dump. Lightweight, but without sacrificing range or accuracy."

Collins hefted the gun and looked through the scope. It smelled new, felt new, and was definitely lighter than a hunting rifle.

Harlan said, "Quiet, accurate. Got the 416R stainless-steel barrel, dichromate seal, of course, which cuts down on bore residue."

Collins nodded like he knew what Harlan was talking about.

"Comes with a hard-shell case, ten twelve-gram CO_2 cylinders, a pack of ten-cc darts and a pack of one-cc practice darts. Pretty much the only projector the Fish and Wildlife guys use anymore. For cougar. Black bear. Even grizzly."

"How much?" Collins asked.

"Two thousand one hundred and twenty-two dollars and eighty-three cents," said Harlan. "Not including tax."

Collins nodded. "Great. I'll take two. Please."

Harlan gawked, and Pimple Boy, for the first time, lifted his eyes from his computer screen.

"Seriously?" Harlan asked.

Collins set a credit card and driver's license on the counter. "Completely. And some fentanyl or M-99 to go with. A good supply—in case there's more than one cougar."

Harlan stiffened slightly. "Sure. Need to see a prescription for that. From a local-area vet."

Collins had anticipated this demand and had his reaction ready. He stared at Harlan blank-faced. Played dumb. "A prescription? For animal medicine?"

Pimple Boy chortled into his sleeve this time, but Harlan stayed serious. "Oh, most definitely. Those are powerful narcotics. Barbiturates. One drop of M-99 can kill an adult man in a couple minutes—if you don't give the antidote." He looked at Collins. "I can sell ya the guns without much paperwork, but not the drugs."

Collins nodded. "Gotcha." He scratched his chin like he was thinking it through. "Okay. Well, they didn't tell me that. Lots to learn, like I said." He smiled. "Ring up the cage and the projectors, and we'll come back for the meds later."

Harlan nodded, retrieved another X Caliber projector from the back shelf, and returned to the register.

Collins raised his iPhone. "I have an idea," he said, as if it had just dawned on him. "Could I take a picture of the different drugs—whatever you recommend for a big cougar—so that I can show the boss the options?"

Harlan shrugged. "Sure. I guess." He stepped to a refrigerator against the nearest wall, took a key from his pocket, and unlocked the padlock on the door. Pulled out some boxes, shut the fridge, and returned to the counter. Positioned the boxes in front of Collins and lifted one of them.

"Etorphine hydrochloride," he said. "Also known as M-99. Made by Novartis. Probably the best for a big predator, but definitely ask your vet."

Collins took a picture of the boxes and said, "They probably know how to load the darts, up at the ranch, but could you show me anyway?"

Harlan shrugged again and removed one of the one-cc darts from its plastic-wrap package. "Premeasured capsule goes here," he said, pointing with his finger. "Dart hits the animal, and the momentum makes the little steel ball at the rear of the injector fly forward and drive the syringe plunger. Needle injects the dose, and the drug causes torpor and prostration within minutes. Gotta monitor the animal's vital signs after that and be ready with the antidote."

He held up another box. "This is the antidote for the M-99. Large Animal Revivon it's called. Technical name, Diprenorphine. But your vet or Fish and Wildife rep will know all this."

Collins smiled. "This is really helpful. Thank you."

Harlan nodded and began gathering up the little boxes. There was a loud click, and when Harlan lifted his eyes again, he found the barrel of a Glock 19 a few inches from his face.

"This is a handgun," said Collins. "I think they still call it that."

Harlan froze, eyes wide behind his battered glasses. He lifted his hands slowly then, without being asked.

Pimple Boy had the same kind of shocked expression, the smirk finally absent from his acne-riddled face.

"Get your hands up, too," said Collins, "Or I'll shoot your pal here in the head."

Pimple Boy complied. Raised his hands high.

"Great," said Collins, turning and fixing his eyes on Harlan once more. "Now. Think carefully. Is there anything else we might need to tranquilize and detain a large, aggressive predator?"

Harlan kept his hands elevated and shook his head slowly, swallowed twice, and said, "No. I think this would cover it." His eyes flicked to the pile of merchandise on the counter. "This is really all you need. More than you need."

Collins nodded. "Great. Good. Thank you." He glanced at Pimple Boy, then back at Harlan. "And thanks for the attitude, as well."

Harlan's mouth opened in an awkward smile, like he didn't understand the compliment. A vein throbbed in his neck, and sweat glistened on his pale forehead.

"Makes it easier to kill you," said Collins.

He shot Harlan in the face, twice. Then turned to find Pimple Boy frozen in his chair, as the roar of the first two rounds faded to silence. Collins fired again—three quick shots this time. The kid flew puppetlike against a filing cabinet and crashed to the ground, tumbling out of his wheeled office chair as he hit the faux-tile floor. The boom of the shots faded once more and the cheery, brainless Muzak continued as if nothing had happened. As if it were just another boring day at Gallatin Veterinary.

Collins put the Glock away, stuffed the drugs into his pockets, and grabbed the "projectors" off the counter, along with his credit card and ID. He walked outside and got in the truck. Exited the gravel lot at normal speed and two minutes later was on I-90, bound for the Buffalo Jump exit, twenty-three miles to the west.

CHAPTER 90

THE SOLO HIKER STRODE toward the helicopters. A big guy wearing a sun hat, long-sleeved shirt, and shorts, and carrying a daypack. They all watched him approach, and Ella felt a flicker of hope.

Beck crouched in front of Ella and Joe. Looked them in the eye one at a time. "Keep your mouths shut. Guy says anything to you, just give a short, friendly answer and leave it at that. No long conversations."

Ella said "How are we supposed to give short, friendly answers with our mouths shut?"

Beck leaned closer. Glared at Ella. "Make this difficult, princess, and you'll suffer more than ever. That's a promise."

Beck turned to Dodd and said, "Give me your hat."

Dodd removed his baseball cap, reluctantly, looked at it, and tossed it to Beck. Beck passed it to Joe. "Put it on," he said. "Keep it on. Keep your bandages covered."

The hiker was only a couple of hundred yards away now, and they could see that he was young—mid-twenties—and tall. He had a long, loping gait.

He stopped fifty yards from the nearest helicopter and took a picture with his iPhone.

"Nice rides," he called. "What're you guys up to?"

Beck stepped from the shade of the nearest helicopter and gave a little wave. "Film crew," he said. "Making a documentary."

"Whoa! Sweet." The hiker came forward and shook Beck's hand enthusiastically. "Edwin Kohl," he said. "Nice to meet you."

"Same here," said Beck.

The hiker grinned. Looked around. "This is *so* cool!"

His gear looked brand-new. Fresh from REI or L.L.Bean. New long-sleeved hiking shirt. New sun hat. New boots. New daypack with a *100 Best Bozeman Area Hikes* guidebook jutting out of a side pocket.

He reminded Ella of a big, friendly puppy. A nice guy. And a bit of a nerd. *Engineer*, she thought. *Maybe a software guy. Probably new to Bozeman. Maybe new to the West. He's exploring his new home. Seeing the sights.*

Edwin Kohl lifted his iPhone for another picture. "So you guys filming from the air or just using these to get around?"

"Both," said Beck. "Taking a break at the moment—waiting for the light to get better."

"Got it," said Kohl.

Ella caught Kohl's eye as he was finishing his picture.

Smiled at him. He smiled back.

"Hi," he said, ambling toward her. He swung his pack down in front of Ella and Joe and fished a bag of trail mix out of the top compartment. Offered it to them. Joe declined, but Ella scooped out a handful of nuts and raisins and M&M's. Then, instead of handing the bag back to Kohl, she set it inside the top of his open pack—the note she'd written on the Erebus jet folded into a little square underneath.

Ella looked up slowly, worried that Beck or one of his men had seen what she'd done, but no one seemed to be watching.

Kohl was turning this way and that, gawking at his surroundings. "A film, huh?" he said enthusiastically. "What about?"

"The Plains Indians," said Beck. "The people who used to live here."

"Cool." The hiker removed his hat, revealing curly, dark hair wet with sweat. "So where's your gear? All your cameras and stuff?"

Beck waved at the tarp covering the weapons. "Under cover. Keeping it out of the sun, you know."

Ella feared Kohl might ask to see the gear, but he said nothing more, just looked around, munching on trail mix and smiling.

Donaldson and Wicks were still sitting in the Bell 206L4. Talking quietly with the doors open.

Kehler and Dodd were resting in the dirt, staring absently at the plain, avoiding eye contact with Kohl, or so it seemed. Wilden was busy scanning the prairie with a huge pair of binoculars, tracking two coyotes as they zigzagged through the tall grass. Ring was beneath the open-sided tent, tapping away on a laptop—also not paying Kohl the slightest heed.

"Solo trip today?" Beck asked the hiker, in his most relaxed, congenial tone.

"Yep," said Kohl. He laughed. "I hike fast. Tend to leave my buddies in the dust. Solo's easier."

"Gotcha," Beck replied.

Kohl looked at Joe and seemed to notice the exhaustion in the priest's face. "They make you carry all the gear or something?" he asked, laughing.

Joe peered up at him. Smiled. "Something like that."

Kohl laughed again, stuffed everything back in his pack, and cinched it shut.

Ella guessed the note had fallen to the bottom of the pack. Kohl would find it when he got to his car. Or back home. Hopefully.

The hiker gulped some water from a bottle and glanced at Ella again. "Man, I'd love to stay and watch you guys film, but I'd better be gettin' back."

Alarms were ringing inside Edwin Kohl's big, gregarious skull, and he wanted now only to leave the helicopters and the odd group of people assembled around them and to hike directly back the way he had come.

The scene just didn't make sense. For one thing, Beck's team didn't *look* like a film crew. The big guys sitting in the dirt looked like bodybuilders. Tough guys. Soldiers.

The couple was weird, too. The guy looked sick. Sick enough to be in a hospital. And the gorgeous woman? She was smiling, but didn't seem happy at all.

The leader was strange, too. Another military guy—but with a crazy gleam in his eye.

Edwin Kohl felt the hairs on the back of his neck rise as he shouldered his pack. Then berated himself for being fearful.

I'm in a state park, for God's sake. The sun is shining. There are tourists just below the cliffs. I'm overreacting.

Still, he wanted to leave.

"Okay," he said, tightening the straps on his pack. "Good luck to you guys. Hope the filming goes well."

Edwin Kohl glanced at Ella one final time as he turned to leave. Beck wasn't watching—no one was watching—and her expression had changed utterly.

Help us! She mouthed the words. Eyes wide. *Help us!*

The hiker's Adam's apple jumped, and he gave a small nod.

"Okay," he called cheerfully, backing away. "See you guys."

Kohl had gone about three paces when Beck said, "Wanna see the camera we use?"

Kohl turned toward the tarp Beck had pointed out earlier. "Oh, thanks. But I better be gettin' back."

Beck smiled. "Camera's in the helicopter."

He gestured to the Bell 206B3 "Just take a second. The lenses are all laid out on the seats. Pretty cool setup."

The hiker hesitated. Stood there in the sun, trying to decide whether to run or play it cool.

He relaxed. What could it hurt to look in the window of the chopper?

Beck walked to the far side of the Bell. To the back. Away from Ella and the others.

"We use all German lenses," Beck was saying as the hiker leaned toward the window.

Beck's hunting knife was out in a flash. An eight-inch Gerber. Razor-sharp. He grabbed the hiker's shirt collar and a handful of his curly hair from behind, jerked the man's head back, and cut his throat.

Kohl flailed briefly. Made choking, gurgling noises. And crashed to the dirt, blood gushing from his neck.

Through the Bell's undercarriage, Ella saw him fall.

"Oh no!" she screamed. "God, no! No! No! No!" And then she was on her feet, running for the cliffs. Hysterical. "Help! Help!"

"Shut her the hell up!" Beck yelled.

Dodd and Kehler sprinted after her. Wilden tossed his binoculars aside and lunged for one of the gear bags. Tore it open and yanked out another medical kit, then followed the other men.

The pilots watched Ella run but stayed in their helicopter. Ring glanced up from his workspace and gawked, seemingly surprised by the commotion.

Kehler caught up with Ella after a hundred yards and grabbed her wrist.

"Help!" Ella screamed. "Somebody help us!"

Dodd was there a second later and grabbed Ella's other arm.

Not tightly enough.

She twisted away and pushed Kehler, trying to writhe free.

"Help!" she screamed.

Kehler pulled Ella into a headlock as Dodd caught up once more. They heard footsteps in the dirt behind them and figured it was Wilden.

It wasn't.

Kehler—one hairy forearm locked around Ella's neck—turned just as Joe Stanton's fist smashed into the side of his face, breaking his nose with a crack. Kehler stumbled back, tripped on a rock, and pulled Ella down on top of him.

Dodd lunged at Joe, low and fast—like a wrestler. Threw the priest to the ground. And now Wilden was there, jumping on top of Ella, a syringe in his hand. Ella twisted in the dirt, surprising Wilden with her strength and ferocity, and swatted his hand away. Swept it toward his thigh where the needle pierced his khakis and stabbed his leg.

"Aw, Goddamnit!" Wilden howled. He yanked the syringe free. Cast it into the weeds. "Shit!"

Dodd held Ella down as Wilden fumbled with the medical kit, withdrew another injection-ready syringe, and jabbed it into Ella's leg.

"Help!" Ella shrieked. "Help us!"

"Shut up, bitch!" Dodd slapped her across the face with the back of his hand, drawing blood, and now Joe was on his knees, trying to get up, trying to come to Ella's aid.

Kehler was behind the priest, blood gushing from his broken nose. He kicked Joe in the ribs—hard—then hefted a toaster-sized rock over his head and prepared to heave it down. Smash Joe's skull.

"Stop!" roared a voice. Kehler looked up. Dodd and Wilden turned as well.

It was Ring, standing a few paces away, silver headphones around his neck. Like he'd just run over from his computer station. Which he had. "Don't do that!" he commanded. "We need him."

Kehler grunted and heaved the rock into a bush a few inches from Stanton's face.

Beck joined the group—wiping the hiker's blood from his hands with a rag—and gawked at his men.

"Jesus, what the hell happened? Guys can't manage a girl and a sick preacher?"

Beck's men made no reply. Wilden got to his feet and immediately collapsed back to his knees. His eyes swam in their sockets.

"He was trying to sedate the girl," Dodd explained, "and she jabbed him, instead." He looked at Ella, lying on her side in the dirt with the same glassy-eyed expression as Wilden. "She's down now, though."

"Un-fucking-believable," said Beck. He nodded at Dodd. "Put Wilden in my chopper—backseat—and strap him in. Do it now—while he can still walk. I don't want to be lugging his sorry ass around in the dark."

Dodd hauled Wilden to his feet and put his arm around the man's waist. Wilden's eyes were still open, but his limbs sagged and his head lolled on his neck like a deadweight. Dodd put his back into it, and together they staggered toward the 206B3.

Beck turned to Kehler. Stared at his nose. At the blood streaming down his face and onto his shirt. "Jesus H. Christ. Clean yourself up and get the hell back here."

"Yes, sir," said Kehler.

Beck looked at Joe, gasping in the dirt, and Ella lying on her side, eyes closed now as she succumbed to the drug. Her cheek was red and raw where Dodd had hit her.

Beck scanned the plain spread out below them, then the ridge overlooking the butte. He could see no other people. No hikers. No bird-watchers. No rescuers running to see what Ella had been screaming about.

There was something new on the horizon, however.

"Weather's changing," said Ring. "Big-time."

Beck nodded. The gray line of clouds over the Gallatin Range had metastasized into a towering wall. A big, muscular front that colored the sky to the east like a purple-black bruise. A sudden breeze rattled the sage and made the buffalo grass on the plain below dance and sway.

Beck sensed a growing tension in the air; a faint, thrumming electrical charge that prickled the skin. A foreboding that pervaded every cell of the body.

He swallowed. Froze. He could feel the Thing that had retreated into the recesses of his mind waking up, slinking forward, rejoicing at the sight of the approaching tempest.

Standing there, looking out, Beck felt a mounting sense of helplessness. Helplessness mixed with dread. The sky had an end-of-the-world pallor to it.

The end of the world. He wondered if that's what was coming.

CHAPTER 91

THE PILOTS INTERCEPTED BECK as he made his way back to the helicopters.

Donaldson gestured at the approaching storm. "We should evacuate. Get these machines out of here before it really kicks up."

"We're staying," said Beck.

Donaldson looked at him. "Then we need to reposition both aircraft. Face them into the wind. And they need to be tied down. Secured."

Beck shrugged. "So do it. What the hell are you waiting for?"

Donaldson and Wicks glanced at each other, then retreated to their respective aircraft and started them up. Rotors began to turn, slowly at first. Then faster. The engines screamed and the rotors became a blur. The choppers lifted off a few feet, hovered, and turned ninety degrees, so that they were facing the Gallatin Range.

The wash from the rotors upset the food table, blasted Ring's open-sided tent down the hill, and left Ring hunched over his computer gear, cursing and screaming.

The helicopters set down once more and the pilots killed the engines and scrambled out. Found tie-down kits in the storage compartments and worked on securing the craft, one at a time. Starting with the L4, they attached straps to the main rotor—two in front, one in back. The front straps they clipped to the skids. The rear to the tail boom. They repeated the process on the B3, then used other tie-downs to secure each helicopter to ground stakes, which they drove into the dirt with fist-sized rocks.

When they were done, Wicks wiped his hands on his pants and nodded at the two aircraft. "Should be good unless it gusts above sixty-five. According to the manual."

Donaldson regarded the eastern sky, which was growing uglier by the moment. "What would be 'good' would be to get the hell out of here," he said. "But what do I know?"

Kehler and Dodd carried Ella to a level spot between the two helicopters and placed her limp, unconscious body on the ground.

Kehler walked away, but Dodd lingered over Ella, fondling her chest and moaning at the feel of her breasts in his hands. "Won't be long now, princess" he whispered in Ella's ear. "Boyfriend's almost history. Gonna be you and me."

They dragged Joe to the spot where Ella lay and threw him, groaning, into the dirt. Shoved the couple together.

On Ring's order, Kehler and Dodd rummaged through the gear bags and found a shelter for Joe and Ella—a Mountain Hardware tarp secured by stakes on one side and guy-lines terminating in more stakes on the other. The tarp was open to the elements on the side facing the prairie and the cliff, but the opening was low to the ground—a single graphite pole creating the triangular entrance. If someone wanted to check on Joe and Ella, they'd have to get on hands and knees and crawl inside.

Dodd pulled the shelter's guy-lines tight just as the first rain began to fall—big, heavy drops that spattered and hissed on the dusty ground.

"Bag the hiker," Beck told his men, when they were finished with the tent. "Put him in the back of the L4. I don't want to have to deal with it later."

Dodd and Kehler set about the task, quickly, silently. Found the body bags and got one prepped. Dodd guessed the hiker was six four and 220 pounds. Horsing him into the bag and then into the L4's gear compartment was no easy task and they grunted and cursed as they worked.

Ring gathered his computer gear from the folding table and hustled everything into the front passenger seat of the B3. It took two trips, and by the time he'd climbed into the chopper and shut the door, the wind was gusting and the rain falling in earnest.

Donaldson and Wicks retreated to the front seats of the L4. Dodd and Kehler made a final sweep of the camp—covering, securing, or stowing all the remaining gear they could find—then retreated to the same aircraft.

Beck alone remained outside in the rising storm.

He found Wilden's binoculars on a rock, dried them with his shirt, and walked to the edge of the sage-covered bench. Bracing himself against the wind, he brought the lenses to his eyes, focused, and slowly panned the plain, east to west. The lush grass filling the prairie danced before the storm in wide, accelerating waves, in cascading patterns, in fast arcs and sweeps and swooshes that resembled hurrying eddies in a tumultuous sea.

Beck could find no animals on the plain. Nothing in the broad reach to the east—in the direction of the storm. Nothing below the bench, and nothing near the cliff edge. No creatures—as far as he could tell—had gathered near the school-bus-sized boulder at the lip of the precipice. Beck lowered the binoculars and scanned for birds.

Nothing.

No hawks. No eagles. No prairie falcons pirouetting against the dark, vengeful sky.

Beck listened to the rain. To the wind buffeting the helicopters behind him—whistling and singing around the rotors and airframes.

The scene on the prairie was disappointing, to say the least. If a terrestrial Exodus was imminent, where were the animals? Where was the migration? The torrent of life, akin to what they'd witnessed in the ocean?

Disappointing.

And yet…

The electricity Beck had felt earlier was still there.

Not simply *still there*, but building. Intensifying along with the storm.

The scene on the prairie was disappointing. To Beck.

But not to the Thing lurking in the folds of his mind.

Beck could feel the *other* looking out, bristling with excitement, gawking with rapt anticipation, as if, through his eyes, it could see things he could not.

Beck turned into the wind, staggered to the B3, and climbed into the pilot's seat.

Surrounded by computer screens, as usual, Ring acknowledged Beck's arrival without looking up.

"The Nexus Animal is close," he said. "At least, I believe so."

Beck shrugged the water from his jacket and shut the helicopter door tight, blocking out the wind. He looked at Ring, then glanced out through the windows. "What? What do you mean? How do you know?"

Ring turned one of his laptops so that Beck could see the monitor. It reminded Beck of an air-traffic-control screen: black background, a fluorescent green dot in the middle, concentric green circles radiating out from the center point.

A glowing green line swept across the screen every few moments, like a second hand on a watch.

"Joe Stanton," said Ring, "sick as he is, is still receiving a robust data flow from Mia's counterpart. Images of the new gate, similar to what we witnessed in the War Room."

Beck said nothing. Just stared at Ring's screen. Wilden snored in the backseat, inert and unconscious from the accidental injection. Beck turned and looked at him. The man's head sagged against his chest, and drool trickled down his chin. If not for the harness, he'd be in a heap on the floor.

Ring said, "I decided to see if I could get a fix on the telepathic signal. Ascertain where it's coming from."

"And you did?" said Beck.

"Sort of."

Beck made no reply.

"This isn't like triangulating a cell phone signal, or tracking a radio transmission. Not exactly. With the kind of electrocorticographic tap Dr. Heintzel installed on Stanton, I can only ascertain proximity. Distance to subject. The 'subject' being Stanton."

Beck stared at him. "So...you know the Nexus Animal is close—but not its exact location?"

"Correct," said Ring.

"So how close is it?"

Ring stared at columns of data flowing along the periphery of the "radar" screen. Watched the data for almost a minute.

"If my measurements are accurate," said Ring, "The creature is within five hundred meters of Joe Stanton, and holding steady. Five hundred meters *maximum*. It could be closer."

Beck's eyes widened and he scanned the surrounding landscape through the Bell's rain-spattered windshield. Then he opened the door and climbed back out, scooping the binoculars off the floor with one hand as he went.

The wind gusts were stronger now and it was a struggle to shut the door.

Beck tottered back a step and watched the front of the Bell levitate a half an inch off the ground; straining against the tie-downs as if it wanted to take off.

The tie-downs held firm.

Beck turned into the wind, lowered his head, and staggered back to the edge of the sage-covered bench. The rain was blowing sideways now, and Beck zipped his jacket tight.

Lifting his head, he scoped the prairie once more. No animals to the east. No animals below the bench. Nothing to the west. Nothing that he could see.

Nothing.

Turning east again, his eyes fixed on the nucleus of the approaching storm and stayed there. Widened.

It was an impressive, terrifying sight.

The snowcapped Gallatin Mountains had been replaced by a mountain of clouds. An impossibly tall, broad mass that seemed to morph and mutate second to second. The sky at the epicenter of the tempest was black, bloated, and now, flecked with lightning—fine traceries of electric illumination that stood out against the volatile mass like cracks in a wall.

Beck panned the plain once more, then turned, slowly, 360 degrees. Took it all in. The sagebrush tossing in the wind. The slope rising to the ridge. The makeshift camp. The gear piles. The tarp covering Joe and Ella. The helicopters—windshields wet with rain—shimmying in the gusts.

He saw everything.

Everything, except an animal.

The Nexus Animal is close, Ring had said. *Within five hundred meters of Joe Stanton.*

Beck turned again, 360 degrees.

Nothing.

No wolf or bear or cougar. No deer or elk or buffalo. Nothing.

There were plenty of places to hide, of course. The creature *could* be close at hand. Hiding behind brush. A boulder. Concealed in a fold in the land.

In this weather, in the failing light, it was impossible to tell.

Ring had said it was close.

And, with a chill, Beck realized that the thing in his head agreed. He could feel the thing, rapt with anticipation. Eagerness.

Beck looked forlornly toward the cliff edge. The Buffalo Jump. There was more light in that direction—to the west, away from the storm. But there was no sign of a gate.

Not yet.

Beck was getting soaked, and getting nowhere. He made his way back to the B3 and was about to climb inside when he saw lights descending from the ridge. Headlights.

He stared through the rain. Shielded his eyes. Waited. It was a truck. A big, beefy 4WD pickup winding its way down through the scrub.

Collins.

Beck thought about waiting outside to talk to him. Then thought better of it. He climbed back in the helicopter and shut the door.

Collins pulled level with the B3 and stayed in his truck. Talked to Beck via cell phone. Told him about the tranquilizer guns and the cage in the back of the truck. Left out the part about killing two store employees.

The storm intensified, settling over the plain like open war. Gusts blasted the helicopter, shunting it side-to-side. Turbulence on the ground. Rain hammered the roof. Lightning cut the darkness. Thunder crashed overhead.

Beck pushed the pilot's seat back as far as it would go and watched Ring work. The scientist was wearing headphones, so there was no sound, but Beck got the gist of what he was studying: images of the terrestrial gate. Blips on the "radar" screen. Streams of data concerning the Nexus Animal. And news feeds.

Beck read one of the subtitles as it crawled across the bottom of Ring's tablet PC:

Scientists rush to find cause of vanishing sea life. Penguin rookeries emptied overnight. Sea lion beaches desolate. Fish stocks decimated in matter of hours.

Beck could see the U.S. president on another part of the screen, talking to reporters at a news conference. Other world leaders were holding similar press conferences in their countries. Beck watched news clips from fishing vessels and whale watching boats.

From the multiple feeds rolling across Ring's screens, it seemed the marine Exodus was all anyone was talking about.

Beck glanced at his phone and saw messages. Lots of messages. Urgent messages from Erebus vice presidents and board members trying to get in touch with him to talk about his father and sister, the tragic helicopter crash, and the state of the corporation.

Beck put his phone away.

Leaning back, he shut his eyes and tried to ignore the screaming wind, the vibrations of the helicopter, and Wilden's raspy snoring.

The thing in his head was quiet, for the moment, and fatigue was settling in, at last. Defying Heintzel's stimulants.

Beck sat still. Tried to empty his mind. After a time he fell into an uneasy sleep.

Joe Stanton lay on the ground, curled against Ella's back, and stared out at the storm through the small opening in the tarp.

Rain pummeled the shelter and wind tore at the doorway as if it were a predator trying to claw its way inside. It seemed to Joe that the wind changed direction every few seconds. One moment it was blasting down from the ridge, flattening the tarp on its rush to the plain. The next it was roaring uphill, causing the structure to billow like a sail. On the upward gusts, a little mist was pushed inside.

Joe didn't mind. He and Ella weren't getting really wet, and he found the cool mist invigorating. So far, the stakes and guy-lines were doing their job, and the shelter was keeping them covered and—relatively—protected.

Thunder crashed directly overhead and Joe pulled Ella closer to his chest. Watched the lightning illuminate the prairie like the noonday sun.

The situation he and Ella faced was beyond dire, but the storm was not adding to his misery. If anything, he found it reassuring. Joe Stanton loved storms. He'd even sought them out—hiking into wilderness beaches on the Olympic coast to watch big Pacific weather systems smash their way ashore.

Listening to the storm, and Ella's rhythmic breathing, feeling the warmth of her body against his own, he gazed out at the tiny splinter of wild universe he could see through the opening in the tent, and his mind felt clearer than it had in days.

He thought first about escape, and if he had felt like his normal self—or anything close—he would've attempted it at once. He was not handcuffed. Not chained or shackled. At normal strength he would've lifted Ella into his arms and carried her through the darkness, through the storm, to safety.

But he was not at normal strength. Nothing like it. And the adrenaline-fueled brawl with Dodd and Kehler had driven him to the brink of death.

His systems were failing, at last. His body disintegrating. He wondered, lying there, if the calm clarity he felt now was due to his proximity to the end. He'd read somewhere that drowning victims—after fighting for their lives—experienced an almost Zen-like state of alertness and peace as they drifted toward death. Was that what he was experiencing now? He didn't know.

He guessed that Ring was somewhere close by, probably in one of the helicopters, monitoring his thoughts, strip-mining his subconscious for more messages from the terrestrial leader. Mia's counterpart.

Joe wondered who the counterpart could be and why Mia had linked the two of them in the first place.

He thought about it.

Found no answers.

His breathing slowed and his contemplation grew so deep that he almost forgot about the storm raging around him.

Time passed, and he lay there. Alert. Watchful. Quiet.

The sky to the west, over the Buffalo Jump, went fully dark—the blackness broken only by occasional angry bursts of lightning.

Joe stared through the darkness. Through the wind and rain and flashing light.

And then he felt it—the connection he'd briefly experienced in the War Room. A connection in his conscious mind.

The link was faint—like a whisper—but real. A reassuring voice in the darkness.

The whisper moved around him. Over him. Under him. Soothing his mind and broken body like a delicious summer breeze. There were words hidden in the whisper. Faint. Beautiful. He understood none of them. Not a syllable.

Who are you? Joe asked.

No reply. Not for a long time. And then the answer was there, fully formed, in his mind.

The other half. Mia's counterpart.

Where are you? Joe asked.

Seconds passed. Then, *Near at hand.*

What are you going to do?

No reply.

Joe closed his eyes and tried to clear his mind. Tried to shove his questions and fears and worries aside in hopes of hearing an answer.

Nothing.

No response.

And then it came. A reply surprising in its gentleness, innocence, and candor.

I don't know.

Joe marveled at the answer.

The creature doesn't know what it's going to do.

The creature is here. Close at hand. Ready. And yet…it doesn't know what's going to happen. It's waiting, along with the rest of us.

The hair on the back of Joe's neck prickled as he recalled what Dieturlund had said about Mia.

Mia is brilliant. One of a kind. But there's more to her than even she comprehends.

And Joe thought maybe he understood.

Something is working through this creature.

Grace.

The inexplicable.

The infinite.

Grace. In play. Unfolding on its own timetable. On its own terms.

And yet, Joe thought, *I'm still connected.*

For a reason he could not fathom he'd been given a window seat. He wondered why this was so. Decided the fact of it was enough. He had a place. And he'd watch for as long as he was able.

He lay there, holding Ella. Aware. Awake. Ready.

CHAPTER 92

IT WAS THE MIDDLE of the night when Beck's cell phone buzzed. He was asleep in the B3's pilot seat and didn't hear it.

Ring lifted the phone off the center console and shook Beck's shoulder. "It's Donaldson. Other helicopter," he said.

Beck opened his eyes and looked blank-faced at Ring. Then sat up straight in his seat. The cabin felt stale and reeked of body odor. Wilden was snoring louder than ever.

Through the pilot-side window, Beck could see Collins's truck parked a few feet away. The truck was dark. Just sitting there.

A hundred feet or so beyond the truck, he could make out the outline of the Bell L4, a faint glow emanating from the cockpit.

He heard the rain dashing in wind-borne bursts against the glass. Felt the gusts pulling the helicopter this way and that, trying to get it to move. Though not like earlier. The storm had diminished. At least a little. The digital clock at the top of the console read 3:13 a.m.

Beck looked at the phone in Ring's hand, took it, lifted it to his ear, and said, "Beck."

"Sorry to wake you, sir," said Donaldson.

"What is it?"

"Sir. This helicopter is equipped with thermal-imaging gear."

"So?"

"So we just turned it on. For the hell of it. Aimed the thermal cameras at the plain."

"And?"

"Sir. You have to see this."

Beck stared out the window at the L4. "You want me to walk over there?"

He heard the other pilot mumble something to Donaldson in the background.

Donaldson said, "There's a short-arc xenon on the B3. Try the narrow beam."

Beck frowned. "What the fuck are you talking about?"

"Sorry, sir," said Donaldson. "It's a spotlight mounted under the front of the aircraft. Joystick in the middle of the dash. Turn the light on and aim it at the plain."

Beck pushed the "on" button. The light came on slowly, then built in intensity. He could see it through the glass floor of the cockpit, pointing straight down.

The beam grew blindingly bright, casting harsh shadows on the plants and stones around the B3.

Beck teased the joystick back, overdid it, and suddenly the light was slicing laser-like through the darkness, a hundred feet above the prairie. Beck watched the rain fall through the beam and gently nudged it down, down.

He stared at the circle of light and trembled.

There were things moving on the plain, shapes drifting past—as if he'd aimed the light at a debris-choked river.

Beck leaned forward and squinted through the windshield. Tried to get a better look. But the view was obscured by glare and condensation. He wiped the glass with the sleeve of his jacket. No good.

"Move the spot around when I tell you," he said to Ring. He grabbed the binoculars, opened the door, and climbed outside.

The wind was blowing steadily—though not as hard as earlier—and the air felt fresh and invigorating. Lightning flashed away to the west, over the Madison River, but the bursts were sporadic now, the thunder low and muffled—out of sync with the light.

Beck stared at the western sky, watched the lightning, and wondered if the storm had really moved on, or was merely regrouping. Gathering strength for another assault.

He stepped to the front of the helicopter, knelt next to the spotlight, and lifted the binoculars to his eyes, following the beam down, to where it hit the plain. He gasped.

There were animals everywhere. Creatures of every size and shape and description. Predators and prey, clustered together, moving slowly, inexorably toward the precipice—the Buffalo Jump. He could see hundreds of pairs of eyes reflected in the glow from the spot. Red. Blue. Translucent yellow. Glinting in the darkness. He could see breath rising in steamy clouds, the clouds disintegrating in the wind.

Beck's body quivered, head to toe, and the Thing in his head leapt forward so abruptly he thought his skull might explode. The thing shivered with exuberance.

"Move the light around!" Beck yelled, wondering, as he said it, if it was him or the Thing that most wanted to see what was on the plain.

Ring panned the light slowly to the right and Beck followed with the binoculars, marveling at the impossibly heavy concentration of life below. Bison—enormous creatures with shaggy heads and horns. Antelope. Deer. Bucks with racks large and small. Does. Fawns. Wild horses. Coyotes. Wolves. Mountain lions. Bears. He could *hear* the animals now, too, snorting and grunting, stamping and braying, and he could smell them. When the wind turned and flowed uphill, the scent filled his nostrils. Rich. Redolent. Earthy.

Ring tilted the spotlight down a couple of degrees. Same scene: animals large and small, lithe and lumbering. An assemblage of organisms akin to what they'd witnessed in the sea. Beck saw an enormous buffalo shaking water from its fur, gyrating like a dog, the droplets flashing like diamonds.

"Pan left," Beck yelled. "Toward the mountains."

Ring moved the light steadily east, to where the alley broadened into the larger prairie. Beck followed with the binoculars and whistled in astonishment.

It wasn't just the channel leading to the cliffs that was full of creatures, but the lands behind it as well. As if the plain were a great reservoir filling to capacity.

Beck guessed that virtually every wild creature from a hundred miles around had gathered—or was gathering—on the plain below.

He turned toward the Jump.

Dead dark in that direction. Utter blackness save for when sporadic bursts of lightning revealed the outline of the precipice and the giant boulder perched near the edge.

Beck remembered the thought captures they'd seen in the War Room—images from Joe Stanton's subconscious that showed the terrestrial gate fully formed at sunrise. He looked at his phone: 3:35 a.m.

Ring had said sunrise would be at 5:41, which meant that the sky would begin to lighten around four. Which meant they didn't have much time.

He pounded on the Bell's windshield with the heel of his hand. "Turn the light off!" he yelled. "We need to get moving."

Beck ran to Collins's truck and opened the door. Collins was bleary-eyed but sitting up. He'd heard the yelling and seen the spotlight.

"Moving out," said Beck. "Pull closer to the other helicopter. Most of the gear's over there."

Collins said "Yes, sir," and Beck continued on, toward the L4, guided by the electric glow from its cockpit.

The ground was muddy where they'd trampled the soil, and Beck slipped a little on the wet Earth.

He pictured the mile-wide thoroughfare on the prairie below, the waist-high grasses obliterated by the unprecedented movement of life. He pictured people walking the land in the days to come, searching the ground for clues, trying to figure out what the hell had happened.

Beck heard Collins fire up the truck behind him.

Thunder reverberated on the horizon, threatening, but distant, like an angry conversation faintly overheard. Rain fell around him. Wind shook the sage and rattled the helicopters.

Beck shivered. Stopped walking. Turned and stared into the darkness toward the plain.

He'd seen the animals. Seen the vast river of life with his own eyes. But he still couldn't believe it.

A lifelong hunter, he'd observed an abundance of wild creatures over the years and possessed a deep understanding of animal behavior—or so he'd always believed.

What was happening here was completely counter to everything he knew, and the facts of the situation made him tremble.

The laws of nature—at least as humans understood them—were here and now being bent. Broken. The animals on the prairie were hearing something, perceiving something, responding to something that humans knew nothing about.

Fearsome power was in play. Moving. Flowing. A mind and will unknowable.

Beck shivered because what was happening was beyond his comprehension. His control.

But then the Thing in his head lunged forward again, gleeful and alive and emphatic.

I can control the events on the plain. The leader is the key.

Beck's eyes moved, this way and that, seeking to penetrate the darkness. Somewhere near at hand the leader was resting. Watching. Waiting. Waiting for the moment when the laws of space-time, just for an instant, would slip.

The moment was almost upon them.

The Thing in Beck's head throbbed and thrummed with joy.

We will capture her. Hold her. Subdue and control her.

Ring had said the leader was likely a predator. Cunning. Stealthy.

Beck smiled. Yes. *And I am a predator also.*

He reached the L4 and opened the door. "Let's move. We've got work to do."

CHAPTER 93

ON BECK'S ORDERS, Kehler and Dodd crawled under the tarp sheltering Joe and Ella, and Kehler dragged Joe outside, into the wind and rain.

Ella stirred, twisted in the dirt, and tried to reach for Joe. The sedative Wilden had injected her with was wearing off.

She fought to sit up, but Dodd was there, headlamp blazing directly in her eyes, blinding her. He jabbed her in the thigh with another dose of the drug, and she collapsed back in the dirt.

He smiled—looking at her limp and defenseless—then leaned forward and stroked her hair. His breathing grew heavy.

"Dodd, for Christ's sake, let's move." It was Kehler, waiting outside the shelter.

Dodd backed out of the tight space and helped Kehler yank Joe to his feet.

Joe was too frail to fight, but he yelled to Beck as the men escorted him to the truck, his words coming in pained, wheezy gasps. "Beck. Listen to me. I'll do anything you want. A hundred percent cooperation. Just let Ella go. Let her go."

Beck went on loading gear.

Dodd shoved Joe into the backseat and strapped him in. Patted him on the leg. "Don't worry, Father," he whispered. "I'm staying here. I'll take care of your girl."

Joe lunged at him—or tried to—but Dodd slammed the door in his face, laughing.

They loaded the truck with weapons and supplies—to complement the gear Collins had acquired—then piled into the vehicle: Collins at the wheel and Beck in the front passenger seat; Joe in the middle of the back bench, with Kehler on one side and Ring on the other. Ring had his ever-present computer gear in bags at his feet. Kehler had a wad of cotton gauze taped to the bottom of his nose, the gauze orange with dried blood.

Donaldson and Wicks remained in the L4 and Dodd stayed behind as well—per Beck's instructions to guard the camp.

Collins flicked on the high beams and aimed for an opening in the scrub. For a way down, to the plain.

Rain pounded against the windshield, and the wipers thumped back and forth. The truck bounced over the rough ground and the engine groaned as Collins shifted into low.

Joe leaned forward, straining against his shoulder harness. "Beck. Please. For God's sake—"

Without turning, Beck said, "Shut your mouth, Father, or we'll duct-tape it shut."

Joe fell silent. Sat back. Sick. Weak. Miserable. He tried to think.

The warm feeling of connection he'd experienced earlier—while lying under the tarp and holding Ella—had been shattered. The emotions circulating in his mind now consisted of fear, terror, and rage.

He tried to calm himself, think rationally.

The air in the SUV was humid and stale and smelled of sweat. Nerves. Tension. The men were tired, running on adrenaline and caffeine and God knew what else.

The big 4x4 descended from the sage-covered bench, toward the prairie.

The ground was soft in places and the truck sank in the mud, tires spinning, the body of the vehicle shimmying side to side, so that Collins had to correct the trajectory every few seconds as they angled down the face of the bench.

They cleared some tall brush and now the headlights shone on the prairie, and on the sea of animals waiting there. The men gasped. Stared. Even Ring gawked at the scene before them, his computers forgotten.

Beck cracked his window, letting in the cool night air and the sounds and smells of thousands upon thousands of living things.

The truck was almost to flat ground now and the animals loomed like a wall. Shining jewel eyes turned toward the truck. Huge shaggy heads. A myriad of inscrutable faces.

The animals arrayed on the phalanx of the fantastic congregation watched the truck's approach, silently. Impassively. Bodies glistening with rain.

The truck thumped and groaned to within fifty feet of the "wall" and all at once the dark line of animals parted, creating a path. A road through the multitude.

The men stared in wonder. Listened to the animals snorting and grunting, chuffing and moaning. Hooves and paws patted the earth as the creatures pulled back. Stepped aside. But there was no sign of panic or aggression.

It almost seemed that the truck's arrival had been expected.

CHAPTER 94

ELLA LAY ON HER SIDE. Eyes closed. Face slack. Respiration steady.

The drug Wilden had injected—and that Dodd had readministered—was a narcotic analgesic designed to maintain unconsciousness for at least six hours. She'd feel groggy and incoherent for another three hours after that—assuming she lived that long.

She lay curled in the dirt as if Joe were still holding her. Kissing the back of her neck. She lay still. Limbs leaden. Useless. An explosion would not have roused her. She wasn't dreaming, either. Her sleep was too deep. Her brain activity too subdued.

An anesthesia team observing the situation would have agreed: The chance of Ella dreaming was low—maybe one in a hundred. The chance of waking anytime soon: Zero. Impossible.

A gust of wind momentarily flattened the tarp, then re-inflated it, filling it like a lung.

The same gust came again.

And again.

A light flickered on in the deepest recesses of Ella's mind then. A thin, frail, ghostly light. A tiny sputtering candle in a vast darkness.

Now—deep in Ella's brain—there was a breath of sound to accompany the flame. A whisper. A delicate rill of words at once strange and familiar and reassuring.

Ella's breathing changed and the light in her brain strengthened. Flared. Her limbs felt dead, still, but her mind was humming.

It was impossible. Shouldn't be happening. But it was.

Thoughts unfurled. Flowed, like the power in a darkened house coming back on. Her hands moved. Her feet. She stretched. Opened her eyes. Looked out at the plain. Watched the lightning dance across a distant ridge. Felt the wind and moist air on her cheek.

The whisper in her mind intensified, and Ella *felt*, more than heard, the sound.

The words flowing inside the whisper were incomprehensible but achingly beautiful. Full and poignant, joyful and playful, funny and melancholy, all at the same time. Too beautiful for human speech, this language; far beyond human speech, yet freighted with relevant meaning and importance.

Ella lay still. Fragments of the whisper clarified in her brain, like phrases of verse recalled from earliest childhood, as if, somehow, she'd learned the language long ago. Ages ago. Forgotten most of it but retained a little in her subconscious—a sound here and there, a syllable or two.

She listened to the voice, drawing sustenance from it. And suddenly the meaning was there, clear and bright.

You are needed, the voice was saying. *The time has come.*

Ella listened.

Are you awake? The time has come.

She lay still. Thinking. Considering her task. Her responsibility.

And then she accepted the task. Put it on, like a soldier donning armor, new and shining and unfamiliar.

The whisper flowed on, around her, through her, and she felt vitality returning to her core, spreading to her legs and arms, hands and feet, fingers and toes.

Her emotions were surging now, too, but she let them go, though they frightened her. Terrified her, in fact.

CHAPTER 95

DODD STOOD IN THE RAIN in the middle of the makeshift camp and watched the GMC's taillights bounce their way steadily downhill. The rumble of the truck faded beneath the rain and wind after a minute or so, but every now and again a gust would bring a murmur of engine noise to Dodd's ears—the whine of the truck's drivetrain groaning over rough ground, toiling downhill in low gear.

Dodd watched the lights until they were perhaps a half mile away—until he was sure Beck wasn't coming back anytime soon.

He looked around the camp.

The pilots had retreated to the L4, eager, they'd said, to get some more shut-eye. The L4's cockpit was dark.

He'd seen something in Donaldson's face that told him the man knew what he had in mind for the girl, but what did that matter?

He turned toward the other helicopter—the B3. Wilden was still in the backseat—belted in and virtually comatose. Even when he awoke from his drug-induced stupor, he'd probably stay put. Sleep off his hangover.

Dodd turned toward the tarp sheltering Ella and smiled. Rolled his head in slow circles—as if warming up for an exercise--and flexed his limbs. Stretched.

This is going to be fun.

He walked to the tarp and squatted down at the entrance. Edged his way inside, out of the rain.

He put his hand on Ella's leg. Felt the warmth of her body through the denim. Already his breathing was heavy, his heart thumping with anticipation.

He flipped on his headlamp and slid forward, until he was hovering over her.

She was magnificent. Perfect. Even with the blue-green bruise on her cheek—where Kehler had smacked her. Even with the dirt and grime and sweat.

She was amazing. Stunning.

Dodd leaned closer. Touched her hair. Stroked her cheek.

This is going to be fantastic.

Her eyes were closed. Her breathing slow and intermittent.

Of course her eyes are closed, thought Dodd. *She's drugged out of her mind. Won't feel a thing. Won't remember a thing.*

He chuckled and reached for her jacket. Rolled her onto her back and climbed on top of her. He tugged her zipper down and put his hands on her breasts. He was moaning now, practically gasping.

He turned the headlamp off, set it on the ground, and kissed her. Threaded his hand inside her jacket, inside her shirt, until he found warm, soft skin. With his other hand he reached for her jeans. Found the top button.

"Oh," he moaned.

He was inches from Ella's face when lightning again flashed behind him.

He froze.

Her eyes were open.

Open.

Staring right at him.

Impossible. A trick of the light. Must've imagined it.

There were two quick sounds behind Dodd then: a soft footfall, and a muffled grunt.

He twisted like a snake. Whipped his body around so that he was facing the entrance to the tarp.

Nothing.

Just the wind and rain. As before.

Then another far-off spasm of lightning revealed something new. Something that hadn't been there before.

A boulder just beyond the opening of the tarp.

A rough, hulking mass about the size of a picnic table.

Dodd's brain searched for possible explanations for the shape.

There were none.

There was another soft grunt, and Dodd saw two points of light glimmering in the gloom.

Eyes.

"What the fuck?"

Dodd slammed his heels into the dirt and threw himself back.

The "boulder" lunged—a single fluid motion—and Dodd screamed as huge white teeth locked on his right leg, on his calf muscle, and bit down with savage, crushing force.

Dodd screamed again and then he was flying out of the tent—jerked out by his leg and whipped through the air like a rag doll.

He twisted, shrieking in agony, digging for his gun.

He felt the flesh in his leg tear. Heard bones cracking. Tendons rupturing.

Lightning flashed again and the beast lunged for his chest, breaking half a dozen ribs as it landed on top of him.

A bear, Dodd realized, dazedly, as shock set in. A grizzly. He could see the massive hump on its back, muscles rippling as it slashed his chest with daggerlike claws.

Dodd was vaguely aware of more ribs snapping and of the beast's jaws dripping—chunks of his own bloody flesh hanging from the canines.

Dodd's eyes swam in their sockets and he fixed on the girl. Ella. She was standing over him now, buttoning her shirt, watching him, her expression flat. Emotionless.

Impossible.

Dodd knew he was in shock, and figured the girl hovering over him was an apparition. An illusion.

"Help me," he said anyway.

The girl seemed not to hear. She cocked her head and vanished into the gloom

CHAPTER 96

THE TRUCK CRAWLED through the darkness, through the surreal corridor of living things, headlights washing across the muddy, uneven ground.

The men gawked at the ruler-straight "road" before them and at the thousands of faces staring their way. Faces intent. Watchful. Uncertain. Eyes iridescent in the glow of the hi-beams.

The rain sputtered to a stop and the storm clouds over the corridor broke apart, disintegrating like bolts of moth-eaten fabric.

The truck rolled on, the sky burning with the white fire of a million stars, and all at once they could see an end to the strange road—an impassable barrier a few hundred yards ahead. The boulder.

From a mile-thick sheet of retreating glacial ice, the bus-sized stone had one day crashed and tumbled, ages and epochs past, coming to rest precisely in the middle of the mile-wide plain, just at the edge of the precipice, as if its resting place had been marked and chosen. Dark and imperturbable it lay before them now.

Watching from his place in the backseat, Joe had a vision of the frenzied stampedes that had long ago shaken the plain. In his mind's eye he saw freight-car-sized buffalo thundering past, the herd breaking like river current as it approached the stone. He saw warriors leaping up, lunging forward, burying their own terror for the sake of the hunt, the tribe.

He wondered if the Earth remembered the stampedes. If the boulder remembered. If the events had somehow been burned into the ground so that rumors of those days reverberated still.

He thought so. And he guessed that the animals massed around them now could hear the rumors. Feel the power of the place.

As he watched the creatures watching them, he had an epiphany.
A shared dream, he thought.
They're experiencing a shared dream. Dreaming, with their eyes open, hearing something…a voice? Music? That we can't hear.

The strange faces looking at them now—faces canine, ungulate, feline, ursine, and more—were dreaming, moving in a languid dance whose choreography had been set down before the beginning of time.

A dream. Yes.

He focused his mind, and thought he could almost make out the song they were hearing, faint and far away. Impossibly beautiful.

He listened longer, and thought maybe he understood. The song was a gentle summons. Sweet. Inviting. Impossible to resist. A refrain that had days ago begun and continued even now.

Listen children, the time has come. Prepare to leave.

Prepare to leave.

With joy they'd received the song, all of them. Heard it. felt it in their bones. Heeded its gentle call.

Now though, as the truck rolled forward, toward the stone, Joe sensed new emotions spreading across the plain, rippling out in waves, interfering with the sweet refrain.

Worry.

Tension.

Discord.

With a shudder, he realized that the source of their worry was something in the truck.

Someone.

Joe sensed the entire host pivoting reluctantly. Turning together, like a single organism. Turning toward the truck. Coming around to face the source of this new unease.

Kehler spoke from the backseat. Gestured at the granite behemoth before them. "That what we're making for, Collins? That rock?"

Collins eased the big truck on and responded without turning. "Not sure we have much choice." He nodded toward the wall of animals lining the road. Laughed humorlessly. "Not a lot of room to maneuver." He glanced at Beck, seated next to him. "Boss?"

Beck stared straight ahead. Said nothing.

The truck rolled on, drawing closer to the stone.

"Boss?" Collins said again.

Beck gave no reply, just stared, as if in a trance.

Collins made eye contact with Ring in the rearview mirror. Ring caught the look and said, "The stone is our goal. Park in front of it and we'll look for a way up. Ferry the gear to the top and use it as a platform."

Collins nodded and drove on.

Inside Beck's head, a storm raged.

For the moment, the old Beck was at the helm, running the show, taking stock of his own condition.

It was not a pretty picture.

The drugs Heintzel had given him had all but worn off and he felt now weaker than he ever had. Weak. Withered. Profoundly fatigued. The antithesis of the robust, vibrant, powerful man he had always been.

The truck rumbled to a stop before the boulder—the gray, lichen-flecked stone rising over them like a castle wall—and Collins killed the engine and turned out the lights.

He sat there with the windows down, letting his eyes adjust to the darkness. The aroma of the rain-drenched prairie mixed with the smell of thousands upon thousands of wild animals had by now so thoroughly permeated their senses they could no longer smell anything.

The engine *tick-ticked* its way to silence, and now Collins could hear the wind caressing the stone, water dripping from cracks and crevices on the boulder's granite face, and the murmur of the host massed around them: heavy hoofs shifting uneasily on muddy ground, low snuffles and grunts, breathy *woofs* and guttural, reverberating growls.

Kehler racked the slide on his handgun and whispered to Ring. "What if they charge when we step outside?"

"They won't.

Kehler glared at him in the darkness. "Guarantee that?"

"No, but it's a reasonable assumption. The animals around us are in a sort of stasis at the moment. Waiting for the leader. For the cue to move on. The next phase to begin. They're not following normal behavior patterns."

"No shit?" said Kehler.

Collins chuckled softly in the driver's seat.

"No shit, Ring," Kehler repeated. "I had no idea. I thought they always did this."

Ring said nothing.

Collins flicked on a headlamp and aimed it at the boulder. Found the zigzag crack in the stone he'd noticed driving up. The fissure ran from the base of the boulder to the top, and there were natural hand- and footholds here and there, worn into the rock, so that it appeared climbing would be a simple matter.

Under the watchful gaze of thousands of eyes, the men quickly, quietly, off-loaded bags of gear by the light of their headlamps.

Collins scrambled to the top of the boulder first, followed by Ring, wearing a backpack filled with his computer equipment.

Collins eased himself back down and helped Kehler drag Joe toward the crack in the stone.

"Climb," Collins commanded, and Joe lifted his foot to the first rain-slick foothold, shocked by the weakness in his legs.

"Climb," Collins repeated. "We'll push."

Collins and Kehler hefted Joe as far up the fissure as they could, and then Collins pushed on the heels of Joe's boots, boosting him skyward. "Ring," Collins grunted. "Take his hand. Pull him up."

Ring lugged Joe onto the flat top of the massive stone—perhaps fifteen feet above the prairie, and Joe collapsed into a heap on the cold, wet granite.

Collins dropped back to the ground, where he and Kehler collected the remaining bags of gear. The light from their lamps washing randomly over the surrounding host.

"Collins. Look."

Collins lifted his head, followed Kehler's gaze and shivered at what he saw.

The road they'd traveled, from the sage-covered bench to the boulder, had vanished. The animals had filled it in, erasing it completely. Now there was just a narrow envelope of space around the truck.

Two more quick trips and all of the gear was on top of the boulder—everything except the cage, which they left in the back of the truck.

Collins leaned through the driver's-side window. "Boss?"

Beck was still in the passenger seat. Still belted in. Still staring zombielike through the windshield.

Collins and Kehler exchanged looks.

"Boss," Collins repeated. "Ring says we need to be on top of the stone—that it's a good lookout. Come on. You can climb up between me and Kehler. Use our light."

Beck nodded absently, like he'd barely heard, unclipped his seatbelt, exited the truck, and followed Collins to the fissure. He climbed, robotically, without assistance. Reached the top of the stone, turned a full circle and sat down.

They arranged themselves amid the piled gear—Beck and his men—beneath stars glittering like shards of blue ice in a black ocean. Constellations wheeled big and bright beyond the cliff, so that it looked as if one could run, leap from the edge, and fall directly into another galaxy.

Lightning still pulsed, periodically, silently, beyond a far mountain range, brightening the horizon like a war in a neighboring country.

Beck sat hunched and suffering on the stone, fighting the creature in his head. He was in profound physical pain now and moaned and rocked back and forth on his heels, clutching his scalp and hair like a madman.

Beck's men stared at him, and they weren't the only ones. The murmur of the vast host faded to silence, so that it felt as if the entire multitude was holding its breath, watching, waiting to see what would happen next.

"No," Beck hissed. "No."

The Thing was slinking forward now, grinning, gloating, ready to claim his broken mind and body for its own, once and for all.

Beck recoiled at the beast's approach.

Raw, weak, and violated he felt, yet possessed also with a keen understanding that he had not known for days. The truth revealed before him now appeared so obvious that he could not imagine how he'd missed it.

Started on Marauder. *On the weather deck. After the fight with Ellis.*

The Thing had been there that day—just a shadow then, a phantom skulking around the bulwarks, watching, weighing its options, deciding it liked what it saw.

Like a virus, it had somehow infiltrated his body. His consciousness, settling in gradually, slowly, so as not to damage its host.

On Beck's own aggressive nature and violent tendencies the Thing had played, driving him to explore the phenomenon in the deep. To push ahead regardless of cost or consequence.

Tricked.

Duped.

The Beast's agenda, he saw now, was far different from his own. Always had been.

It used me. Made me act the way I did.

Used me.

The fact of it enraged him.

Beck whispered defiantly to his nameless, invisible foe. "Won't work. I've been fighting my whole life. Have the best training in the world. I'm disciplined. Battle-hardened. I'm tired and worn down, maybe so, but I am not defeated and not about to give up. So get the fuck out of my head!"

He screamed and pushed against the Beast with all his might, his body contorting and convulsing across the stone.

After twenty or so seconds he crumpled, gasping, onto his side, all eyes staring at him in the dark.

Beck's mind went quiet. Numb. And for a long while he felt nothing.

Nothing.

Nothing at all.

Then, tentative relief. Relief, followed by swelling, surging joy.

"It's gone!" he whispered. "Gone."

He sat up slowly, smiling. Exhausted and weak, but free.

Free!

The Thing was gone. The parasite—the entity that had caused him so much suffering—had been banished.

He closed his eyes and celebrated the feeling of peace.

Too soon.

The Thing leapt forward from its hiding place and smashed through Sheldon Beck's last defenses like a battering ram, overwhelming his nervous system and seizing control of his brain and body once and for all.

Beck screamed—a long, shrill, agony-filled wail that made his men quiver in their boots.

And then the organism that had always been Sheldon Beck got to its feet and stood, gazing into the darkness.

Joe watched Beck struggle and writhe and cry out, and he felt a change in the air—a fleeting, electric tremor—as if the prairie were a magnetic field and the polarity had in an instant swapped positions. Negative to positive. Positive to negative.

Joe rolled over so that he was facing the vast assemblage of animals and felt their sudden despair.

He didn't understand the reason for the emotion. Didn't know what it meant. But he felt it now spreading like a rumor across the land. Spreading out in waves from the boulder, the epicenter of the change.

Collins whispered to Ring, "What's happening?"

Ring shook his head. Said nothing.

Beck stood rooted, motionless in the center of the great stone. Shut his eyes. Breathed.

Minutes passed, and the tension on the prairie seemed to dissipate a tiny bit. The animals shuffled. Shifted positions. Murmured.

Wind whistled around the boulder, and Beck stood frozen beneath the stars. A statue.

Ring pulled Collins and Kehler close and whispered, the fatigue in his voice evident, "I don't know what's going on with Beck—but I know we have work to do."

Kehler and Collins regarded him skeptically.

Ring said, "I still believe events here will unfold much like they did in the sea, and we need to be ready. When the Nexus Animal appears, we'll be able to spot her. She'll be the last to transit the gate, so there should be plenty of time to locate, track, and sedate her, before she gets near the cliff."

Collins nodded and reached for the duffel bag containing the tranquilizer guns. He looked at Kehler. "We should prep. Run through this."

Collins heard a noise and turned to find Beck standing over him, eyes open, face relaxed and confident in the starlight. "Weapons won't be necessary," he said mildly.

He lifted his eyes toward the sea of creatures waiting on the plain.

"The leader will come here," he said. "To me. She has no choice."

CHAPTER 97

ELLA TOLLEFSON STOOD on the edge of Beck's makeshift camp, staring into the darkness and breathing the cool, rain-washed air. The great bear sat nearby, relaxed, watching her closely.

Ella closed her eyes and listened to the sounds on the plain, to the animals massed in the tens of thousands. She could hear deeper sounds, too: music, soft and ethereal. Flowing, it seemed, from the Earth itself.

She felt the energy and the music uniting the great host, gently calling to it, animating it, filling it with anticipation.

And now she sensed an unwelcome thread in the conversation. A discordant note in an otherwise perfect composition.

She sighed and turned toward the great boulder at the edge of the cliff. The truck had reached the foot of the massive island of granite and the men were sitting inside the vehicle.

Far from the truck though she was, Ella could hear the men. Their voices. Their heartbeats. She wondered at this. Then accepted it as fact.

She heard them exit the truck and ready the gear. Heard Collins and Kehler drag Joe toward the stone and force him to climb. Joe's heartbeat was weak. Fading.

She focused her mind on Joe. Focused as hard as she could.

I'm here. Awake. Alive. I love you.

No response. He was, she guessed, too weak now to receive her thoughts.

She turned, tears in her eyes.

There isn't much time, she told herself. *Not much time at all.*

Pilot Jeff Donaldson awoke to the sound of footsteps outside the Bell L4. He opened his eyes and looked around. Heard Wicks, asleep in the copilot seat, snoring softly.

Sitting up, Donaldson saw a ghostlike form glide past the front of the cockpit, assumed it was Dodd, and opened the door.

"That was quick. You even give her a kiss?"

It wasn't Dodd. It was the girl. The prisoner. The woman who'd supposedly been sedated out of her mind.

"Where's Dodd?" Donaldson managed, a quiver in his voice.

The woman just stared at him, an odd glint in her eyes.

Donaldson reached for his sidearm, and the woman stepped clear of the door just as an enormous shape surged forward, out of the darkness.

Donaldson squawked and fumbled for his weapon. The bear roared and smashed into the open cockpit with such force and velocity that the helicopter rose off of its left skid and shuddered sideways a few feet, tearing free of its tethers.

The bear bit down on Donaldson's bicep and ripped him screaming out of the aircraft, into the night.

Waking instantly, fully, to screams, roars, and a shower of his friend's warm blood, Wicks punched open his door and threw himself onto the dirt. An instant later he was on his feet, sprinting into the darkness.

Ella stepped to the L4's rear door, opened it, and flipped on the interior light.

The dead hiker was there—a bulky, rigid form inside a zippered body bag.

The bag lay twisted and askew atop other bags, as if it had been tossed into the compartment quickly, haphazardly, like a sack of trash—as a sort of final insult against an innocent young man.

Ella climbed into the compartment and knelt over the bag, straightened it as best she could, and found the zipper at the top. She tugged the zipper down a few feet, the sound grating and offensive in the still compartment.

The hiker's eyes were open, but unseeing. His skin green and waxy in the glow of the overhead light. His hair matted, his mouth locked in an expression of pain. Shock. The area around his neck was black in the light. A pool of sticky, slowly drying blood.

Ella placed her hands gently on either side of the hiker's head. Kept them there. Closed her eyes.

CHAPTER 98

THE HIKER SAT ON an ice chest a few paces from the helicopter, and Ella stood beside him, holding his hand.

There was a touch of gray in the eastern sky now—a slowly widening band above the Gallatin Range that glowed like polished steel.

Ella watched the sky and thought about the hiker. What had just happened. She'd known that she would be able to wake him. The knowledge had just been there.

I can walk and speak and breathe. And I can wake this man from his sleep.

Part of her had protested, of course, saying, *This is insane. Absurd. This man is dead. Has been dead for hours. He was murdered.*

But then she'd taken his face in her hands, and something had passed between them, like a secret. He'd woken up then. Just as she'd known he would.

Now he was sitting. Staring into the darkness. Breathing.

"What's your name?" Ella asked softly.

The hiker lifted his head, looked at her. His face was blank, eyes glassy—not quite registering. He stared in the dim light some more and then there was a flicker. A pulse like a darting candle flame.

"I was hiking," he said slowly.

"Yes," said Ella.

He nodded as if confirming his own memory. "Guidebook said there were fewer tourists above the cliffs. So I hiked up."

"And you saw the helicopters," said Ella. "Came to find out what was going on."

The hiker nodded. Stared his blank stare. Kept hold of Ella's hand.

He stretched out his free hand, flexed it. Probed his neck with his fingers.

There was blood everywhere. On his clothes, his skin. But the slash across his neck had heeled completely, as if the wound had never happened.

"He cut my throat," he said matter-of-factly. "The leader dude."

"Yes," said Ella.

The hiker stared into the darkness again, probed his neck some more, as if assessing the quality of a shave.

"What happened," he whispered. "Is happening? I can't remember anything after—" He looked up at her. Searched her eyes. "I thought I died."

"You did die," said Ella. "But I need your help."

The hiker gave her a puzzled look. Then seemed to accept her words as fact.

"Edwin," he said.

Ella squinted at him.

"You asked my name. It's Edwin."

"Hi, Edwin," said Ella. "I'm Ella."

The hiker watched her for a long time, studying her face in the growing light. "You don't understand everything that's happening either, do you?"

"No," said Ella.

"And you're worried about what's coming."

"Yes. I think we're going to fail."

CHAPTER 99

JOE STANTON LAY SHIVERING on the cold, rain-slick boulder, wet clothes clinging to his skin, wet hair plastered to his forehead. Beck's men hadn't bothered to cover him with anything, and he curled into a fetal position, drifting in and out of consciousness as he faced the sunrise.

A part of him knew that this sunrise would be his last, but he wasn't frightened or alarmed. He wasn't even sure he was cold anymore. His discomfort actually seemed to be diminishing.

I could just go to sleep, he thought. *Sleep would feel so good right now. Sleep.*

His eyes snapped open and a pulse of adrenaline shocked him into full wakefulness.

Going to sleep now means never waking up again. I'm not ready for that. Not yet.

He was weak—too weak even to push the wet tangle of hair from his eyes. But he had some life remaining. A spark, flickering inside of him still.

He decided to focus on something he could control.

I can keep my eyes open. Watch the sunrise and see what it brings. I can do that much.

This simple resolution cleared his mind and calmed his nerves.

Yes. Stay awake. Alert. Something is happening. Something fantastic.

He thought about Ella and tried to find her with his mind. Send her a message. Speak to her.

No luck.

Not thinking clearly enough for that anymore.

He heard Ring behind him, tapping on a keyboard, eavesdropping on his subconscious. On the flow of information from Mia's terrestrial counterpart.

Joe didn't know what Ring was seeing on his screens, but he felt violated all the same. Ring, Heintzel, and Beck had collaborated to hack into his private thoughts. Into a stream of communication meant only for him. He wished he could leap up and sweep Ring and his computers off the boulder, but he didn't have the strength. Nothing close to the strength required for something like that. Not anymore.

He focused on the sunrise, on the broad swath of prairie revealed in the growing light, and realized his eyesight had worsened.

The landscape before him resembled an impressionist painting. The shapes made sense. But appeared soft. Indistinct. The snow-topped Gallatin Mountains seemed to Joe disconnected from the Earth, as if the entire range were levitating above the plain. Even the animals massed around the great boulder—stamping, breathing, turning, swishing tails and shaking dew from their bodies—seemed to float in soft, individual halos that blended and overlapped with one another to make a larger, shimmering, respirating organism.

Joe watched and felt anew the tension and despair radiating out from the host. It seemed to him that the whole of the assemblage—perhaps all of the creatures massed before all of the nascent gates across the world—was teetering on a knife-edge, walking the thinnest of lines between joy and fear, ecstasy and sorrow.

On one side of the equation: Beck, or, rather, the thing that Beck had become—floating over the stone, radiating darkness, warping, bending and distorting the energy on the prairie, like an enormous black hole. On the other side: the leader, whoever and wherever she was, coming to show the way.

For the umpteenth time, Joe wondered about the identity of the leader. What kind of animal she was. How she and Mia had managed to connect. He believed he could feel her now: A reassuring presence. A friend slowly approaching through the gray dawn mist.

Ultimately, as always, his thoughts returned to Ella, to the woman he loved more than anyone he'd ever met. More than anything in the world.

Ella. Where are you?
Ella, I love you.
Ella.

He wished he could see her again, or at least touch her, with his mind. He knew that neither wish was likely to come true, and tears filled his eyes.

Beck's men could feel the growing tension, too, and for Kehler, it was becoming unbearable.

He hadn't slept. His nose was swollen to the size of a tennis ball—and exquisitely painful to the touch. Blood still oozed from his nostrils.

He sat in the predawn light next to Collins, eyes flicking between Ring—hunched over his glowing screens—and Beck, standing rigid and immovable in the center of the great stone. Beck's eyes were closed still and his body moved not at all. Kehler watched for the rise and fall of his boss's chest—to confirm that the man was breathing—and couldn't even see that.

More blood dripped from Kehler's nose, through the filthy cotton wad taped to his nostrils, and he lost the battle to control his temper. He twisted on the stone and grabbed Ring by the arm.

"What the hell is going on?"

Ring looked up, blinking, a superior, impatient twist to his mouth. "With what?"

Kehler grunted and made a sweeping gesture with his arm. "With Beck. With the goddamned animals. With everything."

Ring turned back to his screens like the question barely merited a response. "That's what I'm trying to ascertain."

Kehler batted Ring's laptop with his hand and leaned closer. "You don't need a fucking computer to tell you this is messed up." He cast his eyes toward Beck. "That the boss is messed up."

Ring pulled his laptop stiffly back into position. "Thank you for that valuable insight, Mr. Kehler. I'll keep it in mind."

Kehler leaned back next to Collins and sat there, staring out, nose bleeding, as if weighing what to do. He relaxed. His shoulders sagged. Then smoothly, abruptly, he rose to his feet and swung toward Beck in a fluid arc.

"Kehler!" shouted Collins.

Too late.

Kehler raised his gun so that it was an inch from the side of Beck's head.

Beck moved not at all and his eyes stayed shut, but as Kehler squeezed the trigger the gun melted in his hand and his arm burst into flame.

Kehler screamed, fell back on the stone, and a reverberating, excruciatingly loud *boom* shook the plain—as if the bones of the Earth were breaking, exploding, directly beneath the prairie.

The *boom* faded into a steady, sustained rumble that merged with the sound of tens of thousands of animals suddenly moving—running—all at once.

Beck's eyes snapped open, the sun flashed above the distant mountains, and a single blade of golden light sliced through the mist and shot across the prairie, toward the cliffs—the Buffalo Jump.

One moment the vast assemblage was waiting patiently, in the thrall of music only they could hear. The next, everyone—everything—was moving.

Collins and Ring were on their feet, facing east. Beck and Joe Stanton stared the same direction, at the sea of animals; at the great congregation of creatures, moving now, in unison. Running, but not panicked.

Kehler lay moaning on the stone, ignored by all, his right arm charred and smoking, wrist to shoulder, his gun an unrecognizable blob of bubbling, molten metal and plastic resin.

Animals flowed around the boulder—around the truck—like rushing water, a surging stream of bison and bear, elk and fox, deer, porcupine, antelope and a dozen other species large and small. Birds and bats there were as well, endless columns of wings silhouetted against the sunrise, hurrying, east to west.

A lithe young mountain lion sprang from the river of creatures, onto the boulder, glanced disinterestedly at the men, and bounded down the far side. Collins scooped an automatic rifle from an open gear bag, and then all of the men—even Joe—turned to see where the animals were going.

They turned, and gaped, dumbfounded.

A delicate archway, hundreds of feet tall, spanned the mile-wide alley leading to the Buffalo Jump. Or rather, what *had been* the Buffalo Jump.

Where before there had been a cliff followed by a drop of eight-hundred-feet, there now was level ground.

No longer were they looking down, into the Madison River Valley, but into a new land.

And what a land it was.

Wide, verdant prairie they saw, with grasses waving and bending to the winds of an alien world. Farther out: forest, and foothills leading to stupendously tall peaks, jagged and impenetrable.

The blade of sunlight from behind the Gallatin Range pierced the shimmering arch—light from one world entering another—and fell on faraway spires—towers of granite thousands of feet tall—and flashing waterfalls.

The view rendered them speechless. Made Collins drop his weapon limply to his side, and Ring forget his computers. And the scene near at hand was just as surprising as the land beyond.

Studying the arch more closely, they saw that the ground did not flow continuously from one world into the next. Directly beneath the towering arch there was a narrow gap in the soil, perhaps two feet across. A break between worlds. A hard black border line. A narrow chasm that even the smallest animals could jump.

And jump it they were—thousands every second. Millions of animals leaving Earth and flooding into the rich and fecund world beyond.

Looking at the arch, at the gap, they had the sense that they were seeing two long-separated continents momentarily, impossibly, rejoined. As if Africa and South America had, just for an instant, melded back into one stupendous, Pangaean land mass.

Or, *almost* melded. Except for the gap. The chasm between worlds.

Into this chasm fell a shimmering, translucent, impossibly delicate veil of water.

Along the entire length of the arch, the water fell, continuously, endlessly. Where it went after it entered the chasm, or whether it was really water, none of the observers could tell.

Lifting their eyes once more beyond the gap, peering through the shimmering, lens-like veil into the new land, they saw the animals spreading out, running with reckless, joyous abandon.

And Joe had a revelation. It wasn't heaven they were looking at. The new land was achingly beautiful, yes, but also wild and harsh and unforgiving. Life there, as on Earth, would be both kind and violent. Benevolent and cruel. Savage and sweet and abundant and deadly.

Not heaven, yet a place where wild creatures could live as they were meant to live. Where there was room to move. Food, water, and air free of poison. A place where they might thrive, unmolested by a mad species bent, it seemed, on extinguishing all of nature's gifts.

Lying there, Joe perceived something else: The joining of worlds would be fleeting. Over in an eye blink. The gears in some vast and unknowable cosmic machine had turned now just so, aligning at the appointed location in space-time. But it wouldn't last. Couldn't last.

For one glorious instant, doors rarely opened stood wide. Across the Earth, barricades had fallen, revealing a sister world familiar and yet a million billion miles distant. A place one sometimes sensed out of the corner of one's eye, yet never could reach.

The men stared, unable to turn away.

All except for Stanton. For he could feel an energy behind him now. The terrestrial leader, approaching from the east.

CHAPTER 100

SUMMONING ALL OF HIS remaining strength, Joe Stanton rolled over on the stone, and saw something as remarkable as the gate.

Advancing steadily amid the running beasts, perhaps a hundred yards from the boulder and closing fast: a pillar of blue fire.

Roughly circular, the girth of a redwood tree, the column of flame came on, and Joe could see shapes moving inside, behind a cascading, slowly rotating curtain of shimmering heat.

Peering deeper into the strange vessel, straining to see, he perceived a familiar form.

Ella?

His heart hammered in his chest, and the truth unfurled in his mind.

Ella is the leader.

Ella.

His thoughts spun back two days, to the Pike Place Market stairs, when Mia had appeared in his mind and asked to trade places. It wasn't—he understood now—to show him her world, though that was a gift beyond measure. It was to connect with her other half, with Ella, the terrestrial leader—though Ella, at the time, knew nothing of her role or the task ahead.

He thought about the massacre Ella had survived years earlier, at the mall, and remembered her words:

It was like the gunman didn't see me. Like I was invisible—though I was right in front of him.

He wondered if grace had been protecting her that day. If her place in the great dance unfolding around them now had even then been set.

Whether the mechanism of her ascendance was something written in her DNA—something that had always been there, waiting, or a thing wholly different, Joe could not guess, but Ella was before him now, moving quickly toward the stone.

He heard the others turn and gasp. All except Beck, who seemed already to know who and what the Leader was. He simply stared, an arrogant, mocking expression on his face.

Ring whispered something to Collins, who dropped the automatic rifle, grabbed one of the tranquilizer guns, aimed at Ella, and fired. The dart flared as it hit the spinning curtain of fire and dropped to the earth as ash.

The pillar was twenty-five yards away now, and Joe could make out the identity of Ella's companions: A man—the hiker Beck had killed—and a huge grizzly bear.

Outside the pillar, close on either flank, walked two enormous bison. Like giant guards or sentinels. Impervious to the flame they seemed, for they brushed now and then against it. Blue tongues of fire flicked and danced across their shaggy coats.

Collins grabbed the other tranquilizer gun from the ground aimed carefully, and fired again. Same result: the dart vaporized as soon as it touched the wall of flame.

Ring started to say something—give different instructions—but Collins didn't seem to be listening. He scooped up an M4 carbine and fired a burst—a hundred rounds—into the shroud of molten blue. No effect.

Ignoring Ring's screams, Collins flicked the barrel to the right and shot one of the bison.

The gun roared, the great animal bellowed and crumpled into the dirt, collapsing awkwardly on its forelegs. Then, pandemonium.

What had been a steady, stately migration turned instantly into a rout. A mad, thundering stampede for the gate. Most of the creatures that had gathered the night before—filling the alley for miles back—had already passed into the new realm. But not all.

Beasts large and small now leapt or sprinted or galloped forward in an instantaneous surge of panic, and the plain suddenly resembled a violent, stormy sea. Beasts collided with one another, fell, and flew headlong for the gate, grunting and roaring, howling and shrieking.

Ring screamed at Collins over the cacophony. "Don't shoot! What the hell do you think you're doing? Don't—"

He stopped midsentence—eyes fixed on the pillar.

The column of flame had ceased turning, and the people inside were staring at the dying buffalo, lying inert, like a small hillock, a few feet away. Blood gushed in miniature geysers from holes across its thick brown coat, and its eyes dulled.

The flame enveloping the walkers winked off and now Ella was stepping to the fallen animal, kneeling alongside of it.

"Shoot!" Ring screamed. "Shoot!"

Collins lunged for the M4, but Ring batted it away. "No. With the dart rifle! Hurry!"

"Shoot what?" Collins cried, dropping to his knees and lifting the nearest tranquilizer gun to his shoulder.

"The girl! The leader. The girl is the—"

The column of flame reignited around the girl and her companions just as Collins fired. As before, the dart dematerialized as it hit the shimmering wall.

Ring put his hand on Collins's arm and they watched—through the flame—as the woman set her hands on the bison's head. Fifteen seconds passed. Thirty. The creature's chest heaved. Its head swung from the ground in a massive arc and then it was rolling and rising—bellowing—to its feet.

And now the pillar of flame was moving again, leaving the massive bison alive and standing, and coming closer to the stone.

The edge of the flickering pillar brushed the side of the 4x4, melting the metal, blowing out the glass and incinerating the vehicle's insides as it passed.

And now the fire was rising—the woman, the hiker, and the bear climbing to the top of the boulder inside of its protective, ever-shifting walls.

Ring and Collins fell back to the far side of the massive stone, stumbling over Kehler as they moved.

Ring screamed over the roar of the stampede. "We'll have one more chance! Be ready with the dart."

Collins looked confused. "I thought the leader would be an animal."

"What the fuck do you think humans are?"

Collins said nothing.

"She's coming for Stanton. The flame will go off again—momentarily. That's our chance."

Collins readied the gun, and now they could feel the heat of the approaching flame.

Joe lay still, watching, as Ella and the others reached the top of the great stone. Beck stood near to the advancing fire, but appeared impervious to the heat.

Ella looked around, peering at Joe and Beck, Ring and Collins, through a veil of constantly changing blue.

Collins had the tranquilizer gun to his shoulder, his face coated in a sheen of sweat.

The gear bags nearest the flame sizzled and flared.

And suddenly the pillar of fire was gone. Extinguished completely. Instantaneously.

Collins aimed for Ella's neck and squeezed the trigger.

Too late.

The bear exploded from its place alongside Ella as if fired from a cannon, and smashed, roaring, into Collins and Ring with the force of a speeding car. Together the three of them flew from the great stone and landed in the midst of the stampede. Collins and Ring died beneath the hooves of a thousand fleeing beasts, as the great bear, without a backward glance, ambled on toward the gate.

Joe lay dying on the stone, pulse weak, heart stuttering. His breath coming now in short, ragged gasps.

He opened his eyes to find Ella kneeling beside him, smiling, bright tears streaming down her cheeks. She caressed his face with warm, gentle hands and, leaning closer, kissed his lips slowly, softly.

The feeling was so blissful Joe wondered if he was dreaming. Having another hallucination. Certainly, what he was seeing didn't make sense.

Ella, the leader?

Ella had been heavily drugged. The hiker, murdered. And yet, here they were.

My own neurochemicals easing me pleasantly toward death, the less spiritual side of him reasoned now.

Except…it wasn't *all* bliss and joy. The tears on Ella's face and the pain behind her smile made that clear. Something was terribly wrong. Something his cloudy brain couldn't process.

He tried to puzzle it out but then Ella and the hiker were helping him to his feet, guiding him down the far side of the boulder.

He was aware of Beck following them. Aware, even though he wasn't looking at the man. He could feel him, somehow, dark and foul, spinning an aura of pain and malaise as he moved. The aura seemed to push against Ella, the two of them sparring as they walked.

Toward the arch; the veil, they hurried, stopping where the cliff had been, next to the surreal curtain of … *light? Water?* Joe looked up—watched the luminous, translucent material falling, flowing, a continuous, endless sheet, fine and delicate as spun glass—but could discern little of its true nature.

Around them, the remaining animals were dashing and springing through the veil. And Joe saw that the creatures, all of them, gave Beck a wide berth—swinging far to the right or left.

Beck approached to within twenty feet of Ella and her companions and stopped, a grin on his face, a knowing look in his eyes.

Joe realized, as he stood there, holding Ella's hand, that he felt better—much better—than he had in days. He glanced back at the boulder, startled to realize that he had walked to the veil unassisted. Looking at his hands he saw that they were no longer shaking. His thoughts were clearing, as well.

He turned to find Ella watching him, and this time he reached for her, pulled her close, kissed her, drank in the warmth of her body, the delicious taste of her lips, the familiar feel of her skin against his.

"You saved me," he whispered, "I'm okay, I think."

She nodded, tears still glistening in her perfect green eyes. "I love you, Joe Stanton."

"Ella—"

"I love you and always will. You must know that."

"Ella. We can go now, right? Cross through? Ella, what's wrong?"

The veil between worlds shimmered not an arm's length from Joe—a wonder beyond imagination. And if he'd been studying it now he would have noticed that the curtain of light was thinning, fading, as the last stragglers on the plain bolted across. If he'd been paying attention he would have seen that the chasm—a mere two feet wide for most of the Exodus—was growing now, as if the momentarily rejoined worlds were preparing to slide apart. To separate for another hundred or thousand or million years.

Joe saw none of it, though, because all of his attention was on the woman standing before him. On his friend. His partner. His lover. The one he cared about more than any other. Alarms rang in his brain, loud now. She was afraid. Sad. Not for him but for the two of them.

"Ella—"

Joe sensed Beck, approaching like a shadow, bumping into the veil, warping it, distorting it.

"Ella—"

She touched his cheek with one hand, shining tears in her eyes. "No time," she said. "Listen to me."

Joe nodded, shaking now.

"You *are* healing. Will continue to heal, in the new world, and there only. Other people are passing through this day. A few who see things clearly. You will find them."

"We'll find them," Joe said. "Let's go." He grabbed Ella's hand, intending to pull her forward, into the new realm. But she moved not at all.

And then Beck's voice was booming out behind them, saying what sounded like a name, an ancient name, a jumble of syllables lost in the wind. "Yes!" he cried. "Lead. Lead so that I may follow, as ordained in laws older than time."

The awful ring of Beck's voice died away and the luminous veil continued to fade.

Ella pulled Joe close, kissed him deeply, and then she was stepping away, and the hiker was there, taking Joe by the arm, turning him, pulling him, leaping with him, over the widening gap.

Joe hit the veil and felt suddenly weightless. As if he were frozen and hovering in an ocean of light, a newborn galaxy of a million, billion stars. Time passed—it might have been seconds or hours or days—and then he and the hiker were coming down on the far side of the veil, landing in soft grass, the air warm and fragrant, creatures fanning out all around. They stumbled a few paces and Joe spun to see Ella, still on the other side, watching him. And the truth pierced his heart like a dagger.

Ella saw Joe spin free of the hiker and rush back, toward the veil, but there was no passage that direction. Not today. She tried to touch his hand through the shimmering curtain. Saw him cry her name but no longer could hear his voice.

Then she felt Beck moving close and she sent Joe one final thought. *I love you, Joe. I always will.*

Beck spoke, five paces away now, and there was a quiver in his voice that hadn't been there before. A touch of doubt—though he tried to conceal it. "Lead," he said, "So that I may claim my place in the new land."

Ella turned. Said nothing.

"Delay is no good," Beck sneered. "Where you go, I may follow. You know this. Haloed light. Deadly dark. I am half of the equation. There is not one without the other. Immutable and older than either of us is the maxim."

Ella lifted her eyes to his. "What you say is true. Where I go, you may follow."

Beck's face twisted into a grin.

Ella turned back and saw that the veil was almost gone. The chasm had widened and the view into the new land was growing faint now. Indistinct.

"Where I go, you may follow," she said again. "And this time, I'm not going."

The veil winked and Beck screamed, sprinted forward, and leapt into the air, clawing at nothing. He hung there, a moment, as the last trace of the shimmering archway vanished in the sunrise. And then the cliff—the Buffalo Jump—was there once more and he was falling. Falling—not into a new world but to the rocks eight hundred feet below.

The thing that had subsumed Beck's mind and soul fled shrieking as he fell, and Beck the man saw what had transpired the instant before he died.

Ella pulled back, shaking, from the brink of the Buffalo Jump, a woman once more, the woman she had always been—the power briefly bestowed upon her now gone.

With fresh tears in her eyes, she made for the trail, hoping to find her way home.

AFTERWORD

Dear Reader,

Thank you for reading EXODUS 2022. I hope you enjoyed the story. I welcome and appreciate honest reviews so please take a moment to share your thoughts on Goodreads and on the site where you purchased the book. Also, please feel free to get in touch with me at ken@kennethgbennett.com. My author website address is www.kennethgbennettbooks.com, and we can also connect on Twitter at @kennethgbennett and on Facebook at www.facebook.com/Exodus2022.

AUTHOR'S NOTE

This book has many friends. My sincerest thanks to the story's early readers: Randy Nargi, Jerry Brown, Mark Slater, Debbie Allbritton, Bill Harper, Chad Cary, Suzanne Cary, Carolyn Greer, Larry Weiner, Melissa Morris, and Joanne Moudy. On matters police and FBI, I am indebted to Matt Cary. Thanks also to Schuyler Boone for his advice on navy and sonar issues. To Susan and Eli: thank you for your encouragement, patience and unwavering support. I would not have made it to the end without your help. My gratitude to you all.

PROOFREADING: Toddie Downs

PUBLICATION MANAGEMENT: Christina Boyd

SOCIAL MEDIA MANAGEMENT: Vanya Drumchiyska

MORE GREAT READS FROM BOOKTROPE

Cathedral of Dreams **by Terry Persun** (Science Fiction) A compelling tale of a dystopian future and personal heroism, pitting the outsiders against the mind-control machine of New City.

The Water Sign **by C.S. Samulski** (Science Fiction) In the post-diluvian world of the future many children find themselves lost in the fog of war.

Phobia **by Daniel Lance Wright** (Thriller) Heights, crowds, small spaces… How does a psychologist handle three phobia sufferers on a cruise ship in the Gulf of Mexico when the ship is overtaken by Lebanese terrorists?

No Shelter from Darkness **by Mark D. Evans** (Paranormal) In the post-Blitz East End of London, orphaned teenager Beth Wade is bullied for looking different. But it goes far deeper than looks. With a growing thirst for blood and the arrival of a man who could kill her just as easily as help her, Beth must fight for control of her life… and of herself.

Discover more books and learn about our new approach to publishing at: **www.booktrope.com**

Kenneth G. Bennett is an author and wilderness enthusiast who spends his free time backpacking, skiing and kayaking. Ken lives on an island in the Pacific Northwest with his wife and son and two hyperactive Australian Shepherds. His other books include the YA novels THE GAIA WARS and BATTLE FOR CASCADIA. THE GAIA WARS series was optioned for film by Identity Films, LA in 2012, and both GAIA and BATTLE have been featured as Top 100 Bestsellers in Teen Literature and Fiction on Amazon.

Made in the USA
San Bernardino, CA
17 December 2015